PRAISE FOR THE WRITING OF ANTHONY GREY

Saigon

"This superb novel could well be the *War and Peace* of our age. By using a technique of historical progression, author Anthony Grey does for the Vietnam wars what Leo Tolstoy did for the Napoleonic wars."

—*San Francisco Chronicle*

"Like James Michener and James Clavell, Mr. Grey is a master storyteller. Unlike them, however, he has something pertinent to say and does so in distinguished fashion. . . . *Saigon* is a novel of terrible importance."

—*The Kansas City Star*

"A long overdue epic masterpiece of twentieth century Vietnam . . . The author balances the political intrigues and wartime horrors with a story of human sensitivity and love." —*Library Journal*

"One of the most memorable love stories of our time has been delivered with a firm literate hand by Anthony Grey who with this novel establishes himself as one of the finest storytellers plying his trade today. . . . It's a book which no doubt will stand the test of time." —*West Coast Review of Books*

"A political statement, a great adventure story, and an accurate window on that war-ravaged country, Vietnam . . . Anthony Grey has produced a masterpiece." —*Leatherneck Magazine of the Marines*

Peking

"A magnificent epic novel of modern China . . .The book is worth reading solely as a factual reminder of the chaos and calamity of China, as a quarter of the world's people struggled and suffered toward modernity in the stormy and cruel decades between 1920 and 1980." —*Toronto Star*

"Grey's depth of feeling makes Peking a compelling epic."

—*The Sunday Telegraph*

"Skillfully narrated, the book is a parable of China and the West's love affair with it." —*Far Eastern Economic Review*

"Outstanding . . . Balance, sanity, serenity and realized human love in the face of a shifting and violent and mostly hateful world." —*Sunday Record*

TOKYO BAY

TOKYO BAY

A Novel of Japan

ANTHONY GREY

OPEN ROAD
INTEGRATED MEDIA
NEW YORK

Cover design by Cameron Shepler

ISBN: 978-1-5040-4923-8

This edition published in 2018 by Open Road Integrated Media, Inc.
180 Maiden Lane
New York, NY 10038
www.openroadmedia.com

Anchorages of the American warships in the
BAY OF TOKYO
July 1853
Tokyo (Yedo)
Shinagawa
Kawasaki
TOKYO (YEDO) BAY
Kanagawa
Yokohama
Mt Fuji
50 MILES
N
W
E
S
Cape Kamisaki
FRIDAY 8 JULY:
Saratoga
Susquehanna
Mississippi
Plymouth
Kamakura
Uraga
Kurihama
THURSDAY 14 JULY:
Susquehanna
Mississippi
Uraga Channel
Cape Sagami
Cape Susaki
American ships
Japanese forts and batteries
MILES

TOKYO BAY

In future as long as the sun shines on the earth, let no one sail towards Japan, not even an ambassador. This declaration will never be revoked and will be maintained on pain of death.

Japanese edict issued after execution of foreign missionaries, 1640.

PROLOGUE

Midnight, 7 July 1853

White later flew from the heaving flanks of a dying courier horse as its helmeted samurai rider spurred the exhausted animal fiercely across the arched bridge spanning the last of three concentric moats in front of the Shogun's massive castle at Yedo.

'*Chokurei da!*' yelled the rider to armoured pikemen who stood guard beside the inner bastion's tall iron-and-wood gates. '*Kinkyu chokurei da!*' He drew a small scroll, bound with golden thread, from the sleeve of his dark blue fighting kimono and flourished it pointedly above his head.

The scowling sentinels, who wore broad helmets and ribbed body armour of leather and bamboo, had begun to lift their pikes menacingly in his direction. But the commanding shout of the obviously young samurai stopped them in their tracks. His words constituted a secret password indicating that he carried a rare 'urgent message' from the Emperor, who lived in seclusion in Kyoto, three hundred miles to the south-west. Also, close up, they could see the heraldic six-pointed star of his clan emblazoned on his sleeveless *jimbaori* battle-coat in gold filigree, denoting that he was a nobleman of the very highest rank.

'*Hayaku!*' yelled the rider impatiently, wheeling the unsteady horse as the startled sentinels swung open the ponderous gates. '*Hayaku!*—Be quick!'

As soon as the gap between the gates was wide enough, he sent the horse surging into the castle's inner courtyard. He rode hard through a succession of further guard-points, yelling and brandishing the scroll each time, until he reached the flight of stone steps that led up to the main entrance of the stronghold. The moment he flung himself out of the saddle, the horse collapsed, blood reddening the foam at its mouth. It shuddered and squealed pitifully before expiring. But the young samurai nobleman did not stop or glance back as he bounded up the steps, his twin swords jutting from the sash belt of his kimono. On showing the scroll and its imperial seal to a chief sentry officer, he was granted immediate entry.

Running and walking by turns, he raced along successive high-vaulted passageways, where the walls shimmered with gold leaf. Ascending staircases three steps at a time, he passed beneath painted wall panels depicting mythical birds in groves of bamboo and mountain pines. Overhead, wooden beams lacquered in black and gilt supported ornately decorated ceilings, but the young samurai scarcely spared them a glance. Pausing only to ask directions from spear-bearing sentries dressed in formal uniforms of bright brocade, he rushed on.

Approaching the gilded doors of the Shogunate council chamber, he removed his helmet and again plucked the scroll from the wide sleeve of his kimono. His expression was ablaze with urgency as he addressed the senior officer of the council's guard. A moment later he removed his thonged *zóri*, to be ushered inside barefoot.

A hundred pairs of eyes swung silently to focus on him as he stepped, panting, into the chamber. They belonged to gaudily dressed *daimyo*, the feudal overlords of Japan's provincial regions, who were assembled in kneeling ranks around a low central dais on which the Shogun himself was seated. Garbed in court dress of stiff-shouldered jackets, loose trailing trousers of silk, and shiny black-lacquered bonnets, the *daimyo* stared in astonishment at the dishevelled, travel-stained young nobleman. When he sank to his knees and bowed his head to the floor, they could see that his shaven crown and its coiled topknot of hair were covered with sweat and dust. Before prostrating himself he had pulled his twin swords from the sash at his waist, to place them reverently beside his helmet on the tatami-mat floor; like his garments, their scabbards and embossed hilts were also damp and mud-stained.

From the centre of his raised and cushioned dais, the Shogun watched impassively. Under flowing robes of grey silk his legs were invisible, giving him a Buddha-like appearance, but although he was sitting stiffly upright his thin face was unnaturally pallid, and the sheen of perspiration visible on his brow suggested he might be suffering from some serious illness. The dramatic entry of the breathless messenger had produced a momentary flicker of alarm in the Shogun's eyes, but he recovered his composure quickly and made a slight movement of his head. This prompted one high official of the council below the dais to rise to his feet and bow very low in his superior's direction. Moving forward, he bowed once more, then gestured for the young messenger to assume a kneeling position and explain himself.

'Sire, I am Tanaka Yoshio, a prince of the Kago clan from Kumatore,' said the samurai in a ringing voice. 'I have been entrusted to bring you a message of the gravest urgency from His Divine Majesty the Emperor in Kyoto.' He extracted the scroll from his sleeve, bowed very low again in the direction of the Shogun, then handed the message to the grey-haired official, who also bowed low in accepting it.

'It is not usual, O Tanaka-san, for a nobleman of such high rank to act as a common courier,' said the official quietly. 'Why have you chosen this role?'

'I volunteered for this sacred duty because of the vital nature of the message,' replied Tanaka breathlessly. 'I started out with other couriers, who either fell exhausted or sacrificed their horses to me so that I might arrive as speedily as possible!'

'It is clear now.' The older man nodded, but as he turned and began to move back towards the dais with tantalizing slowness, the young samurai found he could not contain his impatience.

'Sire, a fleet of smoking black ships is bringing many foreign barbarians from the outside world to Yedo!' he burst out, remembering just in time to lower his head once more in a formal gesture of respect. 'There is grave danger . . . The vessels carry many mighty cannon and hundreds of soldiers . . . They are driven by great wheels which churn the water into white waves . . . They can even sail strongly against the wind!'

He paused once more, struggling to catch his breath. He had just used the pejorative expression *gai-jin* meaning 'outside country barbarians', and his eyes flashed as he repeated it. 'The *gai-jin* are all Americans. Some are black giants! They forced their way ashore in the Satsuma tributary islands of Lew Chew, to the south-west. They appear to be intent on conquest! Travelling fast, they will arrive very soon in the bay before Yedo!'

An audible gasp rose from the assembled *daimyo*, but they fell silent again as the high official reached the Shogun's dais. When he opened the scroll and bowed very low, a hush of tense expectancy fell over the chamber.

'Powerful ships bringing armed beasts from the outside world are approaching Yedo,' began the official, reading the imperial message aloud with alarm in his voice. 'Their clear intent is to violate by force the sacred soil of Nippon. The barbarians falsely believe that the Emperor resides in Yedo castle, and it is hoped nothing will be said to enlighten them. The task of treating with the outside country beasts will therefore rest entirely in *your* hands. At this time of great national danger we hope and pray fervently that the sanctity of our land and its people will be protected and preserved.'

Pale-faced and visibly shaken, the high official closed the scroll and bowed low towards the Shogun once more, before adding: 'The message, sire, as anticipated, bears the personal seal of His Divine. Majesty, Emperor Komei.'

For several seconds a tense silence reigned among the *daimyo* and none of them moved or spoke. Then the Shogun made another small movement of his head towards the messenger and, without rising fully, the young samurai picked up his swords and his branched helmet and backed respectfully out of the chamber, bowing low at every step. As the giant gilded doors swung closed on his exit, he heard a single angry voice break the stillness.

'*Jo-i Gai-jin! Jo-i Gai-jin!*—Expel the Barbarians!'

Quickly other voices took up the cry, and soon the council chamber was filled with an angry chorus: '*Jo-i Gai-jin! . . . Jo-i Gai-jin! . . . Jo-i Gai-jin!*'

After pausing to listen for a moment, Prince Tanaka thrust his twin swords securely into the sash of his kimono and put on his helmet. Slipping his feet into the thonged *zóri* he had discarded a few minutes earlier, he turned and raced back swiftly towards the castle entrance, by the way he had come.

High in the distant, starlit darkness above the unseen coasts of Japan, a strange cone of white light suddenly appeared. To Second Lieutenant Robert Eden of the United States Navy, who was watching from the gently heaving quarterdeck of the steam frigate USS *Susquehanna*, the shimmering light had seemed to float silently upward out of the black depths of the Pacific Ocean without any warning. He stared hard at the ghostly apparition with a mixture of awe and fascination, unable to tear his eyes away from it.

The cone of brightness seemed to hover motionless, two miles high in the heavens. Below it the coastline of the closed and secret land towards which the wooden sidewheel frigate was steaming lay still and indistinct in the darkness. Eden stood alone by the rails on the quarterdeck, and the steady churning of the ship's great side-wheel paddles was the only sound in the night.

As he watched, the image became almost hypnotic, and a thought of astonishing irrationality flashed through his mind: was this a vision he was seeing? Suspended halfway between heaven and earth, the perfect pyramid of light seemed to pulse with its own luminescence. Could he, he wondered wildly, be gazing at some miraculous manifestation of a God in whom he no longer believed? In the stillness of the middle watch, was he being rebuked for his angry abandonment of belief in a compassionate and loving creator of mankind? Despite the wildness of this notion, some intuitive reflex forced him to lower his gaze. Continuing to stand motionless by the ship's rail, he bowed his head slightly without knowing clearly why he did so.

Six feet tall and in his twenty-fourth year, Lieutenant Robert Eden was an impressively athletic figure in his gold-epauletted officer's frock coat and white drill pantaloons. His shoulders were broad and powerful beneath the dark blue double-breasted coat, and his left hand rested with an easy physical confidence on the gleaming brass hilt of his sheathed sword. Alert and keen-eyed, his demeanour in all was that of a vigorous man who loved nothing more than the challenge of physical action. His gold-braided blue cap with its patent-leather visor hid a shock of dark brown hair and his weatherbeaten complexion was obviously Anglo-Saxon. Yet his broad, handsome face was incongruously high-cheekboned and his eyes were dark, narrow and deep-set, betraying a distant mingling of North American Indian blood with that of the hardy European pioneer-settlers of New England who had been his ancestors. In his expression too there was a fierce, brooding quality which hinted that he might be nursing some inner emotional pain. He smiled only rarely, and consequently the brawny gunners who manned the massive spar deck port cannons under his command never wasted a moment in responding to his crisply given orders.

While standing with his head still bowed, Eden was aware that he was not praying in any way taught to him during his conventional Episcopalian upbringing in a small town on the wooded heights of eastern Connecticut, a few miles inland from Long Island Sound. Instead he found his mind had filled with a deep and awesome silence. The thrashing of the *Susquehanna*'s paddle-wheels and the sounds of the sea seemed to be momentarily blotted out, and he felt strangely spellbound.

The stillness appeared to vibrate gently at some mysterious frequency, producing a feeling far more profound than prayer, and quite unexpectedly images of memory that had haunted him waking and sleeping for six years flashed unbidden into his mind. But now they were more intense than ever before, almost as vivid as real life. *In a darkened, storm-lashed Connecticut woodland his very young wife lay splayed limply at the foot of a tree. The wheels of an overturned buckboard still spun slowly nearby. A spasm of agony twisted her smooth features and he clutched despairingly at the slippery, newborn infant not yet severed from her dying body.* With an almost unbearable intensity Eden felt his own agony again; then the images melted away as swiftly as they had come, and to his astonishment a gentler sense of ease as quickly took possession of his senses. For an instant this feeling of peace was as intense and tangible as the previous pain; then it too was gone, leaving him feeling baffled as to what had prompted such powerful sensations.

'Fuji! . . . Fuji-san!'

As though answering his unspoken question, a voice close beside him in the darkness spoke in an urgent whisper. Higher-pitched in contrast to the slow-drawling speech patterns of the *Susquehanna*'s American crew, the voice was sibilant and unfamiliar. Turning, Eden saw a diminutive Asian had stolen up beside him, and he recognized the man instantly as Sentaro, a Japanese castaway whom the *Susquehanna* was carrying homeward for repatriation. Rescued from a sinking fishing junk in mid-Pacific, he had been carried to San Francisco by an American merchant ship, and spent almost four years there working as a port stevedore. Eden was about to remonstrate with him for slipping unseen onto the quarterdeck, but the scrawny Japanese had already fallen to his knees, his face turned towards the shimmering triangle of light. As Eden watched, he bent his thin body double in an elaborate self-abasing bow, until his face was pressed against the planks of the deck. He held this reverent posture for some moments and when at last he sat up and turned his head to glance at Eden, the American saw that his broad cheeks were agleam with tears.

'Many times since my shipwreck I dream of this sight of Mount Fuji,' Sentaro whispered in Japanese. 'When it catches the moonlight, it becomes a silver spirit floating in the night. I am very happy to see it again—but I am frightened too.'

Finding himself moved by the simple fisherman's tears, Eden decided to offer no reprimand. Before the US Navy squadron's departure from its home base, and during the long voyage, he had befriended the castaway who slept and lived in a cramped and uncomfortable storage space under the fo'c's'le deck. He had visited him there frequently and on occasions had invited him discreetly to his own cabin as part of his effort to master the rudiments of the Japanese language. Sentaro had already confided to him that he was approaching his homeland with a mixture of exhilaration and fear; after long years away he yearned to see his family and native country again—but, knowing how fiercely laws banning all travel outside Japan were enforced, he was deeply fearful for his personal safety once he landed.

'Everything will be all right, Sentaro,' said Eden soothingly in Japanese, gazing out over the rail again. 'I am sure this first beautiful sight of Mount Fuji is a good omen . . .'

The Japanese stared up at him doubtfully, his expression anxious. 'I hope so, master.' He bowed his head for another long moment, then turned and crept silently into the darkness, heading for the ladder that led down to the spar deck. Eden watched him go, then peered once more towards the ethereal image of Japan's sacred volcano. The moonlight was strengthening, and he was able to make out for the first time the shadowy outline of the entire mountain, which rose from the inky darkness beneath it in the shape of a perfect cone. The newly risen moon, he could see now, had illuminated the snow-flanked summit suddenly to create the illusion that it was drifting free in space like a disembodied wraith. He had been searching previously much lower in the sky to catch his first glimpse of the spectacular mountain, and its first appearance high in the night-time heavens only added to the aura of mystery which seemed to surround it.

Eden remembered suddenly the passage describing Fuji in the history book translated from Dutch which he had flung down on his cabin bunk before coming up on deck to begin his spell as second officer of the middle watch. The book had described how the fiery mountain had been hurled aloft from the flat eastern plains during a ferocious night of earthquakes some two thousand years before—at the same period that Japan's first emperor was said to have become the nation's ruler. Ever since, both emperors and the mountain alike had been worshipped as sacred divinities, and as Eden continued staring towards its snow-covered summit, another shudder of awe moved up his spine.

'That must be the most beautiful mountain in the world,' he murmured to himself. 'It hardly seems real.'

As the steam frigate and its three sister ships drew nearer to the coast, the pyramid of light appeared to glimmer ever more intensely. Eden wondered melodramatically whether it had emerged suddenly from the darkness to act as a timely guiding beacon, to show the way to this host of strangers now approaching silently from the outside world. For more than two hundred years foreigners of every race had been resolutely barred from these mysterious islands—and it was this fact, which he had uncovered in the library of the new US Naval Academy at Annapolis during his last cadet year, which had prompted him later to volunteer for the voyage. Now, he reflected, that long period of Japan's seclusion was about to end, and he would play a small role himself in its ending. On the silvered sea around the *Susquehanna* he could see the dark silhouettes of the other three slow-moving US Navy ships: two high-masted sailing vessels, the *Plymouth* and the *Saratoga*, and a second barque-rigged wooden sidewheeler, the *Mississippi*, were forging slowly northwards through Japan's coastal waters, under the command of Commodore Matthew Calbraith Perry.

In the grandest cabin of the *Susquehanna*, which he had made his flagship, the commodore was carrying strict orders from the President of the United States. His mission was to break down the barred gates of this tantalizing oriental land and open it to American ships and trade. Perry was carrying a formal request to the present Emperor from President Millard Fillmore, inscribed on parchment and secured in a polished rosewood box. But he also possessed a well-armed body of US marines and enough heavy guns to do the job by force, if necessary. Robert Eden remembered this as he watched the moonlight shimmer on the far-off mountaintop, and for the first time his feelings of exhilaration were tempered by a stab of unease.

Might the brilliant white peak of Mount Fuji, he wondered, be flashing a warning to the approaching American naval squadron instead of acting as a beacon? Could this be interpreted as a last firm warning to retreat? Or at least to draw near to an ancient and mysterious land only with the greatest caution?

From the same Dutch history book that he had devoured avidly during the long voyage from the United States, Eden had learned that fierce hordes of warriors equipped with metal and leather armour still loyally served their feudal lords in medieval crag-top castles. In mountain temples, warriors and peasants alike worshipped the sun goddess, their divine emperor, and a host of mysterious spirits. These same warriors rode and fought beneath multicoloured heraldic banners; in victory they beheaded their enemies without mercy, but if defeated they slashed open their own bowels before shame could demean them.

Their divine emperor, the book explained, was believed to live in mysterious seclusion. Rural towns were often ablaze with street processions and theatres. The earth of the islands was green and fertile, the trees were famous for their dazzling spring blossoms, and the graceful, delicate-limbed women of the land traditionally cultivated the arts of music and singing to a striking degree. Some, the book added archly, were trained to perform the duties of love with a grace matched by no other nation.

Coloured sketches, which had imprinted themselves in his mind, depicted these Japanese females as diminutive, doll-like creatures. Swathed in bright-coloured silken gowns, they wore their dark hair piled high in elaborate styles bristling with ornaments. The male warriors, narrow-eyed and fierce of expression, also dressed their hair strangely—in topknots and pigtails—and garbed themselves in silks that were loose-sleeved and exotically baggy. As Eden continued to peer towards Fuji's moonlit outline, the keen sense of curiosity and excitement which these words and images had generated at first reading intensified. How, he wondered, would cold reality compare, once they set foot on land?

He pondered the question endlessly as he paced the deck during the rest of his watch, glancing frequently towards the shadowy land. On returning to his cabin after being relieved, he stretched out on his bunk without undressing. Taking up the discarded history book, he thumbed through it until he found the same section on Mount Fuji. A verse written in praise of the volcano by a Japanese poet of the ninth century caught his eye and he read it through several times, until the last vivid stanzas were instilled in his memory.

Great Fuji-yama towering to the sky,
A treasure art thou, given to mortal man,
A god protector watching o'er Japan
On thee forever let me feast mine eye.

After he'd laid the book aside and closed his eyes Eden found that the haunting image of the shining mountain still filled his mind. For a long time he could not sleep, but lay listening restlessly to the thump of the *Susquehanna*'s paddle-wheels driving them nearer to landfall. Twice he rose and peered out through the port scuttle, searching the darkness to landward. To his disappointment, however, the mountain was no longer visible. Taking a leather-bound private journal from his cabin trunk he wrote in it avidly for several minutes, still glancing occasionally towards the shore.

When at last he slept, the glittering peak reappeared immediately in his dreams. His eyes seemed to fill with dazzling light, as he found himself on the mountain, ascending easily and lightly across the snow, heading towards the lip of its volcanic crater. Above, in the deep darkness of the sky, millions of stars were shining brilliantly, and on reaching the very top, instead of looking down into the crater, he found himself reaching up with his arms into the midnight heavens. Without difficulty he began pulling at the sky, and drawing down the dark stuff of the night. It came easily into his hands like glistening silk. The silver stars continued to shine as he wrapped them around his body in a loose and beautiful cloak which trailed across the snow behind him. Pulling this cloak tighter about himself, he felt a sense of wonder and contentment suffuse his mind and body in a way he had never known before.

Turning, he saw a temple had appeared on the mountain peak, its roofs curved and its woodwork red. A giant silver mirror to one side reflected a second image of the temple, and he hurried towards this. Just short of the mirror he halted, afraid suddenly of what he might see in it. Then he caught a glimpse of his marvellous new garment in the mirror, and to his relief the stars still shone dazzlingly in the deep blue darkness of its folds.

Reassured he stepped nearer. But when he studied his reflection, he suffered a sudden deep sense of shock. In place of his own familiar features, he found he was staring into the unsmiling face of a Japanese samurai. The top of the warrior's head was shaven, and a long oiled pigtail was tied in a topknot across his crown. Dark eyes bore into his unwaveringly, their expression hostile one moment and enigmatically quizzical the next. Then, as Eden watched, this fierce male face dissolved slowly, to be replaced by the softer countenance of a beautiful Japanese girl. This time the almond eyes were downcast and the hair was enchantingly glossy, pierced by glittering silver pins. Like the samurai before her, she also inhabited the blue silken gown of stars in his place. After a moment she began to lift her head to look at him but, before their eyes could meet fully, the mountain-top and all the stars above it exploded without warning in a sudden blinding flash of white light—and the dream ended as abruptly as it had begun.

PART I

The Black Ships Arrive

8 July 1853

The necklet of green, mountainous islands known today as Japan was in 1853 the most mysterious major country in the world. An isolated nation of some thirty million people—who believed themselves and their emperor to be divine descendants of heaven—had been deliberately sealed off from all other countries for well over two hundred years. Separated from the mainland of Asia by a hundred miles of sea, historically the Japanese had always been fierce defenders of their independence and racial purity. They had traded guardedly during the Middle Ages with near neighbours in India, China and South-East Asia, but otherwise had largely kept themselves apart. Consequently the arrival of European traders on their shores in the sixteenth century had set alarm bells ringing in the minds of the shoguns, the hereditary military dictators who then ruled the nation. Zealous Christian missionaries quickly followed the trail-blazing Portuguese and Spanish traders, and subsequently made hundreds of thousands of Japanese converts. Feeling their authority menaced, the shoguns publicly crucified many foreign priests and, in a bloody climax to a forty-year campaign of persecution, thirty thousand Japanese Christians were finally slaughtered in their castle stronghold. Strict laws were immediately enforced, forbidding all Japanese to travel abroad, and it even became a crime to build any large seaworthy vessel. Simultaneously all foreigners were barred from the country, and an edict was issued instructing, 'In future as long as the sun shines on the earth, let no one sail towards Japan, not even an ambassador.' The edict added, even more ominously, 'This declaration will never be revoked and will be maintained on pain of death.' During this era foreign sailors unfortunate enough to be shipwrecked on Japan's shores were sometimes exhibited in public in cages like animals.

These draconian laws turned Japan into one of the world's most isolated nations, and preserved its late medieval society intact until the middle of the nineteenth century. From 1192 onwards the shoguns had relegated the emperors to a role of purely theoretical supremacy. They ruled with the support of regional feudal lords known as daimyo, who sallied grandly forth from mighty castles in this self-imposed vacuum and exercised supreme control over the lives of their peasant-farmer vassals. These daimyo maintained large standing armies of loyal samurai warriors to fight their causes, and between 1638 and 1853 the turbulent currents of world history passed Japan by. In the eighteenth and nineteenth centuries the French Revolution rang the death-knell of feudal privilege in Europe, George Washington led Americans into a new era of modern democracy in the United States, and British inventors and engineers fomented the movement destined to change the whole world from ancient to modern—the Industrial Revolution. With steam-driven ships, railways, the telegraph, and superior weapons of war, the trade-hungry Europeans and, to a lesser extent, the Americans began exercising an ever-widening influence which led to the colonization of many weaker nations. Treaty ports and foreign concessions were snatched from China by both Americans and Europeans—Britain seizing Hong Kong in the first Opium War—and trade and territorial aggrandisement went hand in hand in Africa, Latin America, India and many other parts of Asia.

News of these historical tides sweeping ever nearer to Japan was conveyed to its rulers by a tiny, unique group of foreigners. Although British, Spanish and Portuguese merchants had finally submitted to the xenophobic exclusion laws and departed from Japan in the early seventeenth century, a few tenacious Dutch merchants had hung on determinedly by their fingertips. Because the Japanese believed that their land was exclusively sacred to them—Nippon, or Nihon the country's indigenous name, means 'land begotten by the Sun'—the Dutch traders were humiliatingly confined throughout two centuries to an artificial, man-made island in the southernmost port of Nagasaki. Closely watched and supervised without let-up, they left this virtual prison only once a year, under escort, to attend an audience granted by the Shogun in his capital, Yedo—now called Tokyo. During their journey, great canvas curtains and screens were often hung along the route in towns and villages, to deny their foreign eyes any genuine glimpse of Japanese life. To retain their exclusive position, these Dutchmen, among other indignities, had to perform like circus bears before the Shogun, demonstrating European dances for his amusement.

But the commercial advantages gained by these traders from Holland were nevertheless considerable, and in return they acted as a channel of information from the outside world. At the Shogun's command they prepared regular reports describing political developments in Europe, America, and other parts of the Far East. This information made Japan's rulers uneasy—and greatly increased their determination to maintain the country's inviolability. During the first half of the nineteenth century a few isolated foreign ships tried without success to put into Japanese ports. One tentative visit to Yedo Bay by American Navy men-of-war in 1846 ended abruptly when guard sampans rowed furiously by brawny samurai attached ropes to the two US sailing ships and dragged them back out to sea. Other foreigners who tried to land were denied entry with similar warnings and threats until, in 1853, a determined United States Navy squadron under the command of Commodore Matthew Calbraith Perry hove in sight. Because of what had happened to their sailing ships seven years earlier, the Americans arrived this time in more powerful steam-driven warships. They also carried the latest cannon and a strong force of marines to back up their demand for trade and port facilities for all American shipping. During the long centuries of seclusion and ignorance, the Japanese people had been encouraged by their rulers to think of all other races in the world as 'hideous barbarians'. Therefore many frightening images of foreigners abounded in the uninformed popular mind. En route to Japan, this US Navy squadron had called at the Ryukyus, tributary islands hundreds of miles to the south-west, the largest of which is Okinawa. As a result, fast courier junks had raced ahead to the southern regions of Japan to warn of the imminent arrival of foreign barbarians travelling in fearsome, smoke-belching machines, the like of which had never been seen before in Japanese waters. As rumours about these approaching newcomers spread northward towards the city known today as Tokyo, the ordinary people of Japan panicked en masse. In their fevered minds they were convinced they were about to be invaded by hordes of ape-like giants as monstrous and terrifying as alien creatures from another planet.

1

Matsumua Tokiwa was stepping naked from her bath at the instant when a great commotion began in the city beyond her *shoji* screens. She was lost in a reverie, gazing reflectively at the tiny pearls of condensation that shimmered on her bare arms and shoulders. In the fading evening light, she thought, they glowed like miniature teardrops against her golden skin. Looking absently down at her youthfully pointed breasts, her shadowed flanks and the flattened curve of her belly, she noticed other such beads of tear-like moisture. Could it be, she wondered, that her soul was always silently weeping within her? Was her spirit sobbing soundlessly and invisibly all the time she smiled her bright, professional smiles, recited *haiku* verses, or played her plangent three-stringed *samisen?*

Thinking these melancholy thoughts she moved gracefully across the soft tatami floormats to where she had laid out her favourite kimono of midnight blue silk. Worn only on special nights, this kimono was decorated with silver stars that glistened luminously amongst its silken folds. Although not yet ready to put the garment on, she reached out a hand towards its shimmering fabric, anticipating the familiar sensual pleasure of close contact with its smooth richness. It was in that moment that she first registered fully the frantic sounds of raised voices and running feet from beyond the wood and ricepaper *shoji* that separated the room from a balcony overlooking the narrow, flagstoned street outside.

The excited night-time murmur and bustle of the Yoshiwara—the walled-in entertainment and pleasure district of Yedo—was not in any way strange to her ears, despite the fresh bloom of youth on her cheeks. Although not yet twenty, she had already spent three years delighting the high-ranking clientele of the Golden Pavilion geisha house. The distaste she felt for her current role in the Yoshiwara had always been successfully masked behind her smiling professional poise; for she had entered the Golden Pavilion reluctantly, to gain for her ruined father the high lump-sum payment that beauty such as hers commanded. A former samurai who had turned merchant, he had recklessly gambled away a fortune in the Yoshiwara's gaming houses, and Tokiwa's reluctant sacrifice had been made solely to help ward off the total impoverishment of her family. She had long since learned to close her ears to the harsh and boisterous sounds which nightly filled the street outside—but never before had she heard anything like the hysterical din now rising towards her balcony.

Still naked, she carefully drew back the nearest *shoji* and peered discreetly down into the street. Amidst the seething crowd her eye fell first on a man who was stumbling under the weight of a frail, white-haired woman clinging to his back. Fear was etched deep in the face of the woman, who Tokiwa guessed was his mother, and, as he staggered along, she peered constantly backward, as though fearing pursuit by all the demons of hell. Tokiwa also saw younger women casting terrified glances over their shoulders as they hurried past with babies clasped in their arms. Weeping children clung to their fathers, and several families were frantically trying to push handcarts piled high with their meagre belongings through the milling throng.

From all over the city temple bells were beginning to toll with an unfamiliar urgency, and men and women called out panicky warnings to one another as they ran. In an effort to hear what they were saying, Tokiwa clasped her arms about her naked breasts and took half a pace out onto the balcony.

'The barbarians are sending floating volcanoes to destroy us!' shrieked one man to another as they passed beneath her. 'They've been seen from Cape Idzu . . . belching great clouds of black smoke!'

'Twenty thousand brave samurai are already manning the cliffs!' yelled another. 'But they're all doomed.'

'Hundreds of hairy barbarian giants are following the volcanoes,' called another male voice desperately.

'They'll burn and rape all Yedo,' screamed a despairing female. 'Nothing can save us!'

Tokiwa shuddered with apprehension and lifted her eyes above the rooftops, seeking a glimpse of the smoke rising from these terrible floating volcanoes. But only the silent stars were visible above the city, shining bright and unobscured, as always in the July night. There was no visible trace of danger anywhere and in the immensity of the heavens the stars seemed to sparkle like magical gemstones. The sight of them reminded Tokiwa suddenly why she had laid out her favoured kimono just half an hour earlier, after receiving a secret written message that Prince Tanaka Yoshio of the southern Kago clan had arrived unexpectedly from Kyoto.

The same note explained that he had ridden non-stop to Yedo from the imperial capital, and would pay a discreet visit to the Golden Pavilion some time that evening. Looking down again at the panic-stricken crowds below her, she wondered whether he would come after all, now that the city was in such an uproar. And should she even bother to wait for him? Shouldn't she perhaps take to her heels and join the rest of the crowds in their headlong dash to escape the clutches of the invading barbarians?

Caught in an agony of indecision, she turned her head and listened carefully. Behind her the interior of the Golden Pavilion was still and silent. With a sudden stab of fear she realized that the other geishas and maids must have all fled from the house while she bathed. Looking down agitatedly into the street, she searched for the familiar, proud-striding figure of Prince Tanaka, with his twin samurai swords jutting from his hip. But amongst the confused mêlée there was no sign of him. Nobody, she noticed, even paused now before the inviting, lantern-lit doors of the Golden Pavilion—except the hunched figure of a mendicant monk in muddied brown robes. Something unnatural in his demeanour caused her glance to linger on him, and in that same instant the beggar lifted his cowled head to stare directly up at the balcony.

Stifling a murmur of alarm, Tokiwa hurried back into the room and quickly covered her nakedness with a full-length under-kimono of translucent white gauze. She began hurriedly to dress her loose hair before a mirror, snatching up pins and tortoiseshell combs to hold the elaborate chignon in place. But before she had half finished the task, the *shoji* screens behind her slid silently apart and the ominous figure of the hooded beggar appeared in her mirror.

A cry of fear escaped her lips, but she did not move. Slipping one small hand into the bodice of the under-kimono, she withdrew it in the moment of turning, and faced the beggar with a short, glittering dagger held determinedly in front of her. For several seconds he remained motionless too, his face almost invisible beneath the cowl. Then suddenly his right hand emerged from beneath the mud-stained robe, holding out a long curved sword. After flourishing it once, the beggar lifted the weapon in front of his face, as if in an elaborate formal salute. With his other hand he swept aside the hood, and she found herself staring in astonishment into the unsmiling face of Prince Tanaka Yoshio. His stern, handsome features remained expressionless as he studied Tokiwa—then he bowed and lowered his sword.

'Your remarkable courage matches your rare beauty, O Tokiwa-san,' he said approvingly. 'I have already learned to admire your *haiku* and your playing of the *samisen*. But this new aspect of you I have never seen before.'

Tokiwa put aside her dagger in turn, and sank to a kneeling position. 'My lord is not the only one to be surprised,' she said quietly, bowing her head respectfully in his direction. 'Beneath that beggar's hood I did not recognize you.'

After studying her further in silence, Tanaka took a pace forward, the shimmering sword still unsheathed at his side. Aware of this, Tokiwa kept her head bent.

'Perhaps I should arrive in disguise more often,' he said quietly, trying to hide the tremor of excitement in his voice. 'To find you unprepared in this way is not unwelcome to my eyes.'

Beneath the filmy under-kimono her golden body was effectively naked, and neither of them moved as he gazed down at her. Her back was narrow and long but her haunches, although slender, were generously rounded, and her dark-tipped breasts pressed full and youthfully ripe against the revealing garment. His eyes lingered for a long moment on the indistinct shadow at the apex of her loins, then returned to the exposed curve of her graceful neck.

'Is it safe to remain here?' asked Tokiwa in an anxious voice, still without raising her head. 'Or will the floating volcanoes of the barbarians destroy the city tonight?'

Instead of replying, Tanaka used his long sword to flick her dagger expertly into a corner, putting it well beyond her reach. Then he raised his blade slowly to the nape of her bared neck and rested its tip gently against her glossy black hair. With only a slight movement of his wrist he removed an ivory comb and two silver pins, which tumbled noiselessly to the tatami at her side. He watched her long hair cascade down over her shoulders, then manoeuvred the weapon into the loosely tied sash of the undergarment, and unfastened it. Using the sword-tip with great delicacy, he drew open the front of the kimono to unveil her breasts fully to his gaze.

'The danger to our country is grave and very urgent,' he murmured, and swished the sword suddenly across her body to throw open the lower half of the kimono. During another long silence he stared down at the nakedness of her lower belly and thighs; then he sucked in his breath fiercely. 'Perhaps it has already come to your notice: you are in personal danger too, because of your liaison with me!'

For the first time she raised her head to look up at him, and her expression showed alarm. 'Shouldn't we then flee at once, my lord?'

Without replying he moved the sharp point of the sword until it touched the fullness of one of her breasts. After a moment's pause he continued to draw it upwards, and she shivered as she felt its needle-sharp tip trace a fine line across her flesh. When it encountered the collar of the kimono, he lifted part of the flimsy garment to expose all of her arm and her right shoulder. His eyes were growing bright with desire, and he rested the blade of the sword on her shoulder to study his handiwork.

'While the dangers are great,' he said huskily, 'they are not as simple as they seem. The fears of the people of Yedo are somewhat exaggerated . . .'

From outside in the street the sounds of panic were increasing. The clatter of feet and shouts of alarm grew louder and more confused. Still intensely aware of the sharp-edged blade on her shoulder, Tokiwa struggled to control her breathing. 'But the seaborne volcanoes will bring death to many people of Nippon! Surely it's not foolish to be frightened.'

'Those rumours are false. The barbarians have not sent floating volcanoes against us.' With the blunt edge of his sword Tanaka caressed her hair, smoothing it downward along the curve of her spine. 'The smoke comes out of their ships—which have iron machines on board. The machines can burn coal inside them and somehow help the ships sail against the wind. They are very powerful, and can tow other sailing ships easily behind them.'

Feeling the cold steel now against her back, Tokiwa shuddered involuntarily. 'But what do they want here, my lord? Why have they come?'

'They have come to humiliate our nation—perhaps to enslave and colonize us. At the very least they will try to force us to welcome their trading ships, against our will!'

Tanaka matched the fierceness of his words with another swift movement of the sword, which lifted the undergarment from her body and dropped it in a heap on the tatami beside her. Uncertain what to expect, Tokiwa kept her eyes averted from his face, and waited. Although she could not see his expression, she could sense that the sight of her entirely naked body had aroused his desire to a new pitch of intensity, and she was not surprised when a moment later the sword reappeared in her range of vision. Its point descended very deliberately to rest on one of her bare knees, then probed down between her thighs until it touched the matting on which she knelt. The cutting edge of the blade was turned inward and she parted her legs with a sharp intake of breath as Tanaka began to move it with slow deliberation towards the most vulnerable point of her body.

'Why am I in danger because of our association, my lord?' asked Tokiwa desperately, her eyes still fixed on the moving steel. 'And how does the coming of the barbarians put you at risk?'

'Because their arrival has caused great strife among our ruling factions. We are badly divided on how to respond!'

'I don't understand, my lord . . .'

'Perhaps you understand more than you admit, O Tokiwasan! And perhaps already you know my enemies! Perhaps they even paid you, and armed you with that dagger, to assassinate me—is that what happened?'

He continued to shift the sword steadily, forcing her to spread her thighs ever wider to avoid the blade's lethal caress. Risking a quick glance at his face, she saw that his eyes were hot with a terrible mixture of suspicion and desire. She wondered desperately if she should try to rise to defend herself, but some deep instinct rooted her to the floor. The ancient Bushido code, she knew, impelled a samurai to act without hesitation on his first instinct to kill—and the law of the land gave him impunity to do so. Every geisha who entertained samurai was acutely aware of these facts, and therefore behaved with the greatest discretion in the company of warriors. Remembering this, Tokiwa lowered her head in the coy, submissive manner which her training and experience had taught her was erotically pleasing to all men of Nippon. Half turning from him, she slowly brushed her long hair aside with one hand, to reveal completely the vulnerable curve of her naked neck.

'My lord, please believe me,' she said softly, speaking over her shoulder. 'I wished you no harm. I have been much honoured by your past visits. They have always brought me the greatest pleasure. Today I was merely preparing to defend my life against an unknown intruder. I know nothing of the danger to you or the disputes among the ruling factions.'

The sword had arrived within an inch of the fine whorls of dark hair that shadowed the naked arch of her thighs, and it was still moving. But although she wanted desperately to shrink away from it, she held to her decision not to show fear openly, and remained motionless on the tatami. Hardly daring to breathe, she watched the approaching blade with a calm, expressionless face.

In the absence of any spoken words, the noise from the street seemed to grow louder. Above the frenzied tolling of temple bells, the angry voices of several running men increased in volume as they drew nearer. The sword, now almost touching her, stopped moving, and she guessed that he had paused to listen to the disturbance outside. But she found that she dared not raise her head in case it provoked him further in some way she could not anticipate.

'Those of us close to the Emperor in the south believe it is wiser to try and learn the secrets of these barbarians!' said Tanaka suddenly in a fierce whisper. 'Leaders of the great Satsuma and Chohshu clans are in agreement with my father and others like him who lead the smaller southern clans. We believe we must try to find out by guile what makes the foreign barbarians so strong. Only then can we strengthen and save our nation.'

'And who is it that opposes you?' cut in Tokiwa quickly, sensing her chance might have come.

'Several clan leaders here in the north wish to strike against them at once! They believe it's the only way to expel the barbarians from our sacred soil once and for all. Men like Lord Daizo of Haifu and his many supporters are determined to fly in the face of fortune, no matter how many thousands of lives they may sacrifice.'

With a muffled exclamation of anger Tanaka began edging the sword towards her again, and it took all her courage to remain still.

'Your cause is clearly the wisest, and I could not oppose you,' said Tokiwa quickly. 'I never had any reason to betray you. I give you my assurance you will always have my complete loyalty.'

She lifted one hand from the matting and gently caressed the shimmering blade. With her heart pounding inside her chest, she turned her head at the same time to look directly into his eyes.

'Won't you sheathe your fine steel now, my lord,' she whispered urgently. 'And replace it quickly with what I most desire—yourself!'

Turning slightly on the mat, she arched the whole of her upper body invitingly around the sword. Lifting both arms she held them out towards him in a beseeching gesture. For an uncertain moment he stared down at her, his breath quickening, his hand tightening on the weapon's hilt. Then he relented and the sword ceased its movement. She saw the flame of desire brighten in his eyes and his chest heaved.

'As I rode here, I prayed fervently to the *kami* that you would prove yourself loyal, O Tokiwa-san,' said Tanaka thickly. 'But I could leave nothing to chance. I had no choice. I had to test your true feelings with my sword. I hope you understand.'

'I understand, my lord,' whispered Tokiwa, struggling to hide her desperate sense of relief. 'I understand perfectly.'

'Good . . . Anticipating such an outcome I've already arranged a secret hideaway for you, where you will be safe from both the foreign barbarians *and* my enemies.'

'Where is that, my lord?'

'It's a remote country inn with a distant view of Mount Fuji, some twenty miles or so from Yedo. Servants and guards of mine, who have followed me here from the south, are waiting nearby to escort you there now!'

'I am overwhelmed by my lord's kindness.' Tokiwa bowed her head while whispering her formal expression of gratitude. Then, acutely aware that she had still to consolidate her victory, she looked up and held out her arms to him again. 'But surely my lord wishes what I also crave? To share a fleeting moment of passion before we part . . .'

Holding her gaze, he slowly lifted the sword clear of her loins. After reversing the blade, he inserted its tip into the opening of the lacquered scabbard which he had concealed under the beggar's robes, and slid it home in a single fluid movement. Laying down the weapon within easy reach on the tatami, he quickly discarded the muddied disguise, leaving himself bare-chested. Dropping to his knees at her side, he unfastened the waistband of his loose *hakama* and, with a muffled cry, took her roughly into his arms.

Tokiwa closed her eyes tight as she prepared to yield to the blindness of his desire. As she had expected, he clutched at her nakedness selfishly, without making any attempt to arouse desire in her in return. With practised obedience she allowed herself to be forced roughly down onto her back, simulating a small cry of pleasure to match his mounting excitement. Then she tensed, anticipating the fierce, conquering thrust of his loins. But, before this happened, his embrace suddenly froze and he lifted his head to listen.

Harsh voices rising above the commotion in the street could be heard outside the Golden Pavilion. A sudden crash was heard from below, followed by the pounding of feet on the stairs. Rising quickly, Tanaka refastened his *hakama*, lunged for his sword and snatched it up in one hand. After glancing desperately around the room, he ran to the *shoji* that partitioned off the small balcony. Drawing back the screens, he motioned urgently with his head towards the outside steps which led down into a dark passage flanking the Golden Pavilion.

'Quick—follow me!' He held out his hand towards her. 'If you stay, you'll be killed!'

Running feet could be heard growing louder on the inside stairs, and Tokiwa rose from the tatami with a look of alarm in her eyes. But, after taking a few steps in his direction, she hesitated, aware suddenly of her total nakedness. Rushing across the room to where she had laid out the midnight-blue kimono, she snatched it up and hurried to join him on the balcony.

Outside, he beckoned her to follow, and dashed ahead down the steps. As she ran, Tokiwa could do no more than fling the kimono about her shoulders. A moment later they were swallowed up by the crowds fleeing heedlessly for their lives and in the seething throng only the silken, star-spangled folds of the glossy garment billowing behind her marked their frantic progress.

2

As dawn broke, Lieutenant Robert Eden was standing watchfully beside an open gunport on the main deck of the *Susquehanna.* In one hand he clutched an unsheathed cutlass and his other hand rested on the holster of his .36 calibre Colt Navy pistol. He was staring hard towards the shore, straining his eyes for a first glimpse of unknown Japan, but a dense shroud of white mist clung to the spars and furled sails of the slow-moving flagship, making it impossible for him to discern the slightest detail of the coastline.

The sea was flat and calm: the night breeze had dropped suddenly and there was no hint of wind. An eerie silence had descended with the morning mist, as though nature, aware of the drama of the moment, was watching a unique event with bated breath. In the stillness even the thumping of the steam frigate's engines and the slap of its paddle-wheels against the water seemed muted. From the tall, single funnel amidships, dark smoke was billowing lazily upwards to dissolve from sight in the mist astern.

'It's a ghostly-looking dawn, sir,' murmured a young marine nervously at Eden's side. 'Do you think we'll find armed troops on the beaches, when this fog lifts?'

'It's anybody's guess, marine,' replied Eden shortly. 'You'd best maintain discipline and stay silent.'

All along the length of the flagship's rails, other United States Marines stood pugnaciously alert at their battle stations. Dressed in peaked caps, blue jackets and white twills, their chests crisscrossed with white bandoliers, they held fully loaded carbines at the ready as they peered expectantly towards the shore. All the other gunports had already been opened, and their heavy cannon had been loaded and run out. Beside every weapon lay a neat pile of round shot and four stands of grape; muskets had been stacked on the quarterdeck and all boats had been armed with carbines, pistols and cutlasses. Sentinels who had been posted fore and aft and at the gangways were leaning out over the rails and bulwarks, their bodies tense, their eyes straining for the faintest glimpse of trouble.

As Eden peered vainly into the mist he found himself pondering in which direction Mount Fuji lay. Would the volcano that had dazzled his eyes so overwhelmingly during the night still be visible by day, he wondered. And could it possibly prove to be as extraordinary a vision in daylight? While he was reflecting on these questions, the first memory of his dream about the mountain rushed back into his conscious mind, and the force of this waking recollection was so strong that he started inwardly. For several moments the starkly beautiful dream-image of the peak filled his thoughts to the exclusion of all else. The very clarity and vividness of this image seemed initially to imbue it with the quality of genuine memory; then he remembered gathering in the star-filled night to wind about his body and he smiled faintly with relief at recognizing the dream for what it had been. But then he recalled the dream's strange climax, and saw again the temple and the giant mirror at the volcano's peak. In its silver surface the disturbing reflections of Japanese faces that had replaced his own swam into focus, and this merging of rare beauty with something ominous and undefined made him shudder physically in the cold damp of the dawn.

'Looks like we're going to find out something now, sir,' breathed the marine guard at Eden's side, gesturing in the direction of the shore.

Realizing suddenly how distracted he had become, Eden gathered himself and screwed up his eyes to follow the direction indicated. Through the mist he could see the smudged outline of a towering headland, flanked by a lower mountain range. His dream memories, both exhilarating and disturbing in the same moment, had heightened the sense of excitement he felt at finally coming in sight of their goal, and this long-anticipated glimpse of land quickened his pulse. He screwed up his eyes, trying to pick out figures who might bring life and depth to the coastline but only the stark grandeur of the cliffs and mountains could be seen.

'This is Cape Idzu,' whispered a voice in Japanese, at Eden's elbow. 'We're now entering the Gulf of Yedo.'

Glancing round, the American officer saw that Sentaro, the Japanese castaway, had appeared beside him and was peering intently into the mist. As he scanned the hazy shoreline, his narrow eyes became bright with emotion.

'It's nearly four years now since I saw my homeland, master,' he murmured anxiously. 'So many times I've longed for this moment—but, as I said before, I'm very afraid . . .'

The light coastal mist was dispersing slowly to reveal a calm, mirror-like sea. No boat or vessel of any kind disturbed its glittering surface and the rocky shoreline, becoming clearer with every passing moment, also lay quiet and deserted, as far as the eye could see.

'There doesn't seem to be much to worry about here,' said Eden quietly, returning his cutlass to a nearby weapons rack. 'No sign at all of any armed men.'

'There are no fortifications here, master,' replied the Japanese, still peering towards the shore. 'Nearer to Yedo in the bay itself there are many forts. High on the cliffs . . . everywhere . . . a lot of guns. No foreign ship has ever dared to sail past them.'

Through the retreating mist the three other ships of the squadron were gradually materializing and taking on distinct form. For safety's sake the *Susquehanna* and the *Mississippi*, both named after great North American rivers, had taken the sloops-of-war in tow and the strengthening sun revealed the squadron to be an impressive sight for their crews, as well as for the many unseen Japanese eyes already watching fearfully from the shore. Weighing around two thousand tons each, the steam frigates embodied two contrasting historical epochs in their appearance: each was barque-rigged with three masts and a full complement of sails from the past, but both also possessed massive, side-mounted paddle-wheels and tall smokestacks that foreshadowed the future. Hauling the lighter sailing ships easily in their wake, the steam-driven vessels looked majestic and impregnable as they moved through the brightening day at a speed of eight knots, with all sails tidily furled.

At the end of the *Susquehanna*'s taut hawser, which minutes before had seemed to haul nothing but a dense cloud of fog, the thousand-ton *Plymouth* was now fully visible. Almost abeam, a quarter of a mile off, the *Mississippi*, belching similar clouds of black smoke, was carefully keeping station, with *Saratoga* gliding silently at its heels. Eden could see that contingents of marine guards and sailors were drawn up at their battle stations on all of the four warships, and the signal flags fluttering from the mizzen mast of the *Susquehanna* visibly confirmed the dramatic command of the hour: 'Clear ships for action.'

For the past three days Eden and his fellow officers had put the gun crews repeatedly through their paces, clearing the decks, shotting and running out the massive sixty-four-pound cannon. The firepower of all the warships had also been augmented with newer eight-inch Paixhans, which fired explosive shells in deafening salvoes, and their small teams of specialist gunners had been trained to a peak of readiness. All the ships' longboats had been armed with small brass cannon and readied for launching; extra lookouts had been posted aloft, in the bows and at the stern; drills to meet all contingencies from landing attacks to repelling boarders had been practised over and over again, and stacks of sharp, long-handled pikes stood ready for use in defending the decks against any attempt by the Japanese to swarm aboard in overpowering numbers.

The strait leading to the Bay of Yedo was some eight miles wide but because no detailed charts were available, as it advanced across the lower gulf the US squadron slowed its speed and moved forward with greater caution. The bigger warships needed a draught of three and a half fathoms beneath their iron-braced wooden hulls and constant soundings were also being taken by leadsmen who swung out weighted lines from the 'chains' of the narrow bows. With the *Susquehanna* at its head, the squadron forged on through the morning hours, following a course that took it to within two miles of the bay's northern shore.

As the coastal mist cleared in the early afternoon, Eden caught sight of the first signs of habitation: a thatched village nestling in the shadow of a rocky bluff. Almost at once figures began spilling from the houses, and soon the beach was black with running, gesticulating men. Higher up the strait a dozen high-prowed fishing junks with ribbed, bat-wing sails were emerging from a cove. On catching sight of the American ships they milled confusedly in a circle for a minute or two before half their number broke from the rest and sailed away rapidly in the direction of Yedo, as though to raise an alarm.

Two or three of the junks approached and crossed the path of the thundering warships before, apparently, realizing the speed at which they were moving. As the *Susquehanna* bore down on them, the Japanese fishermen panicked and brought the sails clattering down their masts. Manning long oars, they desperately rowed their lumbering craft shoreward, passing so close to the American ships that Eden and the marine guards were able to see the fearful expressions on their faces.

As he watched them, Eden felt a tug at his sleeve. Looking down, he found Sentaro pointing out through the gunport towards the beach. Following the direction of his finger, Eden saw a flotilla of twenty or more narrow boats had been launched and were being rowed skilfully towards them. Each boat bore an identical coloured flag on its stern marked with a single Japanese character, and it was evident that they carried an organized defence force.

Sentaro's face furrowed into a despairing expression and he began muttering distractedly, repeating the same words over and over again. '*Shimpai! Taihen shimpai*—I'm worried, master . . . I'm so worried.'

Eden watched the boats for several seconds, then patted the castaway reassuringly on the shoulder. 'Look, they're falling behind already. They're not fast enough to catch us. Don't upset yourself.'

Turning, Eden glanced towards the quarterdeck, where the bulky authoritative figure of Commodore Matthew Perry was silhouetted, standing determinedly alone at the weather rail. Resplendent in a dark blue tunic festooned with gold epaulettes and double rows of gilded buttons, his dark leonine head jutted aggressively from his high collar as he surveyed the misty strait through a long Dollond telescope. When they approached Cape Sagami around noon the squadron had come to on his orders and he had spelled out his feelings very clearly to all the officers and men of the four ships through their captains whom he called to his cabin on the flagship. There were only two ways, he had said, to open Japan to trade—by a *show* of force or by the outright use of that force.

If displaying their mighty steam-driven warships bristling with guns and armed men was not sufficient, he had emphasized, he was fully prepared to go further and use them—even though the squadron carried a total force of only one thousand men to be pitted against innumerable Japanese. Boldness and confidence, therefore, were all-important. In previous years, he had recalled, some American ships which had sailed into this same bay had been boarded, and their commanders had been harassed and humiliated. This would not happen again, under any circumstances! It was for this precise reason that he had ordered the repeated drills at battle stations to bring the crews and the marine guard to a high pitch of readiness. He had particularly reminded all ranks that the formal letter which they carried from the President of the United States to the Emperor of Japan was of crucial importance. It was essential that this letter be presented with the utmost dignity—but as a last resort he would threaten to land and march by force into Yedo, to deliver the letter personally to the Emperor. And that threat was not an idle one . . . Studying the proud, ramrod-straight figure who had made these decisions, Eden could almost feel his steely, unflagging determination. It was widely known that Perry himself had proposed this expedition several years earlier, and he seemed now to swell visibly with the ambition to impose his will on the mysterious country that was at last sketching itself before his eyes through the mist.

The sudden boom of a gun from the shore interrupted Eden's thoughts and wrenched his attention from the quarterdeck. Looking westward through his gunport, he saw a great fist of dark smoke rising slowly from a clifftop fort. He guessed a rocket or a cannon had been fired—either in an attempt to warn the ships to proceed no further or to give notice of their coming to defenders higher up the bay. Realizing this, he swung back quickly to check the reaction of Commodore Perry at the quarterdeck rail. His flag lieutenant was waiting respectfully for orders a few paces away, and eager midshipmen were also hovering, ready to run headlong to all quarters of the frigate with messages and commands. But the burly figure of the commodore remained impassive and unmoved. Almost nonchalantly he continued to study the smoke of the explosion and the fortified shoreline through his telescope, yet he made no comment and issued no new orders.

Glancing quickly about himself, Eden noticed that crewmen and marine guards alike were showing signs of tension. Other forts were becoming visible on distant cliffs and, although no further shots were fired, when he drew a small pair of personal binoculars from his jacket pocket to scan the distant heights, he was able to see that most of their ramparts bristled with guns. More and more fishing junks and fast mosquito boats with official-looking stern flags were putting to sea to swarm in the direction of the squadron, and he realized from their faces that some of the sailors around him were beginning to fear that their own ships might be moving into the jaws of a trap.

'I will be accused, master, of bringing forbidden thoughts back to Japan . . .' Sentaro was back at Eden's side, his expression more anxious than before. 'Arriving home in a barbarian warship I can see now will look very bad for me. I may even be executed.'

'You don't have to remain in Japan, Sentaro,' said Eden quietly, still studying the coastline through his binoculars. 'You could stay on board this ship and return with us to America.'

'How?' asked the castaway frantically. 'I asked to be brought back here. Who would help me now?'

Eden did not reply at once. As more hilltop forts emerged from the haze, dark swarms of armed men could be seen drilling purposefully around them. The afternoon sunlight was also illuminating a landscape of extraordinary beauty: precipitous cliffs were giving way to deep ravines cloaked in rich green vegetation, which in turn opened onto inlets of rich alluvial land at sea level. Small villages were clustered around these inlets, and crowds of people could be seen rushing towards the beaches to watch the American ships pass.

'*I* would help you, Sentaro,' said Eden at last. '*I* would support your request to Commodore Perry. And my home is near Long Island Sound, where many seafarers live and work. I could help you get a job there, and start a new life.'

'If you'd take me back to America, I'd do anything for you, master,' said the castaway in a desperate whisper. Falling on his knees at Eden's feet, he embraced the officer's lower legs.

'Get up, Sentaro,' said Eden hastily, stooping to pull the Japanese to his feet. 'And don't ever do that again! If I help you, it is because you are a friend. Do you understand?'

'Yes, master, I understand—I'm very sorry. Thank you.'

'We'll talk more of this later. Meantime, try not to be afraid.'

Raising the binoculars, Eden turned his attention back to the coastline, and again studied the passing heights. The uplands above the villages were now dotted with cultivated fields as well as shady woodlands; beyond, a low range of mountains rolled away to merge darkly into the haze and, despite the dangers the squadron faced, Eden found himself searching the distant landscape with a curious sense of dissatisfaction.

'Why can't I see Mount Fuji in daylight, Sentaro?' he asked at last, shaking his head in puzzlement. 'There doesn't seem to be any sign of it.'

The castaway plucked at Eden's sleeve, and motioned upward with his head. 'You are looking too low, master. You must raise your eyes higher to find Fuji-san.'

Frowning, Eden lifted his gaze—then drew in his breath sharply. Higher in the sky than seemed possible, the sun was bathing the volcano's white peak with light. As on the previous night, the mountain seemed at first sight to be defying gravity and floating free in the middle heavens. But on peering more closely he realized that low clouds were totally obscuring its broad base. So powerful was the impact of this vision on Eden that for a minute or two he could only stare in silence. Then he closed his eyes and the images of his dream flooded back into his mind. Before he opened them again he wondered whether he might have imagined the extraordinary sight. But, to his relief, when he looked the summit was still visible, soaring with majestic grace into the morning sky. Even as he watched, its peak brightened and gleamed whiter through the thinning haze and the surrounding air deepened to a softer blue. Infinitely moved by this sight, Robert Eden felt a fierce new ambition spring to life inside him.

'Sentaro, do people ever climb your sacred mountain?' he asked softly, turning to face the castaway. 'Do they climb to the very top?'

'Yes, master.' Sentaro nodded eagerly. 'They call it the Supreme Altar of the Sun. All who respect the ancient gods must climb up to its summit once in their lives. So for hundreds of years pilgrims have come to climb Fuji-san from all parts of Nippon.'

'What's to be found at the summit?' asked Eden quickly. 'Is there a temple?'

'Yes, a temple to a beautiful Shinto goddess. Many pilgrims claim they see her hovering like a cloud above the crater. They go there to pray before her shrine, and to salute the rising sun from the peak . . . But that can be dangerous. They say her guardian spirits hide at the precipices—and they may throw down any pilgrim who climbs up there with an impure heart.'

For a moment Eden glanced at the sea, watching the swarms of Japanese boats advancing rapidly from the shore towards the *Susquehanna*.

Then he looked quickly towards Fuji once more. 'One day, Sentaro, I would like to climb your sacred mountain.'

'But you can't, master!' gasped the castaway in horror.

'Why not?'

'No *gai-jin* has ever climbed Mount Fuji. Even the women of Nippon are forbidden to set foot on our sacred mountain.'

Eden considered this statement in silence, still looking thoughtfully towards the mountain. 'Such beauty can't be the sole preserve of any one nation,' he said at last. 'It belongs to all peoples of the world.'

'If you tried to climb Fuji-san, master, you would be killed without any hesitation,' exclaimed Sentaro. 'You must never try.'

'But I've already climbed it,' said Eden quietly.

'How could you, master? You've never been here before.'

'I mean I've already scaled Fuji-san in my heart.' Eden turned to face the castaway who was now crouching by the gunport. 'Last night in a vivid dream I reached the summit. And I felt something very beautiful and strange that I can't explain . . . I still can't forget that feeling. It made me want to go up there more than anything else in the world.'

'I hope you never do, master,' said Sentaro fearfully, after a long pause. 'Because if you do, I'm sure you'll die.'

3

On the Quaterdeck, Commodore Perry's flag lieutenant, John Rice, waited dutiful and alert at a suitable distance from his commanding officer. By the lieutenant's side a fresh-faced midshipman stood eagerly at attention, his body as taut as a tightly coiled spring. Like their august superior, both men were tensely watching the ball of smoke curling up from the hilltop battery which had fired the single warning shot. Their faces showed that they too were wondering anxiously whether further shots would follow.

Lowering his gaze, the lieutenant studied the imposing figure of Commodore Perry as he stood at the port rail. Holding his long telescope to his eye, he was watching the smoke of the explosion drift skyward, but he made no move to issue any further commands and Rice relaxed.

'I'd guess the commodore has decided that disdain is the appropriate response to a gnat bite,' whispered the flag lieutenant. 'I don't think he's going to be lured into making any false move.'

The eighteen-year-old midshipman, flattered by the flag lieutenant's confidential aside, beamed and nodded his agreement. 'So it would seem, sir!'

Rice glanced casually down towards the spar deck, making a routine check that all his previous orders were being carried out, and by chance his eye fell on the Japanese castaway at the moment he flung himself prostrate at Robert Eden's feet. The strangeness of this act beside an open gunport arrested the flag lieutenant's attention, and he continued to watch as Eden dragged the Japanese upright and began to speak sharply to him. After a second or two, Rice looked round in Perry's direction to see if the incident had attracted his superior's attention; but the commodore was still scanning the fortified shore through his telescope. With a thoughtful expression, Rice drew out the notepad on which he normally jotted details of the commodore's orders. Beneath Eden's name he quickly scribbled an informal message, and, folding the paper in half, he handed it unobtrusively to the midshipman.

'When you next have reason to go down to the spar deck, Mr Harris,' he said in a low voice, 'give this quietly to Lieutenant Eden with my compliments. It's a private message, not an order.'

'Very good, sir.'

The midshipman, who had followed the flag lieutenant's gaze, tucked the note carefully into a pocket of his tunic and together they watched further animated exchanges take place between Eden and the Japanese castaway. They noticed that, while they talked, both men turned frequently to look towards the shore and the spectacular outline of Mount Fuji.

'I've heard his men say that Lieutenant Eden is a very brave man,' said the midshipman hesitantly. 'They've got the greatest respect for him.'

'That respect is certainly deserved,' said Rice pensively. 'I know Lieutenant Eden better than most because we did our first year at Annapolis together when the Naval Academy was founded. We were just acting midshipmen in the Mexican war—but he volunteered to go ashore with landing parties to spike enemy guns—and showed exceptional courage.'

'I hope I'll have the same courage when my time comes, sir,' said the midshipman, peering excitedly towards shore. 'I have a lot to learn from Lieutenant Eden—and yourself.'

'I don't think his kind of courage can be learned, Mr Harris,' said Rice distractedly. 'Many years ago, Lieutenant Eden's great-grandfather was captured as a youth by Iroquois Indians when they raided a settlement in eastern Connecticut. A few years later he was seen leading Iroquois braves himself in another raid. Later in his life he returned to the same settlement, bringing with him a half-Indian son. That boy was to become Lieutenant Eden's grandfather . . .'

Surprised and pleased by the flag lieutenant's confidences, the young midshipman stared down at Eden with increased admiration in his eyes. 'I hadn't known all that, sir. Perhaps it explains the lieutenant's remarkable character.'

'Maybe. But there's more to it than that . . .' Rice paused and frowned, his expression suggesting that, in confiding in the young midshipman, he was consciously attempting to order his own thoughts about his enigmatic brother officer. 'Although he grew up in a wealthy merchant family, he clearly was a rebel like his great-grandfather. At sixteen, he ran off to marry his childhood sweetheart. She was only sixteen too—and she died tragically. I think he still blames himself for her death . . .'

The midshipman waited impatiently for Rice to continue, his curiosity fully aroused; but he dared not pose a direct question about a superior officer, in case he appeared insubordinate. 'That sounds very sad, sir,' he ventured at last.

'Yes, it was—at the time she was in the pangs of a premature childbirth,' continued Rice after another pause. 'He was driving her to a doctor through a storm in the middle of the night. Their buggy overturned on a forest track . . . The baby, a son, survived—but she didn't.' Rice hesitated again, as though reluctant to give voice to possibly unreliable thoughts. 'I'm only guessing, but perhaps his bravery comes from not valuing his own life very highly as a result of that . . .'

'I've noticed Lieutenant Eden always keeps himself very much to himself, sir,' said the midshipman tentatively.

Rice nodded. 'He once told me he cursed God on that night in the wood . . . and he swore he would never pray again so long as he lived. He joined the Navy then—and ever since I've known him, he's been remote and withdrawn.' The flag lieutenant shook his head in puzzlement, still watching Eden and the Japanese. 'I think for some reason, Mr Harris, he finds it easier to talk to that castaway than to us . . .'

'Lieutenant Rice! Take a fresh signal for the squadron!'

The deep baritone voice of Matthew Perry rang out across the quarterdeck and Rice hurried to his side, readying his notepad and pencil.

The commodore was making one last imperious sweep of the bay with his eyeglass, watching the fast-moving Japanese guard-boats that were now appearing on all sides. Growing numbers of high-prowed coastal junks were also darting out of the creeks and havens of the rocky shoreline, angling their sails to the wind in an attempt to draw near to the thundering warships—but none could match the speed of the intruders, and all were falling quickly behind.

'My new signal shall read, "Have no communication of any kind with shore,"' boomed Perry. '"And *allow* none from shore!" Start the flags on the starboard forward halyards to emphasize the gravity of this signal!'

'Aye, sir! Very good, sir!'

Lieutenant Rice barked out his acknowledgement, saluted and moved smartly away to hand the written signal to the midshipman. He watched the junior officer make haste down the ladder to the spar deck and race to the signal officer's post amidships. Within seconds the first coloured message-flags were fluttering up the mizzenmast and the midshipman made a detour on returning to the quarterdeck to hand over the private message to Robert Eden.

'With Lieutenant Rice's compliments, sir!'

The boy saluted smartly as he passed on the slip of paper. Close up, he realized that traces of Eden's Indian ancestry were indeed visible in his broad face; but, although the trainee officer stood respectfully to attention before him, Eden did not look at him directly. Instead he merely nodded his thanks before dismissing him, then glanced briefly towards the flag lieutenant on the quarterdeck to acknowledge the note's delivery. Before opening it, Eden scanned the surrounding sea and the distant beaches, to check whether his gunnery crews might be called urgently into action. Only when he was satisfied there was no immediate danger did he unfold the piece of paper.

> The message read: *Robert—first, may I offer a friendly word of advice. I think our Japanese castaway should remain invisible in his quarters during this dangerous period of our approach—for his sake as well as ours. Perhaps you would give him appropriate instructions. Secondly, a personal request. The commodore, for protocol reasons, has ordered me to conduct any initial negotiations on his behalf. He wishes to remain unseen, and will eventually meet only the very highest imperial dignitary. If any Japanese, armed or unarmed, come aboard, I want you and nobody else to head my guard party. I hope you'll agree—John Rice.*

Eden folded the note away into a pocket and glanced round at Sentaro. The Japanese was still crouched on the deck, staring intently through the gun-port. Following his gaze, Eden saw that Mount Fuji seemed to have grown suddenly in size, and for the first time its broad base had become fully visible. But because the lower slopes glowed grey in the growing light, they still seemed to melt and merge moment by moment into the paleness of the morning sky, renewing the impression that the dramatic peak had the power to detach itself from the earth whenever it chose, and to soar majestically into the heavens. The enchantment of the mountain, he found, was as great by day as by night—and it was with an effort that he turned away and bent to tap the Japanese castaway on the shoulder.

'The next few hours could be difficult here on deck, Sentaro,' he said firmly in Japanese. 'It would be best if you went back to your place under the fo'c's'le.'

'Yes, master, of course,' gasped the castaway, his eyes widening with apprehension. 'I'll go at once.'

'And you'd better stay there until I tell you it's safe to come out.'

'Yes, master!'

As the Japanese rose to hurry away, Eden found himself moved by the fearful expression in his eyes, and he dropped a kindly hand on his shoulder. 'We're all in danger here, Sentaro. But try to stay calm—I'll do everything I can to protect you.'

4

On a clifftop in the lower reaches of the bay, Prince Tanaka Yoshio stood among a tense group of high-ranking Japanese, watching the American warships move inexorably northward towards Yedo. It was mid-afternoon, and they could see their own Nipponese guard-boats and coastal junks still buzzing like an ineffectual gnat-swarm in the wake of the massive, black-hulled steam frigates. Occasional puffs of smoke continued to rise into the still air as successive warning shots were fired from shore batteries, but nothing interrupted the steady progress of the US Navy squadron.

'They have already penetrated further into the bay than any other foreign vessel,' rasped one scowling *daimyo* as he stared southward towards the distant ships. 'They must be stopped now by force!'

'You know it's impossible for us to halt them by force of arms, Lord Daizo,' said Tanaka quietly. 'At present we have no adequate defence against such power.'

'We have innumerable brave samurai who will fight to their last drop of blood,' said the richly robed *daimyo*, his face darkening with anger. 'Don't forget that!'

'They are truly *kurufune*—black ships—just as the rumours said,' muttered a shogunate official who wore a more modest wide-sleeved gown of patterned green silk and a lacquered bonnet. 'Only a divine wind from the gods, like the *kamikaze* that wrecked the fleet of Kublai Khan, will drive them away . . .'

A second official, a scholarly-looking interpreter, garbed in similar fashion, looked up anxiously at the clear sky, shaking his head. 'There will be no great wind today—but we shall forbid them to anchor, as the Council of the Shogun has directed. I've composed a command in Dutch, ordering them to leave at once for Nagasaki. The leader of the delegation can display it from our boat . . .'

'What sort of "command" have you prepared, Haniwara Tokuma?' demanded the scowling *daimyo* contemptuously. 'Let us see it!'

Holding out both hands, the interpreter unfurled a giant scroll for the inspection of the other dignitaries. Inscribed with big, hand-written Dutch words that would be visible from a distance, the message constituted a defiant order for the American ships to sail back to Nagasaki—Japan's southernmost port where, during two centuries of total foreign exclusion, a handful of traders from the Netherlands had been permitted to supervise the trickle of trade and other contacts with Western nations.

'Your feeble message will be ignored, Haniwara-san,' said Lord Daizo explosively, waving the banner aside. 'It will prove quite useless.'

'It is my duty to exhibit it nevertheless, my lord,' replied the interpreter, bowing nervously towards the *daimyo* as he closed the scroll. 'I have been instructed to do so. It will at least make our position plain.'

'Unfortunately the Lord Daizo is right,' said Tanaka, glancing round at several other *daimyo* who were watching the approaching warships with distracted expressions. 'The Americans have too many guns—they won't obey such a demand.'

'But we must show the enemy that we are ready to fight. And very soon we *will* be prepared!' A burly, heavy-chested man still strong and forceful in middle age, Lord Daizo glowered at Tanaka in response, then gestured with his arm along the clifftop to draw attention to the growing numbers of foot soldiers and mounted warriors being hastily marshalled into positions overlooking the bay. 'A force of twenty thousand fighting men has been raised from my own estates and from other fiefs in the region. Soon they will all be in position—and *none* will fear the barbarians and their black ships.'

Amongst the squadrons of fighting men, who were arrayed in the colours of their clan lords, a few ancient-looking cannon were being dragged into place on the heights by sweating peasants clad only in loincloths. All along the coastal ridges, coloured canvas screens were being hastily erected to help conceal the movement of troops and weapons from the bay. By the minute, new contingents of men in leather and metal body armour were pouring up the hillsides, clutching pikes, spears, or bows and arrows, and the infantrymen among them carried long-barrelled, muzzle-loading muskets and flintlocks on their shoulders.

'It will not be to our advantage to provoke an outright attack just now,' said Tanaka carefully, after studying the visible strength of the defences. 'The American guns are very powerful. And although they are comparatively few in numbers, those who man the ships are extremely confident in their strength.'

'Those could be the words, Prince Tanaka, of one who is reluctant to fight for other reasons,' said Lord Daizo slightingly. 'How do you know all this?'

Tanaka eyed the *daimyo* steadily, giving no sign of having taken offence at his implied insult. 'My lord, reports brought from the last anchorage of the American ships in the Lew Chew islands make all this very clear. The extent of their power is at present unknown. So it would be most unwise to provoke them into giving us a demonstration . . .'

'The power of the samurai's sword has always been *our* surest weapon!' declared another young nobleman who until then had stood silent at Lord Daizo's side. 'We should be the first to demonstrate that.' He paused and stared hard at Tanaka, one hand on the hilts of his twin swords. His brooding features were recognizably heir to those of the older man at his side, and before speaking again he looked round challengingly at all the other members of the gathering. 'I am sure most of us here agree that we should be ready to sacrifice our lives without hesitation. Then our enemies will know we are fearless in defence of our sacred territory.'

'The sentiments of my son Yakamochi are those that should spring naturally from all your hearts,' said Lord Daizo vehemently. 'So I'm glad that someone of his courage will accompany the officials who are to make the first approach to the American ships.'

'Why do you say that, my lord?' enquired Tanaka, suddenly concerned.

'Because if the American ships can be boarded by some subterfuge, a lightning strike could be made against their commander or his senior officers! That would convince the foreign barbarians of our fierce determination to resist them to the end!'

Before replying, Tanaka looked slowly round the circle of silent faces; in varying degrees all their expressions betrayed alarm and uncertainty, and he noticed that many in the group avoided his eye. 'Nobody doubts the courage of our fighting men—or their readiness to die gloriously. But if we provoke a skirmish at the outset and manage to kill just a few of our enemies, what will be the immediate result?'

'They will realize their purpose is futile and withdraw!' said Yakamochi fiercely. 'They will leave us alone.'

Tanaka shook his head decisively. 'No, they would almost certainly proceed to bombard us with their heavy guns from a safe distance, without any risk to themselves. They can cause enormous loss of life. They might also land a strong force to march into Yedo. And if they did, what would they find there?'

He waited but, because they were puzzled by the unexpected question, neither the officials nor the *daimyo* spoke.

'They would discover first their own ignorance. Our spies from the Lew Chew islands have reported that the Americans think our Emperor himself resides in Yedo castle. And that is why they have come here—to deliver a letter of insulting demands to our sacred ruler. If they land and march on Yedo castle, they will find that it is the Shogun who resides here—but that he is very sick and close to death. They will also discover that our governing council is weak and undecided on how best to resist them.'

'They will never reach Yedo!' exclaimed Lord Daizo. 'Fighting men are already being summoned from all the fiefdoms in the surrounding provinces. They are streaming in from the north, south, east and west. Eventually there will be one hundred thousand warriors defending these cliffs . . .'

'We have no understanding yet of the power of their ships or their weapons,' replied Tanaka coolly. 'And once they are ashore they will certainly see that our guns are few, small and ineffective—no match for their own superior weapons.' He paused and gestured towards the canvas screens that snaked along the bluffs. 'They will also find our whole coastal defence system is feeble. Once they realize that we conceal weakness and not strength behind those screens, they may be encouraged to return quickly with an even larger force and attempt to conquer our entire homeland—which the Dutch tell us has been done elsewhere. Above all we need to win time to prepare our defences . . .'

'The warriors of Nippon are always ready to defend their sacred soil,' proclaimed another robed *daimyo* standing close to Lord Daizo. 'They are as ready now as they have ever been!'

Prince Tanaka again shook his head firmly in disagreement. 'For two hundred years Nippon has shut itself off from the world. That has been a time largely of peace, so our fighting men are no longer hardened and experienced in battle. Their fighting spirit is low, their spears and their muskets are rusted, their arrows are unfeathered . . . On the other hand, the boldness of the enemy ships is a sure sign that the *gai-jin* have a great willingness to fight—'

'You are suggesting that we capitulate to whatever the barbarians demand of us, without a fight,' cried Yakamochi accusingly. 'You are urging a total surrender!'

'That's not true. If we antagonize the barbarians, the shogunate may be humiliated before our people. This could lead to turmoil—and even rebellion! So it is essential that we strive to deceive the enemy. We should negotiate skilfully so as to mislead them about our true strength.'

'This is dangerous,' interjected Lord Daizo. 'If we behave like cowards, they will surely sense our weakness. It would be madness for us to rule out the use of force!'

'If we make the wrong choice, have you not thought how easy it would be for the foreign barbarians to strangle Yedo?' asked Tanaka mildly, looking again towards the bay where the four black warships were cutting a broad white swathe through the growing swarms of merchant junks and sampans dotting the water. 'Look how many supply craft are plying back and forth to feed our great city. The enemy will already have noticed that most of its food is brought in by sea. A simple blockade by their ships at the narrows would quickly bring one million people in Yedo to the brink of starvation!'

'You may be right,' said Yakamochi fiercely, stepping forward and confronting Prince Tanaka directly. 'But we believe it's better to fight than to starve! That's why I've volunteered to help escort our delegation to the barbarian ships, disguised as an ordinary samurai guard.'

Yakamochi paused and, with a flourish, drew his short sword from its scabbard. Turning the weapon, he concealed it expertly inside one of the voluminous sleeves of his kimono, then looked hard at Tanaka again.

'If an opportunity to kill one or more of the foreign barbarian leaders arises, I shall be prepared to act swiftly in this fashion. My father approves of this. And we believe that all of us must act as boldly as the enemy, if we are to save Nippon!'

For a long moment Prince Tanaka held the challenging gaze of the other young nobleman in silence; then he bowed his head formally to Lord Daizo to indicate that the exchanges were at an end.

'I, too, have volunteered to accompany the boat delegation disguised as a guard, my lords,' he said evenly. 'But I intend to do all I can to ensure that we do not use the sword until the moment is ripe.'

'We shall see who is right—and very soon,' snapped Daizo, bowing perfunctorily in return. 'It's time now to confront these barbarians and their black ships!'

Swinging on his heel he motioned impatiently to his son and his bodyguards, and led the way towards their tethered horses.

5

Action stations!'

Robert Eden yelled his order sharply, and watched eagle-eyed as his gun crews surged towards the row of massive sixty-four-pound cannon drawn up before the open firing embrasures on the port side.

'Load shot—and prime!' he shouted, and nodded with satisfaction as the crewmen wielded their ramming poles with lightning speed to force charges of gunpowder, wadding and huge balls of cast-iron roundshot into the gaping muzzles of the guns. As soon as this had been done, slender friction tubes with lanyards hanging loose were dropped into the rear touch-holes, readying the guns for use.

'Run out!' barked Eden, striding quickly along the deck, his hand gripping his sword hilt.

As one man, the sailors strained and heaved at the thick ropes threaded through block-and-tackle fittings on the wheeled wooden gun-carriages. In deadly unison the long muzzles of the guns slid out through the bulwarks of the *Susquehanna* and nosed threateningly towards the Japanese shore. Eden had been timing each action with his pocketwatch, and he counted off the seconds loudly to hasten their actions. While the sweating sailors were still checking the breech ropes that restrained the guns on recoil, he drew his sword, flourished it aloft for all to see, and shouted the final order.

'Fire!'

Leading gunners moved swiftly forward to seize the lanyards of the friction tubes that hung from the vent holes. But, instead of tugging sharply at the cords to fire a match and ignite the gunpowder charges, they merely tapped the stocks of the cannons lightly with their hands before turning away to simulate the evasive action they would have taken if the guns had genuinely fired.

Nodding his approval, Eden moved quickly from one gun to another, speaking a few words of encouragement and praise to each group of gunners in turn. Drills had been ordered every hour during the voyage up the bay, and the gun crews, keyed up by the tension, were already working to their highest pitch of efficiency. When he had finished his rounds, Eden halted and stooped low to gaze out along the barrel of one of the cannons. He saw that the waters of Yedo Bay were dotted more thickly than ever with the dark shapes of Japanese craft. Amongst the slower-moving fishing and cargo junks he noticed a growing number of long, sleek guard-boats that were being propelled forward swiftly and expertly by their crews. As the boats drew nearer, he could see that each one was rowed by six or eight Japanese stripped to the waist. The men were standing upright at their task, facing forward and swinging the whole weight of their slender bodies in unflagging unison to ply the oars. All of the boats, he noticed, were decked with coloured pennants and streamers, and identical insignia flags bearing Japanese characters fluttered at their sterns.

Seated in each boat was a force of twenty soldiers commanded by two officers standing fore and aft. The fighting men wore leather body armour, wide-sleeved cloth jackets and loose trousers. Some clutched muskets in their hands, and all wore twin swords in the sashes of their garments. Their narrow-eyed faces, Eden could see, were set in hostile expressions, and their mouths were wide open. Although no other sound was audible above the thud and roar of the warships' engines, both oarsmen and warriors were chanting and roaring under the direction of the officers who gestured belligerently towards the American vessels.

Another boat caught his eye, heading with greater determination than the others through the mêlée. Black ornamental tassels hung from its bows, and it contained half a dozen sword-carrying samurai who were glaring aggressively towards the US ships. The heads of the warriors were distinctively shaven and pigtails were coiled in topknots on their heads, but amongst them Eden could see a group of unarmed officials dressed in brightly coloured silk gowns and black-lacquered bonnets.

As he watched, the brawny, bare-chested oarsmen redoubled their efforts, straining to match the steam frigate's speed through the turbulent waters that were still being churned white by its huge paddle-wheels. The unflagging determination of the Japanese rowers was evident in their fiercely knitted brows and rippling muscles, and after a minute or two of this intense effort they pulled their craft ahead of the flagship and turned to manoeuvre close in beneath the port bow, where its rail was lowered.

'They're going to try and board us,' said a firm voice at Eden's side. 'Prepare a squad to fend them off with pikes!'

Eden turned to find Lieutenant Rice standing close behind him. His eyes were fixed intently on the intruding longboat and he continued to watch it as he spoke.

'Commodore Perry intends to keep the squadron moving very steadily up the bay. We shall anchor before the township of Uraga. Until then, his orders are that nobody should be allowed to board us without observing the strictest standards of respect and protocol. But you are all to use the utmost discretion. We don't want to provoke a fight to the death.'

Eden nodded quickly and turned to his nearest gun crew. Gesturing towards the sharpened pikestaffs stacked in a pyramid on the deck nearby, he spoke to the men briskly, without shouting.

'Gun drills are finished! Arm yourselves now with pikes. This is the real thing!'

The flattened steel of the pike heads glittered and flashed in the sun as the sailors seized one apiece, then looked expectantly towards Eden.

'Prepare to repel boarders on the port side!' he snapped, and led the squad in a dash along the deck to the nearest open gunport.

Without fuss he formed the men quickly into a tight line and, bracing themselves, they thrust their pikes out threateningly towards the encroaching guard-boat. All over the ship similar orders were shouted, and within moments all the gunports and rails of the *Susquehanna* were bristling with clusters of pike blades.

Amidships in the heaving Japanese boat, an official wearing a gown of sea-green silk had stood up. On catching sight of Eden's gold-braided officer's cap above him, he plucked a giant scroll from his sleeve. Holding it up above his head with one hand, he let it fall open vertically, and gestured with his free hand in Eden's direction. The turbulence created by the *Susquehanna*'s huge paddle-wheels caused the Japanese boat to pitch and toss, but the official managed to remain upright and he turned so that words on the scroll became fully visible. At first sight they appeared to be written in English but, as the boat moved nearer, Eden could see that a message had been scrawled in large letters in some other European language. From the bridge platform built athwartships between the two giant paddle-wheels Eden heard the sonorous tones of Matthew Perry asking his interpreter to decipher the scroll for him.

'It's in Dutch, Commodore,' replied Samuel Armstrong, the China missionary-linguist who had joined the ship somewhat reluctantly at Hong Kong to act as the squadron's interpreter. 'It says: "Depart at once! Foreign ships are forbidden to anchor here." What shall I reply?'

'Say nothing at all!' commanded Perry who was taking care to remain invisible to the Japanese. 'We shall ignore all inappropriate communication.'

After waiting in vain for a response, the Japanese official rewound the scroll around its batons and secured it with ribbons. Along with all his fellow occupants of the moving boat, he continued to stare intently up at the American sailors, as though trying to turn the warships from their aggressive progress by a silent act of will. On realizing that his message was to be completely ignored, the same official suddenly began making further dramatic gestures.

First he pointed angrily towards the *Susquehanna*'s anchor, then towards the mouth of the bay, clearly urging the warships to turn back to sea again. To augment his demand, he drew back his arm and sent the furled scroll wheeling in a high arc over the port bulwark. It clattered onto the deck, close to the gun crew, and one man quickly laid aside his pike-staff to rush over and pick it up. He handed it to Eden, who immediately looked up towards the bridge platform for guidance.

'Toss it back to them right away, Lieutenant,' boomed the still invisible Perry. 'We don't want it aboard.'

After a moment of hesitation Eden leaned out through the gunport and looked down into the guard-boat below. Beside the official in the green gown, he noticed a topknotted samurai staring up at him unblinkingly. The samurai's expression was watchful and intensely curious, rather than hostile, but this first sight of a Japanese warrior close up reminded Eden immediately of his dream and of the fierce male face that had appeared so startlingly in the mirror in place of his own. Although this face was not identical to the one in his dream, Eden could only stare in surprise, and Prince Tanaka—now disguised in the plain brown kimono of a lower-ranking samurai—found himself equally fascinated by this first real glimpse of a foreign barbarian officer.

Their eyes remained locked on each other for several seconds, then with a gentle flick of his wrist, Eden threw the scroll down towards the boat, aiming it for the same seated samurai who had only to lift his right arm to catch the scroll cleanly. Tanaka's watchful expression did not change and, after returning the document to the grave-faced interpreter seated behind him, he continued to stare steadily back at Eden.

At his side, however, the green-robed official grew more furious at this summary rejection of his demand, and above the uproar of the *Susquehanna*'s churning wheels he began yelling one word over and over.

'*Nagasaki! Nagasaki! Nagasaki!*'

'They're trying to indicate, I think, Commodore, that we should return five hundred miles to Nagasaki,' called the voice of Samuel Armstrong. 'Do you wish to give any response?'

'None whatsoever,' roared Perry. 'My orders stand: *Continue to ignore all improper communication and allow no encroachment whatsoever on our ships!*'

Watching tensely through his gunport, Eden saw that the rejection of the scroll had induced a new frenzy of movement around the *Susquehanna* and the other three warships. A number of fortified, junks had appeared, their high fore and aft decks crowded with fighting men bearing spears, lances and crossbows. More of the sleek guard-boats, which seemed to skim effortlessly across the surface of the bay under the skilful manipulation of their standing oarsmen, were putting out from the shore to augment the throng of craft closing around the American ships. The shouting that had gradually become audible above the pounding of the steam engines increased suddenly, and at that moment Eden saw three guard-boats peel off from the encircling ring of craft and begin darting towards the bows of the slow-moving flagship.

'Here they come,' called the voice of Lieutenant Rice from the bridge rails. 'All hands steady now.'

As the guard-boats arrived under the moving bows of the *Susquehanna*, lines tipped with grappling hooks snaked out to find lodging points. One caught in the fixed rungs of a ladderway beneath an entry port and moments later half a dozen Japanese guards, wearing only loincloths, began swarming up the ropes, still shouting as they came.

'Use only minimal force to dislodge them!'

Robert Eden shouted this order in a firm voice, and drew his sword. With a flourish of the weapon he urged his squad forward to block the threatened entry port. Bracing themselves in an arc across the opening, the small knot of American gunners grasped their pikes firmly and thrust them outward to form a glittering thicket of steel points.

'Wait!' called Eden sharply. 'Wait for the right moment!'

The leading Japanese were scrambling hand-over-hand up the iron rungs bolted below the entry port, and their wild shouting grew suddenly louder as they caught sight of the threatening pikestaffs. For a second they hesitated, then, with renewed roars of anger, they continued climbing. When the first Japanese climber came within range, the brawniest American gunner let out a roar and leaned as far as he could through the entry port, preparing to jab the point of the pike into his face.

'Stand back!'

Eden lunged forward with his outstretched sword and knocked the pikestaff aside. The startled sailor recoiled in astonishment as Eden sheathed his sword and wrenched the pike from his hands. Turning the weapon swiftly end over end, he planted the butt of the shaft squarely against the chest of the Japanese who by now was reaching for the top rung of the gang-ladder. With a single heave he unbalanced the intruder and sent him somersaulting backwards into the foaming water.

'Use minimum force!' commanded Eden, taking a pace back and motioning his men towards the entry port once more. 'Try to avoid bloodshed!'

Following his example, the other sailors quickly turned their pikes around and dislodged successive climbers by rapping their hands or jabbing the pike shafts at their upper bodies. As one Japanese after another tumbled, yelling, into the water, renewed roars of anger rose from the guard-boats. Those who had been toppled into the water clambered quickly aboard whichever of their own craft closed in to rescue them, but no further attempts were made to board. At another order from Eden, one gunner swarmed nimbly down the ladder and cast off the grappling lines, and his crew cheered raucously as the two guard-boats were carried rapidly away towards the stern on the foaming turbulence churned up by the paddle-wheels.

On seeing how determinedly these boarding parties had been repulsed, the other guard-boats closing around the flagship slackened their pace. Their rowers fell into a steadier rhythm, designed to keep them on station around the *Susquehanna*, but warriors and oarsmen alike continued to shout ferociously as they kept up their pursuit.

'Good work!' boomed Lieutenant Rice from the bridge through his loudhailer. 'But remain alert. They'll come at us again when we anchor.'

Glancing aft and to starboard, Eden saw that the bulwarks of the *Mississippi* and the two sloops-of-war *Plymouth* and *Saratoga* were also bristling with clusters of pikes. Guard-boats were manoeuvring in hostile fashion around all three vessels, and a single craft had already succeeded in attaching a line to the *Saratoga*. But, as Eden watched, the last of several loin-clothed Japanese invaders was hurled back into the sea, their boat was quickly cut adrift, and the *Saratoga*surged onward.

As the US squadron continued up the narrowing bay, the crews and marine detachments on all four ships remained at action stations. Soundings were still being taken continually because they had moved to within a mile of the eastern shore. The flagship led the way along an uncharted channel of about twenty-five fathoms and gradually, through the distant haze the outline of a craggy bluff came into view. Along its heights, Eden saw that a string of forts had been built, and cannon emplacements had been set up on strategic headlands. But as the ships rounded the foot of the bluff and came within range of these same guns, to Eden's relief they remained silent.

Eventually a small township of traditional wood-and-paper houses became visible beneath the high wooded cliffs. Eden calculated that they must be approaching Uraga, where it was planned to anchor the four ships and bring their sixty powerful cannon to bear on the town and its protective forts. As the *Susquehanna* lost speed and began edging its black bulk closer to the shore, the late afternoon sun finally dispersed the last of the distant haze to reveal a range of low mountains in the distance. Noticing this, Eden raised his eyes to scan the heights, and in that same instant the spectacular snow-covered cone of Mount Fuji materialized silently in the empty sky directly above them. The sun, already beginning to dip towards the west, illuminated its snowcap suddenly with a flood of golden light, and its stark beauty again riveted Eden's attention as he stood alone beside a gunport. Then, as the heavens were split by the roar of a gun firing from one of the hilltop forts, he ducked quickly behind the bulwark. A few seconds later another gun exploded, and a fresh cloud of smoke billowed above the heights, suggesting a signal rocket had been launched.

All four American warships had been edging in line towards their anchorages, still taking careful soundings and moving with great caution, but the roar of the guns prompted an immediate order from the *Susquehanna*'s bridge for the whole squadron to heave to. In quick succession the massive iron anchors of the two steam frigates and the smaller sloops-of-war crashed from their mountings into the placid waters of the bay. The deafening noise of the huge anchor cables running out echoed alarmingly from the surrounding cliffs and Eden saw crowds of Japanese soldiers on the beaches and clifftops begin to scurry back and forth in apparent panic.

The sight of the great, smoke-belching ships being manoeuvred into line of battle, with their cannon muzzles jutting threateningly towards the shore, galvanized the oarsmen in the pursuing fleet of guard-boats. Redoubling their strokes, they spurted forward and began to swarm at close quarters around the now stationary US Navy squadron. Looking down through his gunport, Eden saw that each guard-boat contained boxes of provisions, water barrels and sleeping mats, which suggested that their crews were preparing to lay a siege around the foreign ships. He also saw a new flotilla of guard-boats put out from the shore in front of Uraga, and begin speeding towards the anchored squadron.

A moment later the two steam frigates stopped their engines. As the paddle-wheels ceased to churn, Eden heard clearly for the first time the wild cacophony that was rising from the shore. Gongs were being beaten discordantly all along the clifftops, and mobs of soldiers and civilians were shouting and chanting raggedly on the beaches. Temple bells could be heard tolling out insistent warnings, dogs were barking frenziedly and long lines of figures carrying bundles could be seen scurrying away up the steep cliffside footpaths that snaked away from Uraga and the threatened coastline.

'It looks very bad, master,' whispered a frightened voice at Eden's side. 'They are sounding the gongs of war now.'

Eden glanced down to see Sentaro kneeling in concealment beside the wheeled cannon. Taking care not to be seen by the crews of the Japanese guard-boats pressing all around the ship, he was peering fearfully out over the gun barrel towards the land. Remembering that he had been crouching in the hot darkness of the storage space beneath the fo'c's'le for some hours, Eden bit back a reprimand.

'You should stay in your berth, Sentaro,' he said gently. 'For your own sake you must remain out of sight until we see what happens.'

'If they decide to fight, we may all be killed, master,' moaned the castaway.

Another gun exploded on the clifftop, and another ball of smoke drifted lazily skyward—but no shell or cannonball whistled overhead. Eden gazed grimly down at the guard-boats and their yelling crews, which were still closing in from all directions; then he looked up again towards the hilltop forts, where hundreds of tiny armed figures were now visibly gathering.

'Perhaps—we will know soon. Go back now to your berth.'

The Japanese castaway crept off obediently and Eden looked again towards the shore—but he found he could not decide whether the bedlam of sound all around them indicated that the Japanese were about to launch a desperate attack, or whether it was born out of fear and apprehension. Glancing sideways at his silent gun crews and the ranks of young marines drawn up along the deck in battle order, he saw that they too were watching the scene before them with taut and mystified expressions.

As he waited with his hand resting on the pommel of his sword, Eden found his eyes were drawn again to the distant skyline where the ethereal white cone of Fuji was now sharply visible. Under the daytime blue of the heavens its flanks also glowed like azure and, in striking contrast to the turmoil gripping the Bay of Yedo, the mountain remained, as always, a vision of serene tranquillity. All around him the noisy tumult continued to grow, but Eden found he could not entirely forget Fuji's presence in the distance. Despite the imminent threat of danger to the flagship and its crew, part of his mind was still distracted by the prospect that one day he might climb to the volcano's extraordinary summit.

6

When she drew aside her creaking *shoji* in a shabby village inn some twenty miles west of Yedo, Matsumura Tokiwa looked out at the same distant image of Mount Fuji. In the brightness of the late afternoon sun, the mountain's pyramid-shaped flanks, previously shrouded in a heat haze, glowed with a deep reflected blueness from the sky. Beneath the summit of peerless white, grey lava gullies slashed downward with mathematical straightness, and the perfect symmetry of all its lines gave the impression that the volcano, far from being real, was etched like a simple silk-screen painting on the clear backdrop of the sky.

To Tokiwa, who had grown up in sight of Fuji and had loved its simple majesty all her life, the mountain seemed to have moved dramatically nearer since her last hazy glimpse of it a few hours earlier. Fuji, she well knew, was famous for creating such illusions, but on this occasion the impression was so striking that she murmured aloud in surprise and raised one hand to shade her eyes as she stared at the captivating sight.

'Get back inside! It's most unwise for you to be seen!'

Tokiwa's attention was brought sharply back to the courtyard below her balcony by the fiercely hissed words of the chief samurai guard who had been posted at the inn by Prince Tanaka for her protection. Dressed in bamboo and chainmail body armour and wearing a steel helmet with leather protective wings sloping to his shoulders, the stocky, beetle-browed guard was glaring angrily up at her through narrowed eyes. His armour gave him an ominous appearance but she noticed too that his eyes lingered hungrily on her as he barked his orders, with his right hand clasped pointedly around the hilt of his long sword.

'You must remain in your room—and keep the screens closed at all times!'

After speaking, the guard glanced quickly round at the seething activity in the yard of the modest inn, which had clearly been chosen for its anonymity. Travel-weary merchants and farmers, travelling on foot or on horseback, were scurrying in through the archways from the dusty tracks outside, anxious to secure early lodgings for the night. The professional messengers who habitually jogged between all such country inns were also hastening in and out, to hand over their lacquered despatch boxes to fresh runners. Long columns of gaudily dressed archers and pikemen hurried past on foot in all directions, while some of their samurai officers dismounted from sturdy ponies in search of refreshment. The evening air was filled with raised voices and, on catching sight of the slender female figure standing on one of the front balconies, many of the hurrying men cast quick, curious glances in her direction.

'Please come in now!'

A young peasant maidservant in a plain brown kimono appeared silently in the room behind Tokiwa and laid a hand on her shoulder to draw her inside. She closed the screens quickly, then turned and bowed once with an anxious expression on her face.

'Gotaro-san, the chief of guards, says we will all be in danger if somebody recognizes you. He says it could provoke an attack!'

Tokiwa drew in her breath sharply. The frantic night-time dash from Yedo had been long and uncomfortable. After a hurried parting from Prince Tanaka, she had been carried rapidly through the darkness in a curtained *norimono*travelling chair, with a mounted escort of three guards. They had ordered her not to show her face, and had halted only briefly at wayside staging posts to change horses and coolie bearers. Whenever she had dared to peep out through her drawn curtains, the shadowy roads had been crowded with marching soldiers, and she had felt exhausted from the jolting journey when they arrived dusty and dishevelled at the shabby inn at around mid-morning. The maidservant, hired locally by the guards, had appeared wordlessly to help lay out a sleeping pallet in the small, austere room that was furnished only with scuffed tatami matting, a single low table and a rush-wick lamp. The same maid had been hovering discreetly in attendance when Tokiwa awoke a few hours later from fitful and troubled sleep, but until that moment she had not spoken except to enquire softly about her temporary mistress's needs for food or bathing.

'What do you know of all this?' demanded Tokiwa in surprise. 'What have the guards told you?'

'Nothing except what I have said already,' replied the maidservant, bowing again. 'Only that it is very important for you to remain hidden.'

'What is the latest news in the courtyard about the smoking ships?' asked Tokiwa. 'Have they yet reached Yedo? Have they begun to attack the city?'

The maidservant's face grew anxious as she glanced towards the screens separating the small room from the corridor. She listened for a moment, wringing her hands in front of her, then spoke in a low whisper.

'There are many rumours from the coast which say the ships of the foreign barbarians can move very swiftly without oars, wind or tide! They say that the barbarians are not at all like us. They are sorcerers, magicians, half-man and half-beast! They say they have the power to tame a volcano and transfer its power into their ships—controlling that power as they will . . . The temples in all the villages have been filled day and night with people praying to the gods for deliverance from these monsters.'

'But has their attack begun?' pleaded Tokiwa.

The maid's eyes grew round, and she shook her head in bewilderment. 'I don't know—'

She broke off with a cry as the balcony *shoji* were slid open suddenly by the chief guard, who had made his way silently up the outside steps. He stepped quickly inside and stood glowering at them, his hand on his sword hilt.

'You should know that an edict has been issued by the Shogun,' he snapped. 'All public discussion about the barbarian black ships is forbidden. You must remain absolutely silent on this subject.' He paused and turned to Tokiwa. 'And *you* must keep yourself hidden at all times. When you go to bathe, choose a quiet moment and shroud yourself fully!'

He gestured peremptorily to the maidservant, and she hurried from the room, closing the screens quietly behind her.

'How long will I be kept here, Gotaro-san?' asked Tokiwa, lifting her chin defiantly in the guard's direction. 'How long must I be a prisoner?'

'As long as is necessary for your safety!' He paused, his eyes steady on her and she again noticed the disturbing lustfulness of his gaze. 'My only orders, Tokiwa-san, are to protect you until Prince Tanaka returns. That I shall certainly do.'

She studied the guard's face anxiously, conscious that he had laid heavy emphasis on his last words. 'When do you think Prince Tanaka will come back?'

'At a time of war, Tokiwa-san, it's impossible to make predictions with certainty.'

Tokiwa caught her breath. 'Has war already begun then?'

Gotaro continued to regard her appraisingly. Wide-eyed with agitation, she looked strikingly beautiful in the suffused glow of the afternoon sun. Due to her weariness she had yet to dress her long, black tresses, and several locks tumbled about her uncovered neck. Her kimono was crumpled from the journey and lay askew, affording him a tantalizing glimpse of one slender shoulder and the shadowed cleft between her breasts.

'I have heard that the *kurufune* are nearing Yedo,' said the guard. 'Many thousands of men are ready to shed their blood to defend Dai Nippon.

And Prince Tanaka himself will not desert any battle.' He paused, still gazing directly at her. 'But if he fails to return, you need have no fear, Tokiwa-san. In his absence I will assume *personal* responsibility for your safety.'

Tokiwa started. The full significance of his carefully chosen words made her aware suddenly of her unkempt appearance, and she hurriedly closed the front of her kimono and half turned her face from him as she did so. Seeing this, he smiled thinly and, after staring hard at her for a moment longer, inclined his head an inch in a farewell salute, turned abruptly on his heel, and slipped back out through the balcony *shoji*.

After he had closed the screens behind him, Tokiwa continued to stand motionless in the centre of the room, listening to the hubbub rising from the courtyard and beyond. The scuffle of horses' hoofs and human feet, the clink of steel weapons and the creaking of body armour were all overlaid with the throaty shouting of coolie bearers and the yelled commands of hurrying troop officers. Anxiety and unease were evident in every sound she could hear and, because this increased her own restlessness, she moved silently to the closed *shoji* alongside the balcony.

After a moment's indecision she deliberately jabbed the forefinger of her right hand sharply against one paper panel at eye level, producing the kind of small, jagged hole that a disobedient child might make. By pressing her eye to it, she was able to see the track along which armed soldiers were still streaming eastward towards Yedo. The human tide flowing in the opposite direction was composed mainly of peasants and civilian families who she guessed had fled from towns and villages along the way. Many were staggering under the weight of bundles of household belongings and essential possessions; children were clinging fearfully to their parents' hands, and some groups were stopping from time to time to look back at the sky behind them, as though still expecting to be overtaken by some gigantic nemesis.

Beyond them, Mount Fuji towered above the surrounding landscape, and she was relieved to find that the reassuring sight of it helped soothe the apprehension that had grown during her headlong flight from Yedo. Although the sounds of panic were audible all around her and she was a virtual prisoner at the inn, she felt very glad to see the familiar bulk of Fuji-san at such a terrible time of crisis.

Staring out through the torn waxed paper of the *shoji*, first with one eye then the other, she felt this sense of comfort gradually deepen. She continued to gaze at the sacred mountain for some minutes, then sank to her knees and bowed her head to offer a fervent prayer to Fuji-san's all-powerful gods. Murmuring her words very softly, she asked them to protect the Emperor and all the people of Nippon from the terror of the barbarian ships; she asked too that the lives of her family be preserved, and that Prince Tanaka should survive so that he might return to set her free. Lastly, in desperation, she begged the gods to preserve her from the attentions of Gotaro, the corpulent chief guard whom she feared might rape or even murder her in the confusion, if Tanaka did not return.

'If the sacred *kami* of Fuji will look with favour on these secret requests,' she whispered desperately at the close of her prayer, 'I pledge to give dutiful and obedient love for ever to any man whom the *kami* shall deem worthy—and I will follow their wishes faithfully all the days of my life!'

Still kneeling beside the screen, with closed eyes, she tried to imagine the scene at that moment in the Bay of Yedo. In her mind she saw many giant *kurufune* shaped like vast black pyramids; belching out great torrents of dark smoke, they surged along the coast amidst turbulent tidal waves. Strange giants with fur-covered bodies and long, tufted tails swarmed on their sides; the air was filled with the terrifyingly strange roar of foreign voices and the deafening boom of giant guns. Great plumes of white smoke rose on the shore, as exploding shot from the guns displayed their incredible destructive power. Phalanx after phalanx of courageous Nipponese pikemen and musketeers waded breast-deep into the waters of the bay, with their weapons held high above their heads; but the passing *kurufune* swamped and tossed them aside like chaff, drowning them in hundreds.

The horror of those images forced her to open her eyes at last, and she shuddered as they faded from her mind. For several minutes she remained on her knees, listening absently to the unending tramp of marching feet outside the inn. Then, still wondering what was really happening in the blighted bay before the city, she bowed her head and repeated the prayers, whispering her entreaties with an even greater fervour than before.

7

Strike now!' yelled Robert Eden. 'And strike accurately.'

The second lieutenant watched a new wave of howling, loin-clothed Japanese from the guard-boats reach for handholds to help them swing over the bulwarks of the *Susquehanna* onto the spar deck. But as fast as they clawed at the stays and rigging of the flagship, the pike-wielding American gunners rapped and jabbed at their hands and arms, to send them tumbling back into the sea.

Now that the four warships were riding stationary at anchor in the quiet waters of the bay, they were easier targets. Flurries of a dozen guard-boats had closed in around each of them while others circled, watching the determined efforts to board. The order 'Clear decks for action!' had again rung out minutes before, and the blue-jacketed marines and all ratings were drawn up around every likely boarding point. Armed with carbines, pikes, cutlasses and pistols, they were brandishing their weapons and shouting raucously in their efforts to deter the guards. Some of the muscular Japanese were swarming up the anchor cables, while others had succeeded in attaching grappling-hook lines to the ships' sides. As fast as the lines were attached, they were cut or cast off—but the harbour guards did not give up.

'Hold firm now!' Eden called out encouragement to his gunners as he watched a second wave of Japanese swarming upwards, shouting more loudly in outrage at the rough despatch of their comrades. He waited until they were well within striking distance before calling out a crisp new order—then watched with narrowed eyes as the gunners again dealt determinedly with the attack.

One small, wiry Japanese succeeded in reaching the top of the bulwark and was about to launch himself down onto the deck, but three brawny gunners caught him and forced him back bodily over the side. When a third wave of climbers appeared moments later, they were again beaten off with the same furious energy, and the noise of angry shouting from the boats below rose to an uproar.

'If they're really determined on a fight to the finish,' murmured an educated American voice at Eden's shoulder, 'it could all be very uncomfortable. By my reckoning there must be several million of them—against just a few hundred of us.'

Eden turned his head sharply on recognizing the voice of Samuel Armstrong, the veteran China missionary who had joined the squadron at Hong Kong at Commodore Perry's request, because he was the only American in Asia reputed to have any proper knowledge of the Japanese language. A grizzled, frock-coated figure with luxuriant mutton-chop whiskers, he had rarely left his privileged place beside the commodore during the entire voyage, so his sudden appearance by the dangerous entry port surprised Eden.

'Perhaps you would be safer, sir, if you returned at once to the bridge or the quarterdeck,' said Eden firmly, still watching the guard-boats milling below them. 'It could get very unpleasant here.'

Both men could see that the other American warships were being simultaneously besieged by boarding parties. The noise made by attackers and defenders alike was deafening, but the crews of the other three ships were resisting the assaults as vigorously and successfully as those on the *Susquehanna*.

'As a matter of fact, Lieutenant, I've been sent down here on the orders of Commodore Perry himself,' explained Armstrong quietly, pointing to one of the boats bobbing below. 'It looks as though there may be a good opportunity to communicate.'

Following the direction of the missionary's arm, Eden again spotted the boat with the black-tasselled prow. A different scroll was now being held aloft by the same green-robed official, and Armstrong was peering at it through the open port.

'In French, not Dutch this time,' he grunted, 'but the same content as before. It says, "You must depart immediately—all anchoring here by foreign ships is forbidden."'

Leaning out through the opening, Armstrong waved both hands elaborately, to indicate comprehension and a simultaneous rejection of the message. Renewed shouts of indignation greeted Armstrong's gesture, but because of the uproar he was unable to hear what was being said. When he conveyed this by means of a mime involving his hands and ears, the guard-boat was manoeuvred closer to the entry port.

'I-can-speak-Dutch,' called Haniwara Tokuma in poor English, rising anxiously to his feet beside the green-robed envoy. 'Can-you-understand-Dutch?'

'Speak on!' roared Armstrong happily in Dutch. 'I can understand Dutch much better than Japanese.'

'We wish to be allowed aboard,' called the scholarly looking interpreter in his reedy accent. 'We escort an important official! Please prepare to receive us.'

Armstrong looked significantly towards Eden, who was following their exchange closely without understanding the words. 'There's just a chance we'll avoid conflict here,' he murmured. 'We may be able to pull back from the brink . . .'

'We must come aboard and talk to you,' called the interpreter again. 'Be prepared to receive us.'

'We cannot receive you,' yelled Armstrong in response. 'Our chieftain is of the very highest rank in our country. He represents our President, who is the equivalent of your Emperor. He will only speak to the most senior representatives of Nippon.'

Eden watched and listened with bated breath. As though by some invisible signal, the guards had for the moment ceased all attempts to board the flagship. On seeing this, the tense gunners and marines lining the flagship's rails rested their pikes and other weapons and strained their ears to catch some hint of the exchanges taking place between the missionary and the chief guard-boat.

'The Vice-Governor of Uraga himself is here in this boat,' shouted the Japanese interpreter, motioning towards the stony-faced official at his side, who was garbed extravagantly in sea-green silk robes and a gleaming, black-lacquered hat. 'The deputy governor is certainly of sufficient rank to be received.'

Armstrong cupped a hand to his mouth and leaned out through the entry port again. 'The commander of these ships is known as "the Most High Lord of the Interior",' he shouted, drawing his words out slowly to ensure they were clearly understood. 'He is not prepared to meet with anybody less than a high government minister. For its own safety your party should withdraw to the shore at once!'

Disconcerted, the Japanese officials bent their heads and huddled together, talking and gesticulating animatedly. Stepping back into the shadow of the bulkhead, Armstrong watched their deliberations with a faint smile tugging at the corners of his mouth.

'I think it's working, Lieutenant,' he breathed, looking quickly in Eden's direction. 'Your Commodore Perry is a stubborn, highhanded man—but one of uncanny judgement.'

'Aren't these dangerous games to play, Mr Armstrong?' asked Eden sharply, looking down at the growing numbers of armed boats circling the flagship. 'We're already very close to open hostilities. To avoid unnecessary bloodshed, wouldn't it be more prudent just to talk to them without further delay?'

The clamour of drums and gongs from the shore had become noticeably louder, and many temple bells could now be heard tolling urgently around the headlands. The shouts of the guards filling the air about the four warships had also begun to rise angrily, augmenting the atmosphere of tension.

'Every foreign ship that has tried to come peacefully into a Japanese harbour in recent years has been boarded without ceremony, Lieutenant,' said Armstrong mildly, still watching the boat below them with intent eyes. 'Their officers have been jostled and humiliated, and permission to land has invariably been refused. We don't want to experience that again, do we?'

'Customs men of every nation inspect all incoming ships,' replied Eden equally mildly. 'The Japanese can justifiably claim they have every right to come on board . . .'

'There's some logic in what you say—' began Armstrong then broke off suddenly on seeing the Japanese interpreter in the guard-boat stand up again. When he waved an arm to attract attention, Armstrong leaned out of the entry port.

'We have a suggestion,' cried Haniwara, again speaking in Dutch. 'The American High Lord of the Interior should appoint a subordinate aide of equal rank to receive the Vice-Governor of Uraga . . .'

Armstrong hesitated, cocking his head thoughtfully, as though considering this proposal. Then he nodded exaggeratedly. 'I will go to consult with our Most High Lord about your request. I will return soon with his response.'

With a flourish the missionary turned away and took several long, quick paces which carried him out of sight of the Japanese below. Then he stopped, pulled a gold watch on a chain from a waistcoat pocket, and consulted it. After returning the watch to its place, he moved back against the bulwark beside Eden, taking care to remain concealed.

'As we correctly anticipated they have asked that an official be allowed on board and speak with a subordinate of our "Most High Lord of the Interior".' Armstrong smiled confidingly. 'That's how I have referred to the commodore so far in our exchanges—it's terminology they understand. And I've told them I will go and consult with "His Eminence". As I think you already know, the flag lieutenant has been deputed to conduct any low-level negotiations—and he has chosen you as his chief bodyguard. This delay of a few minutes is purely ceremonial.'

Armstrong checked his watch elaborately once more and Eden glanced along the bulwark at his own armed gunners, who were still drawn up at battle stations. Their swarthy faces remained alert as they watched the seething boats below though some glanced anxiously towards Eden and the interpreter, trying to comprehend what was happening.

'When their vice-governor comes up our ladder,' mused Armstrong, 'he'll be the first Japanese official ever to set foot on American "territory", don't you see? And it will be on American terms. So, at long last, we will have put a stop to the insolence with which Japan has always treated foreigners.'

'But under the threat of force,' interjected Eden evenly. 'And coming uninvited—as intruders.'

Armstrong looked hard at the young lieutenant, noticing his high-set cheekbones and his dark, watchful eyes. 'Your family history has perhaps given you a natural sympathy for those you see as underdogs,' said the missionary gently. 'And I'd like you to know how much I admire that—'

'I wasn't seeking your admiration,' snapped Eden, his eyes suddenly ablaze. 'Perhaps we should drop this subject . . .'

'Don't misunderstand me, Lieutenant.' The missionary laid a calming hand on his arm. 'Such independence of mind is rare in a young navy officer. But don't forget all this isn't one-sided. We're offering the Japanese a fair and equal basis for negotiation.'

He checked his watch again, then tucked it away in his waistcoat pocket. Straightening himself, he took several quick steps forward so that he arrived before the entry port looking as though he had just hurried there from a distance. Leaning out once more, he waved towards the Japanese interpreter in the guard-boat.

'It has been decided that your deputy governor may come aboard to parley briefly with one of our junior officers!' he announced ringingly in Dutch, and stood aside as two ratings summoned by Eden ran forward to fix the gang-ladder in place.

When the guard-boat had manoeuvred to its foot, the Japanese interpreter ushered the Vice-Governor of Uraga ahead of him onto the ladder. Among a retinue of three bodyguards who stood up in the boat to follow them, Eden spotted the face of the same young samurai who had so deftly caught the scroll which he had tossed back unopened half an hour earlier, and again his eyes locked with those of the disguised Prince Tanaka. Then he noticed that another, taller samurai wearing a similar anonymous brown kimono, was also gazing balefully up at him. The features of Yakamochi, son and heir of Lord Daizo of Haifu, however were set in more aggressive lines and as the small group of Japanese climbed slowly up towards the entry port, Eden instinctively dropped his hand to the hilt of his sword.

8

'Anatatachi wa Amerika-jin desuka?'

This first question from the Vice-Governor of Uraga was uttered in a hesitant, uncertain tone. Perched on the edge of an upright chair in the oak-panelled captain's cabin, aft on the main deck, the solemn, round-faced official looked ill at ease inside his flamboyant sea-green silks. While his interpreter, Haniwara Tokuma, who was seated beside him, translated the question haltingly into Dutch, the eyes of the vice-governor flickered nervously back and forth around the cabin, settling only occasionally on Flag Lieutenant Rice, who sat ramrod straight behind a plain polished table on which he had placed his tasselled ceremonial sword secure inside its leather scabbard.

Samuel Armstrong, seated beside Rice at the same table, was puffing relaxedly on a briar pipe. After listening to the Japanese interpreter's Dutch translation, he smiled faintly and leaned back in his chair, before repeating it with mock formality in English.

'The deputy governor asks us if we are Americans.'

Lieutenant Rice nodded formally. 'You may confirm to the deputy governor that we are.'

'Yes, we are Americans,' said Armstrong in Dutch, and waited patiently while Haniwara Tokuma conveyed this reply to his uneasy superior in their own language.

'Why have Americans come to Japan?' asked the vice-governor after a short pause. 'What is your purpose here?'

'We have come here for one reason only,' replied Rice carefully. 'And that is to deliver a letter of the utmost importance from the President of the United States to the Emperor of Japan.'

Midshipman Harris and another of the *Susquehanna*'s fresh-faced cadet officers were standing stiffly to attention behind the flag lieutenant's chair. Armed with unsheathed cutlasses tucked into their belts, they stared straight ahead and gave no impression that they heard anything of what was being said. To one side of the table Robert Eden had taken up a watchful position, his feet planted astride and his left hand resting on the pommel of his sword. Although listening carefully to the exchanges, he kept his attention focused on the three Japanese samurai who were ranged in a small semicircle behind the chairs of their two official representatives.

The samurai who had eyed him so intently from the boat, he "noticed, was the only one who wore the traditional twin swords in long and short scabbards at his waist. Prince Tanaka was standing motionless, with his hands at his sides between the two other escorts, who appeared to be unarmed. These two men gazed steadily at the cabin floor and only Tanaka's eyes flicked from face to face around the cabin. Whenever they came to rest on Eden, as they often did, the American officer felt he detected a lively intelligence as well as wary hostility in his expression.

But as Eden scrutinized the other two escorts, who stood with their hands clasped within the wide sleeves of their kimonos, he noticed that Daizo Yakamochi was holding himself unnaturally taut and bending forward a little from the waist. In that moment Eden became convinced that the man was carrying a concealed weapon in the loose sleeves of his gown.

'Why is it necessary for the President of America to send four armed ships to deliver just one letter?'

The vice-governor, who had been conferring in whispers with his interpreter, posed this new question in a more assertive tone and, on hearing Armstrong's translation, Lieutenant Rice raised his eyebrows and motioned with his head to a third midshipman, who was stationed outside the open cabin door, listening intently to the exchanges. The boy, who had obviously been anticipating this signal, immediately dashed away. Leaning close to Armstrong, Rice explained to him in an undertone that Commodore Perry had instructed that all but the most fundamental questions were to be referred to him in his own nearby cabin.

While awaiting the midshipman's return, Rice made no move to reveal to the Japanese what was holding up his reply. In the tense silence that settled over the negotiating group, the distant sound of gongs and wardrums being beaten on the shore seemed suddenly louder and, as the delay lengthened, the expression of the vice-governor became first puzzled then anxious. After a minute or two he began to shift uneasily on the edge of his seat, looking distractedly at each of the silent American faces in turn. Beside him, Haniwara Tokuma appeared composed and outwardly at ease, but behind them the three standing bodyguards grew noticeably more edgy.

Yet another minute passed, before the rapid tattoo of the midshipman's heels on the planks of the deck heralded his return. On entering the cabin he hurried directly to the table and saluted, before bending close to the flag lieutenant and speaking quietly in his ear. As he listened, Lieutenant Rice picked up a pen from the table and wrote several lines on a blank sheet of paper. When the midshipman had retreated to the doorway, Rice turned to face the vice-governor again.

'You asked me why it was necessary to send four armed ships here to carry one letter? Our answer is: in order to show proper respect to your Emperor.'

On absorbing the meaning of this reply, the face of the vice-governor showed new agitation. 'It is impossible to receive any letter here!' he said in a troubled voice. 'By our law, communications from foreign countries can only be accepted at the port of Nagasaki. There is no alternative. You must take your letter there!'

For a moment or two, Lieutenant Rice studied the notes he had made on the sheet of paper before him. Then he cleared his throat and once more raised his head to look the Japanese official pointedly in the eye.

'The commodore and his squadron intend to remain here until the letter from our President is properly delivered,' he said firmly. 'We have come here precisely because this bay lies close to your Emperor's palace in Yedo. And although the commodore desires. nothing more than the friendship of Japan, he is not prepared to see his country or his President suffer any indignity.'

Rice paused to allow translation, never removing his gaze from the face of the vice-governor. When he understood what had been said, the Japanese laughed uneasily and began to make a reply—but the flag lieutenant held up his hand to indicate he had not finished.

'We suggest a properly appointed representative of the Emperor be sent aboard this ship as soon as possible here in Yedo Bay,' he continued in a warning tone. 'He will receive a copy of our President's letter. Then the commodore will be prepared to land with an escort and deliver the original formally himself, at a properly appointed time.'

Robert Eden watched the faces of the five Japanese intently while the flag lieutenant's words were being translated. As the full significance of their meaning dawned on the interpreter and his superior, their demeanour became more grave, their expressions more impenetrable. The handsome features of Prince Tanaka remained blank and inexpressive, but his eyes hardened too as comprehension dawned. At his side the two unarmed escorts exchanged quick glances; then Daizo Yakamochi looked round calculatingly at each of the Americans in turn, before lowering his eyes to the floor once more.

'And whilst I am speaking of armed men,' continued Rice, 'I must give you a solemn warning. We don't intend to allow your guard-boats to surround us much longer. We will not be spied upon or hounded whilst we are here.'

The vice-governor shifted to the very edge of his seat as the translation was completed. 'The presence of our guard-boats is in accordance with Japanese custom and law,' he said insistently. 'We must obey our laws and carry them out.'

'It is my duty then to inform you that the United States Navy also has its own customs and laws,' replied Rice. 'Where our men-of-war are involved, there are laws that forbid other boats from approaching within a certain range.' He paused to add emphasis to what he was about to say. 'You should also know we take it upon ourselves to enforce these laws most stringently.'

The vice-governor again consulted hurriedly with his interpreter in whispers, then he sat formally upright on his chair to address the American officer. 'I demand that you inform us what is the name of this ship—and how many men and guns does it carry?'

Rice in his turn sat up straighter behind the polished table. 'I need only remind you that we are armed ships—and our custom is never to answer such questions. Furthermore *I* must now demand that you act on what I've said. You must go on deck and order your guard-boats to stand off and return to shore. If you don't give such orders, we shall proceed to fire into them.'

Rice paused and took out a fobwatch from inside his jacket. After looking at it for a moment he turned to Midshipman Harris and gave him instructions loud enough for the Japanese to hear.

'Go to the upper deck immediately, Mr Harris, and give orders for two armed cutters to be launched! If the Japanese guard-boats have not withdrawn to the shore fifteen minutes from now, our crews are to fire at selected targets with their prow howitzers! Is that quite clear?'

'Very clear, sir!'

The midshipman rushed from the cabin and Rice looked calmly towards the vice-governor. 'We will allow you fifteen minutes to give your orders. At the end of that time, if the guard-boats are still here, their crews will begin to suffer. The choice is yours.'

The Japanese official leaned towards his interpreter and conferred agitatedly with him. After a brief interval Lieutenant Rice rose briskly to his feet.

'I will take you now to the spar deck, where you will see for yourselves the strength of our armaments. This will enable you to observe that we are in earnest—and from there you may order your guard-boats to retreat!'

Rice picked up his sword, reslung it on his belt and strode from the cabin, with Armstrong and the remaining midshipmen at his heels. The two Japanese officials rose hurriedly from their chairs to follow. Robert Eden brought up the rear, falling into step close behind the three samurai. As they passed the marine sentries who had been stationed outside the officers' cabins and climbed the port ladders, Eden kept the Japanese warriors under close scrutiny, watching especially the tall, fierce-eyed figure of Lord Daizo's anonymous son, who continued to hold his right arm clamped unnaturally close against his chest.

On the spar deck, the port gun crews were still at action stations, and Lieutenant Rice led the Japanese party quickly along the ranks of blue-jacketed marines who remained drawn up in their battle formations. They held long carbines at the ready, their bayonets glittering in the afternoon sun, and each man was gazing watchfully towards the circling guard-boats.

'You may inspect our guns and ammunition if you wish,' said Rice tersely, pausing beside one of the massive muzzle-loading cannons and its ominous pyramid of gleaming black roundshot. 'Then I hope you will understand our resources with the utmost clarity.'

The vice-governor paused and stared with great absorption at the cannon, which had been run back from its open port. On an impulse he bent over and attempted to lift one of the roundshot—but was unable to shift it. With his fingers spread to their widest extent he assessed the width of the cannon's bore, murmuring details over his shoulder to his escorts, who were studying the powerful weapon with equal curiosity. The interpreter drew a pad from his sleeve and jotted down several notes about the gun, then watched the vice-governor crouch down and peer directly into its barrel. The envoy turned with a look of amazement when he saw that his whole head would fit easily into its gaping muzzle, and the interpreter noted that hastily on his pad.

'This is what we call a sixty-four-pound cannon,' declared Rice soberly. 'Its overall length is eleven feet three inches. Each shot weighs over sixty-four pounds, and its bore is fully eighteen inches. The range of this gun—and of all our guns—is very long indeed. They would easily destroy any target ashore that we chose to aim at.'

The vice-governor glanced along the upper deck towards the other gun positions, his face taut with tension. He looked round once again at the well-drilled marine force, then turned to murmur anxiously to his interpreter.

'The vice-governor would like to ask how many guns like this you have?' said Haniwara Tokuma. 'And are all your weapons as powerful?'

'We have more than sufficient guns for our purpose—that is all you need to know,' snapped the flag lieutenant, glancing significantly at his pocketwatch once more. 'Now your time is running out. Kindly come to the side and order all your guard-boats to head for the shore.'

Rice beckoned for the Japanese to follow and ushered them towards the open entry port, where they would be clearly visible. The vice-governor stepped hesitantly to his side and stood looking down at the dozens of craft milling noisily below. His appearance before the open port immediately provoked a new storm of chanting and yelling from the Japanese guards, and several sleek craft started again towards the foot of the gang-ladder, anticipating that permission to board had been obtained.

'*Umike e kaere!*' called the vice-governor shrilly, pulling his fan from his wide sleeve and flapping it emphatically to warn the boats away. '*Umike e kaere!* Withdraw at once to the shore!'

The furious shouting quickly became ragged and confused, but did not subside altogether. Some of the guard-boats turned and began to draw away, but others—whose crews had either not heard or were set on defiance—continued to move closer. Seeing this, the Japanese official waved his fan more frantically, and repeated his order: '*Umike e kaere! Umike e kaere!*'

At that instant Daizo Yakamochi, who was standing a few feet behind the vice-governor, straightened up fully for the first time since boarding the *Susquehanna*. He took two quick paces forward, his eyes fixed on the unprotected back of the American flag lieutenant, who was still staring out over the rail. His left hand groped into the opposite sleeve of his kimono and he was in the act of withdrawing it when Robert Eden clamped an arm silently around his neck from behind.

Thrusting his own left hand into the sleeve of the kimono, Eden encountered the fingers of the Japanese encircling the hilt of a short sword. Tightening his strangulating grip on Yakamochi's throat, Eden wrenched hard with his other hand, and tore the sword free. It fell to the deck and, on looking round, Eden saw Prince Tanaka bend quickly to retrieve it. Tanaka's face was flushed with anger but, to Eden's surprise, it was focused entirely on the samurai still struggling helplessly in his grasp.

'*Baka me!* You fool!' breathed Tanaka. '*Baka na koto o shita suro na!* That was an act of great foolishness!'

Still staring furiously at Yakamochi, Tanaka thrust the fallen sword safely into his sash beside his own weapons; then he raised his eyes to gaze wordlessly at Eden.

'*Honto ni baka dana*,' said the American officer very quietly, pronouncing the recently learned Japanese words slowly and carefully. 'It was indeed very foolish!'

Glancing up quickly, Eden saw that all the other men around them had their backs turned. Oblivious to what had happened just a few feet away, they were watching intently as one of the *Susquehanna*'s cutters swung down towards the water below. The boat, carrying a dozen armed marines, also had a brass eight-inch howitzer mounted in its bows, and as soon as it settled on the water the oarsmen dipped their blades and brought the cannon to bear on its nearest target. This manoeuvre drove off the remaining guard-boats within seconds and a loud cheer rang out from the marines and gun crews lining the bulwarks above.

'I release him into your trust,' continued Eden quietly in Japanese, loosening his grip on Daizo Yakamochi and pushing him towards Tanaka. As he spoke, Eden unbuttoned his holster and eased the butt of his Colt pistol into view. 'We have no wish to shed blood, but we'll protect ourselves as necessary if we are attacked!'

For a second or two Tanaka stared uncertainly at Eden, as though taken aback by the American officer's puzzling actions. Then he moved quickly to place himself in front of the glowering son of Lord Daizo. Glancing round to check that they were still unobserved, Eden moved a step closer to Tanaka.

'You need say nothing of this!' he said in an undertone. 'Just make sure there's no more foolishness!'

'That action was not authorized,' murmured Tanaka, still staring straight ahead. 'It was an unfortunate act of impulse . . .'

The roar of the cutter's howitzer exploding broke in on his words and new cries of outrage rose from the retreating guard-boats, amidst renewed cheering from the *Susquehanna*. Stepping closer to the entry port, Eden looked out and saw that smoke was drifting lazily from the howitzer's muzzle. But there was no sign of any stricken Japanese boat on the flat waters of the bay, and he guessed that a warning shot had been fired across somebody's bows. Most of the guard-boats were heading rapidly towards the shore, though a select few retreated a safe distance to keep a discreet watch on the American warships.

The faces of the vice-governor and Haniwara Tokuma had turned pale and, after a whispered exchange, the interpreter motioned with his fan to show that they wished to descend the gang-ladder immediately.

'It is appropriate for us to leave now,' he said in Dutch, eyeing Rice and Armstrong uncomfortably. As he spoke he signalled towards the chief boatman below, indicating he should prepare to take them ashore at once. 'The vice-governor wishes to inform you that an official of higher rank will come out for further discussions with you tomorrow morning. But for a full answer he says you must wait at least three days.'

They hurried away down the gang-ladder without waiting for any response, followed by their three samurai escorts. Eden watched warily as Yakamochi approached the entry port; but his dark, sharp-featured face was sullenly impassive, and he avoided Eden's gaze as he climbed down into the waiting guard-boat.

Tanaka was the last to leave, and as he passed in front of Eden he paused for the briefest of moments. '*Taihen on ni na ru*', he said quietly, looking Eden directly in the eye. '*Sumimasen!*'

Because the words were uttered very softly for his ears only, Eden was not able immediately to construe a clear meaning from them. He mulled over in his mind what he thought he had heard, as he watched Tanaka descend into the waiting boat; but the samurai did not speak further or look back, and Eden had to content himself with trying to commit the words to memory.

As the boat pulled away, he heard Lieutenant Rice heave a deep sigh of relief. A warlike clamour still rose from the cliffs and beaches, and some guard-boats were still keeping watch from a respectful distance; but a broad expanse of empty water had been established around the warships, and only the movement of the envoy's guard-boat pulling towards the shore now broke its mirror calm.

'Do you think we've avoided a war, Mr Armstrong?' asked Rice. 'It seemed a close run thing there at times.'

Samuel Armstrong nodded, then re-lit his pipe, puffing a cloud of fragrant tobacco smoke into the warm evening air. 'I think we have, Lieutenant—at least for the moment.'

None of the Japanese occupants of the guard-boat raised their heads to look back at the watching Americans as they retreated from the flagship, except for the disguised Prince Tanaka. From time to time he stared towards the entry port where Robert Eden was standing and his demeanour suggested he was still trying to come to terms with all that had happened on board. As the departing boat grew smaller, Eden in his turn found he was constantly replaying in his mind the words the young samurai had uttered before disembarking. But they continued to defeat his attempts at translation, and he watched the tasselled boat fade into the evening, still puzzling over their meaning.

9

As dusk closed in around the modest village inn where she was being held under guard, Matsumura Tokiwa paced restlessly back and forth across her bare room. Dressed only in a light under-kimono of white gauze, she held her slender arms clenched agitatedly about her own waist and her beautiful face was pale and distraught.

The tramp of feet on the road through the village had lessened, but from time to time she stopped pacing to listen to the closer night sounds of the two-storeyed inn, which was filled to capacity with anxious travellers. In the next room a male voice was chanting a Buddhist prayer in a high, desperate-sounding monotone; from not far away she recognized the jangle of an inexpertly plucked *samisen;* more distantly cymbals clashed and drums were being beaten over snatches of discordant song, and a storyteller's voice sometimes raised itself excitedly above the clamour. Every so often running feet pounded along the corridor beyond her *shoji*, startling her, and she could hear shrieks and splashing sounds coming from an unseen bathhouse.

When she paused to peer out through the spyhole she had torn in the rice-paper screen overlooking the courtyard, she saw the last rays of the setting sun suffusing the pale peak of Mount Fuji with a soft halo of pink light. The sky beyond was already a deep, dark blue, and as always the mood of the sacred mountain seemed to be subtly changing with the advancing hours. In the twilight she imagined that, from the dizzying heights of the summit, its mysterious *kami*were silently watching and waiting for events in the regions below to clarify themselves.

Despite the deepening gloom around the inn, her eyes confirmed what her ears had already told her—that the flow of men and animals along the winding tracks had become less frantic in both directions. Civilians were more evident among the dwindling crowds, and she watched a group of horses, richly caparisoned in scarlet cloth and fringed leather, pass the gates of the courtyard, travelling westward, escorted by liveried riders and footservants. From the flanks of the horses large open panniers were suspended, and inside the baskets a number of aristocratic children were visible; under the light of the paper lanterns suspended from the gates of the inn, their tiny innocent faces peered over the basket rims, looking strangely composed, and Tokiwa found herself envying the evident comfort and security which surrounded them as they travelled.

As she watched them jog on confidently into the darkness a vague, unconscious desire that had been growing gradually inside her for an hour or two suddenly became a firm decision: she was not prepared to remain a helpless captive at the inn against her will! Perhaps she *was* in danger from enemies of Prince Tanaka—but how could she be certain? And how could she be sure that the inn itself was a safe haven? In this confused and bewildering situation she knew instinctively that she was in some danger from Gotaro, the chief guard. So many people were on the move, so many were afraid and at a loss; amidst so much turmoil and frenzied excitement she could not bear to remain isolated at the inn, cut off from all contact with what was happening beyond its walls. She felt confident suddenly that she could protect herself more effectively if she understood better what was happening: she would rather, she decided finally, accept whatever risks were involved and try to escape. If the sacred *kami* of Mount Fuji were truly waiting and watching to see how events would clarify themselves below, she would show them that she at least could act decisively!

The long balcony outside her room, she could see, was already in deep shadow. At its far corner there was a fixed ladder leading down into the yard. A guard was posted below, but she calculated that if he dozed off she might be able to get out onto the shadowy balcony unseen and slip away—especially if she could find some disguise. In that moment she wanted more than anything to follow the example of those liveried aristocrats' horses, and disappear quietly into the unknown darkness. Whether she would return to Yedo and the Yoshiwara or travel off in another direction to begin a new life, she did not yet know.

But the very thought that she might somehow be able to begin a new life filled her heart with an unfamiliar feeling of excitement. Of one thing she was quite certain—an irresistible urge was moving her to do what she had yearned for more and more since becoming a geisha: to rebel in some way against the suffocating tradition of unquestioning female obedience under which she had been raised, and which had subsequently pervaded every moment of her life . . . Perhaps, she reflected, she had inherited more of her samurai father's impetuosity and restlessness than was expected in a compliant elder daughter . . . Perhaps it was impossible in reality to fulfil such wild, unspoken desires; but, amid the panic and upheaval that had so suddenly affected everybody in the land, she sensed that seemingly impossible things might now become attainable.

The sound of the corridor *shoji* being slid apart behind her interrupted these thoughts, and she turned to see the peasant maidservant entering. She was carrying a *zen*, a small table with short legs, which bore a bowl of rice, some eggs, a flask of tea and a copper basin of water. The girl closed the screen carefully behind her and bowed her head once towards Tokiwa before advancing to place the table on the tatami in the middle of the room.

'Here is some food, O Tokiwa-san,' she intoned quietly. 'The guards require you to eat now. You've had nothing since morning.'

Before replying, Tokiwa hurried over to the little red lacquered box wrapped in oilskin in which she had carried her money from Yedo. She took out five silver *ichibus*, concealed them in one hand inside the sleeve of her kimono, and motioned the maid towards the side of the room furthest from the corridor. Pressing an index finger against her own lips, she cautioned her to speak softly.

'What is your name?' Tokiwa whispered.

'My name is Eiko,' replied the maid in an anxious undertone. 'Why are we behaving like this?'

'I need your help, Eiko,' whispered Tokiwa urgently, pulling her hand from her sleeve and opening it to reveal the five *ichibus* nestling in her palm. 'This can be yours if you will help me escape from here.'

The peasant girl's eyes grew wide in alarm as she gazed down at more money than she had ever seen in her young life. Then she peered fearfully round the room, checking that all the paper screens remained closed, and that they could not be overheard.

'I am . . . afraid, Tokiwa-san!' she stammered, torn between an evident desire to take the money and her fear of the guards. 'They may kill me if I help you.'

'They need never know,' breathed Tokiwa. 'Don't be afraid. After I've gone, say you know nothing about it.'

'But they won't believe me, Tokiwa-san,' replied the maid in an agitated whisper.

'There's no need for them to suspect anything, if you stay calm,' said Tokiwa soothingly. 'Now, listen to me. With some of this money I want you to obtain a horse and some peasant clothes.'

'What sort of clothes?' whispered the maid, her expression still indecisive.

Tokiwa smiled encouragingly. 'First a broad hat of plaited bamboo. Then a blue scarf for my head, some loose blue trousers, some wooden clogs—and a working shirt.'

Eiko looked at the money, rubbing her own cheek distractedly with one hand, and started to shake her head.

'I will give you ten *ichibus*,' whispered Tokiwa imploringly, adding more silver coins from the red lacquered box. 'Now will you please try to help me?'

She fixed her gaze on the peasant girl, who she estimated was no more than seventeen or eighteen years old. Her dark eyes were downcast, avoiding Tokiwa's searching scrutiny, and she continued to rub her cheek indecisively. With a feeling of panic Tokiwa realized that the maid could simply take the money and flee into the darkness, never to return—or just as easily report everything to the guards, hand over some of the coins as proof and keep the rest for herself. But as she waited for a reply she realized there was no alternative to trusting her, and again she held out the money.

'If you bring me the clothes hidden under your own, Eiko, I will be able to put them on here and steal down into the courtyard after dark,' she said beseechingly. 'Even if a guard sees me then, he won't recognize me as a geisha from the "Yoshiwara . . . But I can't do it without your help!'

The maid's eyes shone with fearful excitement as she listened, and she nodded once, indicating that she understood. 'It will be very dangerous, Tokiwa-san. When do you want the clothes?'

'As soon as possible—tonight if you are able.'

'Wouldn't it be better to wait until tomorrow evening? I could bring some clothes when I come in from my home in the morning.'

'Do your best,' urged Tokiwa. 'But come as soon as you can. I will be waiting.'

'What sort of horse do you want?'

'An old, slow one—and make sure it is equipped with big straw panniers. Fill one of the baskets with rice, so that I can pass for a peasant travelling to market.'

'And what shall I do with the horse?'

'Tie it to the first tree you come to west of the inn.' Tokiwa paused to pluck two ribbons of fine blue silk from her toilet box, and handed them to the maid. 'Tie one of these to its mane—then I will be sure that the horse is mine. The other is a gift for yourself. Wear it in your hair when you wish to look your prettiest.'

'Thank you, O Tokiwa-san.' Eiko accepted the ribbons with a hesitant smile. Her simple face was still shadowed by doubt but, after running the glossy silk back and forth between her fingers, she reached out suddenly to pick up the ten silver coins and tucked them into the folds of her homespun kimono. 'I will try to do all the things you ask.'

The maid hurried out into the corridor, closing the screens quietly behind her. Left standing alone in the middle of the room, Tokiwa found that she was trembling as she listened fearfully for the approaching feet of the chief guard. If the maid reported to him all that had passed between them, he would come thundering into the room at once to confront her. Where that might lead, she could not begin to guess. She suddenly regretted her rashness, but realized it was far too late to have regrets.

For two or three minutes Tokiwa remained standing in the middle of the room, contemplating the boldness of her action with some astonishment; then, still trembling slightly, she began pacing back and forth across the soft tatami once more.

10

What's going on out there, Sentaro?'

Coming up behind the castaway, who was peering anxiously out through an open gunport on the upper deck, Robert Eden patted him affectionately on the shoulder. In the darkness that cloaked the shore, a chain of great beacon fires flamed on the clifftops. Other fires were burning all along the beaches, and the sound of religious chanting rose intermittently on the still air. A single, deep-toned gong sent out an ominous note of warning at long intervals, and in the flickering light from the fires Eden could see that the face of the Japanese castaway was stiff with tension.

'My countrymen seem very frightened, master,' he said, speaking English in a hoarse whisper. 'Many beacon fires all send out the same message.'

'What do they say?'

Sentaro hesitated for a moment, and when he looked up at Eden his eyes were wide with alarm. 'Sorry, master, but they are saying: "Arm to expel the foreign barbarians!"'

'Do you think they really will attack us?'

'I don't know.' The castaway shook his head several times to express his confusion. 'Many of your brother officers also ask me this question. Perhaps . . . maybe . . . I don't know!'

The calm, black waters of the bay reflected the orange beacon fires like a mirror. Close to the beach the crews of the guard-boats were still watching the American warships from a distance and paper lanterns strung on their sterns provided a gentler chain of illumination. In the deep stillness of the night a new surge of impassioned chanting carried clearly to the ears of those who were awake and listening on the American ships.

'At temples and shrines, many people are pleading with our *kami* to drive away "the black ships of the foreign barbarians",' continued Sentaro after listening carefully to the chorus of voices coming from the shore. 'I think nobody is sleeping tonight.'

Eden drew a deep breath and glanced up into the rigging of the *Susquehanna*. The shadowy silhouettes of many additional lookouts were visible aloft, clinging amongst the spars and shrouds, and all were straining their eyes and ears towards the shore. A wisp of smoke curling upward amongst the furled sails and the quiet throb of machinery from below decks confirmed that the engines were being maintained in a state of readiness for action.

As soon as the Japanese negotiating party had left the flagship, Commodore Perry had issued orders for all watches to be doubled, and for extra sentries to be posted fore and aft. During his own evening tours of inspection Eden had checked that sufficient heaps of roundshot and grape were piled beside each of his guns and that muskets were neatly stacked in the open on the nearby decks. Other watch officers had ordered regular inspections to be made to ensure that there was plenty of coal in the bunkers around the engines, and that enough steam was maintained in the boilers to meet any emergency. All the flagship's cutters had been readied for launching, each craft loaded with carbines, pistols, cutlasses and signal lights. As the darkness deepened, Eden had repeatedly reminded all his lookouts to keep their eyes peeled for burning junks which might be let loose among the warships in an effort to fire and destroy them.

A few minutes earlier, eight strokes of the flagship's bell had marked the midnight hour and the termination of another of Eden's tense four-hour spells of duty as second officer of the watch. On descending the port ladder from the quarterdeck he had spotted Sentaro hunched in the shadows of the gunport, peering towards the flame-lit shore. During his earlier rounds, remembering that he had banished the castaway from the decks long before sunset, he had looked in briefly at Sentaro's makeshift berth among the ropes and sails beneath the fo'c's'le. He had told him then it was safe to get some air on deck under the cover of darkness, so long as he kept himself out of sight and returned quickly to his hiding place if any emergency arose.

'Do you think you'll sleep now, Sentaro?' asked Eden, patting his shoulder again. 'Or will you spend the rest of the night praying that your *kami* will drive our ships away—and you along with them?'

'I have two minds, master,' whispered the castaway, straightening up to stand beside Eden. With a quick movement of his right hand he touched first the centre of his forehead, then his chest. 'Part of me wants to stay in Nippon—but part of me wants to return to America.'

'Which part of you wants to stay?' asked Eden quietly.

The face of the Japanese became serious and he again laid the palm of his hand on the centre of his chest. 'My heart is foolish, master. It wants to beat again in the land of its birth. It wants also to see my son and daughter, and my wife. I haven't seen them for four years.' He smiled sadly, revealing several broken teeth. Then he touched his forehead with one grimy finger.

'But my head is wiser. It tells me I should leave. It knows I will be killed if I go ashore—and then my heart will beat no more!'

Eden looked at him thoughtfully, then turned away towards the blazing beacons of the clifftops. 'How far is your home village from here, Sentaro?'

'Ten miles from Uraga, on the western shore of the bay, master.' He pointed southward with one arm. 'It is called Yurutaki.'

'And how old are your son and daughter?'

'Taro will be nine years old now,' he replied wistfully. 'His sister Haru is five . . .'

'Then perhaps you should please both your heart and your head.'

The castaway stared mystified at the American officer. 'How could I do that, master?'

'Are you a good swimmer?'

Sentaro nodded. 'Yes, master, I swim very well!'

'Then you could slip over the side and swim ashore in the dark. You could find a horse and make your way to your home village without anybody knowing. You would at least see your wife and children—but if you find you're still afraid, you could return secretly to the ship in the same way. And I'd keep my promise to help you return to America.'

Sentaro gasped. 'But, master, to go ashore secretly would be very dangerous. In every town and village there are police spies. I would be very frightened!'

Eden had been staring at the blazing beacons, but now he turned to look at the castaway again, his eyes suddenly gleaming with their own inner brightness. 'Would you be so frightened if I came with you?'

'Come with me, master?' Sentaro's eyes widened in amazement. 'Why should you want to come with me?'

'To try to find out what's really happening behind those fires!' Eden spoke his words with a quiet vehemence. 'We know nothing of your land and its people. Yet at any moment we could make a false move and start a terrible war. If I came ashore with you, I could bring back more reliable information!'

'Has somebody given orders for you to do this?' asked the Japanese in an awed whisper. 'Your high chief, perhaps? Has he ordered you to go ashore—like you did in Mexico?'

Eden glanced round to ensure nobody was within earshot, then he shook his head and lowered his voice. 'Nobody has ordered me to do this, Sentaro. But we shouldn't always wait for others to give us instructions. Sometimes we must dare to give them to ourselves!'

'I'm too afraid, master.' The castaway swallowed hard, his expression apologetic. 'I'm too afraid to do this.'

Eden stared at him, frowning; then his face cleared. 'You're wise to be afraid, Sentaro. It's right for you to stay on board.'

'And you, master, what will you do?' asked the Japanese uneasily.

Eden hesitated for a second, then squared his shoulders with sudden resolution. 'I'll go ashore alone. I'll go and find out what's really happening.'

'No!' The castaway let out a stifled exclamation of alarm. 'It's impossible for you to go alone. No foreign barbarians have been allowed to set foot in Nippon for over two hundred years. You'd be executed as a spy—or become a prisoner!'

Eden looked round and smiled faintly. 'No, I won't. You've helped me learn a little of your language, Sentaro. I'll disguise myself carefully. I'll be able to watch and listen. I might even try to find your home village and tell your family you're alive and well.'

The Japanese again peered out through the open gunport. The beacon fires were blazing higher, and the silhouetted figures of armed men were visible, moving against the flames. In the darkness the deep-toned warning gong continued to sound, and when he looked round at Eden again the uncertainty in his face was plainly visible.

'I *am* afraid, master,' he said in an unsteady voice. 'But if you go ashore, I must come with you. You would not survive there without me.'

Eden considered the castaway's offer in silence, then nodded decisively. 'All right, Sentaro, if you're truly sure you want to take the risk. You would be able to help me a great deal.'

'Thank you, master!' The face of the Japanese was lit for an instant by a passing smile. Then he glanced uneasily towards the shore once more. 'When do we go, master?'

'We must go as soon as possible, perhaps just before dawn—but we must make our preparations carefully.'

'What will we need, master?'

Eden thought quickly. 'Some oilskin waist-pouches . . . Go back to your quarters and make two pouches. Sew them onto belts. They will keep our things dry. I'll take a pistol and ammunition, a knife, a good compass and my small binoculars. So make the pouches big!'

'And some food, master?' enquired the castaway eagerly.

Eden shook his head. 'No, I'll take some of the Chinese silver coins I picked up in Hong Kong. You can buy food for us with them . . . But I'll need some of your old clothes for disguise—especially the big Japanese straw hat you made in California. It will hide my face.'

'All right, master!'

'And I'll come to your berth again later to talk some more.'

'Very good, master.' The castaway began to turn away. 'I go there now.'

'Wait,' said Eden. 'One question. Today I heard some Japanese words I didn't understand. A man said, in my hearing, "*Taihen on ni na ru.*"'

'That means "I am greatly in your debt",' said Sentaro quickly. 'Those are words intended very sincerely. Who used them?'

'They were spoken by an escort of the Japanese envoy who came aboard. And he ended with other words I didn't recognize . . . something like "*Sumo ma san*"'

The castaway screwed up his face in concentration. 'Could it perhaps have been one word, master—"*Sumimasen*"?'

Eden hesitated, then nodded. 'Possibly. What does that mean?'

'"*Sumimasen*" is a special way of saying "thank you".' The castaway wrinkled his forehead as he searched for the right English equivalent. 'But for something you really did not expect to get. It's an apology, too, for causing trouble.'

'Thank you.' Eden's expression brightened as comprehension dawned. Then he nodded, repeating the words quietly to himself, '*Sumimasen . . . Sumimasen* . . . Yes, I think that was it.'

'Glad to find you keeping up your language studies under these trying circumstances, Lieutenant!' The jocular voice of Samuel Armstrong cut across Eden's thoughts as the missionary interpreter approached silently out of the darkness. '*Sumimasen*, if you'd like some scholarly elaboration, is one of half a dozen shades of Japanese apology. As befits a nation so obsessed with form and formality, each version is separate and quite precise. *Sumimasen* has an interesting literal interpretation. It means something like: "The obligation will never end."'

Eden looked searchingly at the China missionary, wondering if any other part of his conversation with Sentaro had been overheard. But Armstrong, smiling and wreathed in smoke, was puffing relaxedly on his pipe and he gave no indication of having heard anything disturbing.

'Mr Armstrong speaks my language well,' said Sentaro, bowing formally to the newcomer. 'But excuse me, master. I will go now.'

After bowing once more to Eden, the Japanese hurried off in the direction of the fo'c's'le, and the missionary-interpreter positioned himself carefully beside the cannon so that he could look out along its barrel towards the shore.

'Our castaway's wrong of course,' said Armstrong softly, as he studied the glowing beacons ranged along the cliffs. 'I don't speak Japanese nearly well enough. What little I know, I learned like you, Lieutenant, from a few shipwrecked sailors. My lot got washed up in Hong Kong and Canton. I've been able to add a little scholarly gloss by talking with some of those intrepid Dutch traders who occasionally pass through southern China on their way to and from Nagasaki.' The missionary straightened his back and looked round admiringly at Robert Eden. 'You've done very well in the short time available to you. Your Japanese is as good as mine—but with you I sense it's something more than just idle curiosity. Am I right?'

'I hoped that knowing some of the language might help me understand what we're trying to do here, sir,' replied Eden, remembering the hint of acrimony in their last discussion, and keeping his voice studiedly polite. 'That's all.'

'Most commendable. Few others would go to such lengths.' Armstrong paused and drew thoughtfully on his pipe. 'Has it helped you to understand?'

'Not very much yet, sir. Perhaps it's too early.'

'I sense, Lieutenant, there's much more in your heart than you feel able to say,' prompted the missionary gently after a short silence. 'You can feel free to speak your mind with me. I'm a civilian, remember. We started to have an interesting conversation earlier. Let's continue it. I won't repeat anything of what you say.'

Eden hesitated for a long moment, as though he had previously made up his mind to say nothing further. Then he inclined his head towards the coast, and spoke with a quiet intensity. 'We seem, Mr Armstrong, to be taking grave risks. We're obviously causing great turmoil ashore. And why? These people have done us no harm. Thousands of miles separate our countries. What is it all for?'

'We're standing on the brink of a turning point in history. Lieutenant—for Asia and perhaps the whole world.' The missionary looked out towards the shore again, pointing with the stem of his pipe along the barrel of the cannon. 'These people are still living out a kind of medieval fairytale that hasn't changed for many hundreds of years. They're cut off from the rest of the world and ruled by an Emperor who is supposed to be divine. But nobody ever sees him. The lords of the provinces, the *daimyo*, live in remote castles, hunting and quarrelling among themselves. They still protect their fiefdoms with private warrior bands garbed in the sort of gaudy feudal uniforms last seen in Europe in the Middle Ages. The peasants toil like slaves in the rice paddies, the townspeople are in thrall too, the whole system is oppressive, and there are no real freedoms as we know them. They're hundreds of years behind us, Lieutenant. Tonight we're bringing the modern age to their doorstep.'

Glancing up as he listened to the missionary, Eden noticed that the silhouetted figures of the silent lookouts posted amongst the *Susquehanna*'s furled sails were becoming more clearly visible. The dark sky high above the four motionless warships was speckled with the faint light of many stars, but so far there had been no sign of the moon. Turning his head, Eden saw that to the south-west a faint glow was spreading above the sea, suggesting that the moon was about to rise, and this growing flood of illumination was causing the four powerful American ships to stand out more dramatically on the flat calm of the bay.

'You make it sound, Mr Armstrong, as though it's an unselfish act on our part,' said Eden quietly. 'But aren't we really levelling our guns at them to glorify the Yankee nation? Aren't we just flaunting our superior power? Nobody asked us to come here—just the reverse. The Japanese have told us to go away—at least as far as Nagasaki. What right do we have to ignore them?'

Armstrong stroked his greying whiskers thoughtfully for a moment, then smiled. 'I admire your youthful idealism, Lieutenant. I was once like you as a young man—filled with righteous fire! As you grow older you see things with a greater sense of balance. Yes, the letter from our President to their Emperor seeks to persuade them to open some of their ports officially to our ships and our trade. We want them to sell us coal, water and other supplies. We demand too that they repatriate American whaling crews shipwrecked on their numerous islands. Is there really so much wrong with all that?'

Eden listened to the booming of the distant war gong and the muffled chanting onshore, then drew a long breath. 'Why couldn't we leave them to choose for themselves whether they wished to join the rest of the world—and when?'

The missionary grinned and reached out to pat Eden amicably on the shoulder. 'Humanity doesn't operate quite like that, young man. Never has and probably never will. For its own sake, Japan needs to learn how the rest of the world does things.'

'If they want to find their own way, in their own time, for their own reasons,' said Eden insistently, 'why should we hold guns to their heads now?'

'For two hundred years,' said Armstrong slowly, 'the Japanese have traded with the West exclusively through Dutch merchants based at Nagasaki. They humiliate those Dutchmen by making them prisoners on an artificial concrete island in the harbour, and never allow them ashore. When a Dutch ship arrives, they stop it outside the harbour and ransack it. They always confiscate any Bibles they find—and even crack open eggs to check if anything is being smuggled inside the shells . . .'

Armstrong chuckled and tapped his pipe against the six-foot bulwark, carefully grinding out with his heel the glowing embers that fell to the deck. He continued to smile at the apparent inanities of Japan's customs officers but gradually his face became serious.

'The outside world can't continue to trade with Japan like this—and today your commodore has forced them to abandon some of the terrible humiliations they habitually inflict on outsiders. He's also forced their guard-boats to cease close surveillance of our ships. And he's made their officials come respectfully to him seeking an audience. All that was made possible by *this* fellow and his friends.' Armstrong raised one hand to pat the long, cast-iron barrel of the sixty-four-pound cannon, and he smiled again. 'Perhaps all this sounds a bit strange to you, Lieutenant, coming from a missionary—a so-called "man of God". I'm not used to travelling on warships, but here's where I see the "balance" in this situation. In his mercy, I'm sure God doesn't wish the nations of eastern Asia to remain forever in seclusion and outer darkness. I believe the truth of the Gospels must be made known to all nations. And God can move in mysterious ways behind commerce, diplomacy—and even US Navy steam frigates.'

'These people have their own gods and beliefs,' said Eden with sudden explosive force. 'Very different to ours, admittedly, but surely we should respect that.'

Armstrong looked up in surprise and saw that the young officer's face had become unaccountably tense. At his side his right hand was clenched in a tight fist and he was staring fixedly towards the shore.

'Do you not trust in the will of God, Lieutenant?' asked the missionary quietly. 'Do you have no faith?'

Eden did not reply at once, but continued staring out into the night. Above his head, the strengthening glow from the southern horizon was bathing the masts and spars of the flagship in a faint bluish light, and many of the lookouts had turned to peer towards its source. In his abstraction Eden failed to notice that the light had intensified and he turned suddenly to face the missionary again, speaking in a voice that shook with emotion.

'I lost my own faith seven years ago, Mr Armstrong—when my wife died in my arms. At the time she was in labour . . . '

'I'm very sorry,' the missionary began, but Eden ignored him.

'She was only sixteen. We'd been married eleven months . . . I've never prayed since. I vowed that night I'd never pray again. Never! No matter how long I lived.'

Eden's voice died away and he bowed his head briefly. For some moments the missionary remained respectfully silent, watching him with a compassionate expression in his eyes.

'We often don't understand God's will at the time, Lieutenant,' he began gently. 'I'd like to talk to you again—maybe at a better moment than this . . .

Eden held up one hand suddenly in a gesture of admonition, and when he spoke his words were harsh and cold. 'There's nothing more to say, Mr Armstrong. I don't want to talk to you, or anyone else, about God—now or ever.'

In the uncomfortable silence that followed, the missionary lifted his head and noticed for the first time the luminous glow that was beginning to light up the whole sky above the Bay of Yedo. The furled sails, spars and hulls of the *Susquehanna* and its sister warships were now silhouetted starkly against the sky and, when Armstrong swung round towards the south-west, he let out a gasp of astonishment.

'Look, Lieutenant—what an extraordinary sight!'

Following his gaze, Eden saw a brightly glowing blue sphere rising very slowly above the horizon. Throwing off a great light, it grew steadily larger in the sky, leaving in its wake a wedge-shaped trail of red phosphorescence. This cascade of brightness illuminated a large area of land and sea, and an awed hush fell over the flagship as those on deck watched it ascend into the heavens. On land the sound of the single gong suddenly ceased and even the intermittent chanting died away, leaving the bay eerily silent.

'What are we to make of this, Armstrong?' boomed a voice from the quarterdeck rail above their heads and Eden snapped to attention on recognizing the resonant tones of Commodore Perry.

A moment later he saw the bulky figure of the commander-in-chief come into view. His shock of dark hair was tousled and his gold-epauletted uniform jacket was unfastened at the collar, suggesting he had risen hurriedly from his cabin to observe the strange phenomenon. Like everybody else on board the four ships, he was craning his neck to stare incredulously skyward.

'It's perhaps a meteor, Commodore,' cried Armstrong. 'Or maybe a comet. But, call it what you will, it's like nothing I've ever seen before.'

A buzz of discussion broke out among the lookouts in the high rigging, and many ratings and officers not currently on watch began stumbling sleepily onto the decks to peer up into the night sky.

'The ancients, I think, Mr Armstrong, would have construed this remarkable appearance in the heavens as a favourable omen for any sort of enterprise, wouldn't they?' called Perry, leaning over the rail again. 'What do you say?'

'I'd say they would indeed, sir . . .' Armstrong paused and chuckled. 'But perhaps the Japanese on shore will see it as just the reverse. They may take it as a sign that we "barbarians" are in league with the devil.'

For a long time there was silence from the quarterdeck and Eden could see that the commodore was still staring up at the sky. The brilliance of the glow from the moving sphere was now so intense that the masts and rigging of the flagship themselves seemed to have become an eerie source of illumination, giving off a strange electric-blue luminescence that was reflecting dramatically in the water all around the ship.

'Whatever it is, Armstrong, I think we'll take a leaf from the book of the ancients,' Perry called down at last, a light-hearted note evident in his voice. 'We'll construe the apparition, for all official purposes, as being an encouragement to our expedition.'

'Amen to that,' called Armstrong in reply. 'And your view must be much better up there. I'll come and join you, if I may.'

'You may, Armstrong. You may. Come up at once.'

The commodore disappeared from the quarterdeck rail, and the missionary hurried away to mount the port ladder. Left alone, Eden stood gazing up at the brilliant source of light, which was still climbing as it headed slowly north-east over the sea. Gradually the glow spread inland until it reached the distant mountains, and the perfect, white-topped cone of Mount Fuji came into view. Bathed by this luminous blue glare, the volcano was transformed into a giant beacon of nature that far outshone all the fires on the coast and, as he stared at the extraordinary twin images, Eden was reminded suddenly of his dream of the previous night.

The memory caused a tangible sensation of well-being to spread through his whole body, and he experienced again the same powerful feelings of awe and wonder which had seized him in his dream when he pulled the cloak of stars down from the heavens. Despite the many tensions of the day, he felt calm, alert and clear-minded.

How long he remained by the gunport looking at the sky, he could not tell. The source of light continued to move northeastward in a slow arc, dipping down towards the sea again after it had reached its zenith. But although it continued to move only slowly Eden found he could not tear his eyes from it while it remained in sight.

'Is it good omen, master? Or is it bad? Perhaps it is telling us we should not go ashore!'

Sentaro, drawn out from under the fo'c's'le by the commotion, had crept soundlessly back to the spar deck and was crouching in the shadow of the bulwark. He had posed his questions in an anxious whisper and was now staring up expectantly at Eden, his eyes wide with apprehension.

'I don't know what it is—or what it means,' replied Eden, quietly. 'And I'm not going to try and guess. But I do know it's made me feel one thing for certain.'

'What's that, master?'

'That this isn't the time for hesitation! Go back to your berth now and finish fixing those belts and pouches. We're going to swim ashore tonight!'

11

Matsumura Tokiwa awoke with a start, to find her darkened room at the inn suffused with an eerie glow of blue light. For an instant or two she believed she was caught up in a nightmare and she let out a little whimper of alarm. Then, on hearing a faint, persistent tapping on the *shoji* separating her room from the balcony, she realized that she was not dreaming after all.

Bewildered and confused by the strange blue glow, she rose from beneath her sleeping quilt and tiptoed apprehensively towards the screens, unsure of what she would find if she opened them. As she hesitated with her hand hovering above the latch, the tapping began again and she heard a frightened female voice whispering her name.

'Please let me in, O Tokiwa-san. It's Eiko, your maid!'

As soon as Tokiwa had parted the screens, the maid pushed hurriedly into the room. She was shivering with fright and peered anxiously over her shoulder. Looking past her, Tokiwa caught sight of the radiant blue orb that was lighting up land and sky alike with its unearthly glow. Its nucleus was now dipping close to the distant horizon but its reddish-blue wake of phosphorescence streamed out across the starry heavens in spectacular waves of colour, like paint hurled from an artist's brush. Tokiwa stood rooted to the spot, her fists pressed to her face, staring at the apparition in an awed silence.

'What is it, Eiko?' she gasped. 'What's happening?'

'Close the *shoji*, Tokiwa-san,' pleaded the maid. 'Close them quickly.'

The geisha hurriedly shut the screens and, turning to look at Eiko more closely, she found she had slung a wide hat of plaited bamboo around her shoulders and was clutching a bundle of clothing in her arms.

'Do you want these now, Tokiwa-san?' asked Eiko in a tremulous voice, displaying the blue cotton garments. 'Will you still try to escape?'

'What is that strange light?' asked Tokiwa in a faint voice, looking again towards the garish glow now shining through the screens. 'Is it some terrible device of the foreign barbarians?'

'Nobody knows! But many think it is a sign of anger from our *kami*. The temple in my village is more crowded than ever. All the women are weeping and wailing . . .'

'Is there no other possible explanation?'

'Others say it's an omen revealing that the gods of the foreign barbarians are all-powerful. Or perhaps the barbarians fired it into the sky from their volcano-ships . . .' Suddenly Eiko thrust the bundle of clothes towards Tokiwa as though they were too hot to hold any longer. 'I smuggled these up the ladder to the balcony when I saw the guards had rushed outside the inn gates. For the moment they have forgotten you. They are all standing in the street among the crowds staring at the sky.'

'Quickly, hide them here!' Tokiwa crossed to her sleeping pallet and lifted one end so that the maid could slip her bundle underneath. 'And put the hat under my quilt.'

She watched Eiko unsling the hat from her shoulders and hide it with shaking hands. Then she led the way back to the balcony screens and eased them open once more. The light in the sky was descending faster now, though blazing ever more brightly. In its glare Tokiwa could see part of the large crowd outside the inn gates, staring upward in silence, but the courtyard below her balcony was empty.

'I think this is the time for me to go!' whispered Tokiwa. 'The light is sinking, and it looks as if darkness will return soon. Everybody's attention is distracted now.'

The maid nodded uncertainly. 'But aren't you afraid, Tokiwasan?'

'Yes, I'm afraid,' replied the geisha. 'But what if the gods have sent this light to aid my escape—and I waste my chance? Nobody's watching now. I won't get a better opportunity. Did you find a horse?'

'Yes. It's tethered to a tree at the side of the road half a mile to the west of the inn.' She inclined her head to emphasize the direction. 'It has two big panniers, and your blue ribbon is braided into its mane.'

'Good, you've done very well.' Tokiwa went quickly to the red lacquered box and took out four silver *ichibus*. Her eyes were suddenly bright with excitement as she offered them to the maid. 'Take this extra money, please. And help me to dress quickly.'

The geisha removed her light under-kimono and waited unselfconsciously naked while the maid knelt to gather up the patched and threadbare peasant garments from their hiding place. On rising, Eiko paused in the act of unfolding a rough working shirt, and studied Tokiwa with a mixture of surprise and admiration. The strange light from the sky outside threw into relief the delicate contours of her body: the gentle curve of her cheeks and neck, her narrow back, her small breasts and her darkly shaded belly were all transformed as though by magic from their normal amber colour to a soft, shimmering blue. As Tokiwa stood motionless, with one hand absently touching a stray lock of hair, her whole body appeared to glow with its own inner luminosity.

'I've never seen anybody so beautiful, Tokiwa-san,' murmured the maid, lowering her gaze as she moved closer to help her into the humble shirt. 'This strange light from the sky makes you look for all the world like one of our spirit goddesses of the night . . .'

Tokiwa smiled abstractedly and waited as the maid pulled the upper garment into place. Next Eiko slipped the rough trousers onto her bare legs, and with a strip of hempen rope fixed them at the waist. She pulled a pair of rough, straw-plaited sandals onto the geisha's delicate feet, then, after picking up a comb and pins, she dressed her long glossy hair into a tight chignon to make it as inconspicuous as possible. When she had finished, she fetched the wide bamboo hat and tightened its cord to settle it securely on Tokiwa's head.

Eiko stepped back to check the effect of the disguise, and after a moment of appraisal she nodded her approval. 'Anyone looking closely at you, Tokiwa-san, will see that you are beautiful—even in those field clothes. But if you walk like a peasant with your knees bent, and keep your head lowered, perhaps nobody will notice. I have left a carrying-pole and two baskets in the shadows by the foot of the ladder. Put the pole on your shoulder and run fast with little, short, bouncy steps. That way the guards will never recognize you . . .'

Tokiwa nodded again and bent to gather up her dark, star-spangled kimono and what few other articles of clothing she had brought with her from Yedo. Folding them together, she handed them to the maid. 'Please wrap these and my lacquered box into a small bundle. There'll be room for them in one of the panniers on the horse.'

Pulling the conical bamboo hat lower over her face she led the maid quietly back towards the balcony. They looked at each other in silence for a moment, then Eiko handed over the bundle of the geisha's belongings, and slid open the *shoji*. Very low in the sky now, the strange luminous sphere had become dazzlingly bright, and by its light they could see that outside the inn gates the dense crowd was still gazing upwards in astonishment.

'I think you are right, Tokiwa-san,' whispered Eiko. 'The light *is* sinking fast. Very soon it will be dark again.'

'Good—and the courtyard is still empty. I must go at once.' Tokiwa turned to look at the maid with a mixture of gratitude and affection. 'Please pray for me, Eiko. Pray that good fortune may follow me.'

'I will, O Tokiwa-san. But which way will you go?'

Tokiwa hesitated. 'Perhaps I'll take the road towards Yedo. My family home is in a village north of the city . . . But I'm not sure. I just want to get as far away from here as I can.'

A great radiance, like a sustained lightning flash, flooded the heavens and suddenly new cries of alarm rose from many throats in the crowd before the inn. Then the sphere started to lose its brilliance as it fell towards the sea, and every eye remained fastened on it.

'Go now, Tokiwa-san,' urged the maid in a frantic whisper. 'Nobody is looking this way. May the *kami* protect you always!'

The geisha slipped out onto the balcony and ran soundlessly to the ladder, holding her bundle firmly under one arm. A second flash lit the night as she scrambled down into the courtyard to pick up the carrying-pole, and again the crowd of onlookers cried out in astonishment. A moment later the peasant maid saw Tokiwa steal unnoticed through the gates of the inn and hurry away westward towards the spot where the horse was tethered. Her shoulders were bent theatrically under the weight of the carrying-pole and Eiko, watching her over the courtyard wall, noticed with satisfaction that she was running with bent knees although the baskets were empty except for her small bundle. A second later the glow in the sky extinguished itself completely and, to the accompaniment of more startled shouts from the crowd, a cloak of deep darkness spread itself over the land once more.

12

John, I'd like to volunteer for a secret mission!'

Flag Lieutenant Rice looked up sharply as Robert Eden burst into his cabin a moment after knocking. By the light of a flickering oil-lamp set on his collapsible writing table, Rice was recording in his official log a detailed description of the extraordinary light that had just passed from the heavens; but he stopped writing and raised his eyebrows in surprise on hearing Eden's urgent request.

'What sort of secret mission, Robert? And to where?'

'Ashore—here in the bay!'

The flag lieutenant put down his pen and looked severely at the younger officer. Because only thin wooden partitions separated the cramped officers' cabins on the lower deck, all their occupants were in the habit of keeping their voices low in private conversation, and both men instinctively followed this convention.

'Why do you think we should take such a grave risk now?' asked Rice slowly. 'We're face to face with a brave and stubborn people who've never been conquered. But we're not at war yet. It's still a delicate mission of diplomacy—bluff and counter-bluff.'

'But we don't know enough to judge whether our bluffing is wise,' countered Eden insistently. 'We haven't got the least idea of what's going on out there. Underneath everything, the Japanese who came aboard this afternoon seemed very tense.' Eden hesitated for a moment then decided to hold nothing back. 'I disarmed one of the escorts, who had concealed a short sword in his sleeve. He clearly intended to attack you when your back was turned.'

Rice stared at Eden in consternation. 'What happened?'

'I wrestled the weapon away from him without anyone noticing—except their senior escort, who looked angry as well as relieved. He snatched up the fallen sword and reprimanded the offender. He seemed very glad I'd intervened.'

Rice let out a low whistle and looked thoughtful, realizing suddenly that his life had been in danger. 'I agree they seemed very tense . . . but I didn't spot anything else. Thank you for your vigilance, Robert.'

'There's no need to thank me.' Eden shook his head dismissively, his mind still fixed on the subject he had come to discuss. 'That's what I was there for.'

'Why didn't you report this earlier?' asked Rice with a frown.

Eden shrugged. 'I suppose, as it came to nothing, I felt it was unnecessary to say anything at the time. And since then a lot's been happening.'

The flag lieutenant turned aside to make a brief note in his log. 'I'll need you to write me a detailed report, Robert,' he said over his shoulder. 'Let me have it as soon as you can, please.'

'Yes, of course,' said Eden impatiently. 'But will you support my proposal for a mission ashore?'

'You know well enough that our aim is to avoid bloodshed if humanly possible,' said Rice, laying aside his pen once more. 'For that reason alone, any undercover operation is out of the question.'

'But we might find things easier if we were better informed about what we're up against,' exclaimed Eden. 'What's their real strength? How many heavy guns do they have? Are they really ready to go to war against us? And what are they hiding behind those strange screens up there? We just don't know . . .'

'You're right, Robert. We'd like to know the answers to all those questions. It would make this very dangerous job much easier . . .' Rice paused and shook his head' ruefully. 'But the situation is already as taut as a piano-wire.'

'Yes—and we're working totally in the dark. So a secret sortie ashore is the only thing that makes sense!'

'It may make sense to you, but any incident, great or small, could start a major conflict now,' said Rice, a faint note of exasperation creeping into his voice. 'The interception of a secret landing party bent on spying might just trigger off what we all want to avoid. And I doubt whether there would be many volunteers for such a dangerous mission.'

'There wouldn't be any need for other volunteers,' said Eden shortly. 'Our castaway Sentaro has already agreed to go ashore with me. He's all the help I'd need.'

'Robert, your idea has all the makings of a suicide mission.' Rice shook his head emphatically. 'Your methods behind the lines in Mexico worked brilliantly. But these are very different circumstances . . .'

Eden drew in an impatient breath. 'I'd still like to try.'

The flag lieutenant stood up and took a pace or two around the small cabin, before facing Eden again with a frown of concern furrowing his brow. 'Robert, I'm honoured to count myself a close friend. You're a conspicuously brave man—but sometimes you seem to place too little value on your own life. The risks of a mission like this would be overwhelming.'

'The risks might be high,' Eden persisted, 'but the odds are not impossible.'

Rice smiled despite himself, his respect and affection for the man before him showing in the warmth of his expression. 'You've thought this through carefully, I can see. How long did you plan to spend ashore—just a few hours and back before dawn?'

'Two or three hours wouldn't be enough for a proper survey.'

'But beyond daybreak,' said Rice incredulously, 'the chances of you being detected and captured would be enormous.'

'The Japanese interpreter said at least three days would be needed to obtain a full answer to our demands,' said Eden evenly. 'All that time we'll just be kicking our heels. So a longer reconnaissance might be possible. I was ashore four days with the raiding party in Mexico.'

'But that was a carefully planned intrusion; it was all-out warfare. This is a solo spying mission in an unknown, unpredictable land where the odds of your surviving would be negligible.'

'That would make the element of surprise even greater,' countered Eden calmly. 'Nobody would be expecting it . . . and I'm confident I can do a useful job.'

'I don't understand what drives you, Robert.' Rice shook his head again in a gesture of disbelief. 'I've often wondered if you would be so careless of your own well-being if Mary hadn't died in that storm.'

Eden stared stonily ahead and said nothing; the muscles of his jaw tightened but he offered no reply. In the sudden silence that had fallen between them the deep, disturbing note of the coastal war gong became audible again, reverberating above the renewed swell of chanting from the temples. Both men listened for a moment, then Eden took a decisive step towards the cabin door.

'Will you please pass my proposal up to Commodore Perry,' he asked pointedly. 'This is a formal request.'

Rice gazed back at him for a moment in silence, then shook his head with an air of finality. 'No, Robert, I won't let this go any further. You'll just have to curb your impatience, and play the waiting game along with the rest of us.'

'Is that your last word?'

Rice's stern expression softened and he smiled faintly. 'Yes, I'm afraid it is. But I'm also asking myself whether I ought to place you and our castaway under close arrest for a couple of days—clap you in irons just to make sure you don't do anything rash.'

'And will you?' asked Eden in a challenging voice.

'No, Robert. You know that's not my style.'

Wanting suddenly to be gone, Eden saluted smartly and strode from the cabin. Hurrying through the wardroom, he entered his own smaller quarters, closed the door firmly behind him and took off his sword. As he lit an oil-lamp and glanced around the tiny cabin that was furnished with a bunk, washstand, water-basin and jug, he became aware again of the throb of noise from the shore. Taking out his journal, he picked up a pen, sat down and began to write impatiently.

Through the scuttle, the glow from the beacon fires was faintly visible and, as he wrote, he heard the chanting and the deep tolling of the war gong more clearly. He tried to ignore the noise but after a few minutes the cramped cabin which he knew so well seemed unbearably confining to all his senses. The instinct deep within him which yearned always for action had led him to suggest the secret sortie ashore—but now, in the wake of Rice's rejection of his proposal, that instinct seemed to clamour more insistently for recognition. The inner excitement inspired by his first glimpse of Mount Fuji and the recent strange light in the sky had also heightened his natural impatience and suddenly the prospect of many more long days of cat-and-mouse negotiations with impassive Japanese officials became unendurable. In that moment he finally made up his mind what he would do and to confirm his resolution he closed his journal with a snap and stood up.

Scooping up his holstered Colt pistol and some ammunition from a drawer in his sea chest, he buckled the weapon around his waist. Into his pockets he stuffed a small compass, his small opera-glasses, a knife, a note-pad and some pencils. After carefully extinguishing the lamp, he hurried out to the port ladders and climbed swiftly to the upper deck.

By a weapons rack he paused long enough to select a good cutlass, then keeping to the shadows of the bulkheads he made his way to the hatch which led to the storage space under the fo'c's'le. Ducking inside, he found Sentaro squatting cross-legged on a big coil of rope in the dusty darkness. He was sewing by the light of a single candle stub and he looked up at Eden and grinned eagerly in welcome.

'Everything okay, master?'

'Yes, everything's fine,' replied Eden in an urgent whisper. 'I'm ready to go—now!'

'Now, master?' echoed Sentaro in astonishment.

'Yes, now. Are you sure you still want to come with me?'

The castaway nodded slowly, his face serious. 'I promised you, master. If you go ashore, Sentaro goes too . . .'

'Good!' Eden threw off his cap, laid aside the cutlass and pistol and removed his frock coat, cravat, vest and shoes. 'Prepare yourself then, Sentaro. And be quick.'

The castaway hurriedly finished stitching a second large oilskin pouch to a leather belt. He already wore a similar belt and pouch around his own waist, into which he had stuffed clothing and some of his own meagre personal belongings. Seeing this, Eden nodded approvingly.

'You've done well, Sentaro. Have you found some clothes for me?'

'I have these old ones, master. Maybe not a good fit, but okay I think.'

The castaway held up a faded, wide-sleeved peasant's shirt of blue calico, a ragged pair of baggy cotton trousers of the same colour, and some recently plaited straw sandals. Folding the clothes deftly, he tucked them into the oilcloth pouch on the spare belt, and tied it quickly around Eden's waist. He watched Eden add his pistol, the ammunition, compass, binoculars and other possessions to the sturdy pouch, then wrap the cutlass in a piece of discarded sail cloth and tie it across his back with a strong cord.

'When we get ashore, master, you can wear this.' Sentaro picked up a cone-shaped hat of woven sedge from amongst the dusty ropes and sails, and slung it around his own shoulders. 'Then nobody will see your face.'

'Excellent!'

Eden folded his uniform clothes, placed his cap ontop of them and pushed them out of sight beneath a heap of torn sails. Then he stood up, barefoot and bare-chested, wearing only his narrow white drill pantaloons. His eyes were bright with anticipation and he patted Sentaro encouragingly on the shoulder.

'If you're ready, we'll go now! Follow me closely. We'll make for the starboard ladders. It's vital we get off the ship without being seen.'

He looked out of the hatch to ensure there was no movement on the darkened upper deck. When satisfied it was safe, he beckoned Sentaro to follow and led the way through the hatch, moving swiftly in a running crouch. Hugging the deep shadows of the six-foot bulkheads, they moved warily towards the nearest starboard ladder, taking care not to attract the attention of the overhead lookouts. Two marine sentries had been set to guard the nearest entry and exit port, and from the cover of a ventilation funnel Eden watched them patrolling back and forth with their carbines on their shoulders. Waiting for a moment when both marines had their backs turned and the men on watch aloft were gazing shoreward, Eden tugged suddenly at Sentaro's arm and ran swiftly to the open top of the ladderway. Swarming hand over hand down the iron rungs, they entered the water within seconds. For as long as they were able, they swam underwater to avoid detection from the *Susquehanna*, and when at last they surfaced they stayed on the lee side of the ships, swimming slowly and silently through the darkness, heading south in a broad arc designed to take them ashore a mile or two beyond the most southerly fire beacons.

PART II

The Black Ships at Anchor

9 July 1853

The people of the secluded nation who in July 1853 watched and waited fearfully for the barbarians on the 'black ships' to come ashore were apparently descended from hardy Mongol tribes. Their early ancestors, who are believed to have wandered southward out of the remote deserts of central Asia, had begun crossing the sea to the Japanese islands on rafts and canoes more than two thousand years earlier. The modern Japanese language and some present-day physical characteristics suggest that these wandering immigrants came into contact with Malayan and Polynesian tribes during their journeyings. The first inhabitants of the Japanese chain of islands, known as Ainu, had been bearded, pre-Mongolian hunters similar to Australia's aborigines. The Ainu had possibly arrived from Siberia a hundred thousand years before, when Ice Age land formations connected the islands with the Asian mainland. The later Mongolian arrivals quickly subjugated these backward people and, although some mixing of blood in marriage occurred, the Ainu were largely driven north to the island of Hokkaido, where a few remain today.

Only seventeen per cent of mountainous Japan is cultivable, and the new Mongol immigrants quickly became rice growers in the fertile areas of the southernmost island of Kyushu. Each village was ruled by a matriarch, and the chief of these formidable Kyushu fertility priestesses came to be known as Amaterasu, 'the living sun goddess'. Complex myths and legends enshrine the nation's beliefs in its own divinity, but myth and history came together in the real flesh-and-blood first emperor, Jimmu, a warrior-chieftain who, at the start of the Christian era, was said to have been born of the line of Amaterasu. Japan's present-day emperor is believed to be a direct descendant of Jimmu.

Jimmu proclaimed himself ruler on Japan's main central island, Honshu. He called his realm Yamato, which can be translated as 'Path to New Conquests'. He reigned at first over the area that includes modern-day Kyoto, Osaka and Kobe. During succeeding centuries he and his imperial descendants extended their rule throughout all the islands. Confucian practices absorbed from China in the seventh century AD strengthened the *imperial system and its bureaucratic control. Ancestor worship and an austere form of Chinese Buddhism were at the same time grafted onto the spirit cults of the native Shinto religion. By the ninth century* AD the emperor had become the Mikado, a title that meant 'Worshipful Gateway'. From that time onward, until 1868, Kyoto remained the imperial capital.

At Kyoto's secret heart, rouged and elaborately robed, these successive emperors or 'mortal gods' came to be seen as the spiritual fathers of the nation. They fathered many children by wives and concubines alike, and sons and relatives were granted castles and fiefdoms throughout the land until they had taken over leadership of all the ancient clans. Private armies of samurai warriors mushroomed on these baronial estates, and the daimyo constantly intrigued and fought fierce wars against one another in efforts to retain their influence at the Kyoto court. At the end of the twelfth century the chaos caused by these wars produced a historic change in the way Japan was ruled. Northern princes defeated a hostile alliance of southern clans and set up a ruling military council based at Kamakura, near modern-day Tokyo. The council's head was given the title of Shogun—'Great Barbarian-suppressing General'—by the emperor, and gradually the Shogun and his hereditary successors became the effective military rulers of the nation, creating their own parallel dynasties. During the following seven hundred years, the Mikado was reduced to a powerless puppet cloistered in his Kyoto palaces and the outside world, in its ignorance, came to believe that the Shogun in his Yedo fortress was the emperor. Commodore Perry, along with the President of the United States, the American government and many other foreigners, shared this misapprehension in the mid-nineteenth century and nothing was said or done by the Japanese during the 1853 confrontation with Commodore Perry to correct the error. So the United States and Japan, who one hundred and thirty years later would become the two most powerful nations of the modern world, began their first-ever contacts with each other by employing veiled threats and subtle techniques of bluff and counter-bluff in equal measure. In those few days of drama and high tension, men on both the American and Japanese sides worked with unremitting effort to gain for themselves and their nations a decisive advantage.

13

Prince Tanaka pressed his knees tighter into the sides of his horse, urging it subtly to greater efforts as it galloped at speed through the velvet darkness cloaking the shores of Yedo Bay. When the animal accelerated, he raised himself from the saddle until he was half-standing in the stirrups and balanced his weight more evenly so that he could better sense and enjoy its energy and raw strength.

Four samurai escorts in silk-laced bamboo and metal armour were riding hard at his heels, leaning low along the manes of their mounts, straining to keep up with him. They were racing through hilly, thickly wooded country, passing occasional terraced rice fields that had been cut with great precision into the steep hillsides. The narrow, little-used hilltop track was flanked by lofty pines which towered into the dark heavens, and the pounding of the horses' hoofs on the soft, needle-strewn ground and the rhythmic jingle of harness and armour were all producing a fierce sense of harmony in action which Tanaka found greatly satisfying.

As he rode, Tanaka breathed in the cool night air with much relish. He was conscious that every nerve and fibre in his body had become more alert during that headlong dash through the darkness begun an hour ago when they left Yedo. The confused disputes and intrigues which the arrival of the American warships had sparked off in the Shogun's capital had darkened his and many other minds for endless hours and he had leapt to his saddle in the inner courtyard of Yedo castle, two hours after midnight, yearning for the soothing balm of the open countryside.

Although the mountains that bordered the Yedo plain were invisible in the darkness, Tanaka could sense their powerful presence to the north as he and his companions raced onward. Intermittently he fancied he could detect, too, the fragrance of lilies, hydrangeas, orchids and other wild flowers blooming unseen in the wayside shadows. From time to time the glow from thousands of stars high above his head became visible beneath their feet as they thundered alongside the black-mirror surfaces of lakes, or splashed through river fords. In all these moments Tanaka felt his inner tensions quietening; with every stride of his horse, he came closer to the cherished samurai ideal of feeling at one with earth, heaven and the universe.

Each time he glanced up at the night sky, he found his thoughts straying to Tokiwa and the starred blue kimono she had snatched up to cover her nakedness as they dashed together from the Golden Pavilion in Yedo. As he crested each hilltop he strained his eyes, searching the darkness ahead for a sign of lanterns that would identify the *yadoya* to which he had sent her, under guard, the previous night. The nearer they came to the village where the inn was situated, the more he was aware that this sharpening of all his physical senses was bound up with anticipation of an intimate reunion with his favoured geisha. Remembering again their interrupted passion of the previous night, he spurred his horse with renewed vigour down another long hill-path, which eventually joined a broader track along which armed men and straggling groups of peasants streamed in both directions.

'We are almost there, O Kami-san,' said one of Tanaka's escorts breathlessly, on catching up with him. 'The village is over the next hill.'

Grunting his thanks, Tanaka raced ahead again, and did not slacken his pace until he approached the gates of the lantern-lit *yadoya*. Although two hours or more had elapsed since the disappearance of the dazzling blue glow in the heavens, a crowd of villagers and inn guests still lingered in the road outside its courtyard. They were murmuring together in a desultory way and staring up at the sky, but the thud of galloping hoofs sent them scurrying to the sides of the track. On recognizing the leading rider, the surprised chief guard, who had been standing among the crowd, dashed forward to take up a welcoming position before the inn gates. He bowed low as Tanaka and his four escorts swirled to a halt in a cloud of dust.

'Welcome, O Kami-san,' said Gotaro, straightening up and rushing to catch at the bridle of Tanaka's horse. 'I had not expected you so soon.'

'Yedo is suffocating in its own confusion tonight,' said Tanaka shortly, and strode through the gates towards the inn. 'Is everything well here?'

'Yes, O Kami-san,' said Gotaro deferentially, passing the horse to an inn groom, then hurrying to catch up. 'Everything is satisfactory here—except for that strange light in the sky which frightened everybody so badly.'

Inside its entrance the *teishi*—landlord of the inn—hurriedly assumed the traditional posture of welcome. As Tanaka approached, he folded his hands and prostrated himself abjectly, pressing his forehead to the floor three times. During this brief greeting he mentioned the unworthiness of his establishment repeatedly, then signalled to another servant who was waiting nearby with a flask of warmed sake and some porcelain beakers. In his turn, the servant bowed low before motioning Tanaka and his entourage towards a small private reception room where the screens were drawn back and a large *andon* paper floor-lamp bathed the walls in a gentle glow.

'How is Tokiwa-san?' asked Tanaka softly once the servant had served the rice wine and retreated, re-closing the screens behind him. 'Has she been well protected?'

'She is sleeping now, I expect,' replied Gotaro, who sat cross-legged in front of him. 'Like everybody else, she was no doubt alarmed by the strange light in the sky. But her maid returned from her home in the village and told me that she would stay with Tokiwa-san for the rest of the night to be of comfort to her.'

Tanaka nodded curtly. 'Send now to dismiss the maid. And make my arrival known to Tokiwa-san. Inform her that she is to prepare at once to receive me.'

'Yes, O Kami-san, immediately.' Gotaro motioned for one of his assistants to deliver the message, then looked expectantly towards his master again. 'What news do you bring from Yedo, O Kami-san? May I respectfully enquire if fighting has begun?'

Tanaka shook his head vehemently. 'There is no fighting yet with the barbarians or their black ships! But they are threatening to open fire on us with their great guns, so war could break out at any time. Worst of all, there is terrible strife in the *bakufu*. Constant meetings are being called, and new disputes break out among the *daimyo* every few moments. Many quite insanely wish to launch an immediate all-out attack. Others feel uncertain, because our forces and weapons are too feeble. But they are not sufficient to prevail . . .'

'What does the Shogun himself command, O Kami-san?' asked the chief guard. 'Surely he will decide the issue?'

Tanaka shook his head briefly. 'The Shogun has become very ill. It is likely he will die soon. He is already confined to bed, and is too sick and feeble to participate properly in events . . .'

The chief guard looked closely at Tanaka. 'Why have the barbarians threatened to fire their guns at us, O Kami-san?'

'They say they have brought a communication from their supreme leader to be delivered to our "Emperor" in Yedo castle. They confuse "Emperor" with "Shogun", and are ignorant of our system of leadership. They say their ships will stay and threaten us until their "communication" is accepted. And they will land to deliver it, if necessary.'

'What does the letter contain, O Kami-san? And why have they brought it in armed ships?'

'The Dutch barbarians in Nagasaki have informed southern clansmen that the American communication is a trick to humiliate us. They wish to force us to open our ports to barbarian trading ships against our will . . . And they want to compel us to sell supplies for their ships. Their powerful guns are trained closely on the town of Uraga, just a few miles from Yedo, ready to fire. The whole population has already fled inland.'

'What do you think will happen?' asked Gotaro anxiously. 'Will there be fighting?'

'Perhaps. I went on board one of the black ships with our first negotiators. The barbarians are confident and arrogant. They know they have great superiority. A hot-headed nobleman of the Makabe clan tried to assassinate a barbarian officer—but fortunately he was disarmed and subdued before any damage was done. If he had succeeded all-out war would have begun by now . . .'

Gotaro's eyes narrowed as he listened. 'Could we defeat the foreign barbarians if we needed to?'

Tanaka knitted his brows in thought. 'Hundreds of thousands of fighting men are moving to the coast from many provinces. But our cannon are few and our ancient muskets are no match for the guns of the foreign barbarians. If war breaks out, we shall have to kill them all by the sword. There would be a terrible loss of life—on both sides. And the barbarians could come back again and again with more ships, more guns, and more men . . .'

'Did that great light come from the barbarian ships?' asked the chief guard in a tense voice. 'Or was it a bad omen from our own deities?'

Tanaka drew in his breath slowly. 'I think it was an act of nature. Who can say what it means?'

Gotaro eyed him calculatingly. 'Will you return soon to the black ships, O Kami-san? Will there be still more talking?'

Tanaka nodded, then drained a last beaker of sake. 'If possible I shall go back to the black ships. Higher officials are due to go on board soon after dawn. I have come here for just an hour or two to escape the wearying intrigues of Yedo.' He stood up suddenly and smiled. 'And I have no further time now, Gotarosan, for idle talk . . .'

He was turning away when a great commotion broke out in the corridor outside. A female voice began to wail in fear, and a moment later the *shoji* were slid violently apart, and one of Gotaro's assistant guards appeared. He wielded his long sword threateningly in one hand, while the other was clamped around the slender neck of Eiko, the peasant maid. Her face was already bruising, her hair was dishevelled, and her kimono was ripped and half torn from her shoulders. With a curse the guard flung her into the room sending her sprawling on the tatami and turned to stare white-faced at Tanaka.

'I'm sorry to announce that Tokiwa-san has gone,' he said in a shaking voice, bowing low. 'Her room was empty and it seems she escaped two hours ago . . .' He jabbed at the prone figure of the peasant maid with the tip of his sword. 'I found this wretch hiding in a storeroom. She took money from Tokiwa-san, and sold her peasant clothes to disguise herself. She even provided her with a horse . . .'

Tanaka, who had become very still in the centre of the room, looked down expressionlessly at the half-naked peasant girl, who was sobbing and shuddering with fright at his feet. 'Why did Tokiwa-san do this?' he asked her coldly.

'I don't know,' wailed Eiko. 'She said she felt in greater danger here than in Yedo. I tried to persuade her to stay . . .'

'She took this bribe,' hissed the guard, flinging down a cascade of silver coins beside the sobbing maid. 'She betrayed our trust.'

With a snort of anger, Gotaro drew his long sword and lifted it high above his head. Lunging towards the fallen girl, he brought the weapon over in a high arc, aiming for her exposed neck. Tanaka reacted in an instinctive split second, without moving his feet. Withdrawing his own long sword swiftly from his sash, he swung it upward in a single fluid movement. The blades of the two swords clashed ringingly close to the maid's head, before the chief guard's weapon flew end over end to impale itself up to the hilt in the paper screens on the far side of the room.

Gotaro stood empty-handed and white-faced, staring blankly at his master. His expression indicated that he was awaiting a further blow to finish his life, but Tanaka quickly thrust his blade back into its scabbard.

'If you had performed your guard duties correctly,' he said very quietly, 'Tokiwa-san would not have escaped you. And this maidservant would have had no opportunity to receive any bribe.'

'It must have been the great light in the sky,' whispered Gotaro in shame. 'I rushed outside to look at it.'

'Which way did Tokiwa-san intend to go?' asked Tanaka, dropping to one knee beside the peasant girl. 'And how is she dressed?'

Eiko lifted her tear-stained face and looked tremulously at the clan prince. 'She said she would go towards Yedo. She has an old, broken-down horse . . . with two big straw panniers on its sides and a blue silk ribbon in its mane. She's wearing cotton peasant clothes and a wide bamboo hat . . .'

'Thank you,' said Tanaka gently, gathering up the silver coins and putting them in one of Eiko's hands. 'You're not to blame. Keep the money and go home now to your family.'

Standing up, he looked round at his armed retainers, who were watching him nervously. 'There are three ways back to Yedo,' he said with an icy calm. 'So we will split up into three groups—and find Tokiwa-san!'

He strode from the room and out into the courtyard, calling loudly for their horses. Moments later he galloped out through the gates of the inn, followed closely by all his guards and escorts. Separating swiftly into three groups, they disappeared one after another into the darkness.

14

Because the hill which she was descending was so steep, Matsumura Tokiwa had to half run and sometimes slide and slither downwards, while holding onto the bridle of the old packhorse for support. The loose stones she was dislodging hurt her feet through the flimsy, unfamiliar straw sandals, and she winced and cried aloud in pain when sharp pebbles cut into her soles. Glancing up she noticed that a thin crescent moon was rising late in the east. It was beginning to cast a gentle glow over the darkened landscape, and from a shoulder of the hill she fancied she could see, far ahead to the south, the dark gleam of the sea.

As she struggled down the steep slope, Tokiwa wondered how far she had come and how much time had elapsed since her hurried departure from the *yadoya*. It must be an hour or more, she felt sure—perhaps two hours. But as she pondered these questions she realized she had lost all sense of time in her anxiety to put as much distance as possible between herself and the inn which had become a prison. Columns of armed fighting men still trudged steadily southward, both in front and behind, carrying paper lanterns to light their way. From the wide variety of heraldic crests on their armour it was evident that these marchers had converged from the estates of many different regional *daimyo*, far and near. Struggling groups of individual travellers, on foot and on horseback, were also moving in both directions along the track, despite the late hour, and whilst threading her way amongst them Tokiwa had kept herself strictly to herself, feeling a comforting safety in her anonymous disguise.

But, as she travelled on, she remained keenly alert to the possibility of danger from behind, and stopped frequently to check if she could hear the drum of hoofs which would indicate the approach of Prince Tanaka's guards. So far there had been no hint of pursuit, but Tokiwa already felt very tired from the unaccustomed exertion and, as she stumbled onward down the steep hillside, she promised herself that when she reached level ground she would look for a place where she might rest and hide.

At the foot of the hill the track levelled out onto a banked causeway which stretched across a wide expanse of rice fields. The flooded paddies shimmered under the light of the rising moon, and Tokiwa could see that smaller paths diverged from the causeway on both sides, leading to tiny island villages which were surrounded by trees. Each of the villages, she could see, was flanked by its own neat agricultural plot where wheat, beans, onions and other small crops were cultivated. Many of these communities were silent, wrapped in a deep, night-time stillness but, here and there, despite the hour, some of the inhabitants had left their cottages to gather in groups along the main track and watch the unfamiliar columns of fighting men march by.

Tokiwa realized that she would find it difficult to hide herself on the exposed causeway if the need arose—or to explain herself if any local people waylaid her or called out. These thoughts alarmed her suddenly and she stopped and peered about, seeking an alternative route. While standing undecided, she heard the unmistakable tattoo of hoofs growing rapidly louder, as they neared the brow of the hill behind her. She listened long enough to identify two if not three galloping horses, then yanked hard on her own horse's leading rope.

'*Hayaku!*—Quickly!' she called sharply, trying to drag the animal towards a small grove of trees which sprouted in an arc around the foot of the hill. '*Hayaku!*'

Neighing loudly, the horse shied in resistance to this sudden, unexpected command. Although the animal was old and decrepit, with back legs bowed from carrying too many heavy loads, it still retained a fiercely stubborn temperament. Baring its yellow teeth in sudden anger, it tried to bite through the rope on which Tokiwa was pulling so frantically. The sound of galloping hoofs grew louder as the horsemen reached the brow of the hill, and she knew it would not be long before they caught sight of her below. In desperation she took a firm hold of the horse's crupper and swung herself up on its back behind the panniers. The bony ridge of its sagging spine felt sharp beneath her, but she leaned forward and grabbed its mane with both hands; digging hard into its flanks with her heels, she startled the animal sufficiently to send it rolling in ungainly fashion towards the grove of trees. As soon as it had entered the shadows, Tokiwa slid to the ground again. Taking the leading rope, she tied it firmly to a low branch, leaving the horse whinnying quietly in complaint, then crouched down to watch from behind one of the broader trunks.

Moments later two mounted warriors appeared, riding hard down the steep hill. Tokiwa recognized at once the distinctive armour and branched helmets worn by all of Prince Tanaka's samurai, and as they drew nearer she could see the six-pointed heraldic star of the Kago clan emblazoned on the sleeves of their *jimbaori*. There was sufficient moonlight also for her to identify the leading horseman as Gotaro, the thickset chief guard, and the sight of him caused her to shrink back fearfully behind the tree trunk.

On reaching the start of the causeway, Gotaro suddenly reined in his mount, signalling to his comrade to do the same. They circled and came together, peering across the flat expanse of rice fields ahead; then they began conversing in an urgent undertone.

In her hiding-place Tokiwa held her breath and glanced round at the restive horse behind her, praying that it would not make any sound to betray her presence. It was tossing its head restlessly and still gnawing at the rope but otherwise remained silent. Tokiwa watched Gotaro raise himself from his saddle to look all around, and at one moment she felt certain he was staring straight towards her in the darkness. Despite the warmth of the night she began to shiver, but in the next instant the two horsemen spurred their mounts forward onto the causeway, and, leaning her cheek against the tree trunk, she closed her eyes in relief as the sound of their hoofs faded into the distance.

15

Robert Eden scrambled the last few yards to the clifftop on all fours and raised his head cautiously to peer inland. To his amazement he found himself staring at the silhouette of a massive cannon drawn up close to the cliff edge, only twenty or thirty yards away. Its muzzle jutted seaward through a gap in canvas screens which were ten feet high, and he could see that two or three similar guns had been hauled into position further along the clifftop.

'We've come up close to some important gun emplacements,' breathed Eden, ducking hurriedly back below the lip of the cliff, to where Sentaro was crouching. 'But there's something very strange about them.'

'What is it, master?' whispered Sentaro apprehensively. 'What's strange?'

'There are no gun crews. No troops! In fact I can't see anybody at all.'

The Japanese castaway's face betrayed the extreme unease he obviously felt. 'What are we going to do then, master?'

'We're going to take a closer look at them!'

Eden scrambled quickly over the edge of the cliff, then leaned back to help the Japanese up in his turn. The clifftop was grassy and Eden mimed a silent instruction for them to ease forward through the darkness on their bellies, using their elbows and knees for propulsion. Eden reached the gun first, and the Japanese heard him let out an exclamation of surprise.

'What have you found, master?' asked Sentaro breathlessly, when he arrived at Eden's side.

'It's not real!' Eden shook his head in disbelief, and reached out again to stroke the gun with one hand. 'Feel it! It's made of wood. All these guns could be useless replicas . . . Wait here!'

Bent double, Eden dashed away towards the other guns, while Sentaro remained kneeling nervously beside the first one, watching his every move as best he could in the shadowy darkness. From the ship they had swum for nearly an hour before landing on a deserted beach three miles south-west of Uraga and Eden had led the way cautiously up the steep cliffs, taking no unnecessary risks. He had chosen their landing area with great care and they had eventually stepped ashore a mile from the nearest beacon fire. Its flames provided no more than a faint and distant glow and, because the newly risen crescent moon was not yet shedding much light on the land, they had the protection of near darkness in which to work. Eden was wearing the wide conical hat of woven sedge jammed down over his face, and in the borrowed Japanese cottons and straw sandals, Sentaro was relieved to see that he did not look too much out of place. When they landed he had strapped the pistol belt around his waist inside his shirt, concealing the holstered weapon, and his cutlass was still tied inconspicuously across his back. These precautions freed his limbs effectively for action and Sentaro watched admiringly as the American officer dashed swiftly from gun to gun in a crouching run. When he arrived back by the first gun, Eden's face was triumphant.

'I was right, Sentaro. All these guns are fakes! And the screens are not hiding anything except empty spaces. They're just a cover-up for a severe shortage of weapons . . . !'

'Watch out, master!' Without warning the Japanese suddenly pulled Eden down behind the fake cannon and continued to stare past him, along the cliff.

'What is it?' whispered Eden. 'What did you see?'

'Sentries—two of them! Patrolling this way'

Eden peered hard into the darkness and saw two figures silhouetted against the distant beacon fire. Carrying pikes, or perhaps muskets, on their shoulders they were only a hundred yards away, but their leisurely demeanour suggested they had not noticed any suspicious movement around the fake guns.

'Let's move quickly!' commanded Eden, and ducked away in the opposite direction, to drop into a clifftop gully that ran inland. They sprinted hard for a few minutes, then Eden stopped and pulled the Japanese down beside him in a grassy hollow.

'You did well, Sentaro,' he gasped, struggling to recover his breath. 'I was careless. Your alertness saved us . . .'

The Japanese nodded and grinned shyly but said nothing.

'But I was forgetting something very important,' continued Eden in a whisper. 'You're on your home soil again now—I want you to know you're free to return to your village if you wish.'

The Japanese stared around into the darkness, as though considering for the first time the full implications of being back in the country of his birth. But his apprehensive expression did not change and he shook his head several times in silence.

'How does it make you feel?' prompted Eden. 'Do you want to change your mind?'

'I will be executed, master, if they find out I was on the black ships! If I return to my home they will kill me for sure . . .'

Eden patted his shoulder reassuringly. 'Nobody need know you were on our ships. Don't go home until all this excitement has died down. Find yourself a job as a fisherman for a few months—or work in the fields somewhere.'

Sentaro shook his head. 'Everybody here is registered; everybody is watched by spies. It's impossible to hide anywhere, so my safest home now is on the *Susquehanna*. Please let me stay and serve you, master—and return to the ships when you do.'

Eden studied the face of the Japanese castaway for several moments, then he nodded emphatically. 'All right, if you're sure that's what you really want.'

'It *is* what I want, master!'

'Good. Then follow me.'

Sentaro grinned with pleasure as they began to rise from the grassy hollow, but the soft shuffle of many marching feet became suddenly audible, and both men froze and dropped down again. The noise of the unseen marchers became louder and on raising his head Eden noticed that a narrow track, which led up the hillside from inland, snaked across the clifftop only a few yards from their hiding place.

As he watched, the heads and shoulders of the leading marchers rose into sight, followed by many others. Moving quietly in soft, thonged *zóri*, they advanced steadily towards Eden's hiding place; when they drew nearer he saw that the column was composed of fighting men who were carrying spears, longbows and ancient-looking muskets on their shoulders.

'What shall we do, master?' whispered Sentaro frantically. 'They will pass very close to us.'

'Lie face downward,' ordered Eden calmly, stretching himself full-length beside the Japanese in the bottom of the hollow. 'And wait quietly until they pass.'

Eden pulled the cone-shaped hat down over his face and adjusted it so that the path would be visible through an inch-wide slit. As soon as the marching column came abreast of their hiding place, he held his breath and lay still. The armed men were carrying only a few lanterns, and to Eden's relief their hollow remained in shadow as the front of the column moved past. Without stirring he found he could see the shuffling feet of the marchers passing a few yards away.

After a while he was emboldened to raise his head, and found he could identify ancient flintlock and matchlock muskets among the mixed batch of arms being carried by the column. He could see too that most of the men were wearing iron helmets and various forms of body armour made from bamboo, chain mail and leather, All the men marched silently in orderly, well-disciplined ranks, keeping in close step and listening carefully for new commands from their two-sworded samurai officers. It took ten minutes for the entire column to march past the hollow, and when at last he lifted himself on his elbows to watch its tail-end disappear into the darkness, Eden realized that the armed force was heading for the fake fort, where it would doubtless bivouac and form a garrison.

'It's like stepping backwards in time,' breathed Eden, half to himself, as he clambered out of the hollow and stood staring after the marchers. 'Some of those weapons must be hundreds of years old.'

'We were lucky, master,' murmured Sentaro, standing up beside him. 'If they had seen us, we could both have been killed instantly. In peace or war the samurai warrior always follows his first instinct. He draws his sword and kills in a moment. No questions are ever asked . . .'

'Then good fortune has presented us with new opportunities,' said Eden softly, beckoning the Japanese to follow him. 'Let's make sure we don't waste them.'

Sentaro followed Eden in silence as they skirted the makeshift fort and headed north, staying roughly parallel with the shoreline. There was enough light from the rising moon now for them to pick their way quickly through the clumps of scrub and woodland that covered the clifftop, but enough shadow too for them to hide themselves in good time whenever they encountered moving sentries or other soldiers.

After several minutes they came within sight of another fort that was being extended and reinforced. Small groups of bowmen and footsoldiers, clutching long spears and shields, were milling around a central group of flimsy wooden buildings. Other uniformed men were carrying small roundshot and kegs of powder out of the same buildings, and Eden could see that they were supplying half a dozen genuine cannon mounted at embrasures in the seaward earthworks. Similar low ramparts of packed earth surrounded the fort on its three landward sides, and hundreds of civilians—men, women and children dressed in dark cottons—scurried frantically back and forth carrying bouncing shoulder-poles from which baskets of earth were suspended. With unflagging energy they emptied the earth onto the ramparts, before hurrying back to collect more from an excavated gully two hundred yards away.

'Let's take a closer look,' whispered Eden. 'Keep low.'

Hugging the shadows he led the way to the shelter of a grass hillock close enough to the fort for them to hear the grunting and muttering of the toiling Japanese as they unloaded their heavy burdens. Tugging his tiny, opera-glass binoculars from the pouch at his waist, Eden quickly examined the central buildings and the half-dozen cannons.

'The magazine and the barracks are built of wood,' he whispered incredulously, ducking down again. 'One direct hit would finish the entire fort. And their guns are no bigger than nine-pounders. They couldn't even reach our ships from here.'

'Our defences have not been well prepared.' Sentaro nodded towards some nearby pole-carriers. 'These people are all grumbling. Fishermen, farmers, their wives and children—everybody has been pressed into service to rebuild the fort.'

'What else are they saying?' asked Eden, raising his head again to look cautiously over the hillock.

'They say that for many centuries our ancestral gods protected us from foreign ships. But they think our rulers have now become careless and inefficient. They say the people of Yedo are terrified that they may starve if the foreign ships block the bay for long . . .'

'Look,' said Eden, suddenly pointing towards the earthworks. 'There are some spare carrying-poles lying on the ground. We can join in the work. We'll be able to learn more.'

'No, master, that's too dangerous . . .' began Sentaro in alarm, but Eden had already bounded from their hiding place, tugging his conical hat down over his face, and was scrambling over the earth rampart.

Within moments he had snatched up a carrying-pole, untangled its rope-matting baskets, and hoisted it to his shoulder. Without looking back he set off at an easy lope towards the excavation gully where the Japanese civilians were digging for fresh earth. Reluctantly Sentaro hurried after him, gathering up a carrying-pole in his turn. By the time he caught up, the American was staggering slightly under the weight of two huge loads of earth and heading back towards the fort.

'Follow me,' hissed Eden in Japanese, nodding towards one of the gun embrasures. 'There are some officers in conversation over there. Let's drop our earth nearby.'

Sentaro quickly filled his baskets and hurried after him. When they reached the earthworks facing the sea, Eden edged as close as he dared to the open gun embrasure, beside which five or six red-cloaked samurai officers were arguing heatedly. Struggling to the top of the rampart, he began to unload his first basket slowly with his hands, without appearing to look directly at the group of men below him. At the same time he gestured discreetly for Sentaro to climb up beside him.

'They seem to be angry,' murmured Eden after listening to the raised voices for two or three minutes. 'I think they've been ordered by their *daimyo* not to undertake any aggressive moves for fear of provoking an invasion.'

'Yes, master,' whispered Sentaro. 'Some of these men are complaining that they have pleaded for permission to attack the barbarian ships. But they have been forbidden to do so. They say the *bakufu*—the Shogun's government—is frightened that if they provoke the foreign barbarians, they will invade Nippon and occupy the whole country. They fear we will become colonial slaves, like the Chinese . . .'

'What special commands have been issued?' whispered Eden, as he emptied out his second basket. 'Did you hear?'

'The strictest orders forbid all gunfire,' replied Sentaro. 'These men have been instructed that no matter how insolent the foreign barbarians become, there must be no use of firearms. "Bloody incidents", say the orders, are to be avoided at all costs . . .'

'I heard them complaining that ammunition is very scarce, too,' breathed Eden. 'They do seem very dissatisfied.'

Sentaro nodded, busily spreading the earth from his own baskets along the top of the rampart. 'They have only ten rounds for each of these cannon. And it is the same at all the other forts. One of them claimed some of his guns are so old he is afraid to fire them.'

'It's clear we have nothing to fear from any of their weapons,' murmured Eden, lifting his carrying-pole and the empty baskets to his shoulder again. Still squatting ontop of the earthwork, he glanced cautiously from beneath the brim of his wide hat towards the group of samurai officers below. They were still talking animatedly, and Eden's eyes narrowed in concentration when he heard another reference to the *kurufune*—the 'black ships' anchored in the bay.

'I'm told that the barbarians on the black ships made it clear to our officials that they are determined to fight,' said one officer with explosive vehemence. 'It's rumoured that the *bakufu* are trembling at the knees, and will agree to anything—even receiving the barbarian letter to His Imperial Majesty here instead of at Nagasaki . . .'

'How soon will we be ready to receive it?' demanded another officer.

'Perhaps three or four days from now,' replied the first officer. 'They are trying to delay as much as possible.'

'Why?'

'Because they can think of nothing better to do . . .'

'Did you understand that, master?' asked Sentaro in an excited whisper, scrambling up beside Eden with his pole and empty baskets. 'They say it is rumoured that your President's letter will be accepted.'

'Yes, I understood,' replied Eden, placing a calming hand on Sentaro's shoulder. 'Go steady. We don't want to draw attention to ourselves.'

Despite the warning, some small clods of earth disturbed by the castaway cascaded down the inner bank of the rampart and one of the samurai officers, noticing the movement from the corner of his eye, turned in their direction. Ducking to conceal their faces, they swung away to scramble down from the earthwork out of sight; but something in their manner had aroused the officer's suspicion and he barked out a sharp order.

'Wait! What are you doing?'

After hesitating for a moment Sentaro turned back and mumbled a response. 'If it pleases you, sire, we were enlarging the fortification as ordered.'

'No work was ordered on this section tonight,' snapped the samurai. 'These ramparts were finished yesterday.'

'Our apologies, sire,' stammered Sentaro. 'We misunderstood our instructions. We will go now to work on another section.'

Eden had already slithered halfway down the inner bank and he tugged at Sentaro's sleeve, urging him to follow. The castaway bowed hurriedly towards the samurai, then stumbled down the slope behind the American.

'Stop!' roared the officer. 'You must have been eavesdropping.' He waved forward half a dozen men who had been standing guard nearby with spears and shields. 'Restrain those two for questioning!'

Eden grabbed Sentaro's arm and pulled him bodily down the slope into the fort. 'Run as fast as you can,' he ordered in a fierce whisper, pointing towards the central arsenal. 'There are a few cavalry horses tethered by the ammunition stores.'

They hurled aside their carrying-poles and rushed headlong towards the group of wooden buildings. Because the pursuing pike-men were encumbered by their long weapons and their shields, they were unable to move quickly and they began shouting and gesticulating for others to help cut off the fleeing pair. Alerted by these cries, other members of the garrison began to give chase.

'We can't escape, master,' gasped Sentaro, looking about in despair. 'We're surrounded!'

'Keep running!' urged Eden, still clutching his arm. 'If we can reach the horses, we can get clear.'

He increased his pace, forcing Sentaro along with him, and the shouts of the pikemen grew louder on realizing that they were heading towards the half-dozen horses tethered beside the magazine.

'Ride straight over the bank at the rear of the fort,' gasped Eden. 'Don't make for any of the gates or you'll be stopped . . .'

Disturbed by the growing commotion, the short, sturdy horses were already tossing their heads and straining at the tethers when Eden reached them. Because their pursuers were closing fast, he reached behind his shoulder to snatch his cutlass from its makeshift sheath of sailcloth. With a flurry of quick slashes he cut free all six horses and urged Sentaro into the saddle of one of them.

'Go!' he yelled in Japanese, slapping the horse's rump sharply with the flat of his sword. 'I'll catch you up.'

As the startled animal shot away, with Sentaro clinging frantically to its mane, Eden flung himself onto a second horse, still clutching the reins of two other mounts in his free hand. The shouts of the armed men closing in all around were loud in his ears as he dug his heels fiercely into the animal's sides and turned its head towards the rear rampart.

'Stop, I command you,' shouted one breathless pikeman, hurling himself into the horse's path, with his pike raised in both hands. 'Stop and dismount!'

Yelling an unintelligible battle cry of his own, Eden tried to swerve his own horse and the two he was leading past the yelling footsoldier. But the pikeman dropped to one knee and swung his weapon towards them with furious energy. The heavy, axe-shaped side blade sheared through the neck of Eden's mount, decapitating it at a stroke and, as the animal collapsed beneath him, Eden plunged heavily to the ground. One of the two spare horses broke free and bolted, squealing with fear, but Eden clung fiercely to the reins of the other and struggled to his feet beside it, brandishing his cutlass defensively in front of him. The broad hat of woven sedge had been knocked off in the fall and, as he stood defiantly bare-headed beside the horse, the lanterns carried by those closing in all around him illuminated his tall, broad-shouldered figure, his brown hair and pale Anglo-Saxon features.

For a second or two there was a strained silence; nobody spoke and nobody moved as the circle of armed men stared disbelievingly at the first foreign barbarian they had ever seen. Only six feet away, the pikeman who had brought him down stood rooted to the spot, holding his bloodied weapon uncertainly in front of him.

'*Shu-i!*' he grunted at last, when he found his voice. 'Hideous alien!'

'*Banzoku!*' growled a second man. 'Barbarian bandit!'

'Kill the *banzoku!*' yelled a third voice—and others immediately took up the cry.

'No! Let's take him alive!' urged the soldier with the bloodstained pike. After a moment of hesitation he began moving warily towards Eden again.

For a moment the American officer watched the pikeman approach—then with a cry he sprang into the saddle of the remaining horse. Swirling his sword above his head Eden kicked his mount into action, this time riding straight at the pikeman. The Japanese began to step aside, and lifted his pike in both hands to make another thrust at horse and rider. But Eden was upon him quickly, and he parried the threatened blow so fiercely with his blade that the pike's wooden shaft broke clean in two.

Riding furiously, Eden set the horse at the earthwork embankment, and sped up and over it without looking back. Shouts of rage grew in volume behind him as the horse slithered down the outer bank and he heard voices begin chanting '*Shu-i*' and '*Banzoku*' in unison as the soldiers began to give chase. At the foot of the bank Eden could at first see no sign of Sentaro, but to his delight the castaway emerged suddenly from a clump of nearby trees and galloped towards him.

'Which way shall we go?' demanded Eden urgently, as the sounds of shouting drew nearer to the embankment above them.

'I'm not sure, master,' said the Japanese. 'But whichever way we go, we must go quickly!'

Glancing up, Eden saw that the light of the rising moon was strengthening. In that split second he also caught sight of something else: in the far distance, above the trees, the shimmering peak of Mount Fuji had become faintly visible, glowing palely against the darkness of the night sky.

'We'll try this way,' he cried impulsively, spurring his horse onto a track that led through the trees in the direction of the sacred volcano. 'Follow me!'

16

As Matsumura Tokiwa led her horse gingerly along a narrow footpath that wound like a coiled serpent through flooded rice fields, she, too, caught sight of the towering magnificence of Mount Fuji's white summit. In the distant heavens to the north, the volcano's dominating snowcap seemed to draw all the gentle light of the crescent moon to itself like a magnet, leaving the range of lesser mountains below cloaked anonymously in shadow. In the higher darkness above and beyond Fuji, countless brilliant stars had become visible and, despite her anxiety to push on as fast as possible, Tokiwa stopped her ungainly horse several times to wonder in silence at the beauty of the night.

The pale moonlight was making it easier for her and the horse to follow the deserted footpath which she had taken in preference to the busier main causeway. This meandering trail had led her into another quiet, narrow, rice-growing valley flanked by thick woods and, as she began to climb again from the valley bottom into a new fold of hills, she heard the subdued roar of a waterfall somewhere ahead. The rushing water seemed to offer a consoling promise of refreshment to her tired mind and body, and when she came to a tiny track leading upward through the trees towards the sound of the cascade, she guided the horse onto it without any hesitation.

'That could be her,' said Prince Tanaka softly, as he watched the tiny, solitary figure turn uphill with the packhorse and disappear among the trees. 'Our search could be over.'

A few minutes earlier he had reined in his own mount beside those of Gotaro and two other guards at a bend in a tree-lined road that snaked high across the head of the valley. Gun-carriages and carts laden with arms and provisions were being trundled southward through the darkness, and endless streams of porters were scurrying by, bearing heavy burdens slung from poles. But Tanaka took no notice of this activity because, from that lofty vantage point, hundreds of feet above the rice paddies, he could scan the whole valley below and his eyes had narrowed with an intense interest the moment he spotted the slender, silhouetted figure leading a packhorse down the open moonlit path. He had watched in silence as the figure moved steadily in his direction, but had said nothing at all to his escorts until the horse and its owner finally went out of sight among the trees.

'That path, I am sure, leads up to this road we are on—but further to the south, O Kami-san,' said Gotaro, the exaggerated deference in his voice reflecting his embarrassment at failing earlier in his guard duties. 'We could ride quickly ahead to the junction, and lie in wait at the top.'

'Yes, we could,' said Tanaka thoughtfully, still scanning the wooded hillside. 'But I think I see a temple among those trees—and there may even be a farm or two. Someone may have to descend and search those places . . .'

Gotaro followed the arm Tanaka had lifted to point, and saw the curved eaves of a small temple, reflecting the moonlight, above the wooded skyline of a raised knoll. The darker geometrical outlines of thatched farm buildings were also visible here and there among trees.

'Perhaps the other two guards could wait at the head of the path, while I go down to search in the woodland,' suggested Gotaro quickly. 'I am most anxious to make amends for my error, O Kami-san.'

Tanaka did not respond at once but continued staring down into the valley. 'To be certain of success, somebody else would need to ride down this steep hillside, then follow the path up through the trees—in case she decides suddenly to retrace her steps.'

'Yes, you are quite right, O Kami-san.' Gotaro looked dubiously at the wooded escarpment that fell away precipitously beside the road. 'That would be the very best of plans . . .'

'And I will take on that last task myself,' said Tanaka quietly. 'You, Gotaro, ride to the path with the others. Then post two men at its top, and descend yourself to search. Whether we find her or not, we will all reassemble afterwards where the path meets the road.'

Gotaro and the other two samurai had turned their horses southward when a sudden commotion of galloping hoofs and raised voices reached their ears. They heard loud male shouts of '*Banzoku! Banzoku!*—Barbarian bandit!' repeated again and again and Tanaka immediately lifted his hand in a cautionary gesture that prompted his men to draw back into the side of the road.

As the noise grew louder, they saw a group of armed horsemen approaching, riding north as fast as they were able amongst the congestion of porters, carts and gun-carriages. The men were shouting at the top of their voices, hurling questions at the bewildered carters and porters as they passed. When the front group of riders caught sight of Tanaka and recognized the aristocratic crests of the Kago clan emblazoned in gold on his *jimbaori*, they reined in their horses at once and bowed low from the saddle.

'May I respectfully ask, O Kami-san, if you've seen anything on the road north of here?' enquired their leader breathlessly, bowing again. 'Anything at all suspicious?'

'What are you looking for?' asked Tanaka calmly.

'A *banzoku*—a foreign, barbarian bandit! At least one, O Kami-san. Perhaps two.'

Tanaka's eyes widened a fraction, but he showed no other sign of the astonishment he felt at the news. 'I've certainly seen no *banzoku* on this road. Please explain yourself further.'

'We think he might come from the black ships in the bay, O Kami-san,' said the leading rider. 'He was disturbed while spying at a fort on the coast . . . He disarmed one pikeman with his sword, then stole horses to flee with a companion.'

'What does he look like?'

'He is very tall, he has wide shoulders, reddish hair and a pale face. But you would probably have difficulty recognizing him as a *banzoku* because he is wearing the peasant clothing of our country. He is accompanied by a smaller man also dressed as a peasant—but he could be *banzoku* or *Nihon-jin*. Nobody has yet seen his face.'

'Are they riding together?'

'Yes, O Kami-san—and both drive their horses very hard,' said the leading rider eagerly. 'Do you think you've seen anybody matching these descriptions?'

'No.' Tanaka shook his head. 'Nobody of that appearance has passed us on this road.'

'Strange!' exclaimed the rider, exchanging puzzled glances with those around him. 'Further back we had several reports of them heading this way . . .'

Tanaka glanced up at the forested hilltops. 'Perhaps they have entered the forest somewhere, to escape detection.'

The leading rider nodded. 'Yes, that is possible. I will send some of my men back to search the area where they were last seen. I'll send men on ahead, too, in case they rejoin the road later.'

He turned away to issue crisp commands, and the group of horsemen immediately split into two. Half of them spurred their mounts back the way they had come, while others set off northwards at a furious gallop. Turning back to Tanaka, the leading rider bowed low once more.

'I'm very grateful to you, O Kami-san. It is an honour to receive assistance from such a distinguished nobleman.'

Tanaka made a dismissive gesture. 'I wish you success in your search. But before you leave I'd like to ask what your precise orders are.'

'My orders from the commandant of the fort are to alert all fighting brigades and all civilians in this region to the presence among us of a dangerous *banzoku*. I must also use whatever means are necessary to capture him, dead or alive.'

'It would be far better to try and take the *banzoku* alive,' said Tanaka quietly. 'I'm sure you know that the *bakufu* wishes to avoid bloodshed at all costs—and we might be able to gain important knowledge from them as captives.'

The man before Tanaka bowed low in his saddle. 'I will bear in mind what you have said, O Kami-san. But the *banzoku* appears to be a ferocious fighter. If he tries to resist capture, it may be impossible to avoid spilling his blood . . .'

He lifted one arm in salute and, wheeling his horse, galloped rapidly away, heading back along the road to the south. Tanaka watched him until he was out of sight then turned to his escorts. 'Follow now the plan we have already made—but keep a careful watch for the *banzoku* at the same time.'

When they had gone, Tanaka urged his own horse over the edge of the steep scarp. The animal shied and whinnied in fear at first, but he quickly calmed it and began to weave his way skilfully down through the closely packed trees, heading for the path hundreds of feet below onto which he had seen the straw-hatted figure of Matsumura Tokiwa lead the broken-down packhorse.

Through intermittent gaps in the trees, Tokiwa could see white skeins of water tumbling ceaselessly down a glistening rockface as she climbed the steep hillside. The cascades frothed a brilliant white in the moonlight, and she felt herself drawn ever more strongly to the waterfall each time she caught a glimpse of it. She fancied she could taste the cool freshness of the spray in her throat while she was still a long way off, and the heavy warmth of the summer night seemed suddenly more bearable. Her grimy cotton clothes were sticking to her skin and she began to anticipate how good the water might feel splashing against her naked body. Even the tired, stumbling horse which she was leading seemed to scent the nearness of the water too, and it began to pick its way with greater purpose up the forested slope.

When Tokiwa came in sight of the waterfall she found that it was pouring down smooth, dark rocks to form a sparkling pool on a small plateau.

Natural stepping-stones, roughly circular in shape, formed a path leading towards the main cascade. Other rocks rimmed the pool to funnel its waters down the hillside in a frothing stream, and Tokiwa guided the horse to the quietest edge and released its leading rope. When the animal had drunk its fill, she tethered it to a tree in the shadow of the rocks, twenty or thirty yards away, and returned alone to the waterfall. For a moment she hesitated, peering round among the dark trees that ringed the pool. Seeing no sign of movement, she quickly removed her wide hat, the straw sandals, the blue trousers and the rough cotton shirt. Dropping them onto the rocks by her feet, she unpinned her long hair and let it fall loose down her back.

Entirely naked she stepped onto the path of stepping-stones and walked slowly across the pool towards the main cascade. When she moved beneath it, the sharp chill of the mountain spring-water made her catch her breath. But a little cry of delight escaped her lips too, and she closed her eyes, threw back her head and lifted her face to feel better the caress of the tumbling spray.

Other cascades bounced and splashed down the rockface, and Tokiwa began to wade towards the back of the shallow pool, passing under each rivulet of water in turn. She imagined that she could also feel the softness of the moonlight rippling against her naked body, and she stretched her arms above her head, luxuriating by turns in the gentleness of the light and the sharp, stinging sensual pleasure of the icy water that rushed down over her breasts, her back and the curve of her loins.

Because the noise of the water filled her ears, Tokiwa remained oblivious to the distant sounds of carts, horses and men passing along the road that crossed the head of the valley. The sounds of other men and horses advancing more cautiously and stealthily through the forest also went unheard. Surrounded by the gentle roar of the waterfall, Tokiwa felt a sense of detachment and peace steal over her.

Seeing crystal beads of water glistening in the moonlight on her arms and upper body, she remembered how she had been bathing at the Golden Pavilion when she heard the first commotion in the streets of Yedo, little more than twenty-four hours earlier. So much had happened since then, she reflected. Her life and the lives of millions of others, it seemed, had been plunged into turmoil by the arrival of the black ships in Yedo Bay and people everywhere were openly fearful. She also felt a continuing sense of unease deep inside herself, but at the same time part of her welcomed wholeheartedly the prospect of danger and change. The stifling boredom of her nights at the Golden Pavilion—providing entertainment for an interminable flow of rich, fat, ageing clients—had at least been interrupted;

and those feelings that her soul was always weeping silently within her at her unfortunate plight had been relieved she realised, if only temporarily. Yet intuitively she sensed that, whatever happened now, nothing would be quite the same again, and this thought caused her to raise her arms aloft once more and embrace the next deluge of falling spray with a renewed sense of exhilaration and gratitude.

Alone under the waterfall, in the heart of the darkened forest, she realized she felt more free than she had ever done in all her life—and the feeling made her head swim with a pleasureable giddiness.

17

Let's go off the track here!'

Robert Eden spoke breathlessly over his shoulder, slowing his sweating horse to a walk for the first time and turning in among trees that stood only a few yards apart on the densely wooded hillside. Sentaro, riding a few yards behind him, obediently followed his instructions as the track curved sharply away downhill. For a few minutes they made their way cautiously forward along the same contour line until they reached a point where the moonlight scarcely penetrated the thick foliage. When Eden was certain they could no longer be seen from the track they had abandoned, he raised his hand to call a halt.

'We can rest here,' he whispered, his chest heaving from exertion. 'And we'll be able to hear if we're still being followed.'

Both men strained their ears for sounds of pursuit, but they heard no hint of horses or human voices; only the steady, soothing rush of a distant waterfall broke the deep silence of the mountain woodland. After listening for a minute or more Eden reached over and patted his Japanese companion on the shoulder.

'You ride well, Sentaro,' he said softly in Japanese. 'I think we've managed to shake off our pursuers.'

The castaway nodded, his face serious. 'Yes, master. But news that a "hideous barbarian" has come ashore will spread very fast. Everybody in this region will be watching for us . . .'

'Don't worry. We'll keep a step in front, somehow.' In the half darkness Eden smiled, betraying the fierce feeling of elation which their narrow escape had aroused in him. 'Let's head for that waterfall. We need a drink as much as the horses.'

They trekked on slowly and quietly through the trees with the sound of rushing water becoming gradually louder in their ears. When at last they came in sight of the open plateau onto which the waterfall was cascading, Eden reined in his horse with a stifled exclamation of wonder. The moon, higher now in the sky, was bathing the wooded cliff in its gentle silver glow, and the tumbling water frothed like cream into the pool at the foot of the soaring rocks. The natural beauty of the mountain glade, encountered so suddenly and unexpectedly amidst the darkness of the woods, was breathtaking, and Eden gazed at the enchanted scene in an awed silence.

He felt a strong impulse to plunge instantly into the pool, and only gradually did he become aware that a human figure was already moving in and out of the torrents of creamy water. At first he thought his eyes were being deceived by some trick of the light—that he was mistaking shadows for a long mane of dark hair spreading across slender shoulders and down the beguiling curve of a naked back. But, watching more closely, he began to realize that the moving shadows possessed their own gentle unity; he saw a head turn slowly, and a lovely, delicate face lift among the misty white sprays; he saw moonlight reflected softly by slender arms and the upward curve of a breast; then at last he saw an unmistakably beautiful naked girl wading across the pool with a languid, unselfconscious grace.

'How lovely she is,' breathed Eden, as Sentaro halted beside him. 'A moment ago I thought I must be imagining things—I felt I was gazing at some mythical Japanese water nymph.' He paused and looked enquiringly at the castaway. 'Who could she be, do you think? And why is she here all alone in the middle of the night?'

In his turn Sentaro stared admiringly towards the waterfall. 'This is nothing unusual, master. It's very common in my country to bathe naked. In our cities, and villages, we have many public bath-houses and there is no shame about nakedness here, as in your country . . .' He broke off, pointing towards the shadows at the foot of the rocks, where the horse carrying the panniers was tethered to a tree. 'See, there is her horse. Perhaps she lives nearby. Perhaps she likes to come here by night and bathe alone under cool water, in the silence of nature—I don't know . . . But you are right, she is unusually beautiful.'

'Could we talk to her?' asked Eden impulsively, gazing again towards the pool. 'Could we join her? Could we bathe in the pool too?'

Sentaro shook his head. 'It is better not to, master. She would report us to the authorities. You would give away your presence here. It might even cost us our lives . . .'

Eden drew a long breath, looking longingly towards the waterfall where the naked girl was now moving out from under the cascades onto the stepping-stones of the pool. She shook her head from side to side in an unconsciously joyful motion, tossing her long hair about her face, and as she moved from stone to stone, her slender body glistened like gold in the moonlight.

'Master, there's also another reason to be careful—look!'

Sentaro placed a cautionary hand on Eden's arm, and pointed towards the tethered pack-horse. In the shadows under the rocks, Tanaka's burly chief guard, Gotaro, was in the act of dismounting silently from his own horse. He too was staring towards the pool and the naked figure of Tokiwa and when he was satisfied that his arrival had gone unnoticed, he tied up his own mount beside the pack animal, drew his long sword silently from its sheath and began to creep forward with great stealth towards the waterfall.

'What does he want?' breathed Eden. 'She seems to be in some kind of danger.'

'Yes, perhaps,' whispered the Japanese, watching the samurai swordsman with wide eyes. 'It may be something personal between them . . .'

Eden saw the female figure reach the last stepping-stone, where she had dropped her clothes, but as she bent to pick them up her eye fell on the helmeted figure of Gotaro. By this time he was rushing silently towards her around the margin of the pool, his long sword thrust out before him. She screamed piercingly and turned to flee towards the waterfall but the surprisingly agile guard caught her easily by one arm. She screamed again as he threw her across his shoulder and began carrying her bodily towards the two horses. At every step she kicked and struggled furiously, but her strength was clearly no match for that of the samurai.

'*Matte kudasai!*' yelled Eden suddenly, flinging himself from his horse. 'Wait!'

The astonished samurai stopped at the edge of the pool, then turned with sword raised to face the man sprinting swiftly out of the darkness to confront him. Eden still wore his hat pulled low over his face, and in his blue cottons and straw sandals he looked like nothing more than a burly Nipponese peasant from the fields. But Gotaro's expression became puzzled and wary as the American stopped and drew his cutlass from the gun belt where he now carried it.

'*Kanojo o hanasa nakkatara kiru-zo!*' grunted Eden in a menacing tone, moving closer and raising the sword. 'You will die unless you free her!'

'Don't interfere with what doesn't concern you,' growled Gotaro, standing his ground. 'Or it will be you who dies!'

Without giving any further warning Eden lunged forward and lashed out instinctively with his curved blade, aiming a disabling blow at the samurai's sword arm. But although he was not free to manoeuvre, Gotaro raised his own steel fast enough to deflect the force of Eden's attack. As a result he took only a glancing blow on his shoulder which drew blood, but was not enough to disarm him. Letting out a guttural cry of rage, the samurai released his prisoner and turned to face Eden, his eyes glittering dangerously.

'*Ike! Uma no ho e ike!*—Go to my horse!' called Eden softly to the naked girl who was now crouching fearfully beside the pool. '*Sugu ike!*—Go quickly!'

He backed up slowly and deliberately, drawing the samurai away from her along the side of the pool; but all the time he kept his eye firmly fixed on the warrior's face. 'Help her, Sentaro,' he called blindly over his shoulder. 'Get her away!'

With a loud cry the samurai flung himself forward and, using both hands, swung his long blade through a fast arc, bringing it down from above his own head with all his strength. The stroke was aimed at splitting the American's skull, but, because Eden was watching the warrior closely, he anticipated the direction of his lunge and stepped swiftly aside, at the same time swaying backward from the waist to avoid the blow. Gotaro's weapon passed close enough to his face for Eden to feel a rush of air against his cheek, and its razor-sharp edge sliced away the front part of his sedge hat. When the samurai regained his balance and turned to face Eden again, his features registered shock and surprise, and he stared at the American for a moment in open-mouthed silence.

'You are the *banzoku!*' he shouted suddenly. 'You are the barbarian spy!'

Circling Eden warily, the samurai glanced round towards Tokiwa, who had now struggled to her feet. She had been watching the fight with a numbed expression but on catching sight of Eden's uncovered face, she raised both hands to her mouth to stifle a gasp of astonishment.

'You are in league with the *banzoku*,' the samurai yelled at her in amazement. 'You are helping the spy!'

'No, no! It's not true!' Tokiwa shook her head, her expression suddenly desperate. 'I have never seen the *banzoku* until this moment.'

She bent quickly to snatch up her flimsy cotton clothes and began to pull them on. Sentaro, who had at last emerged from the shelter of the trees, rushed up and tried to reassure her in a low voice, all the time glancing anxiously over his shoulder towards the two circling combatants.

'She's telling the truth!' Eden spoke sharply in Japanese, moving menacingly towards the samurai again, with his sword at the ready. 'But you must leave her alone. She's not to be taken from here against her will!'

'I will decide that—not you!' yelled Gotaro and threw himself furiously at Eden, swinging his sword sideways in a flatter plane this time, aiming a mortal stroke at his opponent's neck.

The American took a quick step backward, then dropped into a half crouch. Following his opponent's example he clamped both hands tightly around the hilt of his own sword, in order to parry the ferocious blow. The clang of steel meeting steel rang loud across the glade, and shocks like electricity shot up both of Eden's arms as his weapon shuddered in his grasp. But because his stance was more balanced he survived the blow better than his opponent.

The samurai, carried forward by his own momentum, was struggling to regain his equilibrium as he stumbled past Eden. Seeing this, the American stepped in close against him; still clutching his cutlass, he raised both fists above his head and drove them downward in a powerful blow which struck the samurai at the base of the skull. The Japanese faltered for a moment, his eyes glazing, then he dropped his sword. A moment later he collapsed into the rocky stream rushing from the pool and, caught by its waters, he slithered away helplessly down the steep hillside.

'Hurry, master,' called Sentaro, as he watched Eden thrust the cutlass back into his belt. 'The noise of your fighting has been heard. Others are coming . . .'

Eden stood still and listened; the sound of many horses descending at speed through the woods from the road above was becoming audible but the snapping of twigs and the quieter drum of hoofbeats nearby suggested that a solo rider was spurring his mount swiftly up the hillside below them. Glancing across the glade, Eden saw that Sentaro and the beautiful Japanese girl had reached the horses; but she looked deeply apprehensive and he raced across the clearing to sweep off the battered remains of his hat and incline his head smilingly towards her.

'I'm Lieutenant Robert Eden,' he said quietly in Japanese. 'I'm honoured to have been of service to you.'

Tokiwa felt herself tremble as she gazed up at the shadowy face of the first *banzoku* she had ever encountered in her young life. She could not see his features clearly but his hair seemed to have the glint of fire in it and his smiling eyes were curiously round in a strong, pale face. He had wide, muscular shoulders and he seemed to tower dizzyingly above her. She could not recall how she had expected a *banzoku* to look, but nothing in her previous experience had prepared her for such a disturbing confrontation, and she found herself reduced to speechlessness.

'This is Matsumura Tokiwa, master,' cut in Sentaro, sensing her difficulties. 'Tokiwa-san tells me she was being held under protective guard. But she escaped because she felt she was in danger.'

'Then we're both fugitives,' said Eden more urgently, lifting his head again to listen to the sounds of the approaching horsemen. 'Shall we take you with us?'

Tokiwa looked apprehensively at Sentaro. 'I don't know . . .' she began in a faltering whisper.

'We have no time for doubts,' said Eden decisively, swinging into his saddle. 'Mount up, Sentaro. And grab those panniers from her horse! We can't go up or down this hill, but I've seen a path leading along the ridge through the waterfall.'

Leaning down, he circled Tokiwa's waist with one arm and lifted her up in front of him. Calling urgently for the castaway to follow, Eden spurred his horse into the pool. As they splashed through the cascading water and onto the ridge beyond, he tightened his arm protectively around the Japanese girl, wondering at the lightness and slenderness of her body. He could feel her limbs trembling with apprehension but she voiced no protest, and she did not struggle against his encircling arm as he sent his horse racing forward into the moonlit forest.

18

It doesn't look like a palace—but it might give us shelter for a while!'

Robert Eden signalled for Sentaro to wait with the Japanese girl, and jumped down from his horse to plunge through a grove of swaying bamboo which had sprouted around an abandoned barn. Its thatched roof had many gaping holes and its timber walls leaned at strange angles to the steep hillside but, inside, Eden found that heaps of straw still littered its earth floor and the planks of an upper loft at one end.

Moonlight entering through the ragged holes in the roof revealed twisted cartwheels, broken pieces of harness and the scattered matting and ropes of worn-out carrying baskets. The interior of the barn, however, was dry and the air was fresh, and Eden immediately rushed back to hold the fronds of bamboo aside and beckon Sentaro forward with the horses.

'Tie them to the ladder leading up to the loft,' said Eden, gesturing to the far end of the barn. 'And see if you can find some fodder.'

'Of course, master.'

While Sentaro was tethering the horses, Eden turned to the Japanese girl who was standing uncertainly in the shadows by the entrance to the barn. Her face was taut and it was obvious, even in the gloom, that she was still trembling.

'Tokiwa-san, your clothes are still wet from the waterfall,' he said in Japanese. 'In your panniers, do you have anything dry to wear?'

She did not speak, but Eden saw her nod quickly. He realized then that the fear triggered by coming face to face with a 'hideous alien' for the first time was being heightened by the shadowy darkness inside the barn.

'Bring Tokiwa's baskets over here, please, Sentaro,' he said quietly to the castaway. 'She has dry clothing stored in there. And if there's a lantern; light it and shade it carefully so it won't be seen from outside.'

He stood still in the middle of the barn and cocked his head, listening for sounds of pursuit. To his relief, the silence of the wooded hills outside was broken only by the occasional shriek of a night bird. They had ridden hard for perhaps fifteen minutes through the forest before slowing and beginning to search for somewhere to hide. After skirting several valleys of terraced rice fields, Sentaro had spotted the deserted barn close to the edge of the woodland.

'I think we'll be safe here for a while,' said Eden soothingly as he watched Sentaro set down the panniers in front of the pale-faced Japanese girl and pass her a shaded paper lantern. 'We should all try to get a little rest.'

Taking the lantern in one hand, Tokiwa knelt to rummage in her baskets. Several times she lifted her head to cast a quick, nervous glance in Eden's direction, and he saw then that agitation was visible in every movement she made. Sentaro, who was watching her closely, also noticed her unease and he dropped to his knees on the earth floor beside her, his face creased in concern.

'There's no need to be afraid, O Tokiwa-san,' he said gently. 'Our people mistakenly call all foreigners "hideous barbarians" and "monsters", but they're not really hideous. I lived among them in America for four years after I was shipwrecked. They treated me well and brought me back here on their black ships . . .'

Despite the reassuring tone of his voice, Tokiwa still did not respond or look up. Instead, she bent her head even lower, and her shoulders continued to shake as she fumbled unsuccessfully in each basket.

'The American who wishes to help you is a good man,' continued Sentaro gently. 'I've known him for many months, and he's been a true friend to me.' The Japanese turned and motioned silently for Eden to come and kneel beside him. 'You can take a closer look at a *shu-i* for yourself now, O Tokiwa-san. Then you will know I tell the truth.'

Sentaro took the paper lantern from her and held it up at arm's length so that its subdued glow illuminated Eden's face. Squatting on his haunches, the American removed his battered straw hat—and waited. When at last Tokiwa raised her head to look at him, her wide almond eyes betrayed her alarm.

'Don't be afraid,' said Eden in Japanese. 'I'm your friend too.'

Tokiwa's long black hair, still gleamingly damp from the waterfall, half covered her face and she lifted both hands to her cheeks in a sudden, nervous gesture, to draw the strands aside. For a long time she stared at Eden in a wondering silence.

'I have no fangs and no horns,' smiled Eden. 'We "foreign barbarians" are just ordinary human beings after all.'

'Your eyes are very blue—like the ocean,' whispered Tokiwa at last. 'And your hair is brown like the leaves in autumn.'

Eden nodded and smiled again. 'That's not unusual in my country.'

'Do all "barbarians" . . .' she began impulsively, then broke off, still gazing wide-eyed at him. 'I mean . . . do all people who live in America look like you?'

'No.' Eden shook his head. 'People of many races from all over the world have come to live in my country. Many have different coloured hair—brown, black, yellow, even red. Their eyes are sometimes blue. But they may also be green, or brown, or grey . . .'

While he spoke, Eden found himself wondering in his turn at the beguiling face of the girl kneeling in bewilderment before him on the earth floor of the barn. Although her hair was wet and unkempt, there was no disguising her rare natural beauty, which was enhanced by the soft light of the lamp held in Sentaro's hand. Her wet peasant shirt, wide open at the throat, clung darkly to the slenderness of her upper body, outlining the soft curve of her breasts and, as they continued to stare at one another, Eden felt himself drawn powerfully to her delicate and apparently unconscious sensuality.

'I've never before in my life seen a man with blue eyes,' murmured Tokiwa, dropping her gaze to begin searching busily in her baskets once more. 'Please excuse me for staring at you.'

Sentaro lowered the lantern and placed it on the ground. Looking at Eden, he smiled. 'Tokiwa has informed me that she isn't truly a peasant girl from the fields. She had to disguise herself for her escape. Normally she lives in Yedo, where she's an honoured and notable geisha. She has studied music, poetry and dance and entertains noblemen of the highest rank.'

'Thank you, Sentaro,' said Eden, still gazing at the Japanese girl. 'Now I understand.' He paused and bowed his head chivalrously in her direction. 'I'm very honoured to know you, O Tokiwa-san. And I'm sorry this "palace" is so humble compared with what you must be accustomed to in Yedo.'

Standing up, Eden crossed into the shadows at the other side of the barn. After unfastening his waist-pouch he peeled off his own wet shirt and threw it across an overhead rafter to dry in the warm night air. He saw Tokiwa pull a dark garment and a towel from one of the panniers, and retreat in the other direction to the darkness beneath the loft. Turning his back on her, Eden moved to the door of the barn and stood quietly listening for sounds of pursuit.

'Master, come and look,' called Sentaro in a low voice a few moments later. 'Up here!'

Eden saw that the castaway had climbed the rickety ladder to the loft, and was squatting beside an opening through which sacks of grain had once been swung into the upper level of the barn. Clambering cautiously up the ladder, Eden hurried over to crouch beside him.

'What is it, Sentaro?' he demanded in an urgent whisper. 'Is somebody approaching?'

'No, master,' he whispered. 'But look!'

The Japanese raised his arm and pointed out through the nearby opening. Following the direction of his finger, Eden saw the same extraordinary image that he had first seen from the deck of the *Susquehanna* at midnight.

'Fuji-san again!' exclaimed Sentaro. 'And looking more beautiful from here than I have ever seen it. Now I know, master, I have truly come home.'

Framed in the open grain-port of the barn, the snow-topped volcano loomed large in the heavens. The crescent moon and a scattering of stars hung like muted chandeliers above its peak, shedding sufficient light to beautify the mountain, but not enough to destroy the illusion that its darker base had melted away into the shadows of the lower regions. Eden stared out into the night in silence, his hand resting on Sentaro's shoulder, and in that moment the impulsive desire to climb to its summit, which he had first felt on board the flagship, became a firm resolve.

'I'm quite sure now, Sentaro, that some time I will climb your sacred mountain,' he said quietly. 'I know no barbarian has yet set foot on its summit—but one day I *will* stand at the very top.'

'If it ever becomes possible, master, for you to climb Fuji-san, I hope I'll come with you,' murmured Sentaro.

'I hope so, too.'

Lost in thought, Eden continued to stare towards the spectacular volcano. Light swirls of night mist were beginning to drift above the nearer fields and forests, softening the contours, and a profound stillness seemed to have settled like a cloak over the abandoned barn and its surrounding countryside.

'I have noticed that there's a little temple on the hill above us, master,' whispered Sentaro, gesturing out through the grain-port again. 'I would like to go there now to thank the ancestral gods for guiding me back to my homeland. May I leave you for a little while?'

'Of course, but be careful.'

'I won't be long, master.' The castaway grinned his. thanks and headed quickly towards the ladder. 'I'll pray to the *kami* for our safety and protection . . .'

In the deep silence Eden was able to hear Sentaro's soft footfalls as he crept away up the wooded hillside. When the sounds had faded, he selected a spot from which he could still see the moonlit peak of Fuji framed in the open grain-port and settled himself on a mound of straw with his back against a wooden partition. Pulling his sword free from his gun belt, he laid it beside him and closed his eyes for a moment, intent on reviewing the frantic events of the past few hours—but instead he fell instantly into an exhausted sleep.

He did not stir again until a faint rustling at his back woke him with a start, a few minutes later. On instinct he snatched up his sword and stumbled to his feet—only to find Tokiwa standing quietly by the top of the ladder, holding the paper lantern in her hand.

'I'm sorry,' he gasped in Japanese, throwing the sword down into the straw and rubbing his face with both hands. 'I must have fallen asleep . . .'

The Japanese girl's alarmed expression relaxed, but she did not move from her position by the head of the ladder. She was barefoot and had brushed and dried her hair as best she could, leaving it flowing loose over her shoulders. She had wrapped about herself the kimono of midnight-blue silk splashed with silver stars, but it was drawn together only casually around her slender waist with a simple sash of braided cord. In the incongruous setting of the lamplit barn, the soft fall of its silken lines against her limbs gave a new, dramatic emphasis to her femininity.

'It was so quiet,' she said in a faltering voice, 'I came to see if you had run away too . . .'

'Don't worry, Sentaro has only gone to pray in the temple.' Eden shook his head to clear away the blurring effects of sleep. 'I apologize—I should have realized you would be puzzled.'

'I found some cold rice in my baskets,' she said hesitantly after an awkward pause. 'I've brought some for you to eat—if you are hungry.'

'Yes, thank you. I am very hungry.'

She began to move tentatively towards him and he saw that she was carrying in her free hand a small wooden bowl bearing balls of cold rice wrapped peasant-style in palm leaves. As she drew nearer, he became aware for the first time that her kimono was the colour of the night heavens, and that it was emblazoned with hosts of gleaming stars. She put down the lantern and held out the rice bowl gracefully towards him, using both hands, but he ignored it and continued to gaze in amazement at the image of the starlit heavens embroidered and printed so vividly into the rich silk of the garment.

'Is anything wrong?' she asked disconcertedly, still holding out the rice to him. 'Are you no longer hungry?'

Eden shook his head in mystification. 'I'm sorry. Last night I had a dream . . . We had just seen Mount Fuji for the first time, from the sea. It was an extraordinary sight. I went to sleep soon afterwards and dreamed I climbed alone to the top of the mountain. It was very vivid—not like a normal dream.'

He broke off and peered over his shoulder towards the distant volcano. Wisps of mist were beginning to rise around the peak, giving it a blurred, ghostly appearance, and Eden continued to stare at it, lost in thought, until he felt the lightest touch of her fingers against his bare forearm.

'What else happened in your dream?' asked Tokiwa diffidently. 'Will you please tell me . . .'

'At the peak it became very strange,' he said, turning back to look at her. 'I reached up above the summit and began pulling down the stuff of the heavens—with all the stars in it. I wrapped the darkness and the stars around my body like a magic cloak. It felt soft and very comforting . . .' He broke off and touched the smooth silk of her kimono very lightly with his fingertips, all the time looking wonderingly into her face. 'Then a great mirror of ice appeared, and I went to look at my cloak of stars. But when I peered into the mirror I found I couldn't see my reflection . . .'

His voice died away and for a long moment they stood facing each other in silence.

'Did you see anything else in the mirror?' asked Tokiwa at last. 'Anything at all?'

Eden nodded slowly. 'Yes. In the mirror I saw a very beautiful girl of Nippon looking back at me. And *she* was wearing the cloak of the heavens.' He hesitated, and again touched the silken kimono lightly at the shoulder. 'Now, in sight of the real Mount Fuji, you appear suddenly to wake me—wearing the very stuff of my dream.'

She gazed into his face in silence, the earlier expression of awe returning to her eyes. Neither moved nor spoke but they continued to look searchingly at each other while, beyond the open grain doors, fine tendrils of mist swirled more thickly about the distant volcano.

'The girl in the mirror was beautiful,' continued Eden, his voice falling to an emotional half-whisper. 'But she was not as beautiful as you.'

Lowering her eyes, Tokiwa moved away and set down the wooden rice bowl on a ledge. Then she returned to stand uncertainly in front of him.

'Thank you for telling me of your dream,' she said softly. 'I too have something I would like to tell you about. It wasn't a dream, but now it seems like one . . .'

'What was it?'

'Before I escaped from that samurai guard you fought, I was badly frightened. I could see Fuji-san from my room, so I prayed very hard to the *kami* of our sacred mountain to save me . . .' She hesitated, looking up directly into his blue eyes. 'I promised that if my prayers were answered and the *kami* helped me, I would follow their wishes always in future.'

'And do you think they have helped you?'

Tokiwa nodded once. 'Soon after I had prayed, I fell asleep. But I was awakened by a miraculous light in the sky, which shone very brightly into my room. I had never seen anything like it before. It made me more frightened at first. But all my guards had run out to stare at it—and I thought then it might be a sign from the *kami*, their way of helping me. So I decided to escape at once . . .'

'I saw that same light in the sky!' said Eden quickly. 'It made *me* feel I shouldn't hesitate any longer. As soon as it disappeared I slipped overboard from my ship to swim ashore.'

Tokiwa's eyes grew wide as she absorbed what he had said. 'I think the *kami* helped you too,' she said in an awed whisper. 'And made it possible for you to help me.'

'Perhaps,' said Eden, smiling amusedly. 'Perhaps it was your sacred *kami* who sent my dream. Who can tell?'

She frowned, unsure whether he was laughing at her; then, lifting one hand, she drew her fingers slowly across his bare chest, lingering curiously amongst the fine whorls of curled hair. Taken by surprise, Eden caught his breath and shivered at the delicacy of her touch.

'You are very different to the men of Nippon,' she said in a voice that trembled slightly. 'Your eyes are the colour of the sea . . . And you are much taller . . . Your shoulders are broader too—yet you seem far gentler.'

She fell silent as though reflecting for a final moment on her intended actions; then she untied the tasselled sash of braided cord securing the front of her kimono and laid it aside on the straw. Without any sign of self-consciousness, she opened the silken garment and removed it, holding it in one hand. She wore nothing underneath and, when she looked up at Eden, the expression in her eyes reflected a quiet pride in the natural beauty of her unadorned body.

'You seemed like a vision when I first saw you under the waterfall,' said Eden unsteadily, gazing down at her. 'But now you look even lovelier than before—I've never seen anybody more beautiful in my life.'

Tokiwa said nothing, but lifted the kimono with both hands and draped it gently about Eden's shoulders.

'Now your dream is complete,' she whispered, still looking into his eyes. 'Now you know what it feels like to wear your cloak of stars.'

The kimono was tantalizingly soft against Eden's shoulders, and he felt his senses stirred by the warmth of her body which he could detect on the silk. Very gently she drew the edges of the garment together and ran her hands lightly over its surface, touching the hard muscles of his chest and shoulders here and there through the silk.

'I think Fuji-san has cast its spell over us,' she said softly, looking past him towards the moonlit mountain. 'Only a short while ago I felt very frightened—of you and all the other foreign barbarians in the world. But now I no longer feel afraid.'

Eden reached out and gently touched her hair. As she looked up into his face he let his hand slowly follow the fall of the long dark tresses, caressing in turn her shoulders, her upper arms and the gentle swell of her naked breasts. She closed her eyes as an involuntary shudder of pleasure ran through her, and Eden leaned down to brush his lips against each of her closed eyelids in turn. She remained motionless, her eyes shut and her head raised towards him, and after gazing at her for a moment longer, Eden removed the silken kimono from his shoulders. Bending quickly he spread it across the pile of rice straw at their feet.

'Lie down with me,' he whispered, taking her by the hand. 'Here—where we can see the mountain.'

He removed his wet cotton trousers and his pistol belt and, when he was naked too, he knelt and took her gently into his arms on the silk-covered straw. Looking towards the mountain, they moved closer, their breath quickening as their limbs touched and entwined.

'There's something else I want to tell you,' said Eden suddenly, his voice taking on a haunted note. 'Some years ago I had a wife . . . She was only sixteen. I loved her . . . One night during a storm there was a tragic accident in a forest just like this one . . . and she died in my arms.'

His voice faded away and he stared out into the night in a tortured silence. Tokiwa waited, saying nothing. Suddenly Eden tightened his arms around her, his embrace fierce and tender in the same moment.

'Since that night I have never been with any other woman. I've never wanted to. But now . . .' He pulled away and looked hotly into her eyes, touching her hair again. With his fingertips he slowly traced the curve of her cheek; then he drew a quick breath, preparing to speak further.

'Don't say anything more.' Tokiwa whispered her admonition firmly, and placed the fingers of one hand against his lips. She felt herself tremble inwardly as she stared into his face, marvelling once more at his extraordinary blue eyes and his reddish brown hair. The closeness of his strong, muscular body was spreading a strange melting sensation through her limbs, and she was seized suddenly by a faint feeling of dizziness.

'Are you frightened?' asked Eden softly. 'You're shivering again.'

'Yes, a little . . .'

'What are you frightened of?'

She touched his chest lightly with both hands then her eyes strayed downward. 'You are so strong and so big . . . I'm so very small . . .'

'You needn't be afraid.'

Moved to great tenderness by her fears, Eden bore her very gently backwards into the pile of straw and bent to kiss her on the mouth. In turn he pressed his lips against her cheeks, her slender neck, the dark tips of her breasts, her belly, her thighs, all the time murmuring quiet sounds of reassurance. When he took her in his arms again, her eyes were open very wide and she gazed unwaveringly at him as he shifted his body above her.

Beyond the open grain-doors the mists around the peak of Mount Fuji had evaporated almost as quickly as they had arisen. The snow on the peak gleamed bright again in the moonlight, and the stars were etched with a triumphant sharpness on the deep blue of the night sky. Eden's eyes were fixed on the mountain at the moment they cried aloud together with the pleasure of entering and receiving one another. The hush cloaking the forest beyond the abandoned barn swallowed up their muffled cries in an instant, but Eden moaned more loudly as his desire quickened and his starved senses exploded joyously into life.

Her glowing, almond-shaped eyes, still wide open in wonder and never leaving his face, seemed to swim before him, merging into the flaring whiteness of Fuji's distant summit whenever he raised his head. Her long black hair spreading across the rice straw beneath them also spun itself like dark silk around the shining cone of the volcano, drawing it into the voluptuousness of their lovemaking. Fired by the beauty of both these images, Eden's passion became swiftly incandescent: desire, dormant for so long, surged like boiling lava through his veins.

In these instants another subliminal image flashed brilliantly in his mind's eye, and he saw with a terrible clarity the lovely face of his wife Mary, lit by lightning in the tragic forest storm. Once, twice, three times he saw her gazing trustingly up at him, love and pain simultaneously visible in her eyes. As Tokiwa clutched him more fiercely, he felt Mary reaching out again for him with desperate arms; hearing Tokiwa's breath moaning in her throat, he felt he could hear Mary's voice too, murmuring to him one last time in a dying ecstasy.

'I love you!' he gasped in English, with an explosive suddenness which racked his whole body. 'I love you. I love you, Mary! I love you!'

Then, through his half-closed eyes, he was looking only at the exotic, living face of Tokiwa and in that instant their pent-up passions burst with shuddering force. A half-stifled yell of physical rapture broke first from Eden; then Tokiwa cried out in her turn. Arching her body furiously against him, she clung more fiercely than ever to his tender strength, giving herself up fully to the pleasures of all her senses for the first time in her young life. As he felt her body melt into his own, Eden groaned in ecstasy once more.

Outside the barn, the dense forest again absorbed their cries within moments. After a long interval a night bird shrieked thrillingly nearby as though in belated response. In the distance, Mount Fuji continued to loom silently above the night-time landscape, its timeless beauty enhanced by the deep darkness that cloaked all the hills around its feet.

19

Sentaro padded softly up the last of several flights of narrow stone steps hewn out of the rocky hillside and paused beneath a red-painted wooden *torii*. Beyond this sacred gateway, a short avenue of tall pines formed a succession of natural arches that led to the simple hilltop shrine. In the moonlight the temple's curved roof of grey tiles shone like silver and Sentaro, overawed suddenly by the realization that he was about to enter a house of his country's ancient Shinto gods for the first time in years, removed his hat reverently with both hands.

Above the entrance porch of the temple a single feeble lantern was burning, and in the gloom of its interior he could see an aged, white-robed priest moving slowly as he set out offerings on a small altar. Clutching his hat against his chest, Sentaro hurried eagerly forward past rows of stone lanterns and snarling lions which flanked the short avenue. At the foot of a flight of worn wooden steps that led into the temple, he stopped and removed his straw sandals. Dipping his hands in a stone urn of fresh water, he rinsed his fingers and his mouth as tradition required before prayer, and without looking back mounted the steps.

Beneath the red *torii* two other shadowy figures, who were also recovering their breath after the steep climb, watched Sentaro enter the temple. Both were wearing samurai helmets and armour, and one of them already clasped a drawn sword in his right hand. As Sentaro disappeared inside the shrine, the swordsman made as if to rush forward but his companion restrained him, laying a firm hand on his arm.

'Wait, Gotaro,' commanded Prince Tanaka in a whisper. 'We will approach quietly to make absolutely sure.'

The air inside the shrine was heavy with incense when Sentaro entered, but its dark walls of ancient wood were devoid of all decoration. Its central altar bore only prayer wands and some of the small ceremonial dishes of fish, fruit and rice which the priest was still setting out. The floor of the shrine was covered in soft tatami mats, and Sentaro's bare feet made no sound as he entered.

'Have you come to this shrine to pray for any special purpose?'

The priest posed the casual question in a sibilant voice without turning his head or interrupting his activities and the castaway stared at his white-robed back in surprise; he had not expected to find a priest in the temple at that hour, and had assumed his entrance had gone unnoticed. Falling quickly to his knees before the altar, he bowed his head and joined his palms reverently before his chest.

'I came . . .' began Sentaro hesitantly, 'to thank the *kami* for protecting me during a long period of danger.'

'Is that all you wished to say in prayer?' enquired the priest softly, still without looking round.

'No, I wish to . . . thank the *kami* also . . . for something else,' mumbled Sentaro, keeping his head bowed.

'And what is that?' asked the priest in the same sibilant tone.

'For guiding me safely back to my homeland again . . .'

'Hold out your hands,' murmured the priest, lifting a small bamboo ladle with a long handle from his tray. 'We will pray together.'

When Sentaro complied, the priest turned from the altar and, moving nearer, splashed a few drops of blessed water over each hand and on the castaway's upturned face. As he replaced the ladle on the tray, the priest's attention was drawn towards the open door of the temple by a sudden movement. Staring out into the darkness, he saw a samurai with a drawn sword dart forward and conceal himself in the shadows beside the door. A moment later a more richly dressed samurai approached soundlessly, and pressed himself into the shadows too.

'I want to pray also for further protection in the face of present perils,' added Sentaro in a low, urgent tone. 'A close companion and myself are in grave danger. I beg the *kami* to hear our prayers . . .'

A flicker of fear appeared in the old priest's eyes as he noticed Gotaro move silently into view in the open doorway. Blood that had soaked through the armour of his right shoulder was clearly visible, and it was obvious that he had overheard every word of the exchange. With a threatening flourish of the sword, Gotaro indicated wordlessly that nothing should be said to betray his presence, and the frightened priest, relieved that his own life did not appear to be threatened, inclined his head a fraction to indicate his compliance.

Keeping his face impassive, the priest glanced down at Sentaro's bowed head. The castaway had become very still, and was waiting in silence with his palms pressed together and his eyes closed.

'You are a stranger to this region, and it is a very late hour,' said the priest, his tone indicating clearly to the watching samurai that he wished to distance himself from his supplicant and anything he might stand for. 'Is your visit to this shrine connected in any way with the present crisis in Yedo Bay?'

Sentaro hesitated for a long moment, obviously torn between the desire to be truthful and the need to protect himself. 'Yes,' he said at last in a loud whisper. 'There is a connection—but I would rather not speak further of these things now.'

'Then remain silent. I will pray.'

The priest joined his hands together but his eyes remained focused watchfully on the open door as he began to intone a low, inaudible prayer. Before him, Sentaro bowed lower and remained in a kneeling position with his back to the door. The peacefulness of the simple, hilltop shrine surrounded by its ancient, gnarled pines had already filled the castaway with a profound sense of awe, and the murmur of the priest's voice in the deep silence intensified this feeling. As the supplication continued, he rocked himself gently back and forth on his knees—but he screamed loudly in fear when a hand grabbed his hair and jerked his head sharply backward. The next instant, a cold, razor-sharp steel was pressed tight against his throat and the scream died quickly to nothing.

'You are the accomplice of the hideous alien!' yelled Gotaro furiously, bending over him. 'You were with him at the waterfall. Answer yes or no at once!'

He tugged brutally at Sentaro's hair, lifting him bodily from the tatami. At the same time he twisted the blade of the sword until it drew a small ooze of blood from the side of the castaway's neck. The priest watched impassively, neither protesting nor showing any inclination to intervene, and he did not pause in his steady recitation of the prayer.

'Answer me!' yelled the samurai again, his voice ringing round the temple's wooden rafters. 'Answer me—or you'll die now!'

'Yes, you are right,' gasped Sentaro at last. 'I have been travelling with the hideous alien.'

'Where is he now?'

Sentaro looked up at the priest with desperate, appealing eyes, but the old man's thin face remained blank and unresponsive. He continued to peer over Sentaro's head towards the temple door, his lips moving indifferently in prayer, his eyes empty of all feeling.

'The hideous alien is sheltering . . . nearby,' said Sentaro in a haunted tone. 'Only a few minutes away.'

'Where exactly?' The samurai twisted the castaway's head and manoeuvred his blade expertly to release another fine trickle of blood. 'You will tell us where—or you will bleed to death here, before the altar to the *kami*.'

'He's hiding in a ruined barn,' said Sentaro in a fearful whisper. 'It's halfway down the hillside.'

'Lead us there now!'

The samurai hauled Sentaro roughly to his feet and dragged him outside. The wizened priest watched them go without protest, and did not offer any comment or judgement; even after they had left the temple he continued to stand unmoving beside the altar in his snow-white robe, still apparently intoning his unintelligible prayer. Outside in the paved courtyard Prince Tanaka was waiting; he had heard all that was said and, as they approached, he motioned for Gotaro to relax his painful grip.

'Make sure you show the proper respect for Prince Tanaka of Kumatore,' rasped Gotaro, reluctantly untangling his fingers from the castaway's hair. 'If you don't, you will answer to my sword!'

Sentaro's face had taken on a dutiful expression as soon as he noticed that Tanaka was richly attired, but on hearing his name spoken and recognizing that the insignia on his *jimbaori* denoted a high nobleman of the Kago clan, he fell quickly to his knees. In silence he lowered his head until his forehead touched the ground, and he remained in this abject posture until Gotaro stirred him with his foot and grunted for him to rise.

'Who are you?' asked Tanaka quietly when the castaway was standing upright once more. 'I command you to identify yourself.'

'I am Sentaro . . . nothing more than a humble fisherman, O Kami-san.'

'Why has a simple fisherman of Nippon allied himself with a hideous barbarian? Explain yourself fully.'

'I was shipwrecked at sea four years ago, O Kami-san,' said Sentaro fearfully, again bowing low from the waist as he spoke. 'Fortunately I was rescued from drowning by a whaling ship sailing home to America. I was taken to the first port of call on the western coast of that country. I had no choice. I had to stay until they offered to bring me home with them on their black ships.'

'So you have lived four years among the foreign barbarians,' said Tanaka reflectively, speaking half to himself. 'In that case you must know something of their ways.'

'Yes, O Kami-san . . . but only . . . through misfortune.' Sentaro had begun to stammer in his anxiety, and as he spoke he searched Tanaka's face frantically for some sign of his likely fate. 'I didn't wish it. It was not my intention to break the laws of my country and leave our shores.'

'Did the foreign barbarians intend to hand you back to our authorities?'

Sentaro nodded respectfully. 'Yes, of course, O Kami-san . . . But as we sailed into the Bay of Yedo I became very afraid. I was sure, when I saw the preparations for war, that I would be executed for defying the ancient laws which forbid all citizens to leave Nippon. So I pleaded with the foreign barbarians not to hand me back yet . . . to wait until things became clearer.'

Tanaka had been watching the castaway closely as he spoke and his expression became thoughtful. 'We will speak more of this later,' he said slowly. 'Now you must lead us to the hiding place of the foreign barbarian.'

The samurai guard seized Sentaro by the arm and began to drag him roughly towards the steps leading down from the hilltop. Halfway along the avenue he stopped and glowered at the prisoner again.

'Is Matsumura Tokiwa with the foreign barbarian?' he demanded, lifting his sword to encourage a truthful answer.

'Yes . . . she is with us,' whispered Sentaro after a moment's indecision. 'She's in the barn too.'

Gotaro darted a quick glance at Tanaka, but the prince's face remained expressionless and he offered no comment.

'Then take us to them,' he grunted, again pressing the blade of his sword against Sentaro's neck. 'And move very quietly! If you try to shout any warning as we approach, I promise you I will sever your head from your shoulders.'

Sentaro swallowed hard and moved off silently along the moonlit avenue of pines, followed closely by the guard and Tanaka. At the top of the steps he hesitated for a moment, reluctant, despite everything, to betray the American officer who had shown him so much kindness and friendship. But the guard immediately struck him between the shoulder blades with the pommel of his sword, and Sentaro stumbled forward again, to begin the descent towards the abandoned barn, realizing he no longer had any choice but to obey.

20

'Will you tell me now why you were being held a prisoner—and why you put on the disguise of a peasant to escape?'

Robert Eden rose to pull on his own shabby cotton trousers and went to stand beside the open grain-doors. As he waited for the Japanese girl to answer his question, he held his breath and listened carefully for the muffled sounds of approaching footsteps, or the drum of hoofbeats among the trees. But no unnatural noises reached his ears and he stood for a moment gazing abstractedly at the shining image of Mount Fuji, marvelling once more at its extraordinary vividness and clarity.

'My story may be difficult for you to understand.'

'I'd like to try,' said Eden, turning his head to look at her again. 'Perhaps if you use only plain words . . .'

Tokiwa was still sprawled on the straw, with her eyes closed and one arm thrown back across her face. In the faint light shed by the lantern, her body seemed to glow like polished amber against the blue silk on which she was lying. As he gazed down at her, Eden felt himself moved anew by the slenderness and delicacy of her naked beauty.

'You speak the language of Nippon well,' murmured Tokiwa.

'Sentaro joined my ship long before we left America. I made him teach me the language of Nippon for many months—and every day on the long voyage here . . .'

Eden walked back across the loft and, kneeling down, took her tenderly into his arms once more. For several moments she lay still, drawing an invisible pattern across his bare chest with the tip of her forefinger. When she raised her dark eyes to look at him, the expression in them was soft and languorous, and her voice was still half drowsy with desire.

'It all happened so suddenly. I had no time to think.' Tokiwa flattened the palm of one small hand against his chest, and continued to caress him with a distant expression in her eyes. 'Panic broke out in the streets of Yedo when we heard that the black ships were on their way. People came running from their houses in fear . . . Many hid their precious possessions . . . Many others fled from the capital—' She broke off and a faint look of alarm appeared on her face. 'What is going to happen? Is there going to be war?'

Eden drew her close, exploring the curve of her naked hip thoughtfully with one hand. 'America wishes only to trade peacefully with Nippon. I know this must seem like a lie to you, but we don't want war.'

'I've heard that the black ships have come with many terrifying guns,' persisted Tokiwa. 'Why are *they* necessary if you don't want to fight?'

Eden shrugged. 'We came in armed men-of-war because we didn't wish to be driven away like other "foreign barbarian" ships before us. For two long centuries Nippon has cut itself off completely from all other nations. The leaders of my country, for their own selfish reasons, decided to drag your country back into the world again . . .'

'Why didn't they just leave us alone?' asked Tokiwa in a small voice. 'Why did they have to come here?'

'Because they believe that what they're doing is right—though I disagree. I believe we shouldn't threaten and bully other peaceful countries. Fighting could begin by accident . . .'

'Will your warriors from the black ships invade Nippon and make us slaves?' asked Tokiwa, searching his face anxiously.

Eden stroked her long hair for a moment. 'I swam ashore secretly, without permission. I wanted to see if I could do something to prevent war. But it may not be possible . . .'

Tokiwa pressed her face against his shoulder, and he tightened his arms around her. Not far away, up the hillside, another large night bird screeched loudly, then flapped off through the tree-tops as though disturbed suddenly from its roost. Eden raised his head and followed the progress of its clumsy flight, his ears straining without success to pick up any accompanying sounds of movement from the ground. He continued to listen until deep silence had settled over the forest again; only then did he lift her chin gently with one hand so that she was forced to meet his gaze.

'Will you tell me now why you were running away in disguise?'

Tokiwa sat up and arranged the silken kimono loosely about her shoulders. 'A young nobleman of high birth, whom I have entertained often in Yedo, came to me soon after the commotion began in the streets. His name is Prince Tanaka of Kumatore. He said there were great disputes about the arrival of the barbarian black ships. Some *daimyo* wanted to attack the ships at once, although it might cost many lives. Others felt certain that course would be disastrous for Nippon and wanted to wait.'

Eden frowned. 'But how did all that affect you?'

'Prince Tanaka said he was deeply involved and his enemies might kidnap or kill me in order to harm him. So, for my own safety, he said I had to leave Yedo with his guards.'

'Where did they take you?'

'To an inn ten miles north of here. They held me there like a prisoner. I was afraid. I had seen so many people fleeing. I thought a war had already begun, and I might never see my family again . . .'

'Why didn't you stay with them at the inn?'

'I became frightened of my guards. The man you fought at the waterfall was their chief. I didn't know what they intended to do with me if Prince Tanaka should be killed or not return. So I bribed a peasant maid to bring me clothes and find me a horse.'

'You are brave,' whispered Eden, 'as well as very beautiful.'

Tokiwa looked gravely at him. 'My father was a samurai. Many like him were made destitute after the clan wars ended. He became a merchant—but sadly he was too fond of gambling.'

'What happened?' prompted Eden gently.

'He lost everything he owned in just one night in the pleasure district of Yedo. To save him from ruin, I agreed to be sold to a geisha house there. The daughters of samurai, as well as their sons, are brought up to face life without flinching.'

Eden took both her hands in his, and held them against his lips. Looking again into her dark, upswept eyes, he felt a new rush of desire stir deep inside him. The dark silk, dusted with stars, seemed to enhance the allure of her now half-naked body, and he bent his head to kiss her fiercely on the mouth. When they drew apart again, both were breathing unevenly.

'Fate is strange,' whispered Tokiwa. 'We both saw the fantastic light in the sky—and we both became fugitives in peasant clothes on the same night.'

'Yes, it is very curious,' said Eden huskily.

'I made a silent promise when I prayed at the *yadoya*,' continued Tokiwa. 'I promised I'd give my love to any man the *kami* deemed worthy, if my prayers were answered.' She hesitated, looking over his shoulder once more towards Mount Fuji. 'That's why I unfastened my sash so readily for you . . . and gave you my kimono of stars to wear. It seemed as though the *kami* wished it.' She turned away from the mountain and searched his face. 'Do you believe it was fate that caused our paths to cross?'

Eden did not answer at once. 'Since that terrible night in the forest I haven't believed in anything,' he murmured at last. 'Often during that time I haven't cared whether I lived or died . . . But I don't feel like that any more.'

The words faded in his throat and he moved against her suddenly, glorying once more in the sensation of her warm nakedness pressed along the length of his body. With a sigh, Tokiwa wound herself more tightly against him, and he was bending his head to kiss her again when a sudden rush of feet on the loft ladder broke the silence inside the barn. Moonlight falling through the broken roof flashed on Gotaro's drawn sword as he leapt from the top of the ladder with a loud cry; in the same instant Eden rolled desperately sideways, to snatch up his own sword and scramble to his feet.

Tokiwa screamed loudly as the samurai's first blow, delivered with great speed and force, was only half parried by Eden's hastily raised blade. The cutlass flew from his hand and Eden staggered backwards off-balance, until he fell to his knees beside the open grain-doors. The samurai bore in on him, lifting his sword high for another disabling strike and Tokiwa screamed a second time as she shrank back against the wooden wall in terror.

'*Tomemas!* . . . Stop!'

The commanding voice of Prince Tanaka rose above the geisha's scream as he forced Sentaro up the ladder and clambered swiftly into the loft behind him. Gotaro froze, with his sword arm raised high, then took two steps backwards to pick up Eden's fallen blade. When he had tucked it safely in his sash, he dropped into a half-crouch, glowering at the kneeling American.

'Watch him carefully!'

The guard flourished his sword threateningly, while Tanaka moved to the lantern and took it down from its hook. Lifting his arm he let its glow fall on Tokiwa, who was still backed up against the wall, watching him with apprehensive eyes. For a long moment he looked at her in silence, then stepped closer.

'Why are you here alone with the barbarian spy?' he asked in a voice which quivered with anger. 'How did you come together?'

'I was bathing at a waterfall after my long dusty journey, O Kami-san,' replied Tokiwa in little more than a whisper. 'I had not seen him. But he caught sight of Gotaro running to seize me. He rushed out of the trees and came to my aid, without any request on my part.'

'That doesn't explain what made you come to this place with him,' snapped Tanaka. 'Why are you here alone with an enemy of your country?'

'Many horsemen were approaching from all directions, O Kami-san . . .' began Tokiwa, but Eden's voice cut across her suddenly.

'I brought her here by force. She had no choice! I snatched her up on my horse!'

Tanaka's eyes glittered with controlled fury in his otherwise impassive face, but he did not turn to look at Eden. 'And did the barbarian spy force you to lie in the straw with him?'

Tokiwa dropped her gaze under the ferocity of his scrutiny, but said nothing. For another long moment the horses shifting in the straw below the loft provided the only sound in the silent barn.

'I kept her here against her will,' said Eden sharply. 'It was my wish to talk with her!'

'Is what he says true?' demanded Tanaka.

Tokiwa hesitated, then nodded. 'Yes, but the foreign barbarian told me that he did not come ashore as a spy. Perhaps you misjudge him.'

'By coming ashore in the dark without permission, he is committing the crimes of a spy, whatever his intentions!'

'He says he landed secretly because he wants to prevent a war . . .'

Tanaka's eyes narrowed in thought, and he turned round slowly in Eden's direction. But before he could speak he was interrupted by a shout from Sentaro.

'I was taken by surprise in the temple, master!' called the castaway desperately in English. 'I was forced on pain of death to tell them everything and show them the way here. This is Prince Tanaka of the greatly esteemed Kago clan!'

'Shut up!' yelled the samurai guard, swinging round to glare furiously at him. 'Or you will be silenced permanently!'

Sentaro bowed his head by way of apology and shrank back shamefacedly into the shadows by the ladder, avoiding Eden's gaze.

'Say nothing more, Sentaro,' advised Eden quietly in English, rising slowly to his feet. 'Don't endanger yourself in any way.'

'Silence! And stay where you are!' Tanaka barked out his order and strode across the loft, holding up the lantern as he approached so that Eden's face was fully illuminated. Tanaka's eyes opened wide in surprise as recognition dawned, and in the same instant Eden also realized he was looking at the senior escort to the Vice-Governor of Uraga, whom he had encountered only hours before aboard the *Susquehanna*.

'You are the barbarian officer who disarmed our rash swordsman on board the black ship!' exclaimed Tanaka. 'We have met before.'

'Yes, O Kami-san,' replied Eden in formal Japanese. 'You remember correctly.'

Tanaka's narrow eyes again registered surprise. 'And you seem to know our language well!'

'I've been able to learn some Nipponese,' said Eden evenly. 'Sentaro here has been a good teacher.'

Tanaka's face remained a blank mask as he continued to scrutinize Eden by the light of the lamp. Staring back at him, Eden noticed how still the Japanese stood, never moving a muscle. Only his burning eyes hinted that he was struggling to subdue a turmoil of conflicting emotions.

'You've dared to land secretly among us at night, while your black ships threaten us with war,' he said in a controlled voice. 'Those are the actions of a spy—and spying against Nippon is a crime instantly punishable by death!'

'Let me finish him now, O Kami-san,' cried Gotaro, stepping forward impulsively, sword in hand. 'He deserves to die!'

'Wait! Not yet!'

Tanaka motioned the guard back with a dismissive gesture. He had not taken his eyes from Eden's face, and he moved a step nearer to him, dropping a precautionary hand onto the hilt of his own sword.

'If you had been hunted down by others you would no longer be alive,' he continued in the same icy tone. 'When news of your capture spreads there will be demands for your immediate execution.'

Eden returned the gaze of the Japanese steadily, but said nothing. From the corner of his eye he had just caught sight of the gun belt which he had removed earlier, when stretching out in the straw. The belt and the holster containing his Colt pistol lay partly concealed by straw on the floorboards of the loft only six feet away, at the edge of the circle of light cast by the lantern. Knowing that a direct glance might draw attention to the weapon, he kept his eyes averted while calculating whether he could lunge to grab it before the hovering samurai guard struck him down.

'You claim you're not a spy,' continued Tanaka stonily. 'You say you came ashore to seek some way of avoiding war. But a spy always lies. Why should we believe you?'

'Because I tell the truth, O Kami-san,' said Eden simply. 'I risked landing against the orders of my superior officers. It's obvious we know too little about Nippon and its people. And to act out of ignorance is always dangerous.'

'Did you expect to return to your ship undetected?'

'Yes.'

Tanaka smiled coldly. 'Then your first mistake was to underestimate the people of Nippon.'

'Perhaps—but am I alone in making such a mistake?'

Tanaka frowned in puzzlement. 'What do you mean?'

'Didn't you underestimate the people you call "foreign barbarians"—when you came aboard our ship yesterday?'

'In what way?'

'You seemed more than a little surprised, O Kami-san, when your hot-headed guard was quietly disarmed—and nothing further was said.'

Tanaka acknowledged Eden's point with a slight inclination of his head, but offered no comment.

'And weren't you practising a little deception yourself, by posing as an ordinary samurai? Nobody informed us we were receiving a nobleman of the Kago clan.'

'I came aboard incognito to ensure no foolish action was taken,' said Tanaka fiercely. 'My intentions were honourable!'

'Then that should help you understand that my intentions are honourable too,' replied Eden evenly.

For several moments Tanaka remained silent, his face set in thoughtful lines. Then he took a pace nearer to Eden. 'Do you think you discovered anything of value here before you were captured?'

'What I've seen confirms the feelings I already had before I left my ship,' said Eden slowly. 'Nothing more.'

'And what were those feelings?'

'That it will be a great tragedy for both our countries if fighting breaks out. There could be a terrible loss of life on both sides. And nobody will benefit.'

Tanaka considered the answer in silence, then turned on his heel and walked a few paces towards the ladder leading down from the loft. Eden watched tensely as his sandalled feet passed within a few inches of the half-hidden pistol but when Tanaka paused by the ladder and swung round again, he gave no sign that he had noticed the weapon.

'Is this the message that you would carry back to your superior officers?'

'Yes.'

Tanaka glanced round at Tokiwa and Sentaro who were watching him uneasily from beyond the circle of light cast by the lantern; but although his gaze briefly fastened on each of them in turn, he did not seem to see them. As he paced slowly back across the loft, the harsh lines in his face softened, and when he stopped in front of Eden again a new curiosity was visible in his expression.

'What is your name?' he demanded quietly.

'Eden . . . Robert Eden. And I am a lieutenant in the United States Navy.'

Tanaka nodded several times in silence, as though committing the name carefully to memory, then he spoke in a lowered voice.

'You're not like your fellow barbarians, Eden-san. You stopped one of our escorts from committing an act of great folly aboard your black ships—and you helped us to conceal it. You're a trained fighting officer, yet you say you want to prevent a war. You've also learned our language. Why are you doing all these things?'

Faced suddenly with a demand to define his motives, Eden hesitated. He had been taking one last mental measurement of the distance between himself and the pistol; he knew that the six-shot weapon was fully loaded, and he decided that there was a slender chance of seizing it if he could distract the attention of his adversaries sufficiently before he threw himself on it. In that moment he made up his mind to create a distraction at the first opportunity, and the decision helped him focus his thoughts more clearly.

'I suppose I'm two men in one skin, O Kami-san,' he said slowly. 'That's one possible reason.'

Tanaka's brow furrowed in a puzzled frown. 'I do not understand you.'

Eden shifted his position slightly, looking first at Tanaka then at Gotaro; as he did so he moved a foot or two nearer to the gun belt concealed beneath the straw.

'A brave and ancient people lived peacefully in America before new settlers began to sail there from the countries of Europe over two hundred years ago,' he said quietly. 'They were called "Red Indians". These new settlers fought them for their land, and conquered them because they had far better weapons. My great-grandfather, who was one of the settlers, was kidnapped by Indians in a raid when he was still a small boy. He grew up with that Indian tribe and because he was a brave fighter he became their chieftain. Later he led the tribe in many raids on the settlers. He married an Indian girl and had three sons . . .' Eden paused, looking at Gotaro and Tanaka in turn. 'Do you understand now?'

The guard scowled, saying nothing, but Tanaka shook his head quickly to indicate that he required further explanation.

'The Indians fought courageously for a long time in many hopeless battles,' continued Eden after a pause. 'Only one of those three sons—my grandfather—survived. In the end he returned to live among the Europeans. So you see I have the blood of those Indian people running in my veins as well as the blood of the settlers from Europe . . .'

'And where does your loyalty lie now?' demanded Tanaka. 'With which side?'

'I've already told you I am two men under one skin,' said Eden uneasily. 'I was raised a European Christian—but I love my Indian ancestors too. And I've always hated the injustice they suffered at the hands of those strangers who came from far across the sea to conquer their land and rob them of all they possessed.'

'Just as today *you* have come across another sea to lands where you are a stranger,' said Tanaka fiercely. 'In a different attempt to conquer and steal and rob!'

Eden looked at the Japanese in silence. Then he shifted uncomfortably again on his feet, but in a way that moved him imperceptibly closer to the pistol.

'What you say about our expedition unfortunately has truth in it. But you already know I feel its aims are unjust . . .'

'If you were opposed to the expedition, why did you come to Nippon at all?' demanded Tanaka, frowning suspiciously. 'Why didn't you stay away?'

'While learning your language with Sentaro, I discovered that the people of Nippon and the ancient Indian peoples of America shared many things in common. Some words are very similar in both languages . . . the faces of the people, too, are often alike. I found that both our peoples worship the sun and the unseen spirits of nature. And, like you, my ancestors revered certain mountains and rivers as sacred . . .'

Eden paused again to make one last check on the position of the Colt, before turning his head to look out through the open grain-doors. He stared towards the distant volcano, deliberately remaining silent, while he gathered himself for the physical effort to come.

'My Indian ancestors would have understood very well your great reverence for Fuji-san and the spirits of your fields and forests. Also Indian warriors rode and fought with spears and bows and arrows, as your warriors still do. Sometimes they dressed in war masks and horned helmets very like yours. And when they went into battle they shouted war cries to bewilder their enemies just as you do . . .'

Without warning, Eden let out an ear-splitting scream and flung himself full-length into the straw. In a single movement he tugged the pistol from its holster, took fleeting aim at the lantern in Tanaka's hand, and fired. The roar of the firearm was deafening inside the loft, and Tanaka shouted in alarm as the lantern flew from his hand and went out.

'Sentaro! Get down the ladder and unhitch the horses!'

Eden yelled his order to the castaway in English as he lurched to his feet and began to back away towards the ladder. He was holding the pistol at arm's length, pointing it towards Tanaka and Gotaro, who were just beginning to move cautiously towards him.

'Don't come any nearer!'

Eden fired another deafening shot into the roof close above their heads as he shouted his warning in Japanese and Tanaka and the samurai stopped uncertainly in their tracks.

'Hurry, Sentaro!' shouted Eden, glancing over his shoulder to find the castaway hesitating fearfully at the top of the ladder. 'Go quickly or we're lost!'

A piercing scream rang out and Eden turned again to see Tokiwa struggling in the grip of the guard, who had clamped an arm around her throat from behind. He was shielding himself from the gun with her body, and Tokiwa was staring fearfully at the sword he brandished in front of her.

'If you fire again, she will die,' roared Gotaro. 'Surrender the weapon at once.'

Another scream from Tokiwa was stifled as the guard tightened his grip around her throat and brought his blade ominously close to her face. Eden hesitated, then glanced towards Tanaka to find he too was withdrawing his sword from his sash.

'Throw away the gun, as he orders!' commanded Tanaka.

'Don't delay—if you want to save Tokiwa-san, master,' urged Sentaro in a desperate whisper from the top of the ladder. 'They will kill her without doubt.'

Eden looked again towards Tokiwa; she had ceased to struggle but her eyes were dilating with fear as she waited for his reaction. In the filtered moonlight her face seemed deathly pale.

'Let her go now,' said Eden in a dull tone, tossing the pistol to the boards at Tanaka's feet. 'Don't harm her.'

Tanaka bent quickly to take possession of the gun, then rapped out an order to Gotaro to release the girl. As soon as he had relaxed his grip, she sank down into the straw and buried her face in her hands. Eden watched Tanaka walk towards him holding the pistol in one hand and his sword in the other. As he came, he barked out another crisp order, calling Gotaro to his side. The guard, whose shoulder was bloodied from the clash in the waterfall, hurried to obey, staring fixedly at Eden as if relishing the expected order to make the final strike.

'I am ready, O Kami-san,' he rasped, moving closer. 'Just give the command!'

'Put up your sword!'

Tanaka quietly sheathed his own blade and waited until the mystified samurai obeyed. For a second or two Tanaka looked Eden in the eye very intently, as though trying to read his innermost thoughts; then he slipped the pistol inside his *jimbaori.*

'Now draw the sword of the barbarian, Gotaro!'

After a moment of puzzled hesitation, the guard pulled Eden's blade uncertainly from his sash.

'You will return the weapon respectfully to its owner,' said Tanaka, without taking his eyes from Eden's face. 'Hilt first.'

The samurai's eyes widened in disbelief. Then, still glowering, he turned the cutlass carefully in his hands, and inclined his head in a reluctant gesture of respect as he offered it to Eden.

Uncertain of the meaning of this gesture, Eden remained watchful and made no immediate move to take the weapon.

'Because of your action on the black ships I owe you a debt of gratitude,' said Tanaka flatly, inclining his own topknotted head a fraction. 'Now your sword is returned to you and the debt is repaid.'

Struggling to conceal his surprise and relief, Eden nodded formally in response and accepted the weapon. Gotaro, who had picked up the empty gun belt, handed it over wordlessly so that Eden could re-fasten it around his waist and tuck the cutlass away.

'Remember, spying in Nippon is punishable by instant death,' added Tanaka curtly. 'I take personal responsibility for waiving that punishment for the time being. And I restore your sword to you on one condition—that you return straight away to your ship. You will be responsible for your own safety on the way there—and if you are captured again, there will be no escaping execution.'

'I thank you for your generosity, O Kami-san,' replied Eden, and inclined his head towards Tanaka and the guard in turn.

In the silence that followed, he glanced into the shadows where Tokiwa was still kneeling amongst the straw. She had straightened up and was watching and listening with a strained expression on her face. Their eyes met fleetingly, then she quickly lowered her gaze.

'Before I begin my journey, O Kami-san,' said Eden, 'I would like to request one assurance from you.'

'You are in no position to request anything,' said Tanaka brusquely. 'You should go immediately!'

'I ask only that Tokiwa-san should not be made a prisoner again,' persisted Eden. 'And that she should be allowed to return unhindered to her family.'

'The safety of Tokiwa-san is my personal responsibility!' Tanaka's eyes hardened. 'That matter need no longer concern you.'

Eden looked again towards Tokiwa, but she kept her eyes averted and after a moment he turned reluctantly away. At the top of the ladder Sentaro was still waiting; his face was very pale and he was trembling visibly.

'Sentaro should return with me to the ship,' said Eden over his shoulder, as he grasped the top of the ladder. 'He fears greatly for his life now. It would be better if he returned home later when matters between our two countries are peacefully resolved.'

Tanaka looked at the castaway, seemingly uncertain of how to react; then he nodded quickly. 'Very well—he may return with you. But make no further requests—just go quickly.'

'I am grateful, O Kami-san,' said Eden shortly.

Sentaro prostrated himself swiftly on the boards, to express his own silent gratitude, and as Eden waited for the castaway to rise and descend the ladder ahead of him, he peered once more into the shadows. Tokiwa's glossy kimono, now gathered more closely about her body, was reflecting the soft sheen of the moonlight and he could see that she had shifted into a formal kneeling posture amongst the straw. She had raised her eyes at last and was looking in his direction but her face was unfathomably expressionless and she did not move or call out. With her long black hair falling softly about her shoulders, she looked to Eden both fragile and hauntingly beautiful.

Beyond the open grain-doors Mount Fuji was mistily discernible, still presiding silently over the events in the barn from afar, and Eden knew instinctively that every last detail of the scene would remain etched in his memory for ever: the distant sacred mountain, the kneeling doll-like presence of Tokiwa, the tumbled heaps of rice straw, the proud figure of Tanaka, the glowering vengeful face of his samurai henchman. He knew he would be able to summon a vivid image of the loft to mind whenever he wished and after one last, lingering glance in Tokiwa's direction, he hurried down the ladder, gathered up his shirt and pouch, and mounted the horse which Sentaro was holding for him. Beckoning for the castaway to follow, he pulled his tattered hat down over his eyes and rode out quietly into the surrounding forest.

21

The hoofs of Eden's horse clattered loudly on the planks of a narrow wooden bridge as he led the way across a winding brook that foamed white in the moonlight. The track he had chosen was leading them up the side of a wooded, boulder-strewn ravine and following on twenty yards in his wake, Sentaro could see that the American was holding his leather-clad compass constantly in front of him as he rode. Whenever they reached a fork in the path or an expanse of open forest which offered a choice of direction, Eden paused to consult the instrument by the light of the moon.

They had not spoken since leaving the abandoned barn, but had cantered in silence across the densely wooded hills for half an hour, following the narrowest and quietest tracks. They had encountered nobody en route and, noticing that Eden's manner was abstracted, the castaway had not tried to address him. Whenever he changed direction, Eden glanced quickly over his shoulder to satisfy himself that they had not lost contact, and Sentaro sometimes lifted one hand briefly in acknowledgement.

The sloping path curved in a wide horseshoe as it climbed the ravine and led on into shadowy woodlands where heavy-scented festoons of honeysuckle clustered thickly in the lower branches of the trees. Their fragrance filled the moonlit woods, and Sentaro was ducking his head low over his horse's mane to avoid the trailing vines when he saw Eden swing suddenly around a dark outcrop of rock ahead of him and go out of sight. To catch up quickly he forced his horse into a gallop, but on reaching the spur he was surprised to find that Eden had halted unexpectedly, and was waiting astride his horse in the shadowy lee of the rock. As Sentaro reined back his mount and skidded to a halt on the soft earth, Eden lifted a hand to his lips to caution silence, and motioned for him to draw in beside him.

'What is it, master?' whispered the Japanese, leaning close to Eden's ear. 'Why have we stopped?'

'I think we're being followed. Listen!'

For a full minute they sat side by side, straining their ears without detecting any sound of pursuit. Then they heard the distant clatter of a single horse passing rapidly over the same wooden bridge that they had crossed and Sentaro nodded his head anxiously.

'You're right, master. But who could it be?'

'Maybe Tanaka has sent his guard after us,' whispered Eden fiercely. 'Maybe he's changed his mind and wants us killed.'

'Whoever it is, he chooses to follow only at a distance,' murmured Sentaro, after listening again to the faint hoofbeats. 'He's two or three minutes behind us. Maybe a rider has been sent to monitor our progress and report back to Prince Tanaka.'

Eden nodded. 'You could be right. But, whatever the reason, we must throw him off our scent.'

Looking round quickly, Eden backed his horse into a cleft in the rocks and beckoned for Sentaro to follow. As they waited side by side in their place of concealment, they noticed that the white peak of Mount Fuji had again become visible from their high vantage point; it seemed, as before, to float silently into view in the far darkness and after glancing at it for a moment, Eden sat straighter in his saddle, straining his ears to pick up the sounds of the approaching horseman.

'He's still at least a minute behind us,' whispered Sentaro after a pause. 'And he's not riding very fast.'

Eden listened again then nodded wordlessly in agreement.

Sighing loudly, Sentaro closed his eyes and inhaled, relishing the heady fragrance of the matted honeysuckle flowers which cloaked the surrounding trees. The rich scents of leaves and earth were also drifting on the still night air and suddenly he smiled. 'I had forgotten how beautiful my country is, master,' he breathed. 'It is very good that I've come back—even for a short time.'

'How long would it take, Sentaro?' cut in Eden suddenly, his whisper urgent. 'Just roughly?'

'For the rider to catch us up, master, do you mean?' queried the Japanese in a puzzled voice.

'No, to climb to the top of Fuji-san!'

Sentaro turned to look at Eden in surprise. The question had been posed in a barely audible whisper, and he found the American was staring towards the glowing volcano with a strange intensity in his expression.

'Eight or ten hours of very hard toil, I think, from the very bottom up to the rim of the crater.'

'Can it really be done so quickly?'

'I'm told it was once climbed in just six and a half hours, master,' whispered Sentaro. 'It takes at least three hours to descend again, but it's customary for pilgrims to spend one or even two nights up on the mountain.

That way they can reach the summit in time for the most wonderful experience of all—to watch from the crater as the sun rises above the eastern horizon, bringing the new day . . .'

'How far are we now from Fuji-san?' asked Eden in the same half-whisper, still staring towards the mountain. 'How many miles?'

'It looks very clear and close, master,' whispered Sentaro after some hesitation, 'but Fuji-san creates many illusions. The mountain lies about sixty miles from Yedo. And from here it is maybe forty miles . . . But listen, the horseman is approaching!'

They instinctively ducked their heads, calming their mounts as best they could as the thud of hoofs grew louder on the soft earth of the wooded ravine. There was no pause or break in their rhythm as the rider drew abreast of the rocks on the spur of the hill and they both recognized the figure of Gotaro when he entered their field of vision, riding steadily away from them along the track, hunched in concentration over his horse's neck. They watched his shadowy shape disappear into the higher woodland then listened to the fading hoofbeats until they were certain that the guard had not turned back.

'Which route shall we take now, master?' whispered Sentaro urgently, seeing that Eden was again studying his compass. 'We must go quickly because Gotaro will soon find he has lost our trail.'

'Fuji-san is due north-west,' said Eden absently, as though speaking his thoughts aloud, and lifted his gaze once more to the far-off mountain.

'Yes, master, but we must head south towards the coast in the region of Uraga.'

Eden remained strangely silent and when Sentaro turned to find out why, he found the American was still looking abstractedly towards Fuji.

'What's the name of your home village again?' he asked without turning his head.

'I was born in the coastal settlement of Yurutaki, master. Why do you ask?'

'Because I want to give you one last chance to consider going home to your family.'

'But I've already told you, master,' protested the castaway. 'I am too afraid . . . I would be executed!'

'Yurutaki can't be more than fifteen or twenty miles from here. You could return under cover of darkness and let your loved ones know you are still alive. You could at least spend a few hours with them. And if it's too dangerous to stay, you could return to the *Susquehanna* secretly . . .'

'No, master, I don't want to leave you.'

'Then I must order you back to the ship *now*,' said Eden, turning at last to look at the castaway. 'Return to the cliffs where we came ashore, and swim back to the *Susquehanna* the same way. With luck you can be aboard before dawn.'

'But, master, please . . .'

Eden held up a hand to silence him, and pulled the notepad and a pencil from his waist-pouch. Turning in the saddle to make the most of the moonlight, he began to write rapidly.

'I want you to give this to Flag Lieutenant Rice as soon as you get back,' he said when he had finished writing. 'I've described all we saw and heard at the cliff fort. And I'm urging them not to launch an attack under any circumstances. You can say I'll give a fuller report on my return—and that I've stayed ashore for a further two days to continue the reconnaissance . . .'

The castaway shrank from taking the note and shook his head. 'I won't go, master! I won't leave your side.'

'This is an order!' Eden held out the folded note more firmly. 'I forbid you to remain with me any longer.'

After a long pause Sentaro reached out reluctantly, took the folded paper and tucked it into his pouch. 'What do you intend to do master?'

'I'm going to climb to the summit of Mount Fuji.'

Sentaro stared at him aghast. Then he too turned and looked towards the volcano.

'Master, perhaps you didn't fully understand! The ruling authorities of Nippon will show no mercy to any foreign barbarian who violates our sacred mountain! No *gai-jin* has ever climbed it. You would be defiling the holy precincts of the *kami*. You would be committing a terrible sacrilege!'

'Nobody will know,' said Eden quietly. 'I will climb Mount Fuji in secret.'

Sentaro continued to stare at the American officer with a dumbfounded expression on his face. 'It's not an easy climb, master. In fact it's very dangerous. No pilgrims would attempt it until much later in July, when the snows have melted. It's summer down here, but it's still winter at the top of the mountain.'

'I shan't be up there very long.'

'But the snow is very thick and the air is thin! There will be avalanches and fog and rain. Typhoons can come quickly, even on the lower slopes. Men have often died on this mountain. You need special warm clothes and experienced *goriki*—mountain men—to guide you to the rest huts. You need to be shown the right tracks up the steep slopes . . .'

'Have *you* ever climbed Fuji-san, Sentaro?'

'No, master! But for a thousand years many villages throughout Nippon have each sent a single pilgrim to climb Fuji-san. They worship and pay homage at the summit for their friends and families. As a boy

I remember listening to a neighbour tell of his experience. On his climb alone, two men fell to their deaths.'

'I shall find a way of climbing safely to the crater.'

'But why, master?' pleaded the castaway. 'Why must you go now?'

'I may never get another chance, Sentaro. And I can feel the mountain beckoning.'

'Prince Tanaka himself warned you: you'll be killed if you're found ashore!'

'I won't be found.'

'But you have so far to ride through fields and villages,' said Sentaro desperately. 'And it will be daylight soon . . .'

'If necessary I'll hide in the forests until darkness falls again.'

'I wish I understood, master,' moaned Sentaro. 'I am sure you will die if you try to climb Fuji-san alone!'

Eden turned to look down at the castaway, smiling suddenly. 'Perhaps Fuji-san has stirred up the blood of my Indian ancestors. Perhaps the marrow in my bones knows better than my brain . . .'

Sentaro wrinkled his brow. 'I don't understand, master.'

'Maybe something inside me knows that Fuji holds secrets long forgotten, secrets that need to be rediscovered . . . Or maybe some ancient part of me just wants to worship the sunrise again from the top of a sacred mountain.'

Sentaro settled back in his saddle, nodding without really understanding. Glancing up at the taller man, he saw the shadows of his features thrown more sharply into relief by the moonlight, and in the half-darkness his eyes looked deeper set, his cheekbones higher and more angular.

'Sometimes, master, I see the ancestors you spoke of very clearly in your face,' said the castaway hesitantly. 'And then I think I see something of my own people there too.'

Eden looked at him in silence. 'When you are two men in one skin, Sentaro,' he said at last, 'you realize that all the races of the world are brothers. Nothing will be right until everybody understands this—and acts every day with such understanding.'

Sentaro took a deep breath. 'You said before, master, we would climb Fuji-san together—when, like us, America and Nippon had become good friends . . .'

Eden smiled and nodded. 'Yes—but that may take too long.'

'But why must you go alone now, master? Why won't you let me go with you?'

'Because I may risk my own life in this wild venture, Sentaro. But I may not risk yours too. You must go back to the ship.'

Sentaro's face tightened with emotion as he removed his broad, mollusc-shaped hat and held it out towards Eden. 'Take this, please.'

'Why?'

'It will be a better disguise for you. And I don't need it.'

Smiling, Eden pulled off the battered remains of his own hat and replaced it with that of the castaway. Then he manoeuvred his horse out from the cleft of rock, and leaned over to clasp the castaway warmly by the hand.

'Thank you, Sentaro. You're a true brother. I'll see you soon on board the *Susquehanna*.'

He moved his horse quickly out onto the track, but ignored the path taken by the samurai guard. He had already tucked his compass away in his waist-pouch and without hesitation, he urged the animal over the edge of the ravine and rode rapidly down its steep side, heading directly north-west towards the visible goal of Fuji.

'Good luck, master! May the *kami* protect you.'

Sentaro called out his farewell in English; then, his face fixed in a grimace of sadness, he sat unmoving beside the rock watching the silhouette of Eden and his horse merge gradually into the ink-black landscape of hills and trees that reached all the way to the horizon.

22

On the morning of Saturday 9 July 1853, dawn broke over Yedo Bay with a sparkling clarity. The first rays of the rising sun chased away a few remaining tendrils of coastal mist, and the unruffled surface of the bay was soon reflecting as sharply as any mirror the outlines of the four American warships that were drawn up side by side with their heavy guns aimed towards the land. In the early light the uneasy sentries and lookouts, who had kept vigil on the ships through the long night, became fully aware for the first time of the striking grandeur of the shores from which they had been nervously anticipating an attack.

Slanting horizontally across the water from the east, the warm sunshine illuminated high coastal cliffs of grey rock on the western margins of the bay. Beyond them successive ranges of green hills rolled inland, intersected here and there by the gleam of a fast-flowing river or stream. Higher up the bay, towards the capital, the same coast was more intensely cultivated, and from the ships small towns and villages could be seen on either side of the water.

The eastern shore, more barren and mountainous, had a wild, uninhabited appearance, but in the crystal-clear atmosphere of the early day every detail of the landscape was sharply discernible. Some of the tiny wood-and-paper houses in the town of Uraga, closest to the ships, were seen to have pyramidal roofs; some were square; others, apparently whitewashed, had peaked roofs more familiar to American eyes. Around the inlets and harbours, fishing junks with distinctive bat-wing sails were moored in groups, and in the quiet dawn a rare natural harmony seemed to exist between the landscape and the visible signs of its human inhabitants.

'We're standing at the gates of a country that's as beautiful as it is dangerous, Mr Harris,' said Samuel Armstrong, appearing silently beside the young midshipman who had been posted at the port-bow gangway. 'This morning the "Land of the Rising Sun" seems to be arrayed in its full glory.'

The greying hair of the missionary-interpreter was still tousled from sleep, and he rubbed his eyes and stifled a yawn before raising a long telescope to survey the coastline in detail. The midshipman, whose eager young face was showing signs of strain, heaved a loud sigh of relief.

'I was mighty glad to see the dawn, Mr Armstrong, sir.' He flexed his stiffened shoulder muscles and shifted the cutlass in his belt to a more comfortable position. 'It's a been very long night.'

The drums and war gongs which had throbbed through the hours of darkness were still audible but, although Armstrong searched diligently with his telescope, he could not locate any visible source of the clamour. Along the nearest beaches he could see long files of uniformed soldiers manoeuvring at the water's edge, carrying banners, pikes and longbows. Marching and countermarching in groups, they appeared to be moving purposefully between the forts on the higher headlands. Other detachments, drawn up in stationary ranks at intervals along the beaches and cliffs, were gazing watchfully towards the ships. The large fleet of guard-boats, which had swarmed around the squadron on its arrival the previous evening, was still standing offshore, fully manned, keeping the warships under surveillance from a distance of three or four hundred yards.

'I've heard a rumour going around among the seamen that we may have lost a man overboard in the night,' continued Midshipman Harris, speaking quietly so as not to be overheard. 'Did you hear anything about that, Mr Armstrong?'

The missionary looked quizzically at the trainee officer, then shook his head. 'No, Mr Harris, I've heard nothing of that.'

After scrutinizing the canvas-shrouded forts on the cliffs one by one, the missionary lifted his glass slowly to inspect the forested hills that rose above the western coastline. Their contours shimmered a deep, thrilling green that contrasted sharply with the frowning escarpments of bare rock rising steeply on either side of the harbour town of Uraga. High in the western heavens, Armstrong suddenly noticed that Mount Fuji towered with great dignity over the whole spectacular scene. In the dawn glare, the cloak of snow blanketing the summit's northern ravines glittered with the brilliance of diamonds, and through his glass old fissures, scoured deeply into its sides by ancient eruptions, were dramatically visible.

'Their sacred mountain is truly magnificent,' sighed the old missionary, lowering the telescope. 'It's the crowning glory of a peerless morning . . .'

At that moment one of the *Susquehanna*'s armed cutters hit the flat water on the starboard side of the ship with a loud smack. Ropes shrieked in their davits and when Armstrong moved forward to look over the side, he saw that the fighting boat was crewed by seamen fully armed with carbines, pistols and cutlasses. Its brass howitzer cannon stood primed in the bows, and raucous shouts of encouragement rang out from those remaining on the ship as the boat settled on the water. Its oarsmen immediately began pulling hard towards the shore, and muffled shouts echoing across the bay made Armstrong aware that other armed cutters had been launched simultaneously from the *Plymouth*, the *Saratoga*and the *Mississippi*. Within a short time the small, aggressive-looking flotilla had formed up and was heading steadily in the direction of the beaches.

'What purpose are the boats to serve, Mr Armstrong, sir?' queried the midshipman, in an alarmed tone. 'Are we making some sort of attack already?'

'I don't know,' replied the missionary, glancing apprehensively towards the quarterdeck. 'But I can see Lieutenant Rice up there at the rail, so I'm going up to find out.'

Retracting his telescope and tucking it away in a pocket, Armstrong hurried up one of the port ladders. When he reached the quarterdeck he found that Rice was following the progress of the cutters closely through his own glass. After greeting him, Armstrong stood patiently beside the officer, watching in silence as the boats continued to move confidently towards the shore.

'Isn't it dangerous to send boats so close to their forces on the beach?' asked the interpreter at last in a worried tone.

'Perhaps, Mr Armstrong,' replied Lieutenant Rice flatly. 'But they're following Commodore Perry's orders to the letter. Do you see what they're doing?'

Armstrong noticed then that a single seaman had risen to his feet in the bows of each craft. At each boat's length these standing men were swinging leads into the water to take depth soundings, while other seamen noted the results on charts spread across their knees. With each sounding, the cutters shifted nearer to the lines of Japanese fighting men watching balefully from the shore.

'This might easily provoke conflict, Lieutenant. Those men on the beach look to me as if they're in a mood for war. Is it really worth such a risk?'

'The commodore has decided to pile on the pressure,' replied Rice shortly. 'It's a very simple tactic.'

'How exactly does he intend to achieve this end?'

Rice continued to study the Japanese movements through his telescope. 'The Japanese are to be told today that we'll land a big invasion column to deliver the President's letter to the Emperor by force, if necessary. So the commodore wants them to see us taking detailed soundings all along the coast. That way they'll know we're making serious preparations to move the squadron further up the bay, to threaten their capital.'

'It's a bold stroke.' Armstrong rubbed his chin thoughtfully. 'But, in my opinion, a very risky one . . .'

A loud warning cry from a lookout on a yard-arm high overhead interrupted the conversation, causing both men to look up sharply. The silhouetted sailor was pointing and gesturing towards a single Japanese boat that was being rowed swiftly towards the *Susquehanna*'s stern. When they turned to scrutinize the craft, both Rice and Armstrong saw that it was filled to the gunwales with civilian Japanese. All without exception were peering intently towards the flagship but they did not appear to be wearing any kind of uniform and there was no sign that they carried any arms.

'How extraordinary,' exclaimed Armstrong, training his telescope on the approaching vessel. 'It looks like it's crowded with artists. They seem to be drawing and painting absolutely everything in sight!'

As the boat came closer, it became unmistakably clear that all those on board were working with a furious energy, recording every visible detail of the looming warships: their masts, sails, paddle-wheels, funnels; their flags, their personnel, and their light and heavy cannon.

Lieutenant Rice quickly summoned a hovering midshipman and despatched him to the main deck with orders for the boat to be warned off with threats. If necessary, he added, a marine detachment should fire a live volley above their heads. Within minutes the Japanese boat was retreating, but the dark heads of its artists remained bent intently over their work as they continued to paint and draw in a controlled frenzy.

'It's obvious we're up against a meticulous people,' murmured Rice as he watched the boat retreat. 'They're not only implacable enemies—they also seem very eager to learn.'

Armstrong nodded in agreement; then another thought struck him and he frowned. 'I've just heard, Lieutenant, that we may have lost a man overboard in the night. That sounds very unfortunate.'

'Where did you hear this rumour, Mr Armstrong?'

'Mr Harris made mention of it.'

Rice remained tight-lipped, peering again towards the shore, and the silence lengthened to a minute or more. 'I want you to treat what I'm about to tell you in absolute confidence, Mr Armstrong,' he said at last. 'No matter what rumours are flying around, the crew is not to be given this information. You must know of it because it will affect your duties.'

'Of course,' responded the missionary, his face suddenly tense with anticipation. 'Who has disappeared?'

'Lieutenant Robert Eden—who I think is very well known to you.'

'Good heavens! I can hardly believe it.'

'Lieutenant Eden failed to take command of his morning watch two hours before dawn,' said Rice grimly, 'so I immediately ordered a search of the ship. His uniform and cap were eventually found hidden beneath some old sails in the stowage area under the fo'c's'le.'

'May the Good Lord preserve him!' gasped Armstrong. 'What on earth could have possessed him . . . ?'

'The Japanese castaway quartered under the fo'c's'le was also found to be absent,' continued Rice, ignoring the interruption. 'And Lieutenant Eden's pistol was missing from his cabin.'

'So he's slipped overboard armed and taken our castaway as his guide,' said Armstrong incredulously. 'Why in heaven's name would he do that?'

'Just after midnight Lieutenant Eden came to my cabin and suggested a secret spying patrol should be sent ashore. He'd been on secret sorties behind enemy lines in Mexico, and believed such a mission might help avoid bloodshed here.' Rice paused and drew a long breath. 'He then volunteered to go alone with the castaway.'

'He's almost bound to be killed!' Armstrong's forehead creased into a frown and he turned to stare towards the forts and the wood-covered hills that stretched inland as far as the eye could see. The throb of the gongs and drums was growing louder again as the US Navy cutters neared the beach and more columns of Japanese fighting men were becoming visible, streaming down from the heights. 'It's hard to believe that he could be so foolhardy. He could start a war single-handed!'

'Maybe he has already,' said Rice heavily.

'Does Commodore Perry know about this?'

'I informed our flagship commander as soon as I was sure that Lieutenant Eden was no longer on board. He went immediately to wake the commodore.'

'I should think steam came out of his ears.' The missionary closed his eyes at the thought. 'This madness could compromise the whole expedition.'

Rice shook his head emphatically. 'It would take more than a moment of madness to deflect Commodore Matthew Calbraith Perry from his great mission. Nothing is to be allowed to stand in the way. His decision was instantaneous—and very simple: Lieutenant Eden is to be officially disowned.'

Armstrong raised his eyebrows in astonishment: 'How?'

'The commodore has directed that, when the Japanese come aboard again, you are to take them into your confidence at an appropriate moment.' Rice paused and lowered his voice. 'After official negotiations are completed, you are to draw aside their interpreter and explain informally that one of our officers has disobeyed orders and left the ship without any authority whatsoever. You're to say we greatly regret this folly and ask their assistance in locating him and bringing him back on board as soon as possible. But you are to explain further that if Eden is harmed or killed during efforts to capture him, they'll receive no protest from us. And tell them too that once he's back on board, he will be placed under close arrest.'

Armstrong let out a long, low whistle. 'And what about our unfortunate Japanese castaway? He'll be in dire danger too.'

'You're to explain that we were bringing him home as an act of compassion and that he also left the jurisdiction of this ship without our permission. Say further that our only wish was to return him unharmed to his homeland. But in view of his disobedience to our orders, his fate is now to be left entirely to their discretion.' Rice paused again and looked Armstrong steadily in the eye. 'Are all those points absolutely clear?'

Armstrong nodded slowly. 'Yes, Lieutenant, you're saying that Robert Eden and Sentaro are really on their own out there now.'

'You may feel the decision is severe,' said Rice vehemently. 'But just because I pass on these orders, don't think I necessarily agree with them. Robert Eden's a good friend of mine . . .'

Armstrong sighed resignedly. 'It's to be greatly regretted—but perhaps there was no alternative course. Eden's actions have been very headstrong.'

'I threatened to clap them both in irons at one point last night,' said Rice fiercely. 'I'm sorry now that I didn't.'

'Don't blame yourself, Lieutenant,' said the missionary in a conciliatory voice. 'You weren't to know. There's nothing to do now but pray for them both—and we might soon need a prayer for ourselves, by the looks of things . . .'

Armstrong took out his telescope again and focused, it on the four Navy cutters that were continuing to forge along the coast. He saw that new phalanxes of scarlet-clad soldiers were marching rapidly along the shore, abreast of the American boats. Some carried brightly coloured banners which they implanted vigorously in the beach at intervals, and the leading ranks were already beginning to embark in a score of empty craft which had been drawn up in readiness at the water's edge.

'It looks as though they intend to intercept us,' breathed Armstrong. 'It will be difficult to avoid a confrontation.'

As they watched, the first Japanese boats formed a disciplined line and moved across the path of the advancing US cutters. Others, as soon as they were launched, began to spread out purposefully in different directions so as to encircle the cutters on all sides. Fast, and identical in design to the guard-boats which had first approached the American warships, these new craft were rowed with a speed and confidence which suggested that they were carrying out well-rehearsed war manoeuvres.

'At the very least this will be a severe test of our resolve,' grunted Rice, watching intently through his own glass. 'The officers on our cutters have instructions not to flinch.'

At that moment orders shouted by the lieutenants commanding the four cutters rang simultaneously across the quiet water. In response, the US seamen were seen to back their oars and snatch up their carbines. With deliberate ostentation they adjusted the caps on the weapons and held them at the ready across their laps.

Silence returned to the bay for a second or two before another order rang out, followed by a sharp flurry of noise as the American oarsmen clamped steel bayonets to the muzzles of their carbines. With the Japanese fighting boats closing in swiftly all around them, the broad, knife-shaped bayonets flashed like tiny mirrors in the bright morning sunlight.

'What orders do our officers on the cutters carry?' asked Armstrong, still holding his telescope jammed against his eye. 'How far are they to go?'

'They've been directed to row four miles up the bay,' grunted Rice. 'Soundings are to be taken all the way. And they're not to turn back or retreat until summoned by the firing of a gun from this flagship.'

The leading American cutter was moving slowly again, nosing closer to the line of Japanese military boats blocking its passage. Only half of its seamen were now rowing; the remainder were cradling their carbines in readiness for use. As the cutter approached them, forests of spears bristled suddenly from the Japanese boats, and Armstrong drew in his breath sharply, seeing that a collision was imminent.

'We need a miracle,' he gasped. 'Surely to God we need a miracle!'

The bows of the first cutter launched from the *Susquehanna* scraped against the side of one Japanese boat, drawing furious shouts of anger from its crew. They brandished their spears more angrily and in response the American seamen lifted their carbines to their shoulders. The shouting from the Japanese grew louder, and with frenzied gestures they indicated that the cutter should turn back. But its commander, now standing belligerently in the stern, continued to urge his rowers on and, by skilful use of the tiller at the last possible moment, he nudged his craft cautiously through the defensive line of guard-boats into open water.

The three accompanying cutters quickly followed and all the American boats spurted ahead again. Amidst howls of anger, the Japanese boats turned and began sculling furiously after them. More craft were being launched from the shore, and the growing Japanese flotilla began fanning out swiftly across the bay to form another defensive line. Amongst the growing throng of boats it was becoming difficult to keep the cutters fully in view from the deck of the *Susquehanna*, and Armstrong shook his head in alarm.

'They won't let our boats escape a second time, Lieutenant,' he said in a worried voice. 'Isn't it time to fire the recall gun?'

A new shout from the lookout in the rigging high above them made them turn their heads. A mile away another fast Japanese craft, propelled by half-naked standing oarsmen, had come into view, heading rapidly out of Uraga harbour. As they watched, it turned its prow in the direction of the *Susquehanna* and increased speed.

'Don't be too sure, Mr Armstrong,' said Rice, studying this new arrival carefully through his telescope. 'It seems the Japanese might be more anxious to parley again than we are.'

Armstrong watched the official boat with renewed hope as it drew steadily nearer. A diminutive, straight-backed Japanese, wearing a dazzling robe of turquoise silk edged with silver and gold, was seated amidships. On his head a black-lacquered bonnet gleamed in the sun, and when the boat pulled alongside the flagship, Armstrong could see that the official's robe was embroidered with the design of a great peacock. Its tail was spread in a brilliant, multicoloured fan and the richness of the decoration as well as the official's exceptionally haughty demeanour suggested he was of a higher rank than previous negotiators.

'We appear to have a visitor of greater standing today,' said Armstrong, relief showing in his voice. 'How is he to be received?'

'All negotiations must be conducted in the same arm's-length fashion,' said Rice, watching the boat manoeuvre towards the gangway. 'Commodore Perry will continue to stay out of sight until a Japanese envoy of the very highest rank is produced. I will represent him as before, and we'll use our midshipmen as messengers again, so that he can control all aspects of the negotiations from his cabin. Please take your time with translations, to assist this process.'

Armstrong attempted hastily to order his tousled grey hair with his fingers; then, as best he could, he straightened his loosely knotted cravat and prepared to descend to the head of the gangway by which the Japanese would come aboard. 'Are we able to offer any small concession to lighten the atmosphere? Are we to offer them any accommodation at all?'

'Commodore Perry has given us permission to show them the original letter from our President, if that seems useful,' replied Rice, summoning a midshipman to his side with a quick gesture. 'They'll be allowed to see the official seal, and the rosewood box in which it's contained.'

'Is that all?' asked Armstrong in a disappointed voice.

'Yes, that's all.' Rice turned away briefly to issue orders to the midshipman, who immediately dashed off down the ladders to the main deck. 'Our standpoint otherwise will be firmer, and more uncompromising than ever.'

'Shouldn't we at least concede something small to help salvage their pride?' insisted Armstrong. 'Perhaps make some gesture of a conciliatory nature.'

'That's not Commodore Perry's intention,' replied Rice, shaking his head. 'We are instructed to remain polite, but very firm. I've just ordered a marine detachment to stand guard at the top of the gangway for greater security. No Japanese escort wearing a sword will be allowed aboard this time. We must all increase our vigilance—so explain that even ceremonial weapons must be left in their boat.'

'Very well, Lieutenant,' replied the missionary, his face serious. 'I'll do as you ask. But I hope Commodore Perry is not overplaying his hand. A cornered rat, if left no room for retreat, will often fly for the throat of an attacker many times its own size.'

Seeing that the Japanese boat had been made fast at the foot of the gangway, Samuel Armstrong squared his shoulders and drew a deep breath. Turning quickly on his heel, he hurried down from the quarterdeck to supervise the reception of the haughty Japanese envoy and his entourage.

23

'Our distinguished fguest identifies himself as His Excellency, Gudai Kasawara, the Governor of Uraga,' proclaimed Samuel Armstrong, enunciating his English translation with a sonorous gravity. 'And his first and most pressing question is: what are those four American armed cutters doing so close to the shores of Nippon?'

'Tell His Excellency first of all that he is most welcome aboard this flagship of the United States Navy,' replied Lieutenant Rice in his most formal tone. 'And secondly inform him that, at first light, our boats commenced a detailed survey of the harbours and anchorages of Yedo Bay. Thirdly, say this survey is being carried out because it may very soon become necessary for our squadron of warships to steam up the bay and anchor broadside on before his capital city.'

Armstrong translated the flag lieutenant's words into Dutch, and listened and watched carefully as the same scholarly-looking interpreter who had accompanied the first delegation conveyed their meaning to the stony-faced dignitary. As before, the two groups were facing one another warily in the restricted confines of the captain's cabin, and Flag Lieutenant Rice, who was wearing his full dress uniform for the occasion, had placed his black cocked hat and sword formally on the table at which he sat. Behind him Harris and two other midshipmen were standing rigidly to attention, flanked by four fully armed marine guards and, to emphasize his position of intermediary, Armstrong had seated himself at the table's end. The Governor of Uraga was accompanied by four new civilian officials, in addition to the interpreter, Haniwara Tokuma, who this time had introduced himself to Armstrong on arrival. All the visiting officials were seated stiffly on straight-backed ship's chairs and as soon as he had understood the response to his query, the Japanese governor rapped out words that the Americans recognized as a protest even before they were interpreted.

'His Excellency insists that the laws of Nippon expressly forbid foreign vessels to make such surveys,' said Armstrong uneasily. 'He also demands that our vessels cease this activity immediately.'

At a nod from Lieutenant Rice, Midshipman Harris hurried from the cabin, leaving the remaining participants facing one another in an uncomfortable silence. As the cadet officer's footsteps echoed across the floor planks of the wardroom, the Governor of Uraga remained ramrod straight on his chair, his narrow eyes focused, like those of his supporters, on the oak panelling behind the Americans. In the absence of conversation, the incessant throb of war drums and gongs from the shore seemed more menacing, and the quiet closing of a cabin door and the rapid return of Midshipman Harris's footsteps came as a welcome relief to the waiting Americans. On re-entering, Harris moved to Lieutenant Rice's side and whispered urgently in his ear.

'I must inform His Excellency the Governor that American laws compel us to make such surveys,' said Rice when the midshipman had resumed his place. 'And we are as much bound to obey the laws of America as the Japanese people are bound to obey the laws of Japan.'

'Is it your intention to make landings from these boats?' asked the governor anxiously through his interpreter. 'Are you planning to put men ashore?'

Lieutenant Rice shook his head firmly and looked towards Armstrong. 'Tell His Excellency that the commodore has no plans to land armed personnel—at present. And emphasize very specially those final words *at present*. Remind him, too, that our sole mission is to deliver a letter from the President of the United States, and to see that it is received with appropriate dignity by a personal representative of His Imperial Majesty, the Emperor of Japan. And that means at least a high minister of cabinet rank.'

Armstrong hesitated before beginning the interpretation, and leaned close enough to the flag lieutenant's ear to speak in an undertone. 'Might it be advisable now to give His Excellency a moment's pause? Could we not suggest that he may send a member of his entourage ashore to inform the defence forces that our men are merely making a survey, and have clear orders not to land? That might help defuse the tension—and perhaps save lives . . .'

The flag lieutenant considered the suggestion for a moment, then nodded quickly. 'Yes, that would be wise, Mr Armstrong. Tell them the commodore wishes to confirm that there will be no landings for the present—while we await a decision about delivery of the President's letter. But phrase your reply very clearly . . . And be sure to re-state the paramount aims of our mission in no uncertain terms.'

After Armstrong had conveyed the officer's reply, a flurry of whispered discussion followed among the Japanese. Then Haniwara Tokuma, who had been making notes on a small table, straightened in his chair. 'His Excellency welcomes your solemn agreement not to make any landings on the sacred soil of Nippon from your longboats,' he said slowly. 'Furthermore we do wish to take this opportunity to despatch one of our officials to convey this information to those defending our shores.'

The interpreter paused as one of the governor's silk-gowned acolytes rose hurriedly from his chair. Upon a whispered order from Lieutenant Rice, one of the junior midshipmen moved forward to escort the official from the cabin. When their footsteps on the ladders had died away, Haniwara glanced nervously towards the American officer, then took a deep breath and continued.

'But His Excellency the Governor has been instructed to make one further point clear to you. Under the laws of Nippon, it is impossible to receive your letter from the President of the United States at the town of Uraga. Even if that were possible, any answer would be sent to Nagasaki. Nagasaki is the port where, under our laws, all dealings with foreign countries must take place. Therefore the squadron of United States warships must immediately leave Yedo Bay and proceed to Nagasaki!'

Rice shook his head grimly to indicate immediate rejection of the point, but offered no comment. Instead, he again motioned for Midshipman Harris to convey the essence of the Japanese statement swiftly to the commodore.

'They are only repeating in stronger terms what was first said yesterday, Lieutenant,' whispered Armstrong. 'Perhaps it might be appropriate at this point to offer our visitors a sight of the President's letter.' He paused and gestured with his head towards the gleaming rosewood casket, decorated with elaborate gold filigree, that rested on a side table. 'Its splendour may be seen as a compliment—it might perhaps have some palliative effect.'

The lieutenant nodded quickly in compliance, and Armstrong rose to pick up the casket. Unfastening its golden clasp, he opened the elegant container and held it out towards Gudai Kasawara.

'Your Excellency, you might like to see the original letter addressed respectfully to His Imperial Majesty the Emperor of Nippon,' said Armstrong politely, tilting the casket sufficiently to reveal its contents. 'You will see it is written in the finest hand on gilded vellum, and is signed by President Millard Fillmore himself. It is also embossed with the Great Seal of the United States in gold, and housed in this silk-lined casket of rosewood that has been specially created for the occasion by one of our finest craftsmen.'

As they listened to their own interpreter, the governor and his supporters gazed suspiciously at the ornate box and its letter; but beneath their bonnets of shiny black lacquer, their impassive faces betrayed no obvious reaction.

'To assist you, we have provided copies and official translations in Dutch, Chinese and English,' continued Armstrong affably, waving an arm towards sealed packages on the side table. 'The copies will be handed over to you for your study well in advance—once arrangements have been agreed for the formal presentation of the original letter.'

'Perhaps you could help His Excellency by translating some extracts from the letter,' suggested the Japanese interpreter tentatively, peering at the document with his pen poised above his writing tablet. 'That would be of very considerable assistance.'

After receiving permission from Lieutenant Rice, Armstrong tilted the rosewood casket towards a shaft of light filtering through an overhead hatch. 'After sending formal greetings to His Imperial Majesty, the President says, "Our steamships can now go from California to Japan in eighteen days and if Your Imperial Majesty were to change the ancient laws of your land so as to allow free trade between our two countries, it would be extremely beneficial to both . . . It also sometimes happens in stormy weather that one of our many ships is wrecked on Your Imperial Majesty's shores. In all such cases we ask and expect that our unfortunate people would be treated with kindness, and that their property should be protected till we can send a vessel and bring them away . . . We are very much in earnest in this . . ."'

As he wrote swiftly on his tablet, the interpreter was murmuring a quiet translation into Japanese. Around him the faces of the governor and his supporters showed that they were concentrating intently on every word.

'The President further says, "We understand there is a great abundance of coal and provisions in the Empire of Japan . . . We wish that our steamships and other vessels should be allowed to stop in Japan and supply themselves with coal, provisions and water. They will pay for them in money, or anything else Your Imperial Majesty's subjects may prefer. We also request Your Imperial Majesty to appoint a convenient port in the southern part of the Empire where our vessels may stop for this purpose . . ."'

Armstrong paused to give the Japanese interpreter time to catch up, then gestured towards the foot of the letter, indicating he was drawing to a conclusion.

'Therefore, to summarize, the President concludes by saying, "The following are the only objects for which I have sent Commodore Perry, with a powerful squadron, to pay a visit to Your Imperial Majesty's renowned city of Yedo: friendship, commerce, a supply of coal and provisions, and protection for our shipwrecked people . . . And we are very desirous of obtaining all these things—'"

Armstrong broke off as a sudden flurry of footsteps heralded the return of Midshipman Harris from the commodore's cabin. When he entered, he was seen to be carrying a single sheet of paper bearing several lines of writing in a firm, bold hand. After placing the paper before the flag lieutenant, the midshipman resumed his position behind the table.

'We wish now to respond formally to your insistent demand that our warships proceed at once to Nagasaki,' said Rice, looking hard at the Governor of Uraga. 'And we would make three very important points. Firstly, we would inform you that our commander-in-chief, Commodore Matthew Calbraith Perry, will never consent under any circumstances to such an arrangement. And, secondly, be assured he intends to persist without any letup in his duty, to deliver the President's letter to your esteemed Emperor right here in the Bay of Yedo.' Rice paused and waited for Armstrong to make the translation; when he had finished he resumed very slowly, to emphasize the gravity of the final point. 'Lastly, if no person of suitable rank is appointed to receive the letter, our commander-in-chief will land at the head of a sufficient force of armed men, and march on Yedo castle. There he will deliver the letter personally—no matter what the consequences of this action might be!'

A tense silence descended on the cabin as soon as the third point was translated. None of the Japanese spoke, and their immobile faces betrayed no emotion; but the sudden stiffness of their postures conveyed more clearly than words the inner sense of affront and apprehension they were experiencing.

'In view of all that you have said, I will return to Uraga now,' said the governor at last in a distant tone. 'It will be necessary for me to send a communication to Yedo and seek further instructions before these discussions can continue.'

'Very well,' replied Lieutenant Rice, nodding agreeably. 'We will, of course, await your answer with much interest.'

'It will take at least four days to obtain a reply,' added the governor, a note of defiance entering his voice. 'Perhaps longer.'

Rice frowned and motioned with his head to Harris once more, and the senior midshipman immediately left the cabin. 'I should perhaps inform Your Excellency,' he said, turning back to the governor, 'that not much more than one hour's steaming will take our warships within sight of Yedo. The distance is no more than thirty miles. Four days seem an unduly long time to obtain instructions.'

'It will take four days,' repeated the governor stubbornly. 'That is the necessary time for a proper exchange of messages.'

The midshipman returned rapidly with another sheet of paper, on which only a few words were written, and handed it to Lieutenant Rice.

'Our commodore will grant you *three* days to obtain a reply, no more,' said Rice brusquely. 'We will expect a communication from you no later than Tuesday, the twelfth of July. Until then, no further visitors from Nippon will be welcome aboard this flagship. And furthermore, with this statement, these discussions are hereby concluded.'

As soon as he had finished speaking, Rice rose to his feet, picked up his hat and sword and waited while the governor and his officials were ushered from the cabin by the midshipmen. Samuel Armstrong followed them up to the spar deck and, by the entry port, he drew the interpreter quietly aside.

'Haniwara-san, I would like to advise you informally of one further detail,' said the American missionary, speaking Dutch in a confiding undertone. 'During the night one of our younger officers disappeared from this ship.'

The Japanese interpreter looked startled. He glanced quickly towards the shore, where the American cutters were continuing to make their soundings, shadowed closely by the Japanese flotilla. A discernible tension still surrounded the manoeuvring of the boats but both sides, for the time being at least, had clearly pulled back from the brink of conflict.

'Has this officer you speak of fallen overboard and drowned?' asked the Japanese, turning to look at Armstrong again.

The missionary shook his head decisively. 'That's unlikely. In defiance of our strictest orders, he seems to have swum ashore. We also had on board a Japanese fisherman who was shipwrecked some years ago and taken to America by a passing vessel. We were bringing him home. He too has disappeared from this ship.'

A shadow of suspicion appeared in the eyes of the interpreter, and his voice hardened. 'Your officer has gone ashore to spy on the people of Nippon! You wish only to mislead us!'

'No, quite the contrary—I'm telling you the truth,' continued Armstrong patiently. 'His disappearance is most unfortunate. Because he has acted foolishly, and without authority, we seek your assistance in tracing him and restoring him under restraint to this ship.'

'If he has gone ashore, he will be found by our fighting men,' said the interpreter nervously. 'And without any question he will be killed.'

Armstrong hesitated, frowning, then spoke with an obvious reluctance. 'I am instructed to say further that if our officer is harmed in any way during your attempts to capture him, or even if he meets his death, no protest whatsoever will be made by us.'

The interpreter's eyes narrowed in surprise as he absorbed the significance of Armstrong's words. The Governor of Uraga had already descended the gang-ladder and was now seated in the boat below with the rest of his entourage. Seeing this, Haniwara made a sudden move towards the entry port.

'I shall convey what you have told me to our authorities,' he said coolly. 'But I fear they will regard this as a very serious matter—and not one where leniency is appropriate.'

Armstrong laid a hand politely on the arm of the Japanese to restrain him. 'What I've told you so far, sir, I was asked to say officially. But I would like to make one last personal plea . . .'

'Please be quick,' said Haniwara uncomfortably, aware that all eyes in the boat below were upon them. 'We are delaying the governor's departure.'

'Our missing lieutenant is somewhat impetuous, and very idealistic,' continued Armstrong in an urgent whisper. 'But he's a fine young man. He has learned something of your language and at this time of great danger for us all I believe he thought by going ashore he could somehow prevent fighting between our countries. His name is Eden, Lieutenant Eden, and I ask you to urge that his rashness be looked on with compassion—and above all please try to ensure that his life is spared . . .'

'I can give you no such undertaking,' replied Haniwara distantly, drawing away and turning towards the ladder. 'No barbarian spy can go undiscovered for long among the people of Nippon . . . It's probably already too late to save the life of your Lieutenant Eden.'

24

Long caravans of packhorses laden with rice and vegetables climbed slowly up a steep, zigzag trail that wound through a wooded ravine thirty miles south of Mount Fuji. The animals, roped together nose and tail, sometimes stumbled under the weight of the produce as they toiled up the long scarp; their teams of drivers, who were transporting supplies to the growing hordes of fighting men lining Yedo Bay, were shouting loudly and from time to time they flailed at the hindquarters of the horses with slender bamboo switches to urge them on.

The ravine rang repeatedly with the cries of the drivers and the neighing of the animals but, inside a shallow cave that opened onto a ledge eighty feet above their heads, Robert Eden heard nothing of the noise; stretched full-length on a rough bed of ferns which he had cut from the nearby woodland, he was sleeping soundly, his head resting on a bundle of clothing. He lay on his back with one arm flung across the makeshift pillow in an easy, relaxed posture and although the sinking sun was beginning to dapple his face through overhanging foliage, he slept on, oblivious to his surroundings.

He still did not stir, even when a crouching man moved silently into the mouth of the cave, casting a shadow slantwise across his body. Small and lithe in build, the man was wearing a broad straw hat, and he looked down at the sleeping figure of the American in silence. Twenty or thirty yards away, Eden's tethered horse was quietly pulling at the sparse clumps of grass that sprouted around the foot of the rocks. Pricking its ears, the horse raised its head to listen to the sound of the packhorses passing below the ledge; but it paid no attention to the crouching man's presence, and soon resumed its contented cropping of the grass.

As the man ducked down to move inside the low-roofed cave, his shadow fell across Eden's face, and in that instant the American awoke with a start. Because the sun was shining into his eyes, he saw only a dark silhouette of head and shoulders close before him and with a stifled exclamation of surprise he rolled himself away towards the back of the cave, groping frantically for his sword.

'Keep your distance!' snarled Eden in Japanese, struggling to his knees and raising the sword in his right hand. 'Who are you?'

'It's all right, master! It is only me—your friend Sentaro!'

'Sentaro!' Eden exhaled explosively in relief and threw down his sword. 'What are you doing here?'

The former castaway bowed low, his face distraught. 'Forgive me, master, for disobeying you. When I watched you ride away into the moonlight, I meant to return to the ship—but, soon after I started out, I knew I couldn't go on. So I turned round and rode after you . . .'

Eden shook his head in disbelief, but his face showed no anger.

'I followed you all the time and left my horse higher up the hillside to watch this cave while you slept. And with the silver coins you gave me, I went to buy a new hat for myself and food for us both. Look! Eggs and rice and pickled cucumber . . .' He held out the food wrapped in large green palm leaves. 'You must be hungry, master.'

Eden smiled slowly and nodded. 'Yes, I'm very hungry.'

'Then eat, master, now.' Sentaro placed the food eagerly on the floor of the cave in front of him. 'I have also brought some feed for our horses. It is still quite a long journey to Fuji-san.'

'What made you decide to follow me?' asked Eden, beginning to eat. 'You could have been safely on board the *Susquehanna* by now.'

The castaway thought for a long time in silence before replying. 'I think I felt ashamed suddenly. . . .'

'Why ashamed?'

'This is my country, master, which I love! This is my country which I have been away from for too many years—and I was running back to your ship like a frightened rabbit to sail back to America without even seeing my family. And although the odds against you were great, *you* were bravely riding towards Fuji-san . . . I felt ashamed because *you* were showing courage, and I was being a terrible coward.'

'That isn't true, Sentaro,' said Eden quietly. 'And you know it.'

'It *is* true, master! You made me think very hard—and I realized it was *me* who should be climbing Fuji-san to pray to the great *kami*—before going home to Yurutaki!'

'So you've decided to risk going home after all?'

'Yes, master, but only after I have climbed our most sacred mountain myself. As I watched you ride off I knew deep inside me it was best for me to go to Fuji-san too—to give thanks for my safe return and to beg the greatest *kami* of all to protect my future life here . . .'

Eden looked at the castaway, searching his face for signs of doubt; but this time he saw none. 'If your mind is really made up, Sentaro, it will be good to have you with me on the climb.'

The castaway nodded. 'My mind *is* made up, master—and at peace with itself for the first time in many years! Your example inspired me. I know truly now what I wish to do.'

Eden ate in silence for a while, looking thoughtful. Through the branches which overhung the mouth of the cave, the hills and the plain above which Mount Fuji towered were clearly visible in the pale evening sunlight. The daytime haze that often shrouded the volcano was beginning to fade, and a blurred outline of the high peak was becoming more apparent as the sun sank towards the horizon; but in partial obscurity the cone itself again seemed curiously small and distant.

'How far are we now from Fuji-san?' asked Eden quietly. 'It seems to have moved further away.'

'From here, perhaps twenty *ri*—about thirty American miles.'

'Then we can reach the foot of the mountain under the cover of darkness. And begin our climb tomorrow.'

'Yes, master.' Sentaro grinned his approval. 'It was good that you found a place to hide and rest before the full heat of the day. You will need all your strength on Fuji-san.'

'I slept much longer than I intended.'

'But that is good too. While you slept I found the best route forward from here. For safety's sake we should wait until darkness falls before we continue . . .'

Eden nodded his agreement, then gestured towards the food and looked up enquiringly at the castaway.

'No thank you, master. I have taken food myself. That is for you.'

'You seem to have been very busy today. Have you slept?'

Sentaro shook his head and grinned again. 'A Japanese fisherman, master, learns to sleep whenever he can. There was no time today.'

'Then sleep for an hour or two now. I'll keep watch, and feed the horses.' Eden gestured towards the soft heap of ferns. 'Take my luxury bed. It's very comfortable.'

He watched Sentaro stretch out on the ferns before turning away to squat at the mouth of the cave. He carefully scanned the zigzag track, up which more packhorse trains were straining, and spent several minutes making certain that nothing had attracted attention to their high, half-hidden shelter. Then, turning westward, he witnessed by chance the instant when the faint, daylong haze around Fuji cleared finally, and the majesty of the solitary violet cone re-etched itself with a dramatic sharpness against a sky beginning to flush rose-pink behind it.

Awestruck by this new example of the mountain's extraordinary and ever-changing beauty, Eden continued to squat on his haunches staring at the hypnotic vision until he he heard Sentaro's breathing become deep and even in sleep. Then he rose and slipped quietly away along the ridge to tend the two horses which would carry them through the night to the start of their climb.

25

At that same moment the plangent notes of a *samisen*, plucked by the graceful kneeling figure of Matsumura Tokiwa, were reverberating softly through an open-sided pavilion thirty miles away to the south-east. In front of it, a small garden blended formal paved paths with groups of smooth rocks and dwarf trees; a miniature waterfall splashed into a carp pool spanned by an arched wooden bridge, and songbirds housed in tiny bamboo cages were beginning to sing sweetly to welcome the dusk. Designed with meticulous precision, the artificial garden had been constructed as a frame for the distant sunset image of Mount Fuji, which rose in perfect symmetry above the bridge. Prince Tanaka Yoshio of the southern Kago clan was seated cross-legged beside the pavilion's open screens, fanning himself and gazing in meditative silence towards the volcano.

'Our sacred peak has a different look this evening,' he said suddenly, without turning his head. 'Something has changed.'

'In what way, O Kami-san?' asked Tokiwa, plucking the strings of her instrument more softly.

'Tonight the proud blush of sunset on its virgin snows looks more like a blush of shame!'

Tokiwa was kneeling on the soft green tatami beside a small central table, the three-stringed instrument resting in her lap. Arrayed now in the full costume of the geisha, her face was whitened with delicate rice powder to accentuate the lines of her eyes and mouth, and her glossy black hair was elaborately coiffured high on her head in the traditional 'split peach' style. She was wearing an embroidered *haori* cloak over a blue-flowered summer kimono, and she stiffened slightly on hearing his words; but she did not raise her eyes, nor pause in her gentle, wistful playing.

'Do you understand my meaning?' asked Tanaka with sudden vehemence, turning from his contemplation of the mountain to look at her. 'Do you know why I see shame in this sunset?'

She continued plucking the *samisen* but, because she sensed what was coming, she did not reply or raise her head to look at him.

'Give me an answer, O Tokiwa-san,' he commanded after an interval. 'I asked you a question.'

'I expect, O Kami-san, what you see is connected in your mind with Nippon's helplessness against the ships of the foreign barbarians,' she said uncertainly. 'Perhaps it would be good to unburden yourself of those feelings in the writing of a *haiku*.'

She stopped playing and laid her instrument aside. Rising to her feet, she picked up from the table a small tray that held an inkstone, a brush, a tiny porcelain container of water and a tablet block of white paper suitable for practising the art of calligraphy. Without making a sound she crossed the pavilion, bowed formally, and knelt to set the tray down beside him on the tatami. With deft speed she mixed ink on the stone, arranged the writing tablet in front of him, and dipped a brush ready for his use. She bowed again, and was rising to retreat to her place by the table when he reached out suddenly and seized her by the wrist.

'What you say is only partly true!'

As he stared at her, his face was expressionless, but his glittering eyes revealed that he was struggling inwardly with a mixture of angry emotions. He was dressed in a kimono of yellow silk, over which he wore a shorter black jacket with wide, stiffened shoulders. A brown sash circled his waist, and on his feet he wore a pair of plaited straw *zóri* edged with gold thread. He had laid aside his long sword on entering the pavilion a few minutes earlier, but now that she was closer to him she could see that the short sword which he retained at his left hip was protruding slightly from its sharkskin scabbard.

'Do you know why it is only partly true?' he asked quietly, still moving his fan back and forth with his other hand, so that the stirred air entered his looped sleeves. 'Do you understand my thoughts at all?'

He pulled her closer to himself, and she saw that his narrow sash was only slackly tied. His bare chest was visible within the loose folds of the kimono, indicating that he wore nothing beneath it and, when he tightened his grip on her wrist, she felt the physical tension in him. But still she said nothing, waiting instead in silence for him to continue, her head partly bowed.

'Since you don't answer, O Tokiwa-san, I will tell you,' he continued fiercely. 'It is *your* actions that have helped me to see shame in the sunset over Fuji-san!'

'You are hurting me, O Kami-san,' whispered Tokiwa, closing her eyes and wincing. 'Please let go.'

He relaxed his grasp a little, but he did not free her arm. Breathing quickly, he continued to stare at her, his eyes glittering more fiercely than before.

'I find you lying in a barn at night in the embrace of a foreign barbarian! I find you almost entirely unclothed! Is it surprising that I should feel anger at the shame you bring on us? Is it surprising that my grip is fierce?'

Tokiwa lifted her head, but she did not face him, and she kept her eyes resolutely closed. The tinkling of the miniature waterfall in the garden outside and the trill of the caged songbirds floated gently into the pavilion, but only his uneven breathing broke the grim silence that otherwise surrounded them.

'Did you . . .' he began, but broke off, his demeanour uneasy. The silence between them lengthened once more; then he took another deep breath. 'Did you . . . unfasten your sash for the foreign barbarian? Or did I arrive in time to prevent that?'

Tears squeezed themselves suddenly from beneath her closed eyelids, and coursed down her powdered cheeks. But she did not move, and continued to kneel in the same straight-backed posture, her head held carefully erect.

'You are still hurting my wrist, O Kami-san,' she whispered. 'Please let me go.'

He released her with a sharp gesture, and sat back, continuing to fan himself with quick, agitated movements.

'Answer my question now, O Tokiwa-san,' he demanded in an ominously low voice. 'And be sure to tell me the truth!'

'The past two days . . . have been a time of great confusion and upheaval, O Kami-san,' she began unsteadily after another long silence. 'I have been afraid and bewildered, like many other women of Nippon. But, remember, I did not seek to place myself in the position where you found me. There was much fear in my heart, for many reasons. And there was much turmoil and shouting in the darkness. At times I was engulfed by doubts and confusion. Events happened by chance and ill fortune. Remembering that, you must judge me as you will . . .'

'You are not answering me,' snapped Tanaka. 'You are evading the question!'

'Your question conceals a dagger within, O Kami-san,' replied Tokiwa softly, dropping her eyes once more. 'I cannot answer in any other way without wounding myself upon the dagger in your eyes.'

'You have not told me whether the foreign barbarian bade you to undo your sash—or himself forced its undoing!'

Tokiwa lifted her head to look at him again, her expression uncertain. Then, as she spoke, tears brimmed again in her eyes and she spoke with a sudden impassioned intensity.

'I was far from Yedo and the Yoshiwara pleasure district, O Kami-san, where I first had the good fortune to entertain your noble self. But, as you know, there I have also entertained countless men of Nippon with dancing and songs and the playing of the *samisen*. I shall probably entertain many more in the future . . .'

'This is a different matter,' interrupted Tanaka angrily. 'You seem to misunderstand deliberately.'

'No, that is not true. Last night I was exhausted, and wearing the muddied cotton clothes of a peasant girl in the darkness of a region very strange to me. There were rumours that the foreign barbarians were great monsters. There were rumours that the black ships were smoking volcanoes! I had travelled many *ri* on foot—the second journey in two nights forced on me by their arrival . . .'

'If you had stayed at the *yadoya*, you would have been safe!'

'I have already told you, O Kami-san, I was afraid there.' She raised her shoulders in a gesture of helplessness. 'I felt abandoned and alone. I didn't know if there would be war, if you would return safely—or ever. I was frightened I would be left at the mercy of your guards. That's why I fled.'

'You did not seem to be unhappy to find yourself at the mercy of a foreign barbarian in a deserted barn!' said Tanaka sharply.

Tokiwa stifled a sob. 'I didn't expect to encounter a barbarian. He came ashore secretly in the darkness . . .'

Tanaka stood up suddenly, grasping the hilt of his short sword. 'I have listened to enough of your evasions! Tell me now what happened. Did you undo your sash for him—or did he force you to do so?'

Without looking, Tokiwa could feel that he was poised for action and she choked back her tears. 'Neither, O Kami-san! I didn't unfasten my sash for him. And he did not have time to force me to do so.' She kept her eyes averted, and began to tremble for fear that he would see through her lie. 'You arrived just in time to prevent it.'

'Are you quite sure you're telling me the truth?' He took a step nearer, leaning angrily down towards her. 'You seem much afraid.'

'I am telling you the whole truth, O Kami-san.' She glanced up imploringly. 'Please believe me. I am trembling because your anger is so frightening.'

He gazed back fiercely at her, his right hand whitening on the hilt of his sword—then slowly it relaxed. 'Very well! You have given me your answer.'

'Thank you, O Kami-san,' she whispered. 'I am grateful that you have understood.'

'I'm *not* sure that I've understood you fully, O Tokiwa-san,' he said, uncertainty still apparent in his eyes. 'Only you can truly know the meaning of your thoughts and deeds.'

'I was numb with shock when the barbarian appeared, O Kami-san,' she said tearfully. 'I can see now it would have been wiser if I could have found some way to run away from him too . . .'

Her shoulders shook again as she wept in relief and he stood looking at her in silence, noting the slender paleness of her neck, the swell of her breasts and the curve of her thighs outlined by the tightly drawn swathes of her kimono. As the moments passed, the gleam of anger in his eyes gave way gradually to the light of desire, and he laid aside his sword and his fan.

'Let us cease this discussion for the moment, O Tokiwa-san,' he said. 'Your tears make your beauty impossible to resist. I bid you to unfasten your sash now—for me.'

After a moment's hesitation, she shrugged out of her *haori* and reached behind her back to undo her broad sash. Still trembling, she drew open the front of the kimono and arranged its folds so that the soft contours of her body were mistily visible beneath the pale white gauze of her undergarment. When she had settled herself again, she raised her tear-stained face to look at him and found he was gazing at her with an expression of fierce longing in his eyes. Still holding her gaze, he untied his own sash and knelt on the tatami beside her.

'You may undress me now, O Tokiwa-san,' he commanded in a whisper, letting his own kimono fall open. 'And make yourself naked quickly, too!'

Tokiwa brushed tears from her cheek with the back of her hand and moved obediently towards him. She reached out to take hold of his outer jacket, then paused.

'What is it?' he asked impatiently. 'Did you not hear what I said?'

Tokiwa lowered her eyes again. 'I heard you, O Kami-san, and it is my pleasure and my duty to obey—but you haven't informed me yet why we've broken our journey at this place. I still feel uneasy in my heart, and I would like you to explain.'

'This castle belongs to a nobleman friendly to my clan,' said Tanaka quickly. 'You are quite safe here and you may remain in this pavilion as long as you wish. You will be well cared for by experienced maids, and you won't be disturbed by any guards.'

'But I believed we were returning to Yedo!'

'A messenger has recently brought news from Yedo. It's not yet safe to return to the capital because the foreign barbarians have threatened to land an armed force and to march on Yedo castle.'

'So the city and all its people are still in danger?'

He nodded quickly. 'Yes—and disputes are still raging about how we should best defend ourselves. There's more bitterness than ever between the group who want to attack the black ships immediately, and those of us who want time to build up our strength.'

'Then how long must I stay here?' asked Tokiwa anxiously.

'Until this crisis has passed. It's impossible to say more.'

'If I must stay, O Kami-san, may I ask you a favour?'

'What is it?'

'That Eiko, the maid from the *yadoya*, be brought here as my personal servant. I fear she might be maltreated for trying to help me. I know she would feel happier here with me.'

Tanaka considered the request for a moment. 'She has not been maltreated. But I will fetch her if it will comfort you.'

She bowed her head formally then raised her eyes to his once more, an expression of surprise spreading across her face. 'Am I also being kept here, O Kami-san, because I know about the presence of the foreign barbarian?'

Tanaka sat up straighter on the matting, a flicker of unease in his expression betraying the fact that he was taken aback by her question.

'What I've already told you is the truth, O Tokiwa-san,' he said quietly. 'There is danger for you in Yedo.'

'But it would be dangerous also for you—if your enemies knew about the foreign barbarian. Wouldn't they condemn you for allowing a foreign spy to go free?'

'We should not discuss the subject further,' snapped Tanaka. 'There might have been some danger, if the foreign barbarian had not returned to his ship. But it is my wish that you should never speak of this to anyone. Is that clear?'

'Yes, O Kami-san,' she said meekly. 'It's quite clear.'

They looked at each other in silence for a moment.

'I have already given you permission to disrobe me,' he said in an urgent undertone. 'I do not wish to wait any longer.'

After lowering her head in a formal bow she reached out with both hands to slip the stiff, half-jacket from his shoulders. She felt his body tense as she took hold of the front edges of the yellow silk kimono and drew it apart, baring his chest. But before removing it altogether, she paused and looked enquiringly at him.

'And what will happen, O Kami-san, when this crisis is over? You know well our liaison is already a subject of widespread gossip in Yedo. Will I expect you to continue visiting me at the Golden Pavilion?'

With an exclamation of impatience he gripped both her hands with his own. Guiding them roughly, he forced her to remove the yellow kimono from his upper body and draw it aside from his thighs. Letting go of her hands he unfastened her filmy white under-kimono, flung it from her shoulders, and gazed hungrily at her nakedness.

'It is right that you should be famed far and wide for such rare beauty,' he said in a voice that was heavy with desire. 'Even before the black ships of the foreign barbarians appeared, I had decided I no longer wanted to make the long journey to Yedo every time I wished to see you . . .'

He reached out suddenly to caress her, running his hands roughly along her limbs and down the front of her body. She closed her eyes and submitted passively to these clumsy attentions, but did not respond in any other way.

'But the barbarian black ships have arrived now,' she whispered. 'Has that changed your wish?'

His breathing had become uneven and suddenly he took hold of her shoulders and bore her backwards onto the tatami. Crouching over her, he parted her legs and manoeuvred himself without ceremony between her splayed thighs. Looking down at her, his expression became intense and he paused, savouring the moment.

'This is not the time to talk of the future, O Tokiwa-san!' Drawing a long, deep breath, he shifted his position slightly. 'In truth this is not the time to talk at all!'

Acting with unexpected suddenness, he lunged downward and entered her. She winced and let out a whimper of pain, but he took no notice. Aroused further by her involuntary cries, he forced himself deeper, covering her body heavily with his own. She moaned in protest once more and closed her eyes, but he continued to move against her with growing force, giving no sign that he had heard.

'Forgive me, O Kami-san, for intruding. I must see you very urgently!'

The guttural male voice calling agitatedly from outside the closed *shoji* at the rear of the pavilion was accompanied by an urgent knocking on the wooden lattice work. Finding no immediate response, the knocking resumed after a pause, and the voice called out again more loudly.

'*Forgive this interruption, O Kami-san! But I must speak to you at once.*'

On recognizing the voice of Gotaro, Tanaka ceased his movements abruptly. After taking a moment to control his breathing he turned his head and spoke angrily in the direction of the *shoji*. 'Your message can wait! Return in a little while!'

He glanced at Tokiwa, to find her staring up at him with an alarmed expression in her eyes. The sight of her lying submissive and helpless beneath him provoked a new rush of desire, and he began to move urgently against her once more.

'My message, O Kami-san, should not wait,' called the samurai uneasily. 'You would never pardon me if I delayed this news.'

'Enter, then!' roared Tanaka impatiently. 'And be quick!'

The *shoji* opened and closed quietly and Gotaro entered. His cloak and armour were stained with dust and mud from a long ride and he bowed low as he stepped into the room. But when he raised his head and saw the naked figures of Tanaka and the geisha, he stopped in mid-stride, at a loss for words.

'What is your message?' demanded Tanaka, without turning or slowing his movements. 'Speak out quickly!'

'I beg your understanding again, O Kami-san,' said Gotaro in a disconcerted voice. 'I would not normally wish to approach you at such a time . . .'

'Speak on, while I continue to ride my horse,' snapped Tanaka over his shoulder. 'And be brief!'

'My message concerns the foreign barbarian, O Kami-san!'

Tanaka suddenly became still and lifted his head to listen. 'What of the foreign barbarian? What news do you bring me?'

'He has failed to return to his ship as ordered. I followed him as you instructed, but he concealed his tracks in the darkness. . . .'

'What do you mean?'

'He hid somewhere—then changed his direction completely . . .'

'Where is he now?'

'I don't know, O Kami-san. I gave chase for many *ri*, but in the end I lost his trail.'

'In which region did you lose him?'

'Almost from the start he headed towards the north—away from the black ships. He rode on for many miles and seemed always to be going in the general direction of Fuji-san—that is all that I can say.'

'Towards Fuji-san?' demanded Tanaka, his tone surprised and angry. 'Are you sure?'

'Yes, O Kami-san, I'm quite sure. Always towards Fuji-san.'

Tanaka forced himself downward again more sharply, expressing anger and annoyance with each repeated movement of his body. Tokiwa, who had flung up one arm to hide her face as soon as the samurai entered, cried out repeatedly, but her cries again served only to heighten the ferocity of Tanaka's passion.

'Assemble twenty of my best warriors . . .' he grunted over his shoulder. 'And saddle fresh horses . . . If the foreign barbarian falls into the hands of my enemies, they will use him as an excuse to start a war. We must recapture him ourselves. Go now!'

'Yes, O Kami-san.' Gotaro bowed very low, relieved to be dismissed from the pavilion. 'I'll see to that at once.'

When the guard had closed the screens behind him, Tanaka shifted Tokiwa's arm from her face and looked down at her. Fearing he was about to demand an answer to some new question, she gazed apprehensively back at him, wincing with each new thrust of his body. But, to her surprise, he remained silent and holding her gaze, he began to bear down on her anew with even greater force. His movements quickened, becoming ever more frantic, and he closed his eyes suddenly and opened his throat to emit a long guttural shout that was a mixture of anger and desire. He did not look at her again and as his passion mounted swiftly towards its climax, he ignored all her pained cries and gave himself up entirely to the gratification of his own senses.

PART III

The Black Ships Close In

10–12 July 1853

Japan's characteristic determination to resist foreign intrusion at all costs, which was demonstrated so forcefully in the summer of 1853, had been greatly strengthened by one momentous experience in its history. Under their shogun of the time, the Japanese fought ferociously to repel several attacks by the Mongol hordes of Kublai Khan, who swept through China and all Asia towards the end of the thirteenth century. When an overwhelming seaborne force of one hundred and forty thousand Mongols was finally sent to Japan's shores in 1281, to put down the resistance once and for all, everything seemed lost; but a kamikaze, a so-called 'divine wind', blew up and wrecked the Mongol fleet at the last moment, drowning more than half of the invading troops. This seemingly miraculous deliverance from all-powerful enemies reaffirmed the belief of the Japanese in their own supposedly divine origins, and helped mould their national character in a manner which endures into the present.

They were also further strengthened as a nation when the most ruthless and successful of all the shoguns, Tokugawa Iyeyasu, unified the whole country under his uncompromising rule at the beginning of the seventeenth century. This military dynasty, although acknowledging the Emperor's spiritual supremacy, remained all-powerful for the next two hundred and fifty years, and its first scion imposed those draconian laws which successfully wiped out Christianity and closed Japan off from the outside world until the mid-nineteenth century. Other ruthless edicts issued at that time compelled all the daimyo, the feudal lords, to spend one year in two at the political capital, Yedo; they also had to leave their wives and families in the city as hostages whenever they returned to their provincial estates, to ensure they did not plot rebellion. It was under this tyrannical and oppressive regime that Japan turned inward on itself for so long. No major wars disturbed the Tokugawa peace for more than two centuries—but it was while slumbering in this unnatural isolation that Japan fell seriously out of step with the march of history in the rest of the world, and so became vulnerable to the might of the steam-driven American warships when they arrived.

That it was men from the United States of America who came across the Pacific to batter down Japan's closed gates at long last was something of an historical irony, because some early drifts of emigration had possibly moved in the opposite direction. There is evidence to support an argument that at least some of the aboriginal tribes of Indians who first populated North America may have originated in the islands of Japan. A great equatorial ocean current, the Kuro Shiwo or Black Stream of Japan, flows by the Japanese islands and onward in a great semicircle past the Aleutian Islands and Alaska, to Oregon and California. For thousands of years countless junks and fishing craft from east Asian shores had been sucked into the Kuro Shiwo by easterly typhoons and whirled across the northern Pacific to wreck themselves on the western shores of America. Facial resemblances between some Japanese and certain North American Indian tribes strongly suggest that prehistoric emigration might have followed this natural ocean track. The two ancient peoples also appear to have shared similar religions, customs and superstitions and both have notably been worshippers of the sun and the forces of nature. Some identical words can be found in the Indian and Japanese languages, and myths surrounding such animals as the fox are also shared. Certain Indian totems, crests and methods of picture writing were also strikingly reminiscent of early Japanese forms but, whether or not this sea-route forged a direct link between the original peoples of Japan and America, both almost certainly had ancestors in common among the Mongols of northern Asia and therefore were of a similar bloodline.

But the powerful American naval force which sailed in the opposite direction from the United States to Japan in 1853 represented those who were then in the last stages of subjugating and dispossessing the North American Indians on their home territory. If the Japanese watching the US Navy squadron so apprehensively from their island fortifications had been aware of such obscure historical cross-currents, they might have been strengthened further in their resolve to resist encroachment by powerful, foreign, white men just as their distant cousins had done so valiantly in the great open spaces of North America. Because Japan was a chain of mountainous islands buttressed by the cultural and national unity of its people, it was a more compact bastion to defend—but awakening suddenly to the realities of foreign military and industrial superiority was to be traumatic and turbulent for them too, although in a different way. To the most astute among the Japanese, this danger had already become very clear as the ominous squadron of smoking warships continued to ride threateningly at anchor in the Bay of Yedo for the third successive day.

26

The big capstan on the upper deck of the *Susquehanna* was draped with the red, white and blue United States flag. Lying open on this canopy of stars and stripes was the oversized ship's Bible, leather-bound and gilded at its edges. Under the misty white haze of Sunday morning which cloaked Yedo Bay, the colours of the American flag seemed to glow with an added vibrancy in the eyes of the three hundred seamen and marines drawn up in orderly ranks below the flagship's quarterdeck for a formal service of Christian worship.

The silver and brass instruments of the squadron's band glowed dully too in the filtered light of the morning sun, as the bandsmen launched into the stirring strains of a hymn. Above the assembled crew and blue-jacketed marine units on the quarterdeck, the squadron's officers led by the towering figure of Commodore Matthew Calbraith Perry were arrayed for the occasion in the splendour of their gold-splashed full-dress uniforms. Staring haughtily ahead, and ignoring the visible Japanese fighting units that were being marshalled and deployed in ever-growing numbers on the cliffs and beaches around Uraga, the commodore added his own deep baritone to the lusty rendering of the hymn. The solemn Christian chant rolled sonorously across the calm waters of the bay, blotting out momentarily the agitated tolling of temple bells and war gongs. Even the sudden boom of a distant shore cannon echoing among the hills did not disturb the flow of the shipboard service, and the three hundred and more voices sang on unperturbed.

'Before Jehovah's awful throne
Ye nations bow with sacred joy,
Know that the Lord is God alone
He can create, He can destroy . . .'

Samuel Armstrong, who was standing at the rear of the group of officers, turned his head from his hymnal as he sang, and saw a column of dark smoke rising above a headland half a mile higher up the bay. The purpose of the distant cannon shot remained obscure but because it presented no immediate danger he turned his attention discreetly to the nearer cliffs, where he could see long files of straining figures hauling additional guns into place in the open embrasures of the forts. Other fighting groups armed with shields and lances were being marched to new guard positions among the fortifications, and some beacon fires which had burned throughout another long night were still blazing in the mist which obscured the hills and mountains beyond the cliffs.

'I think a lot of new guns are being trained on the squadron from south of Uraga, Lieutenant,' said Armstrong, speaking in an undertone to John Rice who was standing stiffly at his side, hymnal in hand. 'There's more activity than before around the forts.'

The flag lieutenant did not pause in his hymn-singing; he had been responsible earlier for making it known throughout the ship that the commodore wished the weekly Christian ritual to be seen onshore as a forceful display of American power and confidence. Hymns considered to have a particular potency for the occasion had been chosen, and all ranks had been instructed to take special care with their dress uniforms and their deportment. Lieutenant Rice's demeanour, therefore, like that of all his brother officers, bristled with the determination to carry this task through. As he continued his spirited singing of the hymn, the lieutenant glanced briefly towards the clifftop Armstrong had indicated; but his gaze did not linger and he volunteered no comment before returning his full attention to the last verse.

As its final notes died away and the squadron chaplain stepped up to the flag-covered capstan to read the lesson of the day, Armstrong glanced towards Matthew Perry and noticed that the commodore's bearing, from which all his subordinates were consciously or subconsciously taking their lead, had become straighter and more determined than ever. Beneath his tasselled cocked hat, thick hair bushed out strikingly around his broad face; his expression was both fierce and composed, and his leonine head and bull neck jutted aggressively above shoulders made broader and more imposing by his gilded commodore's epaulettes. A double row of gold buttons sparkled on the dark blue cloth of his coat and the continuous, mountain-like swell of his chest, which merged with the muscular paunch beneath it, gave his figure a powerful, oak-like solidity. In the manner of Napoleon, he held his right hand across his chest, tucking its thumb between the coat buttons, thereby signifying silently to the world at large that he was a man of force and unshakable convictions.

'We shall now ask our Heavenly Father for the strength to carry through our mission successfully in these waters,' intoned the chaplain, after finishing his reading of the lesson. 'And Commodore Perry, our squadron commander, will first lead us briefly with his own supplication.'

Armstrong watched Matthew Perry close his eyes and incline his head a fraction, standing motionless before the quarterdeck rail. Even in prayer his massive bulk continued to exert its powerful influence, and Armstrong saw a number of seamen and marines on the deck below lift their heads surreptitiously to catch a glimpse of his awesome figure in a rare moment of repose, before he spoke.

'We pray God,' said the commodore in a slow, booming voice that carried easily throughout the ship, 'that our present attempt to bring a singular and isolated people into the family of civilized nations may succeed without resort to bloodshed. And we ask His blessing also on all our thoughts and deeds at this time of difficulty and danger . . . Amen!'

A hearty roar of 'Amen!' rose loudly from the upper deck in response, before the men settled themselves again to follow a longer prayer read by the chaplain; but as he spoke, many raised their heads briefly to snatch a further glimpse of their imposing commander-in-chief in his finest array.

Among the listening crewmen, the deeds and achievements of Perry's extraordinary career were already legendary. At the age of fourteen he had been the youngest midshipman ever commissioned into the American Navy; in the War of 1812 he had fought gallantly as a young officer; and in the more recent Mexican War he had, with resounding success, commanded the largest American fleet ever sent to sea. He had personally supervised the building of the American Navy's first ocean-going steamers, the *Mississippi* and the *Missouri*, and confounded sceptics who predicted that they would be lost in their first ocean storms—by triumphantly circumnavigating the globe in the *Mississippi*. For those deeds he had become widely celebrated as 'the father of the American steam navy' which had added a unique dimension to his growing stature.

Having seen vast tracts of Asia fall under the domination of Europe's imperial powers during his lifetime, however, it had become the crowning ambition of his career to place American power on at least an equal footing with the Europeans throughout the Orient. To expand American trade, he had proposed that a chain of coaling ports and naval bases should be established across the Far East. His detailed proposals had been received with such enthusiasm in Washington that he had effectively written his own orders for the mission to open up an enigmatic and mysterious Japan that had deliberately secluded itself from the predatory outside world for two centuries—and these orders, at his own insistence, specifically allowed him to use force of arms if he judged it necessary.

All these diverse strands of his life, Samuel Armstrong reflected, were inherently visible in the pugnacious Sunday-morning stance of the commodore on the misty quarterdeck of his own flagship. His commitment to his own personal goal, which he had astutely turned into a national crusade, was total; more importantly it was backed by a powerful modern naval squadron spread threateningly across the bay, which he could deploy however he wished. *No matter what happens now*, his silent bulk seemed to declare, *American pride, and if necessary, American force of arms will prevail.*

As he continued to gaze at the imperious figure of the commodore, Armstrong realized too, with a sudden rush of clarity, why the youthful figure of Robert Eden was no longer standing among the group of dutiful, straight-backed officers flanking their commander on the quarterdeck. Eden's birth, his mixed blood, his fierce sense of justice and his instinctive sympathy for a proud people overpowered in their own land by more forceful, better-armed strangers, had made it impossible for him to continue standing unthinkingly shoulder-to-shoulder with the men around him. Only such fierce idealism, given a reckless edge by his own private agonies, could have forced him to dive off the side of the ship in the darkness of Friday night and strike out heedlessly for the shore. The mental turmoil he faced in the moments leading up to that rash decision would doubtless have been painful and, understanding all this fully for the first time, the veteran missionary was no longer surprised. In his own heart, where fading embers of his youthful Christian zeal still glowed faintly, Samuel Armstrong suddenly felt something approaching envy for the young officer's courage and singleness of mind.

'Perhaps it's a pity no Japanese have yet caught sight of our distinguished commander-in-chief,' he murmured at last, leaning close to Lieutenant Rice as the prayer ended. 'If they had seen the jut of his jaw and the glint in his eye, they would surely never have considered resisting delivery of the President's letter.'

The band was launching itself boisterously into the opening bars of another hymn, and again Lieutenant Rice did not immediately reply. Armstrong noticed that his expression was abstracted, and he was looking past him towards the shore. Turning to follow the direction of the officer's gaze, he saw that a Japanese longboat covered with a striped canopy was heading purposefully out of the harbour towards the *Susquehanna*. Rowed swiftly by standing oarsmen, it appeared to be carrying a number of silk-gowned officials.

'The commodore has no intention of changing his policy for the time being,' said Rice shortly. 'He will continue to hold himself aloof from all contact with the Japanese.'

'And what are we to tell the officials who seem to be heading towards us now?' asked Armstrong, watching the canopied boat drawing nearer. 'Am I to talk with them?'

'The commodore has expressly ordered that, out of reverence for the Lord's Day, there be no communication whatsoever with the Japanese authorities until tomorrow,' said Rice quietly. 'No visitors are to be received on any of our four ships. You may go and tell them that—and make it clear they are refused permission to board for the rest of the day.'

Hurrying from the quarterdeck, as the voices of the three hundred seamen and officers bellowed out the verses of another hymn, Armstrong climbed halfway down the port gangway, and waited for the official Japanese boat to come alongside. Four officials wearing black-lacquered caps and embroidered gowns of silk were seated gravely beneath the canopy, flapping their fans slowly before them. But none of their faces was familiar to Armstrong, except that of the scholarly-looking interpreter, Haniwara Tokuma, who rose and hurried towards the bows of the boat when he saw Armstrong hold up a hand indicating they were not welcome.

'Why have you come today, Haniwara-san?' called Armstrong in Dutch. 'What is the purpose of your visit?'

'My superiors wish to come aboard to discover how your admiral intends to deploy his warships in the coming hours,' replied the interpreter. 'In particular they wish to know whether he intends to continue the dangerous practice of sending out armed survey boats.'

One of the oarsmen tossed a rope to Armstrong, who looped it once around a rail of the gangway to make it clear that the craft would be secured there only temporarily. Then he stood up straight and addressed its occupants in a formal tone: 'I am instructed to advise you that no visitors will be allowed to board any ship of the American Navy here today. No communication of any kind will be received by our admiral until tomorrow morning.'

'What are the reasons for that?' demanded Haniwara, clearly puzzled.

'Each week we set this whole day aside for the worship of our God. As you can perhaps see and hear, a service of worship is taking place at this very moment on our upper deck.'

The interpreter explained this answer to the seated officials then turned to face Armstrong again, his expression grave. 'My superiors say that they have come to warn your admiral. They say fighting will certainly break out if your survey boats approach too close to our shore.'

'I can only repeat,' said Armstrong slowly, 'that our admiral wishes to have no communication with your superiors on this important day of worship.'

Haniwara looked at Armstrong steadily. 'My superiors are very disappointed with this response. They wished to receive assurances about your activities.'

'I am unable to go beyond my strict instructions that there should be no communication with you today,' said Armstrong, allowing a note of apology to show in his voice. 'But for myself I would like to enquire whether you have yet received any reply from Yedo about the delivery of our President's letter to a high official of His Imperial Majesty the Emperor?'

'There has been no reply yet,' said the interpreter, beginning to turn away. 'There has not been enough time . . .'

'Wait!' called Armstrong in an urgent voice. 'I would like to raise one further question.'

'What is that?' enquired the interpreter curtly.

'Whether you have any news of our missing officer?' Armstrong bent nearer, keeping his voice low, to prevent others on the ship above overhearing his words. 'Has he been found yet?'

Haniwara Tokuma moved back to the gangway again, and eyed Armstrong searchingly for a moment; then he too lowered his voice. 'It is very unfortunate. Your officer was discovered spying on fortifications above Uraga. There was fighting and some bloodshed.'

'Was he killed?' demanded Armstrong anxiously.

'No, he managed to escape,' said the interpreter stonily. 'Later he was discovered further inland. Again there was fighting, but again he was not recaptured . . .'

Armstrong took a deep breath. 'And what's happening now?'

'He is still being pursued,' said Haniwara sharply. 'He is being hunted by many fighting men. It is impossible to say what the consequences may be.'

In a reflex action Armstrong raised his eyes and looked towards the shore. But, above the cliffs, the landscape was still shrouded in an impenetrable white mist that obscured all the distant hills and mountains beyond.

'Thank you, Haniwara-san,' said Armstrong quietly, unwinding the rope from the gangway and casting the boat off. 'Thank you very much for that information.'

The interpreter, his face a mask of inexpression, bowed perfunctorily before returning to his seat beside the four officials and Armstrong watched the near-naked Japanese oarsmen send their boat scudding back towards the shore with powerful, rhythmic strokes. Above his head he heard a new chanted supplication rising from the upper deck and he stared again into the white mists onshore, trying to imagine where Robert Eden might be at that moment. Then, with Eden's name silently on his lips, he closed his eyes and joined the rest of the crew in prayer where he stood, halfway up the rungs of the gangway.

27

'This mist is very eerie, Sentaro. Do you think we are still going in the right direction?'

As he spoke, Robert Eden leaned low over his horse's neck and peered vainly ahead into the grey-white murk which enclosed the morning all around them. He had tied his hat tight beneath his chin to hide his face, and although there was no other living soul in sight he was still hunching himself unnaturally in the saddle in an effort to disguise the fact that he was more than six feet tall.

'Yes, master, I'm sure we're still going the right way.'

Sentaro, cantering steadily at his side, also screwed up his eyes to peer ahead; but he could distinguish nothing more than a few stunted trees struggling up from the surface of the desolate, rolling moorland, across which they were riding on a track of black shale. The hoofs of the horses crunched loudly on the friable, cinder-like surface of the rising track which wound gently upward in long zigzags, and even on the moorland to either side, patches of the same black volcanic ash were visible here and there among the tufts of sour grass.

'We haven't seen Fuji-san since sunset last night,' said Eden in a subdued voice. 'It seems to have disappeared without trace.'

Somewhere high above their heads they heard the piping song of a rising lark. The tiny bird, however, remained invisible and no sound other than the passage of their horses could be heard in the strange white stillness. They had ridden hard through the night, and when day dawned under its unrelieved cloak of mist they had first found themselves passing through terraced rice fields where indistinct hatted figures wielding sickles were beginning to harvest the grain. Then they had entered a chain of forests, ducking beneath spreading boughs of oak, larch and pine, as they continued to follow the narrow, rising path northward. In between these forests they had encountered scattered groups of high-roofed, thatched peasant houses, from which ghostly family groups were emerging into the grey morning gloom. But they had never slackened their pace and had swept past with heads held low, their broad hats always covering their faces.

Whenever Sentaro risked stopping to seek directions or buy food for them, Eden had either hung back or ridden on quickly ahead, so as to arouse as little suspicion as possible. On these occasions he had turned to peer round cautiously behind them, checking for signs of pursuit. They had rested their horses regularly and when they rode on, their path had continued to rise steadily over the undulating terrain; but because the whole landscape was shrouded by the mist, they had seen nothing in the surrounding highlands which confirmed their bearings. A drizzling rain had also been falling intermittently since daybreak and their thin cottons were damp and splashed with mud.

'We must try to obtain some warmer clothing, master,' said Sentaro, shivering suddenly in his saddle. 'A couple of padded kimonos and some warm *tabi* for our feet. The air up here is colder. I think we are already about four thousand feet above the sea. And at the top of Fuji-san, remember, it is still like midwinter.'

Shuddering himself, Eden nodded in agreement. 'But where will we find such garments?'

'In this region there are several inns and rest-houses for pilgrims . . .'

As they rode on in silence the mist before them began to thin, and Eden found himself looking ahead at what he assumed were patches of storm-dark sky becoming visible above the moorland horizon. He was puzzled at first by the absence of any high contours in these leaden heavens until he realized with a shock that he was looking not at empty sky but at one gigantic flank of Mount Fuji rising up steeply above their heads. It blotted everything from view in front of them and the gentle violet hues of the volcanic cone, which had seduced his senses so completely from a distance, had changed at close quarters to an ominous, dark, primeval colour which made its massive bulk seem overpowering and hostile.

'You see, master, we *are* still going in the right direction,' said Sentaro quietly. 'Fuji-san herself has drawn back the curtain to show us the way.'

Eden nodded, but made no reply. The first harsh glimpse of Fuji close up had brought his shipboard dream images flashing back into his mind: although both brilliant and enthralling, the dream had also possessed a disturbing dimension which had now been echoed in reality for the first time. Furthermore the mist, far from clearing, was closing down rapidly again, like a curtain being deliberately re-drawn for reasons of concealment. Eden just had time to catch a glimpse of the snow-covered peak rearing up with threatening suddenness above them; a few moments later the whole mountain was obscured once more by the shroud of impenetrable whiteness, and he Was left with a vague and unidentifiable feeling of foreboding.

For the first time he wondered if he had been insanely rash in surrendering to his wild impulse to climb the spectacular volcano. He was well aware he had been acting on instinct not reason, and had realized he would face considerable risks; but had he seriously miscalculated the degree of danger? Was the whole venture an act of extreme folly? He closed his eyes, pondering these questions with a mounting feeling of anxiety; yet, despite his misgivings, he found his inner senses did not urge him to abandon the attempt and turn back. Something beyond words, he felt, was drawing him on, and he shrugged his shoulders as he rode forward, trying to push all negative thoughts from his mind.

'Look, there's something ahead, master,' said Sentaro a few minutes later, pointing towards what turned out to be a tiny pilgrim inn nestling in a fold of the land. 'I will stop to get us extra clothing.'

Eden was shivering continually now, and he spurred his horse into a clump of trees while Sentaro reined in outside the inn and dismounted. The former castaway joined him again fifteen minutes later, grinning broadly from under the brim of his wide hat. Across the neck of his horse he carried two black padded kimonos, two traditional pilgrim over-gowns of white cotton, thick white woollen *tabi* for their feet, and several spare pairs of woven-straw sandals. He had filled a new water bottle and also bought climbing staves, which he carried in one hand. Slung around his neck like necklaces, he wore two strings of eggs that had been cooked in their shells; each egg had been tied up individually inside a narrow strip of straw matting and, after riding far enough off the track to be invisible to anyone passing, they pulled on the warm garments, the white over-gowns and the woollen socks. Bowing his head respectfully, and grinning at the same time, Sentaro hung one of the skeins of hardboiled eggs around Eden's neck, as though honouring him with a decoration, and they paused long enough to devour two of the eggs from the other skein.

'I have rice and vegetables in my pouch, master, so we are better prepared now to begin our climb,' said Sentaro, his narrow face become serious again. 'But the landlord of the inn warned me that it is very dangerous to attempt the climb at any time without a guide. When the mist is thick, it is especially dangerous. He also said the snows this year still look very deep near the summit.'

'We will find our own way, Sentaro. A guide would only betray us.'

Eden spurred his horse away with a sudden ferocity, as if trying to calm the sense of disquiet nagging inside him. Sentaro followed quickly and they rode side by side without speaking up the winding track, noticing that the stretches of black sand and ash were growing larger. Very soon the surface of the moorland had become predominantly black, with only occasional splashes of green where small clumps of rank grass had taken root. In the dead grey light the whole landscape had taken on a charred and abandoned appearance as though it had been recently swept by fire, and the two mollusc-hatted riders clad all in white passed steadily across it, moving forward like silent, insubstantial ghosts.

'There was an eruption from this side of Fuji-san a hundred and fifty years ago,' panted Sentaro at Eden's side: 'The ashes rained down for many miles around—even the rooftops of Yedo were covered. The landlord of the inn back there told me this whole area was covered with black sand to the height of a man . . .'

The hoofs of the horses were sinking deeper into the soft, volcanic cinders, slowing their progress, and the track grew steeper. Very soon the last patches of green and even the stunted trees disappeared, leaving the surface of the earth all round them ominously bare. As they climbed higher Eden began to realize that the frowning bulk of Fuji was not even the dark metallic blue it had seemed to be half an hour earlier: the whole of the mountain, like the moorland, was a shocking cinder-black. Framed within lines of extraordinary symmetry, the cone seen from those lower slopes was a daunting pyramid of dead ashes, lava and cinders. Only high above—many miles away, it seemed to Eden—was this grim colour relieved by the sudden whiteness of the snow-covered summit, which by contrast seemed purer and more dazzling than before.

'We must leave the horses soon, master, and continue on foot,' whispered Sentaro, gazing up towards the peak with a bemused expression in his eyes. 'I was told there's one last pilgrim inn where they can be sheltered.'

Half an hour later after Sentaro had stabled the horses, they were standing side by side, holding the staves in their hands, at the bottom of the steep cliff of black scoriae. Whenever they moved, their feet sank deep into the loose cinders, making a sharp crunching sound. A cold breeze was beginning to blow, chasing the fog, wisp by wisp, from the trackless mountain face and Eden stared through narrowed eyes at the harsh contours as they came gradually into focus.

No other human figure was visible on the steep slopes ahead of them to give any clue where invisible paths might lie, and he searched in vain for some logical line of ascent through the drab wastes. A sense of bafflement engulfed him suddenly as he struggled to come to terms with the horror of the grim scene before them. The charred flanks of the mountain, abandoned by all visible life forms, were a seared and deserted realm that reeked of fiery death and destruction. An ominous silence had descended and in those moments it seemed impossible that the spectacular mountain which had captivated him at first sight as a vision of light and beauty could have transformed itself so nightmarishly into the opposite.

'Which way shall we climb, master?' asked Sentaro, speaking in an uncertain voice at his side. 'Have you made up your mind?'

Eden did not reply at once. Unable to formulate any rational plan of action, he jabbed his stave into the black cinders at his feet with a sudden decisiveness.

'Yes, this way! Follow close behind me.'

The next instant he lunged blindly away across the loose scree and Sentaro hurried after him. A sharp gust of wind whipped against their faces and with each step they took, their feet sank deeper into the loose, black sand.

28

Riding fast through the thick mist at the head of a group of twenty helmeted and fully armed samurai, Prince Tanaka failed to spot the tiny pilgrim inn nestling at the edge of the moorland. He had already passed it and was spurring his horse onward along the winding track, when Gotaro, who was riding at the rear of the group, noticed the blurred outline of the little thatched building and reined in his mount.

'O Kami-san, forgive me,' he called out loudly. 'There is an inn here. We could stop and seek information.'

He waited respectfully while Tanaka wheeled his horse and led the rest of the samurai troop up to the inn gates. When Tanaka dismounted, the chief guard followed him to the doorway where the *teishi*, or landlord, had already appeared. Having caught sight of Tanaka's richly embroidered *jimbaori* and the horned helmets of his escort, emblazoned with the Kago clan insignia, the landlord had already prostrated himself abjectly on the threshold with hands folded before him. He touched his forehead to the ground five times as the group approached, and remained in this position until he was addressed.

'Rise,' commanded Tanaka brusquely. 'We wish only to ask you a question or two.'

The *teishi* half rose, still bowing obsequiously, and began backing into the shabby inn, indicating with mumbled self-effacements that his lordly visitor was very welcome to enter his unworthy establishment.

'We don't require the service of your inn at present, Teishi-san,' said Tanaka quickly. 'We wish only to know if any strangers have called seeking refreshment, or otherwise passed by here today.'

'It is at present very quiet in this remote region, O Kami-san,' said the *teishi*, bowing very low again. 'When the snows have melted fully on Fuji-san, many pilgrims will come by as usual. Today only one man has called at my humble inn.'

'What sort of man was he?' asked Gotaro eagerly. 'Did he look anything like a *banzoku*—a foreign barbarian bandit?'

Tanaka shot an angry glance at his chief guard as the *teishi's* eyes widened in alarm; then he bowed again before replying.

'The man who called today at my humble inn was an ordinary Nipponese—a farmer, a fisherman or some such, I should think . . .'

'What did he want?' asked Tanaka, his eyes glowing with sudden interest. 'Why did he call here?'

'He merely bought some warm clothes, O Kami-san, to climb the mountain—and also some food. I warned him how dangerous it would be for them without a guide.'

'Why do you say *for them?*' asked Tanaka sharply.

'Because he bought clothes and food for another man as well, and he said he was preparing to climb the mountain with a companion . . .' The *teishi* stopped speaking, suspicion dawning in his eyes; when he resumed his voice had taken on a faint edge of excitement. 'Yes, O Kami-san, that's right! And one of my servants said he saw another man gallop up with him. But the other man rode on past the inn without stopping . . .'

'What sort of clothing did you sell them?'

'Warm clothes, O Kami-san. Pilgrim robes, *tabi* and thick kimonos . . .'

'And what clothes did he buy for his unseen companion?'

'The same—but the largest size of everything . . .'

'It must be the *banzoku*, O Kami-san,' said Gotaro excitedly. 'And he clearly intends to commit the gravest of crimes by climbing sacred Fuji-san itself!'

'How long is it since they passed?' asked Tanaka, ignoring the samurai's impetuous interruption.

The *teishi* thought for a moment. 'Perhaps three hours or so, O Kami-san. Four hours at the most.'

'And which way did they go?'

He pointed along the black shale track to the north. 'That way, O Kami-san.'

Tanaka reached into a pouch at his waist, extracted two silver coins and held them out. 'I commend you for your assistance, Teishi-san. And I expect you to say nothing of these things to anybody else.'

'O Kami-san does my humble dwelling the greatest honour.'

The *teishi* received the coins in both hands and bowed from the waist again in gratitude. He remained in this respectful posture while Tanaka climbed into his saddle, and did not straighten up until the group of horsemen had swept from the inn yard, to disappear rapidly into the mist. For a moment or two he stood listening to the urgent, fading beat of their hoofs, his face indicating that he was deep in thought. Then he called over his shoulder to a young servant, who throughout the meeting had hovered judiciously out of sight just inside the door.

'Saddle up a horse,' he said to the youth, 'and ride fast to our lord's castle. Tell him it is believed the foreign barbarian bandit passed by here this morning, in the company of a Nipponese fisherman. Say they were last seen moving up the slopes of Fuji-san! Say also that a prince of the Kago clan is pursuing him hotly, with twenty of his samurai.'

'Yes, master!' said the youth, his eyes wide with excitement. 'I will go at once!'

He dashed away towards the stables to prepare a horse and three minutes later galloped furiously out of the inn yard. Bent low over the horse's mane, he swung away in the opposite direction to that taken by Prince Tanaka, and in his turn disappeared swiftly into the mist.

29

A windowless black-lacquered *norimono*, being carried swiftly through the same persistent mists above Uraga, jolted and bounced alarmingly on the shoulders of its four fast-trotting bearers. A group of mounted samurai cavalrymen, holding aloft the fluttering clan standards of Lord Daizo of Haifu, were riding in close formation around the traditional conveyance that for many centuries had been employed to transport noblemen or officials of rank in secluded privacy. Its small wooden cabin was suspended from a single, stout carrying-pole borne by two pairs of brawny coolies front and back, and the samurai escort cast watchful glances in all directions as they hurried them over the crest of a low wooded hill. In the distance the curved rooftops that crowned a *daimyo*'s hilltop castle became faintly visible and, on catching sight of the fortress, the samurai captain shouted urgent new orders to the bearers to accelerate their pace still further.

Inside the wildly bouncing *norimono* the thin, scholarly face of Haniwara Tokuma, who had acted as interpreter for all the encounters on board the American black ships, was already pale with apprehension. He was trying to brace himself more rigidly on the conveyance's narrow seat to lessen his discomfort, and from time to time he clutched frantically at his lacquered bonnet to prevent it being knocked askew. But on hearing the samurai captain's order to speed up, his expression grew more agitated. Even though he could see little or nothing from inside what was effectively a tiny wooden cage, he sensed they must be approaching their destination and the headlong downhill gallop of the bearers, which jolted him more painfully than ever in his seat, seemed to confirm his suspicions.

The unexpected arrival of the *norimono* and its escort, while he was resting in a guest pavilion at the governor's residence in Uraga, had surprised but not alarmed him. The samurai captain had bowed and greeted him respectfully enough in announcing that he was summoned to an immediate audience with Lord Daizo of Haifii. But as soon as they had left the palace, the *norunono* had speeded up alarmingly and the guards had insolently ignored all his shouted demands for an explanation of their haste. His frantic requests for them to slow down had also gone unanswered and he had soon lapsed into a fearful silence, realizing that he was being subjected to these deliberate indignities in preparation for something worse.

After reaching level ground and climbing gradually again, the *norimono* passed through several guarded gateways until at last it halted and the expressionless samurai captain wrenched open the tiny door of the conveyance inside the castle courtyard. He gestured for the scholar-official to disembark, without offering any of the courtesies appropriate to his rank, then turned and strode quickly away towards a portalled door.

'You will follow me,' he called brusquely over his shoulder. 'You are to be received immediately by Lord Daizo.'

Three other samurai fell into step behind him, their hands resting pointedly on the hilts of their swords, and he was marched into the castle. They passed rapidly along wide stone corridors hung with weapons and shields bearing the Makabe clan insignia, and mounted a flight of steps to a small, bare audience chamber where Lord Daizo, a glowering burly figure dressed in a formal kimono of dark blue silk, was seated cross-legged on a small cushioned platform. The taller, more youthful figure of his son Yakamochi, who wore the armour, battle-jacket and twin swords of a warrior nobleman, stood behind the dais, to one side, his features composed in an expression of hostility similar to his father's. After prostrating themselves in their *daimyo*'s direction, the four samurai guards took up station watchfully beside the doorway, and motioned Haniwara Tokuma to step forward. The interpreter bowed low and prostrated himself in his turn, pressing his forehead three times against the tatami; then he looked up with an anxious expectancy towards the grim-faced *daimyo*.

'Nippon's most sacred laws are those which forbid the admission of all foreign barbarians to our country,' snapped Daizo, gazing coldly at the interpreter. 'And because those sacred laws have now been violated, the divine dignity of His Imperial Majesty the Emperor is grossly offended.' The *daimyo* paused and glared challenging across the audience chamber. 'Do you agree, Haniwara-san?'

'You speak the truth, my lord,' said Haniwara uncertainly. 'That is self-evident.'

'If we revere His Imperial Majesty, and believe the land of the gods is sullied by the presence of even a single hideous alien, then we must strive mightily to expel him!' The *daimyo* paused again to stare belligerently at the interpreter. 'Do I speak with truth on that matter also, Haniwara-san?'

'Your speech is very clear, my lord.' The interpreter lowered his eyes evasively. 'Very clear indeed.'

'I'm glad you think so—that will make it easier for you to assist me.'

'Rest assured, my lord, that is my wish,' said the interpreter, still staring down at the tatami. 'I will assist you in any way that is in my power.'

'Good,' said Daizo heavily. 'Because I have brought you here to help me find the foreign barbarian spy who has sneaked ashore from the black ships.'

The interpreter looked up sharply, his anxiety showing more clearly on his face. 'How can I do that, my lord?'

'We shall see,' said Daizo, staring intently at Haniwara to gauge his reaction. 'But, to make your mind rest easier in these dangerous times, I should tell you I have sent guards to the home of your wife and children in Yedo. I have taken them all under my personal protection, and conveyed them to a secret destination. So you can help me now without fearing in any way for their safety . . . or informing anyone else of our conversations.'

Haniwara's face turned pale as he realized that his family had become helpless hostages of the ruthless *daimyo*. In Daizo's hard, narrow eyes he could see a fierce glitter of satisfaction, and again he lowered his head in order to disguise his true feelings.

'I am grateful for your concern about those dearest to me, my lord,' he said unsteadily. 'Tell me how I may offer you assistance.'

'Yesterday I sent my best samurai to hunt down the hideous alien in the region of the coastal fort where he was found spying—but he had disappeared without any trace! I wish to know from you whether he has returned secretly to the black ships?'

Haniwara continued to stare downward, avoiding the *daimyo*'s fixed gaze. 'No, my lord, I am sure he has not yet returned to his ship. This morning the barbarian interpreter asked me in confidence if there was any news of him. And many guards are now patrolling the entire shoreline.'

'But he *still* has not been found!' Daizo's eyes blazed angrily. 'What else do the foreign barbarians say about their treacherous spy?'

'They try to insist he is not a spy, my lord. They say he came ashore without permission, only because he wishes there to be peace and friendship between Nippon and the foreign barbarians. They say that is why they revealed his actions to us.'

'Those are lies!' shouted Daizo. 'That is their treachery! They say such things to mislead us—and to disguise their true intentions.'

'Perhaps my lord is right,' said the interpreter faintly. 'I can only report what has been said to me.'

'Already the foreign barbarians are making slaves of the peoples of China and India,' fumed Daizo. 'And they wish to enslave Nippon in the same way. As usual they are employing a clever mixture of threats and deceit. We will only escape their slavery if we fight to the death—*now* without delay!'

'I follow the orders of others in doing my duties, my lord,' said the interpreter helplessly. 'At present I attend upon the Governor of Uraga. Perhaps you forget I have no say in what is to be done.'

'The orders given to you and the governor come from weak and cowardly men obsessed with compromise,' rasped Daizo, leaning forward and thrusting out his jaw aggressively. 'The Shogun is near to death, too ill to act decisively in the matter of the barbarian ships. Because of this, our ruling council is in the grip of terrible indecision and uncertainty.'

'What will be the outcome?' asked Haniwara, lifting his head diffidently. 'How can the issue be resolved?'

'The fearful nobles who favour appeasement have won the day so far,' said Daizo, spitting out his words contemptuously. 'They want us to appear to do the bidding of the foreign barbarians, while playing for time. They think the barbarians will negotiate fairly! They think that in time we can learn all the barbarian secrets, and so build up our national strength to match theirs. But if we delay so long it will be too late to save ourselves! And I, Daizo Shitomi, Lord of Haifa, will not allow that delay!'

'What will you do, my lord?'

'I shall capture the foreign spy! I shall bring him in chains to Uraga, and expose their gross treachery for all to see. Then everyone who doubts will know there is only one sure way to rid ourselves of these foreign barbarians—by fighting! To our last drop of blood if necessary!'

The *daimyo* sat back on his cushion, looking hard at Haniwara. From his position behind the cushioned dais, his narrow-eyed son also regarded the interpreter with an unwavering stare.

'Perhaps you have some other knowledge that could assist us,' said the younger man in a quieter voice. 'Something you may have omitted to impart previously because of your understandable anxiety at the circumstances in which you have been brought here today.'

'What have you in mind, your lordship?' asked Haniwara, looking towards the *daimyo*'s son with a startled expression in his eyes.

Yakamochi blinked slowly. 'Think carefully. There must be something . . . Something which could perhaps help ensure the safety and survival of your beloved family.'

On recognizing the undisguised threat for what it was, a look of desperation came into the interpreter's eyes, and his demeanour became flustered. 'Yes, yes . . . perhaps there is something . . . In the last hour another suspected sighting of the barbarian spy has been reported—by a courier who had ridden at top speed from the estate of a noble lord in the region of Fuji-san.'

'From Fuji-san?' echoed the *daimyo* angrily. 'Why have you not mentioned this before?'

'I didn't wish to risk misleading you with unreliable information,' stammered the interpreter, looking more uneasy than before. 'There have been many false alarms . . . and so far there is no certain confirmation of this report.'

'What did the courier from the region of Fuji-san say?' barked the *daimyo*. 'Tell us. And be quick!'

'He said that the foreign barbarian was seen near the sacred mountain—at the foot of the south-eastern ascent route.' The interpreter paused nervously. 'He appeared to be disguised in farmer's clothing, and was accompanied by a Nipponese who bought some extra climbing garments and staves . . . The courier also said about twenty samurai of the Kago clan were riding in pursuit with their prince . . .'

'Tanaka!' Daizo let out an exclamation of anger, and after a moment's thought he turned to give orders to his son in an urgent undertone.

'Go immediately yourself! Take fifty of our bravest warriors. And send messengers to find our other search group. Order them to join you at the foot of the south-eastern ascent. And also be sure to send back couriers to bring me regular reports!'

Without hesitation Yakamochi bowed low and ran silently from the audience chamber. On his cushioned dais the *daimyo* remained motionless in his cross-legged posture, staring again at the uncomfortable interpreter. A whole minute passed in silence, but when at last he spoke his voice had become more thoughtful.

'You have been aboard the black ships three times, Haniwarasan. You must have made some estimate of the total number of barbarian fighting men present on their ships. What is your opinion?'

The interpreter shifted uneasily on the tatami. 'I am no expert in martial matters, my lord . . . but their fighting men can only be numbered in hundreds—fewer than one thousand in all.'

Daizo nodded slowly in satisfaction. 'We already have more than one hundred thousand men-at-arms stationed along the shores of Yedo Bay. And more are arriving all the time. By tomorrow there will be one hundred and fifty thousand . . . The next day perhaps two hundred thousand . . .'

The *daimyo* paused to listen to the sound of many horses clattering swiftly across the castle's cobbled courtyard. A shouted command, then another, drifted up to the open window of the audience chamber, confirming that the samurai troop under the command of his son was departing from the castle. As he listened, an expression of satisfaction flitted across his face.

'Soon the barbarian spy will be my captive, Haniwara-san,' he continued quietly. 'Then those who still doubt will be roused to action. And even though there may be many powerful new weapons on board their black ships, the foreign barbarians will not be able to resist a surprise attack by two hundred thousand men of Nippon!'

As soon as he had finished speaking, Lord Daizo dismissed his visitor with a peremptory jerk of his head, and the interpreter was soon hunched miserably on the narrow seat of the black-lacquered *norimono* once more. Fresh bearers, under the urging of the samurai guard, rushed the enclosed conveyance back over the forested hills towards Uraga, at the same breakneck speed as before, never changing their pace and never pausing for rest. As they ran they chanted and sang in a noisy, undisciplined way, as if they were carrying an empty chair, but with each step they took they delivered a newly painful jolt of discourtesy to the kimono-clad interpreter cowering uneasily inside.

30

Traversing slowly back and forth across a steep face of red and black ash, Eden and the former Japanese castaway edged slowly upwards towards a rocky shoulder of the volcano. The almost vertical cliff of crumbling slag was too soft to scale directly, and their feet slipped constantly in the loose volcanic ash as they followed their laborious zigzag course. They were digging their staves and heels in deep to prevent themselves sliding back, and the effort this required caused them to grunt with exertion at every step. The thick white vapour of a dense cloud through which they were climbing blotted out the sun's glare from above and a sharp wind, which had forced them to tighten their hat strings, whipped constantly at their faces.

Both men were panting for breath and perspiring freely as they reached a winding lava gully filled with volcanic rubble and cinders. Big, slag-covered stones jutted through the floor of the gully, giving it the appearance of a crumbling staircase, and Eden took the opportunity to scramble up this natural flight of steps to the jutting shoulder of rock. Resting breathlessly on his stave, he turned to watch Sentaro stumble up behind him. The castaway's straw sandals, he noticed, were badly frayed and worn, like his own, and he could see that the soles of his feet were blistered and bleeding in places; one of Eden's own feet was also gashed and its sandal was stained with fresh blood.

'Sit down on this rock, Sentaro,' said Eden firmly, as the Japanese arrived gasping beside him. 'Your feet need attention.'

Once the castaway was seated, Eden knelt and removed the mangled wisps of straw from his swollen feet. Uncorking the drinking bottle, he poured a few drops of water onto a cloth and wiped away the blood. Taking a fresh pair of straw sandals from Sentaro's waist-pouch, he slid them on and fastened them around the castaway's ankles. Then he tended his own gashed foot, and took out a new pair of sandals for himself.

'Thank you, master,' said Sentaro, still struggling to catch his breath. 'You show me much kindness I don't deserve.'

Eden looked at him for a moment. 'You're a brave man, Sentaro—and a loyal friend. I owe you a great debt of gratitude for all the help you've given me . . .' He looked away and slipped his feet into the fresh straw sandals, tying them quickly. 'And it's not necessary for you to call me "master". Such deference is not needed between friends.'

Eden stared downward, trying to penetrate the grey-white cloud that swirled about them: small, ragged gaps had begun to appear through which fleeting glimpses of the lower slopes were becoming visible, but the main bulk of the mountain remained shrouded in dense vapour. Immediately below them the land fell away with a dizzying suddenness to disappear into the churning billows of cloud and, looking over what seemed to be a virtual precipice, Eden realized for the first time how high they had climbed. This first disturbing view of the mountain's massive black bulk, seen from on high, also renewed more intensely the feelings of foreboding that had seized him soon after dawn and he shuddered involuntarily.

'I thank you for the kind warmth of your words, master,' said Sentaro quietly, bowing his head once. 'But I address you like this to show proper respect and admiration for a good man . . .'

They stared down into the fog in silence for some moments; then the Japanese jumped to his feet and pointed to a dark patch of mountain which had become visible far below, where the forest finally gave way to the harsh expanses of treeless lava and sand.

'Look, master! Down there!'

Eden strained his eyes, unable to see anything. 'What is it, Sentaro? What do you see?'

The Japanese moved closer to him, pointing through a gap in the scudding clouds. 'A line of men—look, master! And climbing very fast.'

Eden looked again, and caught sight of a dozen or more figures, ant-like in their smallness, snaking out of the forest in single file. At their head were three quick-striding figures clad entirely in white, but the remainder wore darker clothing. From time to time the white-robed men stopped to peer up into the racing clouds and, on seeing this, Eden rose and clambered swiftly over the ridge of rocks on which they were resting, calling for Sentaro to follow him. Sprawling face-down in the lee of a lava knoll which made them invisible from below, they studied the line of moving figures more closely.

'The men in white must be *goriki*, master,' said Sentaro in a hushed voice. 'They are men of the mountains who act as guides for climbers. They know every track and path . . .'

'And the other men are samurai,' murmured Eden grimly, after pulling out his miniature field-glasses from his pouch and focusing them. 'I can see they are wearing cloaks and helmets—and twin swords.'

'Somehow they've followed us,' said Sentaro in a surprised voice, watching the line of figures scurrying swiftly upwards. 'I think they know we're here. They're coming after us!'

Eden nodded slowly, his eyes fixed on the moving column of climbers. 'I'm sure you're right. But this is a very big mountain. It will have many hiding places. We have several hours' start and today there's much cloud.'

'What do you plan to do, master?' asked the Japanese with a puzzled frown. 'How can we possibly escape them?'

Eden turned and peered along the face of the mountain, which had previously been hidden from their view. He could see a narrow ledge, wide enough to walk on, that wound away over another shoulder of rock, and he turned back to Sentaro with a thoughtful expression on his face. 'There must be many different routes up Fuji-san, am I right?'

'Yes, master, there are at least five or six. They lead up from different directions, because pilgrims come to Fuji-san from all parts of Nippon.'

'Good.' Eden nodded quickly and rose in a crouch, keeping his head below the level of rocks. With one hand he gestured towards the narrow ledge. 'We'll turn north now—and stay at this level until we can find another route leading up from the other side of Fuji-san. That way we'll get to the summit without being seen—and we'll avoid them by coming down a different way.'

He peered cautiously over the ridge to take a last look at the line of climbers far below. Under the leadership of the white-clad *goriki*, the whole column was moving smoothly upwards, evidently following a more direct path that had not been discernible to Eden from below. The *goriki* had long ropes slung over their shoulders and they were using them frequently to help the samurai clamber up the steepest slopes. They were ascending at more than twice the rate he and Sentaro had achieved and after watching their progress for several moments, Eden turned and laid an encouraging hand on his companion's bony shoulder.

'They're catching us up fast. We must try to move more quickly ourselves.'

'I am rested now, master,' said the castaway eagerly. 'I am quite ready to climb again.'

Eden looked at him for a moment. His narrow, unlined face was serious, its expression calm and determined. In his eyes there was an excited brightness, but there was no sign of doubt or lack of confidence in Eden's leadership.

'Good, Sentaro. Then we'll go on.'

Eden tapped his closed fist gently against the castaway's upper arm and, without speaking further, turned and led the way onto the narrow, northward-facing ledge.

31

From the saddle of his moving horse, Yakamochi, eldest son and heir of Lord Daizo of Haifu, gazed angrily up at the dark mass of Mount Fuji that towered above him. Thick cloud still enveloped its upper regions, but high on an area of its harsh sable flanks that was still visible from below, the file of Prince Tanaka's samurai and their *goriki* could be seen moving steadily upward. As they approached the lower banks of cloud, the leading climbers were already becoming indistinct shapes, and Yakamochi cursed softly beneath his breath.

'How far ahead of us are the men of the Kago clan?' he asked, continuing to watch the tiny moving specks through narrowed eyes. 'How many hours will it take for us to reach that level?'

'At least two hours, my lord,' replied the stocky leader of a group of shaven-headed monks who were trotting beside his horse, carrying staves and coiled ropes of plaited cotton. 'Possibly three hours, if the mist comes down heavily again.'

Yakamochi's face creased into a scowl and as the hillside was becoming too steep for horses to negotiate easily, he reined in his mount. Behind him his troop of fifty warriors immediately brought their horses to a standstill, and the monks who had been hired from a nearby mountain monastery to guide them also came obediently to a halt.

'Is it possible for us to catch them up?' demanded Yakamochi of the leading monk. 'If we dismount now and go forward quickly on foot?'

The monk glanced up the steep slopes of the volcano. 'The guides, my lord, are the most experienced in these regions. They are *goriki*, trained men of the mountains, and they have already led the Kago samurai to a considerable height. By following in their footsteps it would be impossible to catch them up before they reach the summit.'

Yakamochi cursed again and raised his head to look skyward. A lone eagle was floating silently in and out of the mists high above them, and he gazed at it for a long moment in silence.

'If we had the wings of the eagle, we would be able to find the foreign barbarian very quickly,' he said vehemently, watching the great bird glide effortlessly through the lower clouds. 'But, earthbound, we are blind in these mists.'

'My lord, if you wish to look down on the world like an eagle, it would be better for you to fly up quickly above the clouds.'

'What do you mean?' Yakamochi looked down sharply at the leading monk, who had made his suggestion in a calm, gentle voice. 'How can we fly up above the clouds?'

'On such days as this, my lord, the peak of Fuji-san itself almost always stands above the clouds . . .'

'That is possibly true,' broke in Yakamochi impatiently, 'but how can it help us?'

The monk gestured briefly towards two riderless horses that were being led by Yakamochi's samurai guard captain. 'At the inn where you found these horses, the *teishi* said the foreign barbarian and his collaborator left to climb Fuji-san alone and without guides. Therefore they will be moving only slowly. But by riding fast for a few short miles, you could climb quickly to the peak by a route which is little known . . .'

'Do you truly know such a route?'

'Yes, I do, my lord. And by using it you will be able to overtake both the men of the Kago clan and the foreign barbarian at a single stroke! From the summit you could then look down on your approaching enemies before they see you—just like the emperor of all birds.'

Yakamochi stared hard at the monk, his face alight suddenly with excitement. 'A worthy suggestion—that way we will prevent the foreign barbarian from reaching the peak and profaning the most sacred precincts of our gods!'

'We pray so, my lord.' The monk bowed his head low to acknowledge Yakamochi's praise, then glanced up the mountain again to where the last of the distant climbers could be seen disappearing into the bank of low cloud. 'But to ensure we reach our goal in time, my lord, we should leave at this very moment.'

'We shall go on at once! Can you ride?'

The monk bowed low again. 'Yes, my lord.'

'Then you will take the horse of the foreign barbarian.'

Yakamochi turned and signalled to his guard captain, who immediately brought one of the riderless horses forward. After conferring with his fellow guides, the leading monk swung himself easily into the saddle.

'You will wait here for our other search troop,' Yakamochi ordered the guard captain. 'Find enough fresh horses for the remaining monks. When our other troop arrives, ride hard with them and the monks, and follow us as swiftly as possible to the summit of Fuji-san. Is that understood?'

'Yes, my lord.'

The guard captain bowed low to acknowledge his instructions but, before he straightened up, Yakamochi and the monk had turned their horses' heads to the north-east and were spurring them into a fast gallop across the slopes of black cinders, followed closely by all the other samurai.

32

In the luminous white fog of a higher cloudbank Robert Eden felt his heart begin to thud heavily against his ribs. A feeling of tightness in his lungs indicated that the chilled air was becoming more rarefied, and he stopped to lean against a rock, gasping for breath. His head was starting to ache and a dizzying sensation gave him the impression that the steep slope beneath his feet was shifting and rolling. The fog swam before his eyes and when he turned to look back over his shoulder he saw that Sentaro had dropped a long way behind and was barely visible, stumbling with difficulty over a cluster of basalt rocks thirty feet below. Eden stopped climbing and waited for the castaway as he had done many times before, again searching the blanket of whiteness for shadowy shapes that might betray the presence of their pursuers. But he saw nothing to arouse his suspicion and he turned his attention back to the slow-moving figure of Sentaro.

They had struck upward again in the direction of the summit after trudging along the narrow ledge for more than an hour. Remembering the determined speed at which he had seen the group of samurai climbing, Eden had tried to press onward at a much faster pace than before, but as they moved higher he had to wait more frequently for the Japanese to catch up. As the mountainside became steeper and the cold increased, Sentaro's rate of climb had slowed noticeably, and soon he was stopping to rest every few minutes. Although he had not seen or heard anything to suggest that their change of direction had been discovered, Eden found himself glancing back constantly over his shoulder as they moved higher to check that they were not being overhauled.

Above and below them, the slopes of volcanic ash and sand had now given way to ugly escarpments of black stones, gritty pumice and sharp rocks which rattled back down the mountain in streams from every step they took. The wind had recently died away and their laboured breathing and the clatter of these miniature landslides were the only sounds to be heard in the eerie silence. They were climbing beside a high ridge of soot-coloured lava, which had spouted violently from the still-invisible crater during one of Fuji's many past eruptions, and the ferocious energy locked up inside its frowning bulk seemed to add a new dimension of threat to the endless wilderness of stark black rubble all round them.

'Are you all right, Sentaro?' asked Eden, scrutinizing the Japanese closely as he scrambled up the slope to join him.

'Yes, master. Don't worry. My chest hurts a little, that's all.'

'The air is much thinner at this height—try to breathe slowly and evenly until you get used to it.' Eden could see from the castaway's weary face that the long, arduous climb was beginning to take its toll, and he patted him encouragingly on the shoulder. 'You're doing fine—keep going. We'll take a rest soon.'

As they continued to scramble upward, sometimes on all fours, rain began to fall and was soon lancing down in freezing torrents; the wind also rose again to lash the rain against their faces. Eden moved closer to the wall of black lava, seeking its limited shelter, but within a few seconds the rain had turned to hail and bullet-like fragments of ice bounced and cracked ferociously against the lava rock all around them. Behind him, Eden heard the castaway cry out suddenly and he turned to find that he had fallen and was lying motionless face-down among the black stones.

Slithering quickly down the slope, Eden knelt to gather him up in his arms. On turning him over, he saw there was a gash three inches long above his right temple; his eyes were closed and his face was very pale. A faint blueness was visible around his mouth, but after a moment his eyes flickered open and he struggled into a sitting position, a bewildered look in his eyes.

'Forgive me, master! What happened?'

'Don't try to talk,' shouted Eden, leaning closer to protect him from the driving hailstones. 'You slipped and gashed your head.' He looked round desperately. 'We've got to find shelter.'

The rising wind was tearing ragged holes in the cloud and Sentaro raised himself suddenly to point ahead to the foot of the next drift of volcanic rubble above them.

'Look, master, there's a pilgrim hut!'

Following his pointing finger, Eden spotted what appeared at first to be a small tunnel leading into the mountainside. Lifting Sentaro in his arms he bowed his head against the storm and scrambled up the rocky slope at a stumbling run. As he drew nearer, he realised that what he had thought was a tunnel was in fact a square door of discoloured wood. It covered the entrance to a small hut so deeply submerged under tons of rock and cinders that it seemed to be part of the mountain slope. Eden tugged open the door, and ducked into the small dry interior, where bundles of firewood and other pilgrim supplies hung from low wooden rafters blackened by the smoke of countless fires. Rolls of bamboo matting covered the rocky floor around a central stone hearth and, after lowering Sentaro gently onto one of the mats, Eden closed the door and barred it against the wind.

'The gods of Fuji-san have been kind to us, master,' gasped Sentaro, smiling weakly up at him in the near darkness. 'They've led us to a shelter when we most needed it. I'll make a fire now and prepare some food for us.'

Still breathing raggedly, the Japanese tried to struggle to his feet but found he was too weak. Sinking back onto the mat, he began to shiver violently from the cold.

Outside, the wind was moaning and blowing more furiously, and hailstones flung themselves angrily against the door. With each gust, the drifts of rock and stones on the roof moved with a roaring reminiscent of shingle on a beach, sending fine showers of grit and sand drifting down into the hut.

'You need to rest until you recover your strength,' said Eden, hauling a dusty bale of padded quilts down from the rafters. 'Wrap one of these around yourself. I'll make a fire.'

Eden used matches from his waist-pouch to kindle a fire with twigs and wood in the stone hearth. The hut filled quickly with blue wood-smoke which stung their eyes, but the cheering flames soon brought a reviving warmth to their shuddering bodies.

Kneeling beside Sentaro, Eden inspected the gash on his forehead by the firelight; although the wound had not bled profusely, his temple was bruised and badly swollen, and a faint blurring of his gaze hinted that he might be suffering a mild concussion.

'After some food, you must sleep,' said Eden firmly. 'I'll bathe the wound later with hot water.'

Among the rudimentary utensils stowed above the rafters, Eden found iron cooking pots, wooden plates, beakers, and a vegetable-oil lamp. He lit the wick of braided cotton and heated water over the fire to make black tea which Sentaro gulped down gratefully while the eggs, rice and vegetables he had bought were cooking in another pot. Afterwards, Eden washed and dressed Sentaro's head wound with a makeshift bandage, and as soon as they had eaten the food the castaway lay down close to the fire and fell into an exhausted sleep.

Outside, the noise of the hailstorm, which had abated temporarily, grew suddenly loud again as though it were deliberately launching a renewed assault. Shrieking gusts of wind tore at the tiny hut, seeming to snatch away its entire covering of rock and stone one moment, then dashing an unbearable new deluge down upon its roof the next. Furious showers of hailstones were being hurled simultaneously against the door, and the whole hut began to sway under the awful barrage. Pulling a quilt round his shoulders, Eden added more wood to the fire and shifted nearer to the comforting flames himself. Fresh falls of grit and sand were pouring through cracks in the roof and it seemed suddenly to Eden as though the whole mountain might be starting to rumble and sway beneath him.

In his troubled sleep, Sentaro whimpered and groaned as though unconsciously aware of the storm's heightened ferocity, and Eden watched the castaway's eyes flicker repeatedly as though he was trying in vain to wake himself from some unbearable nightmare. A long-drawn-out, growling roar seemed to accompany each new swirl of wind and hail and as Eden looked around at the quivering walls and rafters of their precarious shelter, a cold worm of fear began to wriggle somewhere deep in his brain.

He remembered suddenly, with great clarity, his first moonlit glimpse of Mount Fuji seen from the darkened ocean. The image of peerless beauty had so overwhelmed his senses that it made him wonder whether he was seeing some ethereal vision of God—a God he had long since rejected. But he also remembered, with even greater clarity, the alarming sensation that had swiftly followed: the suspicion that the unearthly vision shimmering in the night might equally be a beacon warning him or the American warships—or both—against some terrible tragedy.

Those moments of matchless beauty had drawn him towards the volcano like a moth to a flame—but even though the great mountain was now shuddering terrifyingly all around him, he found he still did not regret his response to that irrational impulse. Instead, he was seized by a strange feeling of near-ecstasy at experiencing for himself the gigantic power of the natural forces swirling around the volcanic cone. He had felt similar stirrings of awe during violent sea tempests, but never before so intensely, and something deep within him seemed to throb suddenly in response to the wildness of the storm.

With part of his mind he found himself wondering how far they might be from the summit crater. And what thickness of rock might exist between his back and the mighty funnel through which the white-hot lava of any new eruption must gush. Listening to the primal rumble of the wind and earth after climbing Fuji's desolate, black flanks for several long hours, it seemed perfectly possible that at any second the sacred volcano might erupt for the first time in two hundred years, and send molten lava gushing skyward.

The more he thought about it, the more likely it seemed, and his acceptance of the possibility eventually helped to calm his fears. If that same eruption swept away the hut and both its occupants in a sudden blaze of light, as in his dream, that too, he told himself, he was prepared for, because something unimaginably greater than himself had seemed to demand it.

Perhaps, he thought suddenly, that was the whole reason for his coming there—to give sacrificial point to the cataclysmic warning, to become part of it, to become its very essence! But whether that was true or not, in abandoning himself to this invisible force, he felt again the same profound sense of peace and serenity which had flooded into his mind as he looked on the image of Fuji for the first time; and in that same moment he knew with total certainty that, however great the risks had seemed, it had been right to come.

While these extraordinary thoughts and feelings were coursing through him, the wind rose to a howling crescendo, and Sentaro began to moan incoherently in a loud voice as he slept. A new avalanche of rock and sand was hurled onto the roof of the hut with a shuddering crash, and great clouds of grit fell on the fire, smothering some of its flames. The volcanic dust peppered Sentaro's sweating face, too, but still the castaway did not waken. Looking down at him, Eden was seized by an intense feeling of compassion, and in the next instant a cold calm rationality surged back into his mind.

Sentaro was injured and now feverishly ill; and the troop of samurai pursuing them was as great a threat to him as it was to Eden himself. Therefore it was suddenly clear that the wisest course would be to abandon their attempt to reach the summit and head back down the mountain as soon as the storm abated. They had already climbed high, and experienced at first hand something of Fuji's extraordinary power. But turning back now would give them at least a practical chance of escaping unscathed from the region. Exposing Sentaro to further risks, he reasoned, would be a betrayal of the castaway's unflagging loyalty, as well as an act of the greatest foolishness.

Another louder rumble came from the mountain, rocking the hut on its foundations, and the next moment there was a deafening crash as a further shower of rocks and volcanic debris smashed down onto its roof. Dust poured through the rafters in torrents, extinguishing the lamp and the remaining flames of the fire. The interior of the hut was plunged into darkness and Sentaro awoke with a wild shout of alarm. To comfort him Eden lunged across the hearth and cradled the castaway's head in his arms.

'It's all right,' he shouted above the frenzy of the storm. 'Don't be afraid!'

'What's happening, master?' croaked the castaway. 'Where are we?'

'The storm's put out our fire,' shouted Eden. 'We're still in the hut.'

Several more waves of debris broke over the shelter in quick succession, and Eden felt the castaway's body shaking with fear. The wooden walls creaked loudly, as though on the point of collapsing under the assault; then, as abruptly as it had begun, the storm began to subside and the wind slackened. Within minutes the frightening noise had died away and only the faint drumming of gentle rain on the roof could be heard. Soon even this sound ceased, and almost immediately the darkness inside the hut was penetrated by a bright ray of yellow light. It fell directly onto the face of Sentaro, and the Japanese looked up fearfully at Eden.

'Who is that, master?'

For a moment Eden stared uncertainly at the light; entering horizontally through a crack in the door, it fixed itself unwaveringly on the face of the Japanese, growing brighter with each passing second.

'There's no need to worry,' said Eden at last, speaking in a relieved voice. 'It's the setting sun.'

33

The eagle wheeled in a great, slow circle, drifting easily on the wind, its wings straight and unmoving. For several moments it hovered motionless, then it turned and swooped majestically down towards a vast, fleecy sea of cloud that stretched from Mount Fuji to the horizon. Like the clouds themselves its plumage was turned to gold in the dying blaze of the sun and, watching the gilded bird swinging through its graceful gyrations thousands of feet below the open door of the tiny pilgrim hut, Eden marvelled at its grace and power.

'Do you see the eagle, Sentaro?' he asked quietly over his shoulder.

'Where, master?' The shivering castaway pulled his quilts more securely about himself and craned his neck towards the doorway.

'There—look!' Eden pointed into the vast abyss spread before them, to where the eagle, now little more than a glowing speck, was sliding closer to the mountainside.

Peering downward, the Japanese let out a muffled exclamation of awe when he spotted the great bird. 'I've never looked down on an eagle in flight before,' he breathed. 'This must be how the gods see our world.'

The sun was dipping below the western rim of the dense continent of fleece, dispersing and unravelling vast regions of it at the same time with the aid of the wind. Crimson and orange light was flooding over the ragged vapour contours, setting them ablaze, and in the far distance purple peaks of real mountain ranges were coming into view, thrusting up like fingers of smoke through the clouds. Golden veins of light shimmered in the dark landmass emerging below, hinting at the presence of rivers and lakes. Valleys and gorges, forests and foothills were also being revealed as the vast tectonic plates of cloud slowly parted. Some regions remained deep in shadow, others glowed suddenly under the blaze of the dying sun, and as Eden looked at each boundless vista in turn he felt a sense of exultation at the lifting of the oppressive, day-long cloak of cloud. After the harrowing storm and the blind scramble up Fuji's grim black sides, the beauty of the sunset seemed to heal and revitalize all his wearied senses within moments.

Above their heads the immense dome of the sky was fading from blue to a softer, more subdued luminescence, and for the first time Eden was able to see at a glance the whole of the mountain's massive girth below them. The perfect, unwavering line of the western slope nearest to the pilgrims' hut seemed to have been slashed down the sky with an unearthly geometric exactitude, never deviating a degree from its course: a diagonal horizon tipped at forty-five degrees to the earth below, it sped dizzyingly downward, as unerring as an arrow in flight, to disappear into a cluster of cloud still clinging around the mountain's base. The uniformly black surface of sand looked as though it was raked daily with the greatest precision to preserve a total perfection of line, and Eden stared at the slope in silent, awestruck wonder.

'I can understand now, Sentaro, why the people of Nippon have always considered Fuji-san to be a sacred dwelling place of the gods,' Eden whispered over his shoulder. 'It's not like anything else I've ever seen. It looks as if it was shaped quite deliberately with giant hands . . .'

'They say that slope is the best way down, master,' murmured Sentaro, looking in the same direction. 'It is very soft sand, and you can run fast all the way to the bottom.'

Eden craned his neck, following the line of the western slope above their shelter. Because fresh heaps of rocks and black drift had piled up around the hut, he was unable to see very far, but the all-pervasive blackness of the volcano was relieved suddenly, within his range of vision, by the tail of a long gully of white snow. Sparkling brilliantly in the light of the sinking sun, it reached down almost to the level of the pilgrim hut, and the sight of it caused Eden to cry out in surprise.

'Sentaro, we've reached the snow line!'

He rose and moved out impulsively through the door of the hut, trying to see further up the mountain. Then, remembering their pursuers, he dropped into a crouch and retreated into the doorway again. His face thoughtful, he turned and looked back at the shivering castaway.

'While you slept I've been thinking, Sentaro,' he said quietly. 'It wouldn't be wise for you to climb any further. Our best course would be to try and get back down the mountain under the cover of darkness. Then I'll head for the ship and you can begin making your way to Yurutaki.'

The Japanese looked at Eden without replying; huddled in his quilts close to the dead fire, he was still shivering, his face was very pale, and he was perspiring more freely than before.

'I know how much it means to you, master, to climb to the summit of Fuji-san,' he said at last in an unsteady voice. 'In your dream you reached the very top . . .'

'It's not more important than your safety,' replied Eden gently. 'And you'll recover faster if we descend immediately.'

The Japanese bowed his head in a gesture of thanks, but his expression remained dogged. 'I thank you, master, but remember I also want to climb to the peak of Fuji-san for myself. I feel the gods have guided my thoughts, and I want very badly to pray at the peak and give thanks . . .'

'Sentaro, I don't think you have enough strength—'

'But, master, listen,' pleaded the castaway. 'Riding here, I've seen once more the great beauty of my homeland. I've moved among my own people for the first time in a long while. In my heart I feel quite different now. I am very sure my place is here, no matter how great the dangers are. I know something of your country . . . Perhaps I can help others here to know something of it too . . . And I want to pray at the summit of Fuji-san for all these things.' He paused and peered anxiously at Eden. 'Do you understand?'

Eden stared at the castaway's bruised and swollen face. 'I understand, Sentaro—but I still don't think it's wise for you to climb any further. It would be better for you to rest a little, before we go down.'

'Then you must climb on alone, master!' the Japanese persisted. 'Go right to the top for both of us. I'll wait here.' Eden began to shake his head, but a beseeching look came into the eyes of the castaway. 'At least go out now and climb above the hut! You will be able to see then how far it is to the top. Soon the sun will go down—this will be your last chance.'

Eden hesitated; then he smiled and patted the castaway on the shoulder. 'All right, I'll go and take a look. You wait here and keep warm.'

After scanning the slopes below the hut to check that there were no signs of the pursuing samurai, Eden picked his way up onto the cliff of lava, taking pains to conceal himself amongst the black boulders as he moved. Slipping into a crevice which provided cover on all sides, he raised his head cautiously above the rocks until he caught sight of the volcano's magnificent white crown rearing towards the evening sky. The sun was by now sinking fast into the western clouds, but the pyramid of snow was softly reflecting its golden light. A few thin wisps of vapour clung to the high crags of lava rock that ringed the crater, but otherwise the pinnacle of the volcano, remote and austere in its grandeur, had become fully visible in the light of the setting sun.

Eden stared upward, feeling himself gripped by a new sense of excitement and awe. They had come very close to their goal without realizing it, and he felt a sudden urge to rush headlong up a stepped lava dyke which he could see leading across the remaining escarpment. He guessed that no more than five hundred feet separated them from the crater, and he was filled with the sudden conviction that he could spring lightly to the summit within a few minutes, with little or no effort.

It was at that moment that he saw the tiny figure of a man appear on the crater's white rim. Dwarfed by the mountain, the man remained visible only briefly as he moved in front of a column of snow-covered lava. A second figure followed, then a third, and all three men stood still as though looking down towards his hiding place. Then they disappeared abruptly and Eden's heart began to thud faster in his chest as he ducked out of sight himself.

The figures silhouetted starkly against the snow had seemed so minute that he immediately revised his estimate of the remaining distance to be covered: perhaps it was nearer a thousand feet than five hundred. But, more disturbingly, all three men, he was certain, had been wearing horned helmets and ribbed armour, and despite the distance it was clear that they were carrying the now familiar twin swords of the samurai tucked into their sashes.

34

Pacing fretfully along the lip of Mount Fuji's summit crater on its northern side, Daizo Yakamochi seemed to see neither the infernal signs of scorching inside the awful cavity nor the breathtaking beauty of the necklace of mountain lakes that shimmered in the gathering dusk beyond the volcano's northern flanks. Swathed in a long, thickly padded white kimono, his breath steamed from his mouth in clouds in the cold air and he gazed distractedly ahead as he walked, his expression agitated and ill-tempered. The stocky leader of the group of mountain monks, who had guided him and his first troop of samurai swiftly to the summit by the little-known north-eastern route, was trotting respectfully at his heels. Whenever the heir to the leadership of the Makabe clan slowed his pace, the monk slowed down too, taking care always to remain two or three steps behind him out of respect for his exalted rank.

'Why have we not made any sightings of the foreign barbarian yet?' demanded Yakamochi in an impatient tone, stopping to peer down abstractedly at the seared and blackened walls of the crater. 'Why does there seem to be no sign of him?'

'He has probably taken shelter somewhere against the storm, my lord,' replied the monk mildly, as he came to a dutiful halt behind the young nobleman. 'And, until the cloud lifted, it was difficult for anybody to see very far down the mountain.'

'If we don't find him soon, it will be dark,' snapped Yakamochi. 'The night will make our task more difficult.'

The monk glanced quickly across the gaping maw of the half-mile-long crater, checking in turn the positions behind rocks and lava knolls where he had stationed hidden groups of samurai alongside his guides. The second search group had long since caught up, swelling the small Makabe clan force to more than seventy warriors. Some were crouched in hiding; others were stretched out flat on the frozen ground so as to remain unseen, and from time to time small knots of men rose silently to their feet to hurry surreptitiously to new vantage points.

'I am confident all our sentinels are continuing to maintain vigilance, my lord,' said the monk quietly. 'You can rest assured that every known approach to the summit is under our surveillance.'

'What is the latest information on the movements of the men of the Kago clan?' asked Yakamochi, still staring absently into the crater. 'Which route are they following now?'

'They are apparently still moving across the northern face of the mountain at the same level, my lord. They are heading westward. You will remember that, before the storm, one of my monks saw them change direction after they stopped to pick up some discarded sandals. It's far from certain why they are going that way . . .'

The leading monk broke off, watching two samurai who had appeared suddenly in the distance at the western end of the crater. They were running swiftly side by side through the snow, and the monk watched without making any comment until he was sure that the two warriors were heading towards them.

'But I think we can expect, my lord, that before the sun sets our patience will be rewarded . . .'

Yakamochi looked up sharply at him. 'What do you mean?'

Instead of replying, the monk nodded silently in the direction of the fast-approaching samurai. One was Yakamochi's guard captain and, on hearing their hurried footsteps, the nobleman turned quickly. When they slid to a halt to prostrate themselves on the snow before him, he signalled impatiently for both warriors to rise.

'What do you have to report, Motohiro-san?' demanded Yakamochi, addressing the guard captain. 'Have you seen something of importance?'

'Yes, my lord,' gasped the captain breathlessly. 'There is a single climber below the western end of the crater. He was concealed among the rocks when I first caught sight of him.'

'Are you sure he was alone?' demanded Yakamochi.

'Yes, my lord, we are sure! Nobody else was visible.'

'Do you think it was the foreign barbarian that you saw?'

'It's impossible to say for certain, my lord,' replied Motohiro, his chest still heaving. 'He was wearing white clothing, and a broad straw hat—but he seemed to be a very big man.'

'How far down the mountain is he?' asked the monk quietly.

'Just below the point where the snow begins,' said Motohiro, turning to his companion. 'Am I right?'

The other samurai nodded his agreement.

'About a thousand feet from the crater; that would make sense,' said the monk, his voice rising a little with excitement. 'There is a pilgrim shelter there, at that level. And that is also the direction in which the men of the Kago clan have been heading.'

'Was the man you saw coming up towards us?' asked Yakamochi.

'No, my lord. He climbed a little way very cautiously, then stopped and hid among the rocks. We left our companions watching his hiding place.'

'Then we must go down quickly to capture him! Otherwise he may fall into the hands of the Kago clan!' Yakamochi turned to the leading monk, his eyes bright with excitement. 'I want you to lead a dozen of my most nimble warriors quickly down that route.'

'It is a good way up, my lord, but a dangerous way to descend from this peak,' said the monk without any sign of emotion. 'But it *is* possible, with care. If you wish me to lead armed men down there, I will do my best.'

Yakamochi turned back to his samurai. 'You, Motohiro, select the twelve finest fighters and lead them down to capture the foreign barbarian—alive if possible. But don't let him escape or fall into the hands of the Kago warriors, whatever happens. If necessary we can even use his dead body to foment war at Uraga!'

Motohiro placed his hand on his sword hilt and bowed low. 'I have understood, my lord.'

'You, remain here on the peak in command of the rest of our combined troop,' ordered Yakamochi, turning to the other samurai officer. 'Guard all other approaches and be ready to send reinforcements down in case the foreign barbarian evades capture or the Kago warriors appear!'

The second samurai also bowed in acknowledgement, then both men prostrated themselves formally at Yakamochi's feet again, before dashing away to carry out his orders.

'I shall accompany you myself,' said Yakamochi, looking grimly at the leading monk and urging him into a fast walk. 'I wish to be on hand to see the foreign barbarian captured—or killed.'

35

When he thought it was safe again, Robert Eden raised his head cautiously above the ridge of black lava and stared up towards the rim of the crater. There were no further signs of movement, but he feared that unseen eyes might now be watching him from the heights. Yet if they were, how had the pursuing band of warriors reached the summit so quickly? Or had they split into two, he wondered, with one section heading rapidly for the summit while the other continued to follow on behind Sentaro and himself in an effort to trap them? This thought caused him to turn his head to peer back down the mountain; but again he could see no sign of human movement anywhere on the ominous black slopes that were visible to him.

In the act of turning to look southward he noticed that, as the sun dipped lower, the dense clouds were fragmenting and rolling apart more rapidly. An enormous panorama of mountain and forest landscapes, sunlit and shadowed by turns, was now spread before him, stretching for many miles in all directions. Dazzlingly golden in the far southern distance he could see the broad expanses of Yedo Bay and the coastlines. In the crystal clear light of the lowering sun, the sails of junks and other ships were visible, being blown like flecks of gold dust across the shimmering surface of the sea.

Narrowing his eyes he searched the waters of the bay until, with a jolt, he recognized a familiar sight: twin columns of dark smoke were spiralling up in lazy drifts from indistinct black shapes on the surface, and he knew this smoke could only be issuing from the coal-burning engines of the *Susquehanna* and the *Mississippi*. Although it was obvious that the ships were not moving, he sat and stared at them for a long time, astonished that he was able to see evidence of the squadron from the higher reaches of the volcano. He guessed that the two most powerful warships must still be under orders to keep up steam, in case they were required to move into sudden action, and he realized then that he had scarcely given a thought to the ships since slipping silently over the side of the *Susquehanna* nearly forty-eight hours earlier.

The distance between the warships and his hiding place, which he knew must amount to fifty or sixty miles in all, seemed even more immense; snowy floes of cloud still drifted in patches across the face of this vast natural canvas, yet most of the land and seascape surrounding the ships was sharply defined in the perfect evening light. To his astonishment he was able to see the twin capes and the central islet at the distant mouth of the bay, as well as the rugged coastlines which funnelled up towards its head. There he could distinguish a shadowy concentration of buildings which he deduced must be the capital city of Yedo.

As he continued to survey the bay and all the land in between, Eden found himself wondering idly if any of the sailors on the warships might at that moment be peering towards the spectacular peak of the volcano; and, if they were, could they imagine that the missing officer from the *Susquehanna* might be gazing back at them? Thinking these thoughts, he was seized with an irrational desire to make some sign with smoke or a mirror that might be visible to the lookouts posted on the warships. But as soon as these notions entered his head he rejected them as foolish as well as dangerous. Any signal that could be seen from the ships would certainly be detected by the samurai looking down from the summit, and would betray the hiding place they had so fortuitously found.

While he sat staring out towards the ships, other thoughts and questions began to tumble rapidly through his mind. How were the negotiations faring? Had any agreement been reached yet on how the letter from the President of the United States should be delivered to the Emperor? And, if so, had the tension along the shores lessened? Lifting one hand to shade his eyes against the last dying glory of the sun, Eden found he could pick out in silhouette some of the fortifications that were ranged along the coasts. But because of the great distance involved he could not otherwise discern anything that indicated what progress was being made with military preparations. Although he knew for certain a massive force of warriors was being assembled to confront the might of the American guns, the wide evening landscape stretching from horizon to horizon gave an impression only of peace and a vast, silent serenity.

As the light faded, new accumulations of cloud were racing in from the east, and large areas of land and sea had begun to disappear from view almost as quickly as they had been revealed. Within a few minutes the whole Bay of Yedo was again concealed, and the twin capes at its broad mouth had also melted into a misty invisibility. To Eden it seemed as if a gigantic natural veil were being drawn back hurriedly across a beautiful and enigmatic face, rendering it mysterious again at the very moment when it had seemed on the point of revealing itself fully for the first time.

The brevity of the revelation had been tantalizing, and he frowned as he stared down at the thickening belts of new cloud. He could scarcely believe that he had impetuously ridden some fifty miles across a land so different from his own. Ruled by strange and rigid codes which had endured unchanged since ancient times, it still seemed remote and impenetrable, even as he stood on the heights of its most sacred mountain. In the few skirmishes forced upon him during the journey, he had more than once felt the ferocious courage of its fighting men; and, by contrast, in the shadows of the moonlit barn he had also fleetingly known some of the tenderest and most passionate moments of his life. These experiences, he realized, had served to deepen the sense of fascination he had begun to feel months before, when he first set out to learn the language of Nippon, although then, as now, he had not truly understood the reasons for this fascination.

As his mind went back to the ruined barn, vivid images of Tokiwa lying naked in his arms flashed disturbingly through his mind; they lingered to become inextricably mingled with the continuing sense of puzzlement he felt as he gazed down at the canopy of cloud spreading out below the mountain. What had Tokiwa thought and felt during the intense and tumultuous moments of their brief meeting? And what truly were his own feelings? Her beauty had been heady and intoxicating, but like her country and its people she had in the end remained remote and elusive. His own passions had been fiercely stirred and some emotional part of him that had long been dead and cold had been unexpectedly revived. But what, he wondered, could the people of Japan really think of those they so insistently called 'foreign barbarians' and of whom they knew so little? Could understanding, friendship or love grow between peoples of such extraordinarily different experience and history? Could naked emotion ever hope to bridge such an enormous gulf? A breathless feeling of physical excitement tightened his chest as these memories and unanswerable questions chased one another through his mind, and he shuddered suddenly from the cold.

Glancing towards the west he saw that the sun had been swallowed up in the dense cloud, and its light was being rapidly snuffed out. The earlier golden effulgence had turned to a flood of bruised, crimson shadows, and a single bright star was beginning to glimmer in the twilight. The sight of the solitary star in the darkening heavens made Eden turn his head to look up again at the peak of the mountain; but in the gathering dusk he could see no sign of the helmeted figures who had appeared earlier at the crater's edge and, after carefully surveying the slopes all around him, he slipped out of his hiding place. While slithering down the black lava rock, he realized he had left Sentaro alone for some considerable time and he began to hurry, anxious to tell him that he had seen the warships smoking on the distant bay. When he reached the pilgrim hut, its door stood ajar and he pulled it open eagerly to duck inside.

'Sentaro, I saw our ships!' he called softly, dropping to his knees by the hearth and gathering together fresh firewood to relight the fire. 'The clouds rolled back and I could see for about a hundred miles . . . But I believe that there are samurai already up there on the peak.'

Disturbed suddenly by the quietness in the hut, Eden broke off and peered into the gloom. The vegetable-oil lamp was flickering in its jar by the hearth, but no response at all came from the shadows beyond it. Rising to his feet in alarm, Eden seized the lamp and raised it above his head. Its light illuminated all four corners of the dusty shelter, and Eden saw then that the quilts with which Sentaro had covered himself had been abruptly discarded in an untidy heap beside one wall. Eden's belongings lay untouched on the hearth where he had left them, but the castaway, his waterproof waist-pouch and his climbing staff were gone.

36

The covering of crisp snow crunched beneath his sandalled feet as if it were powdered glass when Eden scrambled, bent double, into the mouth of a drift-filled lava gully forty feet above the pilgrim hut. Clutching his climbing stave he ducked down behind a cluster of bare rocks that jutted up through the snow like the serrated humps of a black dragon. His broad hat was pulled down over his eyes, and he was carrying his sword in the gun-belt outside the padded kimono so that it would come quickly to hand in an emergency.

He had selected the cluster of rocks just above the snowline as the closest vantage point to the hut from which he would be able to see down the mountain in all directions. The rocks themselves protected a bulging knoll of basalt and, when he had settled himself, he craned his neck to survey each of the downward slopes in turn, hoping to catch sight of Sentaro's slight figure. But nowhere on the wastes of dark shale could he detect any sign of human movement. He also searched east and west along the face of the volcano, yet still saw nothing. Baffled, he scrutinized all the same downward slopes again, using his miniature binoculars, but without any success.

The light was fading fast and the snow in the gully gleamed whiter in contrast to the sinister sable wastes all around. With the sun sinking rapidly into the clouded horizon below, more stars were beginning to glimmer overhead and, with feelings of desperation mounting inside him, Eden turned to look up over his shoulder. As he did so an indistinct flicker of movement on the snowy cliff two or three hundred feet above him caught his eye. At first he thought a small wounded animal was scuttling up the snow-filled lava gully, but when he turned to focus his gaze more intently, he realized he was looking at the hunched figure of a man scrambling clumsily upward on all fours.

For a second or two Eden stared in disbelief; despite the fading light he could see that the climber was wearing a cone-shaped hat of straw and a long white gown. Lifting his binoculars to his eyes, he trained them carefully on the heights and drew in his breath sharply as the identity of the tiny figure was confirmed beyond any shadow of doubt. In almost the same instant another flurry of movement drew his attention, and he raised the binoculars quickly to scan the snow-capped summit. This time he saw a long line of agile figures descending rapidly from Fuji's jagged crater. Moving purposefully in single file, about fifteen men were heading down a snow-filled ravine towards the scrambling figure, who remained unaware of their approach. Three or four of them were unarmed but Eden could see that all the others were helmeted samurai who wore swords and carried bows and quivers slung about their shoulders.

As he watched the armed men, the rational part of Eden's mind told him that now was the perfect moment to slip away down the black shale of the western slope, at a fast run. In the gathering gloom he could reasonably hope to reach the foot of the mountain unseen and begin his journey back to the *Susquehanna* under the cover of darkness; any other course of action seemed certain to end in disaster. Glancing westward along the mountainside, he wondered if he was right to suspect that other warriors might appear from below at any moment. There was no sign yet of other climbers but the suspicion strengthened his urge to plunge back down the mountain, and with his eye he picked out a likely path that led away through the rocks beneath his vantage point.

On raising his gaze again, however, he saw that the small, lone figure was now sinking repeatedly into the snow, and was having to stop frequently to rest. The armed samurai were taking advantage of every contour to remain hidden from view, but they were clearly moving to cut him off, and Eden watched for only a moment longer before rising abruptly from his hiding place and lunging out into the gully, in full view.

'Sentaro!' he yelled in Japanese, waving both arms wildly above his head. 'Turn round! Turn around and come down—fast!'

Eden's shouts echoed resoundingly across the snow-covered faces of the mountain, but Sentaro did not look back. He seemed to stumble, and stopped for a moment, clinging to a rock as though on the verge of exhaustion; but then he pushed on again, moving—it seemed to Eden—with the strength that comes only from desperation.

High above the castaway, the line of samurai halted for a few seconds and stared down at Eden; then a flurry of shouted commands and responses rang back and forth between them before they resumed their descent, clambering down more rapidly than before. Seeing that his warning had been ignored, Eden shouted the same words again and threw himself forward, jabbing his stave fiercely into the snowdrifts to help lever himself between the jutting blocks of lava.

But still Sentaro did not stop or turn to look back, and Eden fell silent, concentrating all his energy instead on moving as fast as possible up the steep-sided gully. With the disappearance of the sun, the air had become icy cold, and although the wind had quietened, it was still blowing strongly enough to whip flurries of crystalline snow from the rocks into Eden's face. Through these flurries Sentaro remained intermittently visible, appearing and disappearing by turns as he zigzagged awkwardly amongst swirls of snow-dusted lava which Eden could see had long ago burst out from a narrow, lateral side crater less than a thousand feet below the summit. The castaway had to turn eastward briefly to skirt this gaping oval crater before stumbling on above it and, watching him, Eden noticed that his movements were becoming more sluggish and erratic the higher he climbed. Never raising his head, he appeared to be oblivious to everything that was happening around him, and Eden wondered if the concussion he had suffered had disordered his senses.

When they saw that the castaway had changed direction slightly, the samurai, who were lowering themselves swiftly between similar knolls of lava, paused briefly for discussion. As soon as they began moving again, Eden saw that they had split into two groups. Half a dozen of the faster warriors, led by two guides, were striking daringly across the snow-covered rockface in a diagonal line, heading directly towards Sentaro and the side crater. The rest were proceeding more slowly, moving along a well-defined ravine that would bring them downward in a wider sweep to cut off his retreat to the side and the rear. Sentaro's own pace slowed to a crawl as he entered another gully and, on seeing this, Eden began to climb faster, straining every muscle in an effort to get to the castaway before the descending samurai.

Within three minutes Eden had reached the side crater and, after racing around its scorched rim, he caught sight of Sentaro again no more than a hundred feet above him. The castaway had stopped halfway up a funnelled gradient of deep snow, and fallen to his knees beside a ridge of black rock, his head bowed to the ground as though in silent prayer. Some two hundred feet higher up that same snow-covered ridge, Eden suddenly saw the smaller group of samurai come into view. Swinging hand over hand on braided cotton ropes, they were making rapid progress down one of the volcano's steepest cliffs. They caught sight of Sentaro and Eden at the same moment that he saw them, and excited shouts immediately erupted from their throats.

'Kill the traitor!' yelled one warrior.

'Capture the barbarian bandit!' screamed another.

'Take them both now—alive or dead!' roared a third.

The samurai continued to give vent to their battle cries as they came nearer, but the castaway still did not move and Eden broke into a run up the snowy slope.

'Sentaro, get up!' he cried desperately in Japanese. 'There are warriors above you! Come back this way.'

If the castaway heard he paid no heed, and he neither raised his head nor moved in any other way. The shouts of the samurai were growing louder but a longer, more despairing cry rang out suddenly above the din. Looking up, Eden saw that one of the warriors had lost his footing and was tumbling headlong down the mountainside. The flailing body spun and twisted as it fell, and the warrior's dying screams rang eerily through the dusk as he bounced and rebounded sickeningly off the jagged rockface before plummeting down into the black abyss of the side crater.

The remaining samurai and the two guides halted in their tracks, clinging to precarious handholds, and watched in horror as a rush of ice and rock followed the body down the precipice. A moment later a louder noise filled the air as a vast slab of snow, set in motion by the falling body of the samurai, started to shift and detach itself from part of the mountain below them. Breaking rapidly into many smaller waves, it cascaded downward within seconds, rumbling and roaring like an ocean storm.

On hearing the awesome sound of the approaching avalanche, Sentaro stirred himself at last and staggered to his feet. Realizing that part of the moving snow-wall was hurtling directly towards him, he turned and started to run frantically back towards Eden; but before he had taken many paces it broke over the last ridge of black rock and crashed on down the slope at his heels.

'This way!' yelled Eden above the tumult and dashed forward, waving his arms to attract the dazed castaway's attention.

Because he was looking round fearfully over his shoulder, the Japanese stumbled and almost fell. By now the churning bow-wave of the avalanche was no more than fifty yards away, and when Eden reached his side Sentaro was glassy-eyed with fear and exhaustion.

'Hold onto me!' shouted Eden close to his ear, and swung the slight body of the Japanese up onto his shoulder in a fireman's lift. 'Just hold on!'

Flinging himself sideways out of the path of the rumbling snowslip, Eden plunged in amongst rocks flanking the gradient, and lowered Sentaro to the ground. Crouching protectively over him, he covered his own head with his arms, and a moment later the white tidal wave roared past this natural barrier, shaking the ground and filling the air above their heads with a fine mist of whirling snow and grit. For several seconds the mountainside around them seemed to boil with the frothing white turbulence but, as suddenly as the snowslip began, it ceased and a strange, silent stillness immediately closed in all around them again.

'Master, thank you,' croaked Sentaro in a stricken whisper, staring at Eden with feverish eyes.

'Don't talk,' warned Eden. 'Just try to get your breath so we can start down the mountain as soon as possible.'

Pushing his straw hat back onto his shoulders, Eden cocked his head to one side, listening for sounds of movement on the rockface overhead. When he heard nothing, he quietly unscrewed the stopper from the neck of his water bottle. Cradling the castaway's head with one arm, he put the bottle to his lips.

'I don't understand why you decided to climb up here,' he breathed as he watched the castaway drink. 'I came back to warn you I'd seen warriors on the summit—but the hut was already empty.'

'I did it for you, master,' gasped Sentaro, after drinking deeply. 'You wanted to climb right to the peak—but you gave up because of me . . . I knew if I went on, you'd follow.'

'You shouldn't have taken such a risk . . .' began Eden in a severe tone, then broke off, motioning the castaway to silence.

From the rocks overhead the crunch of stealthy footsteps on snow had become faintly audible in the gathering dusk. Easing the hilt of his cutlass higher in his belt, Eden rose in a watchful half-crouch and edged away from the rock wall, peering upward. Narrowing his eyes as he listened, he tried to separate the different footfalls, and hazarded a guess that perhaps four or five warriors were moving cautiously towards the lip of the rocks a few feet above them.

Within moments this suspicion was confirmed, and he found himself staring up at a row of fearsome samurai war helmets. Outlined starkly against the brightening stars, the helmets were fitted with grotesque fighting masks of painted leather, which concealed the features of half a dozen of Lord Daizo's cavalry samurai. Only the narrow eyes of the warriors glittered behind the masks, as they stared down at Eden and Sentaro, but a sudden muttered order and an ominous flurry of metallic noise indicated that six long killing swords had been withdrawn simultaneously from their scabbards.

'Surround and disarm the barbarian spy! But leave the traitor alone. I will kill him myself!'

The voice of Daizo Yakamochi rapped out the fierce commands a moment before he and the five other samurai hurled themselves down from the rocks. Their cloaks spread out darkly around them like wings as they plunged onto the snow, but in an instant they were standing upright and forming a threatening semicircle around Eden. With their long swords extended in front of them, they began to move watchfully towards him.

'Come here, Sentaro,' yelled Eden in Japanese, drawing his own sword and retreating towards the rock. 'Get behind me!'

Taken aback at hearing their own language spoken by a foreign barbarian, all the samurai hesitated, and the castaway, who had been crouching on the snowy ground, struggled upright. Rushing to Eden's side, he shrank against the rock, his face taut with fear.

'Sentaro is not a traitor to his country!' Eden spoke quickly in Japanese, as he watched the warriors edging closer around him. 'He's just a shipwrecked fisherman who was saved by an American ship. Now he's come home to the country he loves . . .'

Yakamochi, who had been staring at Eden, suddenly moved a pace forward, in front of the other samurai. Tugging off his helmet and mask, he studied the American officer intently.

'You are the barbarian who robbed me of my sword on the black ship!' he exclaimed in a surprised tone. 'And now you have become a spy!'

Eden looked back at the samurai nobleman in astonishment as recognition dawned. The man's face was dark, his eyes narrow and deep-set, his lips harshly thin; the front of his head was shaven in the traditional style, and a long pigtail was tied up in the usual topknot across the crown. His expression was glowering and hostile and in the twilight Eden was reminded suddenly of the anonymously cruel Japanese face which had appeared so dramatically before him in his shipboard dream of Mount Fuji. With night gathering swiftly about the mountain and pinpoint stars beginning to glimmer more brightly all around them, the most disturbing image of his dream seemed to have re-created itself in reality with an eerie exactitude. After recovering from his surprise, Yakamochi took half a pace forward, and it was plain to Eden that his fiercest desire was to avenge the intense humiliation he had suffered on board the *Susquehanna*.

'I remember you also,' said Eden, standing his ground and watching Yakamochi's swordtip align itself with his chest. 'But you're wrong to think I came ashore to spy on you . . .'

'What other reasons could a barbarian who speaks our language have for landing secretly among us?' rasped another contemptuous voice from the rocks above them. 'I am Motohiro, guard captain to Daizo Yakamochi, the young lord of Haifu! You are now a prisoner of the noble Makabe clan. Surrender your sword and don't insult us with your lies!'

Eden looked up to see a tall, topknotted figure standing with feet apart on the edge of the rocks. Flanked by three or four other samurai and the mountain monks who had led them down from the summit, Motohiro was still breathing fast from his exertions but his face was alight with the triumph of their capture.

'I'm not lying to his lordship,' said Eden quietly, looking first at Motohiro then at Yakamochi. 'I came in peace to seek understanding. That's why I've travelled as far as Fuji-san.'

'You are lying. You are both spies!' exclaimed Yakamochi, his eyes ablaze. 'You were disturbed in your foul work at the Uraga fort!'

Eden shook his head and spoke again with an added urgency. 'Fate forced Sentaro to spend four years in my country. He learned many new things there—that's why he wished to help me grow in understanding here in Nippon. He has taught me something of your language—and he knows men of different races can be brothers. He could help the people of Nippon to understand that.'

'What the barbarian says is true, my lord!' Summoning his courage, Sentaro shifted uneasily to a position where he could look directly up at Yakamochi. 'I revere His Imperial Majesty the Emperor and I love the sacred land of the gods where I was born. In all truth I am not a spy—'

'You are at least a common traitor who has betrayed Nippon by consorting with foreign barbarians,' bellowed Motohiro, glaring at the castaway and lifting his sword above his head. 'The orders of my lord are that you shall die by this blade!'

The ring of samurai moved threateningly closer behind Motohiro and Yakamochi, but Eden did not retreat: instead he thrust the point of his own sword towards Yakamochi. 'If you want to kill Sentaro, you will have to kill me first!'

'Die—if you wish to die,' hissed Yakamochi, taking another step forward. 'And your corpse will be displayed at Uraga in chains. That will be enough to expose the treachery of the black ships. Every doubting clan throughout Nippon will then join an all-out war to drive off the foreign barbarians!'

Eden froze for a moment as the implications of these words sank into his mind; then Yakamochi sprang forward, swinging his sword through a savage horizontal arc in an effort to decapitate the American with one stroke. Ducking quickly to one side, Eden swung his own blade upward with all his strength and squarely intercepted the blow; Yakamochi's sword flew from his hand and he stumbled, falling momentarily to one knee in the snow. In the same instant another piercing battle-cry rang in Eden's ears, and he saw Motohiro's sword whirling down towards him. He tried to duck and twist away from this new danger but moved too late and could only partly parry the heavy blow. The two swords locked at the hilt and Eden and Motohiro teetered and swayed against one another for a moment before the weight of the samurai's rush carried Eden backwards against the rock with a sickening crash. The collision knocked all the wind from him, and his sword fell into the snow as he sagged forward, gasping for breath. His face came close to his opponent's and he saw an anticipatory gleam of triumph appear in Motohiro's eyes.

'You wished to die for the traitor, wretched *gai-jin*!' grunted the Japanese. 'Now I grant your wish.'

Growling like an animal, the guard captain heaved himself backward, swung his blade behind his shoulder and slashed viciously at Eden's throat. Still struggling to regain his breath, Eden tried to sway out of range, but he was hemmed in too tightly against the rock. At the last moment he ducked below waist level to avoid the blow and the samurai captain's weapon clanged against the rock face, creating a bright cascade of sparks.

While Eden was snatching up his fallen sword, Motohiro closed in again, cursing loudly, aiming to impale him with an underarm thrust of the long, curved blade. Before he completed the stroke, however, the air around them came alive with the whine of arrows. Two or three shafts ricocheted harmlessly against the rock face above Eden's head, while half a dozen others thudded into the flesh and body armour of the watching half-circle of Makabe samurai, scattering them amidst a chorus of curses and agonized screams. A few arrows sped harmlessly wide of their targets to fall unnoticed in the snow, but one drove itself bloodily through the throat of Motohiro from behind, its honed metal head forcing its way obscenely into view beneath his chin as he froze in mid-stride. Choking horribly and pumping crimson blood onto the snow, he pitched forward, dropping his sword, and lay still only a few feet from the spot where Eden was struggling shakily to his feet.

'It's the men of the Kago clan, who were following us, master!' gasped Sentaro, pointing across the slope. 'They're running to the attack!'

Eden looked up and saw a disciplined formation of twenty helmeted Kago samurai charging across the gradient towards them with swords drawn. A handful of their bowmen, standing on rocks amongst which they had previously been hiding, were still firing repeated salvoes of arrows towards Yakamochi and his men, and the swordsmen, leaping determinedly across the broken banks of snow, began to yell loud battle cries as they drew nearer. Some carried freshly lit torches of orange flame which clearly illuminated the Kago clan symbols emblazoned on their shields and pennons, and by their light Eden spotted the fast-striding figure of Prince Tanaka charging at their head.

'Take cover there, Sentaro,' hissed Eden, pointing urgently to a nearby jumble of rocks. 'And get away down the mountain if you can. I'll try to follow.'

'Are the Kago warriors coming to our rescue, master?' asked Sentaro in an agonized voice.

Eden shook his head quickly. 'For their own purposes perhaps—not ours. We seem to have become a battle prize. Go now! Before it's too late!'

As Sentaro scuttled off, Eden realized that Yakamochi had climbed the ridge and was roaring out angry new commands from overhead. Looking up, he saw that a short line of archers, kneeling along the edge of the rocks, were bending their bows furiously to pour a continuous shower of arrows into the ranks of the advancing Kago clansmen. Because the approaching samurai were running with their shields raised to buffet away the arrows, few if any found their mark, and the voice of Yakamochi rose higher in angry exhortation.

The half-dozen Makabe samurai below the ridge, who had been scattered by the first shock fusillade of arrows, were reforming themselves hastily into a new battle group in the lee of a rock, preparing to confront the charging Kago force. Some were still tugging out or breaking off the feathered arrows that jutted harmlessly from their thick body armour of bamboo, leather and chain-mail; other fighters, who had arrived from the summit by the longer route, were jumping down from the ridge to augment them and as soon as he saw that a company had formed up around one of his officers, Yakamochi yelled a fresh command to send them into action.

'*Charge bravely now, men of Makabe! Charge!*'

As his samurai lunged into action, Yakamochi turned and looked down towards Eden. Only seconds had passed since the surprise attack was launched out of the darkness, and in that time he had rapidly marshalled his forces to a disciplined resistance. Without taking his eyes from the American, he barked another order over his shoulder, and three more of his helmeted samurai immediately drew their swords and separated themselves from the protective formation drawn up around him. They ran forward to the lip of the rock and flung themselves down towards Eden, yelling hoarse battle cries as they came.

In response Eden took a step forward, raised his sword, and dropped into a defensive crouch. From the corner of his eye he saw the two opposing ranks of charging samurai crash together in a maelstrom of kicked-up snow and whirling steel. Battle cries and shouts of pain rang loud across the snowy cliffs of the volcano as the warriors of both clans hacked and slashed at one another in a cold, sustained frenzy. Their archers had ceased to fire arrows now that battle was joined at close quarters and some were shouldering their bows and leaping down from the vantage points to rush through the snow towards the heart of the fighting. In the moment before his first attacker sprang at him, Eden saw the white-clad figure of Sentaro dash out suddenly from a cluster of rocks to his right. Keeping clear of the fighting, he started to run unsteadily downhill through the snow, apparently unnoticed, and Eden felt a surge of exultation rush through him; if somehow he could get free and follow the castaway down the mountain into the darkness, there was still a chance that all might turn out well!

The battle scream of the leading samurai who flung himself at Eden seemed to issue from the gaping jaws of a ferocious animal. Beneath the horns of his elaborate helmet, the protective mask was a bestial grimace composed of jagged teeth, a flattened, animalistic snout, and flaring eye-holes. Framed against the starlit heavens and the snow, the lunging warrior looked and sounded like some terrible avenging deity of Fuji, and in response Eden's own throat opened by instinct to roar out a primal Indian war-cry.

The Japanese warrior's long killing sword, held fast in two fists, came flashing down through a perpendicular arc, aiming to hack off his adversary's sword-arm at the shoulder. But as the atavistic war-whoop welled out of Eden, it seemed to send new strength surging through his limbs. Stepping swiftly sideways at the last moment, he swung his own sword in a mighty overhead blow that split the Makabe samurai's grotesque helmet and drove him unconscious to his knees in the snow. The warrior rushing up behind him stumbled over the fallen man, and lost his balance. As he staggered, he slashed wildly at Eden's head, but Eden dodged the wild stroke with ease and thrust his blade swiftly through the samurai's shoulder, withdrawing it in an instant and stepping clear as the man doubled over, groaning in agony, and dropped his sword.

The third warrior threw himself at Eden in a headlong dive, aiming a ferocious killing thrust at his heart. Eden turned his body in time to avoid the jabbing weapon, but the warrior's momentum knocked him to the ground. They rolled over and over in the snow, grunting, grappling fiercely and lashing at each other with their swords—but neither was able to land a disabling blow.

Although night had fallen, and the stars seemed to be whirling and spinning above him in heavens of the darkest velvet, the snow itself seemed to glow with a fluorescent whiteness that bathed objects near and far in a strange bright glare. As Eden rolled and fought and struggled to preserve his life, the shimmering peak of Fuji overhead spun repeatedly through his field of vision, outlined against the starry sky with the unnatural clarity of a giant painting. The continent of fleecy cloud that cloaked the whole world below had turned a deep, thrilling purple—but to his eyes it also seemed to have been etched meticulously from horizon to horizon by some gigantic ethereal artist.

One hand of the samurai was locked on Eden's throat, the other was restraining his sword arm, and the American simultaneously held the warrior in a similar stranglehold. As he strove in vain to break free from this rolling embrace, Eden wondered if he was seeing the mountain, the sky and the battling warriors with such spectacular sharpness because he was about to die. For years he had not cared whether he lived, indeed he had been continually careless and contemptuous of his life; but facing almost certain death amidst a bloody mêlée of feudal swordsmen, to his astonishment he was filled suddenly, as never before, with an overwhelming desire to live. Life in its every detail seemed to shimmer with a new force and, whenever his head turned, he saw Yakamochi on the ridge, watching his struggle with the sharp, intent eyes of a hovering hawk. Then he noticed Yakamochi making angry gestures to despatch half a dozen more warriors in his direction, and the men leapt down immediately from the rock to run yelling towards him.

He also saw archers at Yakamochi's shoulder, pointing urgently down the mountain. When he rolled over again he could see that they were drawing the nobleman's attention to Sentaro, by then a small, diminishing figure descending shakily through the snow towards the rim of the side crater. Eden saw Yakamochi gesture angrily, he saw the bows of the archers bend suddenly to the limit, he saw their arrows fly, and an instant later he saw Sentaro fling up both arms and pitch forward on his face in the snow. He could even see the dark feathered shaft of the arrow protruding from the red stain in the middle of his back—and the castaway did not make any further move.

Eden was making another frantic effort to break free of the Makabe samurai's tenacious grasp, when he saw Yakamochi urge two more swordsmen down the mountain in the direction of the side crater. He still had a troop of two dozen fighters grouped around him on the ridge, and in that instant Eden became aware that the numerical superiority of the well-disciplined Makabe warriors would prove decisive. The Kago samurai led by Prince Tanaka had launched a brilliant shock assault with fewer men, and had even achieved total surprise. At least ten bleeding bodies, most of them Makabe, already lay crumpled on the snow, and bloody hand-to-hand battles were still raging fiercely around them—but whatever the Kago objective had been, he could see that the smaller force was not going to be strong enough to achieve it.

When the new group of Makabe attackers surrounded him, their clan emblems of symbolized clouds and pine trees seemed to Eden to gleam as though freshly painted on their bobbing helmets and sword hilts; their bamboo and chain-mail body armour glowed brightly too, each segment distinctly visible to him. They yelled fresh battle cries as they swung their swords up above their heads and seeing the blades start to descend towards him, Eden made one last effort to break free from the grunting samurai who was pinning him against the ground. He finally succeeded in throwing him onto his back, but still he clung on and knowing it was too late, Eden closed his eyes involuntarily to blot out the falling death blows.

He heard the angry swish of swords, without seeing them; a strangled, gurgling cry followed, then died abruptly, and Eden wondered if it might be his own. Then he was struck by the weight of an inert body, and he felt the shock of other sword blows finding their mark. Screams of agony and rage mingled nearby, and fire flared suddenly, brightening the darkness behind his closed eyelids. At the same moment all the strength went out of his samurai adversary and he went limp in Eden's grasp.

Opening his eyes, Eden found the headless body of another of his attackers sprawled bloodily across him. The man with whom he had wrestled was also dead, his back ripped open by a terrible wound. Frantic feet were trampling the reddening snow all around him, and on looking up he instantly recognized Prince Tanaka: holding a flaming torch aloft in one hand, the Kago nobleman was driving back another pair of Makabe warriors with a flurry of furious blows. In close support, Gotaro and three other Kago samurai were engaging those around them with equal fury and Eden saw them hack down two more screaming opponents who tried to rush Tanaka simultaneously from different sides.

As he dragged himself to his feet, Eden became aware of Yakamochi ranting along the ridge, gesticulating towards Tanaka. Within moments another assault group had been formed from the Makabe reserves and, hurling themselves down from the rocks, they began to charge across the snow towards Tanaka, yelling in unison as they ran. Still clutching his sword, Eden bent low to make himself as inconspicuous as possible in the darkness, and began to run too—in the opposite direction. Skirting the frenzied tangles of fighting men he raced on downhill, still nourishing the faint hope that he could somehow reach the wounded Sentaro in time to escape with him into the safety of the lower darkness.

Ahead of him he spotted the two samurai who had been sent after the castaway. Running surprisingly fast over the broken snow, they had covered half the distance to the rim of the side crater, and Eden gritted his teeth fiercely, trying to accelerate. But a dull pain in his right thigh grew more agonizing with each step, and looking down he saw blood was soaking rapidly through his white kimono below the waist. The wound, which had obviously been inflicted during the long struggle in the snow, made him cry out and he slowed to a hobble. A wave of dizziness swept through him, and he heard a new outbreak of shouting from behind; the voices grew louder, as though they were moving rapidly down the mountain, and although he did not look round he guessed the clamour meant he had been spotted from the ridge and more Makabe warriors were setting off in pursuit. Another fit of dizziness made him stagger suddenly, and he knew then that his hopes of escape were forlorn.

The two samurai despatched by Yakamochi had now reached the inert form of Sentaro, and something in the quick decisiveness of their movements made Eden's blood suddenly run cold. One of them had drawn his sword and he took up a careful stance with his feet apart at the very edge of the side crater. The other warrior squatted quickly, hauled Sentaro's limp body to its knees, and dragged it forward. The arrow which had felled him still jutted from his back and the castaway's head hung down on his chest, suggesting he was not fully conscious of what was happening. The sword swung once through a deadly arc and Eden watched in horror as the kneeling samurai rose to his feet, lifted the headless trunk of Sentaro's body and tossed it casually over the rim of the crater in its turn. The two warriors stood looking down into the scorched abyss for only a brief instant before turning away to retrace their steps up the mountain.

Eden realized then that he had stopped in his tracks, to witness this moment of horror. The two samurai executioners caught sight of him for the first time as they began to jog-trot back up the snowy slope, and in that moment Eden plucked his cutlass from his belt and began moving down towards them at a stumbling run. Another primitive battle roar, in which grief and rage were mingled equally, burst from him and he brandished his weapon wildly above his head as he ran on. Ignoring the fierce pain from the thigh wound, he fixed his agonized gaze on the two surprised swordsmen, his mind emptied of everything except a blind urge to avenge the brutality and humiliation of Sentaro's death. He fell to his knees twice in the deep snow, but scrambled up each time and struggled on, oblivious to all except the two executioners who stood watching calmly from the foot of the slope.

Although the shouting from behind him had grown louder, Eden seemed not to hear it, and when his leading pursuer drew close enough to aim a blow at his head, he did not turn. The sickening impact of the sword, when it fell, spun him around but his eyes saw only the glittering peak of the volcano. His arms flew wide, his own sword spun away into the darkness, and his hands seemed to reach up as they had done in his dream towards the heavens and its countless stars.

As he sank onto the snow, the stuff of which the starlit night was made seemed to tumble easily into his hands like glistening silk, and he wound it softly around his body, luxuriating in the sudden feeling of ease and relief it brought him. Then another blade smashed sickeningly against the side of his head, and the millions of stars exploded in a blinding flash of white light. In the same instant the mountain, along with everything else, dissolved into a cold, silent void.

PART IV

The Black Ships Land

12–17 July 1853

As the dramatic summer days of mid-July 1853 ticked by, the American sailors watching from the US warships in Yedo Bay sometimes relieved their growing tension by poking fun at the antiquated defence works that were becoming ever more visible on the shore. 'Another dungaree fort's gone up, sir,' lookouts would cry jestingly as new lengths of coloured canvas screening were erected to conceal further contingents of Japanese fighting men clad in medieval combat costumes. The banners, pennants and insignia under which the Japanese were gathering did indeed look more like the decorations for a jousting tourney in King Arthur's England than preparations for modern nineteenth-century warfare. Their outdated-ness helped confirm prevailing American feelings of superiority—but the two and a half centuries of self-imposed feudal isolation which those trappings symbolized had in fact been of vital importance for Japan. During a crucial historical period when European nations had begun to colonize and control vast areas of Asia, this fiercely guarded seclusion had helped the Japanese to consolidate and expand unique national characteristics that were to make their country one of the modern world's great powers within a few short decades.

The feudal clan system had inculcated the principles of loyalty, obedience and self-discipline into every Japanese; these virtues were focused towards, first, their immediate clan lords, then ultimately the Emperor, who was revered as the divine head of the national family and the living representative of the gods in 'the land begotten by the sun'. The deep conviction fostered by the national religion, Shinto, that every Japanese was in turn a unique and divine member of this sacred family was consequently further strengthened. No other major nation in history had ever achieved such self-sufficiency over so long a period and during those two hundred and fifty years the samurai spirit, which primarily encouraged cultivation of personal inner strength and determination, also became ingrained in the national psyche.

The term 'samurai' can be translated as 'servant', 'vassal' or, by implication, 'fighting man'. Samurai traditionally formed the upper class in feudal Japan, standing directly below the ennobled daimyo and the imperial court.

But members of the aristocracy and princely families who wished to do so also practised the samurai arts. To win this prestigious status, however, was not easy. A long, rigorous period of training and education had to be endured and this began at a very early age. In an attempt to remove all superstition and fear of death, boys as young as five years old were sent to watch hideous public executions and sometimes had to carry away newly severed heads in their hands without flinching. To strengthen their nerve further, they were also made to revisit execution grounds alone in the middle of the night. In other exercises they were toughened by deliberate exposure to extremes of cold, starved for short periods and forced to remain awake all night. Successful candidates received their swords at the age of fifteen, after immersion in a long educational process that was as much spiritual as physical.

At special élite schools, fundamental precepts of Confucian duty were taught as well as Zen-Buddhist mysticism and the practices and principles of Shinto. Breathing and meditation techniques enabled the samurai to understand the science of energy as it was then perceived and achieve a sense of communion with nature, the earth and ultimately the universe. All this was designed to help him achieve his supreme goal—the development of a sixth sense which made possible a total spontaneity of thought and action and a lightning swiftness with all his weapons. The Christian concepts of original sin and guilt were unknown to Shinto morality and whenever a samurai drew his sword and struck out, fatally or otherwise, the spontaneity of the act was invariably respected and assumed to be justified. It was for this reason that ordinary Japanese behaved with great caution in the presence of the two-sworded warriors. A samurai was also taught to excel in all other forms of combat, including bare-fist fighting, and he trained himself to remain ever alert, even in his sleep, so that he could leap into action immediately if attacked. This entire samurai code of conduct came to be known as Bushido or 'The Way of the Warrior' because in common Japanese parlance samurai were known as bushi or 'warrior knights'. The word do translates as 'the path' so the rules of the code laid down the true way for a warrior to demonstrate unqualified allegiance to his lord and emperor. These warrior knights became the officers of the feudal armies so their ethic spread downward to embrace all other ranks.

Since Japan's long period of seclusion ended, the spirit of Bushido has been frequently detectable in Japan's national behaviour. Carefully studying the enemy's strengths and weaknesses and striking one fast, lethal blow by surprise was the prime ambition of a samurai in combat, and the whole Japanese navy would apply this principle perfectly in May 1905. Then almost the entire Russian Baltic Fleet, the greatest and most modern of its day, was wiped out by surprise while passing through a narrow Japanese strait. Nearly forty years later, in 1941, 'Strike first—and by surprise!' was again the watchword when some 90 per cent of America's Pacific Fleet was destroyed in port at Pearl Harbor by Japan's air and sea forces while her diplomats deceitfully conducted peace negotiations in Washington.

In the very different circumstances of striding towards economic and technological primacy in the world of the late twentieth century, the Japanese continue to draw strength from these same feudal traditions and exclusive tendencies which still set them apart today as a nation. But none of these perspectives were visible to the unknowing American sailors of 1853, who could only see from their warships the quaint outer trappings of Japan's feudalism. Also they had no way of knowing, as they tensely watched the shore, that their brief intrusion into Yedo Bay would be the spur that plunged Japan into a turmoil of change—and that these changes would draw the Japanese people and their formidable energies decisively into the quickening flow of world history.

37

On the narrow bunk in his tiny cabin above the rudder of the *Susquehanna*, Samuel Armstrong pitched and tossed restlessly back and forth between the borders of sleep and a troubled wakefulness. An anxious sheen of perspiration was glistening on his brow and he muttered aloud and twitched every now and then as he drifted towards a hazy state of consciousness. A knocking noise seemed to be intruding into his clouded mind from some unidentified source, tearing at the last shreds of sleep: harsh and persistent, it sounded as though distant hammers were crashing urgently against wooden planks, and the noise was echoing and re-echoing ringingly across the dawn waters of the bay.

He was unsure whether the noise was real or dream-inspired and he tried, still without waking fully, to shut it out of his hearing. Part of his mind was already obscurely aware that the crucial fourth day at anchor before Uraga was dawning—Tuesday 12 July, the last of the three days allowed by Commodore Perry for the Japanese to reply to his ultimatum. Only a few hours were left now for them to decide whether to accept the letter from the President of the United States with due formality, or risk an American fighting force landing to deliver it.

'Today we'll know if it's to be peace or war,' Armstrong's half-wakened self had been whispering in an agitated tone inside his head since long before dawn. 'Today we shall know whether our bluff has been called. Today we'll find out if our marines and sailors will have to try and fight their way into Yedo . . .'

Perhaps, he thought suddenly in his half-dream, preparations for the despatch of the small invasion force had already begun. Perhaps the ship's carpenters had all been ordered to rise early and begin constructing coffins. When fighting began, he told himself sadly, casualties were bound to be heavy. Throughout the long hours of the previous day he had paced restlessly back and forth along the *Susquehanna*'s decks, watching the Japanese fighting units grow in density around the clifftop forts of Uraga and on beaches along both sides of the bay. Archers, pikemen and musketeers were seen being marshalled rapidly into defensive positions along the shores, and occasional cavalry units galloped vigorously into view with pennons flying. Estimates, among the flagship's officers, of the total strengths of the shore battalions varied from ten to fifteen thousand in the immediate vicinity, and if these estimates were true the American marines and sailors on the warships were overwhelmingly outnumbered by at least ten to one. It also seemed certain that many more Japanese warriors would be held in reserve, hidden from sight.

With other members of the *Susquehanna*'s crew, Armstrong had watched apprehensively as the *Mississippi* weighed anchor on Perry's orders at mid-morning and steamed off provocatively up the bay towards Yedo, flanked by a flotilla of armed cutters. When alarmed Japanese officials had dashed out to the flagship in their boats, he had personally translated to them the brusque explanation from the *Susquehanna*'s captain that the bay was being charted so that an American force could sail towards the capital and fight its way directly into Yedo if necessary. In the following hours big flotillas of local guard-boats had swarmed off around the point in pursuit of the steamer, and the land reinforcements arriving to man Uraga's coastal defences had swelled further in volume.

The *Mississippi* had returned safely before dusk to report many tense moments with the guard-boats, and after night had fallen more new beacons had flared above the heights of the bay; the war-gongs and temple bells, which had died away during Sunday, had also begun to beat and toll ominously again, and in response the *Susquehanna* had got up steam, taken in thirty fathoms of her anchor cable, and made the necessary preparations to slip the remainder quickly in any emergency. Guns had been shotted and run out, all the watches had again been doubled during the night, and extra lookouts had been posted aloft on all four ships.

Unable to rest because of the high tension, Armstrong had roamed around the ship into the small hours, anxiously watching the beacons and the troop movements, before falling into an uneasy slumber on his bunk around 4 a.m. Never fully asleep for long, and intensely aware that the rumbling boilers in the flagship's bowels were keeping her in a state of constant readiness, he had first noticed the loud sound of knocking at the moment when he began to dream that hundreds of hangman's scaffolds were being built onshore—one for every crew member of the entire US squadron. Then he remembered, in a bout of wakefulness, that the Japanese had no tradition of execution by hanging; but when he fell asleep again he dreamed with horrifying vividness about the mass crucifixion of Christian converts in Japan two centuries earlier.

This dream, to his consternation, repeated itself later in an even more alarming form and he saw and heard a forest of wooden crosses being erected noisily by leering Japanese carpenters on a hill opposite the ships. Moaning in protest, he was being lifted and nailed to the first cross himself when he was awakened fully at last by the sound of a loud knocking at his cabin door.

'Mr Armstrong, sir!' called the concerned voice of Midshipman Harris. 'Are you all right, sir? Are you awake?'

'Yes, I'm awake,' mumbled the missionary after a moment, opening his eyes in relief and sitting up. 'Come in.'

Through the open scuttle of the cabin the perfect cone of Mount Fuji was just appearing; emerging dramatically from the mist into the early sunlight, its entire outline became fully visible in an instant, glowing with a greater clarity than he had ever seen before. As he gathered his scattered senses, he stared out through the scuttle, wondering silently at the purity of the image, and it was while he was looking towards the volcano that he noticed that the constant sound of hammering, which had invaded his slumbers so persistently, was continuing in reality. Turning to look at the eager young midshipman who was standing to attention in the cabin doorway, he noticed that the youth, in keeping with the flagship's overall state of armed readiness, was wearing a cutlass slung from his waist.

'I'm afraid I've slept rather badly, Mr Harris,' said the missionary wearily. 'What can I do for you?'

'Flag Lieutenant Rice presents his compliments, sir,' announced the midshipman, straightening his posture further and squaring his shoulders. 'And he says he'd like to see you in his cabin as soon as you are ready.'

'Very well.' The missionary rubbed his eyes, realizing he had fallen asleep in his clothes. Straightening his cravat and smoothing his crumpled jacket, he swung his legs stiffly over the side of the bunk and stood up. 'Is the summons for something particularly urgent?'

'I believe the commander-in-chief has composed a new letter to the Emperor of Japan during the night, sir,' said the midshipman promptly. 'Lieutenant Rice has the letter, and a translation will be required before the Japanese delegation appears.'

'Are the Japanese expected?' asked Armstrong sharply. 'Has there been any sign of their boat?'

'Not yet, Mr Armstrong, sir. But Lieutenant Rice says the commander-in-chief is confident they will appear soon.'

Armstrong drew a long breath and knitted his brows in a frown. 'I hope he's right. A thousand American lives may depend on it.'

'The lieutenant asked me to say, sir, that the commodore is very concerned that everybody involved today should be correctly briefed as soon as possible.'

'Thank you, Mr Harris,' said Armstrong distantly. 'You've been very helpful.' The midshipman had begun to turn smartly away but the missionary raised a hand in his direction, requesting that he wait. 'You've heard that constant noise of hammering I suppose, have you?'

'Yes, sir. It's been going on most of the night.'

'What is it, do you know?'

'No, sir. Nobody seems to know, sir. It's coming from the shore—behind the bluff down the bay. The sound carries very clearly over the water.'

Armstrong nodded bemusedly and stood up. 'And what about the enemy fighting units on the shore? How do they seem to be behaving this morning?'

'They're already looking very active, Mr Armstrong, sir. There's been a lot of manoeuvring and marching. Lieutenant Rice thinks they're putting on a deliberate show of force—or preparing for hostilities.'

'I see. Then tell him I'll be there as soon as I've changed my clothes.'

'Very good, Mr Armstrong, sir.'

Although there was no need to acknowledge the civilian missionary formally, the midshipman saluted as a sign of respect before spinning round and marching away with one hand clenched self-importantly on the hilt of his cutlass.

When he had gone Armstrong took off his jacket and poured cold water into a basin from a jug to wash his face and hands. After changing his shirt and his cravat and puzzling for a moment over the continuing sound of hammering coming from the shore, he put on his jacket once more and walked quickly to the cabin of the flag lieutenant. When he entered, he found Rice was poring over a chart, writing in details of the soundings taken by the *Mississippi* and the cutters the previous day. After exchanging greetings with the missionary, the young officer looked up with a pleased expression on his face.

'The cutters found deep soundings all the way up the bay for twelve miles, Mr Armstrong. There's a bottom of soft mud, and the channel very likely continues beyond the furthest point they reached.'

'Is that a cause for celebration?' asked the missionary acidly.

'Yes, it is. The lead gave a depth of twenty fathoms in the centre of the channel. On the sides it struck banks of mud at around five fathoms. So it looks as if the whole squadron could push safely up as far as Yedo itself . . .'

'I hope and pray that nothing so extreme will prove necessary, Lieutenant,' said Armstrong soberly. 'We've made our best progress in the negotiations so far by peaceful methods. That surely is our greatest merit.'

Rice bent over his charts again and wrote in another figure. 'Our commander-in-chief believes the success of peaceful methods is best ensured by being prepared to act boldly and decisively with force of arms—should it prove necessary.'

'Doesn't the commodore have any qualms about the hundreds of American lives he's putting at risk?' asked Armstrong mildly. 'Or does he never think of such things?'

'I can't pretend I know the commodore's every unspoken thought,' said Rice slowly. 'His life will be at risk, too, remember. And I'm sure he believes that readiness to attack is the best means of defence—for his own skin as well as ours.'

'But the odds against us on land are growing hour by hour, despite our superior firepower,' insisted the missionary. 'They've probably got unlimited numbers of men under arms. The arms are ancient, but they're known to be proud and fierce fighters hand to hand. Why should we risk pushing them into a bloody fight to the death at this stage?'

Rice continued to busy himself with his charts, and his voice hardened. 'I don't think the commodore would presume to tell you how to go about converting the heathen, Mr Armstrong. So perhaps it would be best if you deferred your judgement—at least for a while.'

'And how long exactly does the commodore expect to wait for his results?' asked the missionary heavily. 'How long might it take before all this blows up in our faces?'

'A feint was made with the *Mississippi* yesterday,' replied Rice in the same calm voice. 'The commodore deliberately gave the impression the ship was steaming directly for the capital. And she passed further up the Bay of Yedo than any foreign vessel has done for three centuries.'

'That may not seem like a very great achievement if things go badly wrong as a result,' said Armstrong, shaking his head.

'The purpose was to stir up the Japanese and force a quicker response to our demand to deliver the President's letter,' continued Rice evenly. 'And it clearly worked, because the Japanese dovecote has been in a flutter ever since. The commodore doesn't expect to have to wait much longer.'

'Stepping into the unknown like this involves great risks,' said Armstrong severely. 'I had a terrible nightmare before I awoke this morning. I felt I was being crucified for what we are doing here.'

'The commodore has already marched fighting columns to famous shore victories in Mexico,' said Rice, ignoring the missionary's confidence. 'In Africa he also landed an armed force and struck unexpectedly into the heart of a pirate stronghold . . .'

'Japan is a very different kettle of fish to a pirate's lair in Africa,' protested Armstrong hotly. 'It hardly compares—'

'In both actions the commodore achieved his objectives without undue losses. So you can rest assured that he is a man who knows very well from experience what he's doing.'

The flag lieutenant paused and picked up a single sheet of vellum bearing a short letter written in the strong, flamboyant hand of Commodore Perry, and handed it to Armstrong.

'The commodore requests that you make a prompt translation of this new letter to the Emperor into Dutch and Japanese, so that it can be passed to the delegation as soon as they arrive.'

The missionary quickly scanned the short letter bearing Perry's signature. It appeared to do no more than restate formally that, as commander-in-chief of the US Navy's East India Squadron, he wished to meet one of the highest officials of the Empire of Japan as soon as possible, so as to present an urgent communication from the President of the United States. It added that he wished to hand over at the same time his own personal letter of credence. Armstrong read it quickly again, then glanced questioningly at Rice.

'This doesn't seem to add anything very much to our position, Lieutenant. What's the purpose behind it?'

'We've had very little contact with the Japanese for three days,' replied Rice, laying aside his pen and looking up significantly at the missionary. 'I think its primary aim is to re-emphasize the commodore's determination to stand firmly by his original demands until he gains satisfaction—here in the Bay of Yedo. I've also been asked to say that it's most important that you translate every word with those sentiments firmly in mind.'

Noticing from the officer's tone that he was passing on formal instructions that brooked no argument, Armstrong accepted them expressionlessly and without comment. 'Do I assume,' he asked quietly, 'that today's meetings are to be conducted in the same manner as before?'

'Yes. Commodore Perry will again supervise the negotiations invisibly, from the seclusion of his own cabin. But he anticipates the Japanese may try to employ new delaying tactics—or play for time in some way. He thinks they may even try to refer us to Nagasaki again. He will, of course, resist all such stratagems. And once more you are asked to assist by ensuring that every inflection of your translating shows our stand to be firm and unshakable. I trust that's clear?'

'It's perfectly clear, Lieutenant,' said Armstrong, inclining his head in acknowledgement. 'I'll go now and prepare the translation in my cabin.' The missionary turned away towards the door, then stopped, tugging thoughtfully at his whiskers. 'Lieutenant, may I ask if the subject of Robert Eden has been mentioned recently by the commodore?'

Rice shook his head. 'No, Mr Armstrong, there's been no recent discussion at all about Lieutenant Eden in my presence. Is there any particular reason why you ask?'

'None,' said the missionary with a shrug. 'Except he's been missing now for three days. His absence has been noticed by some of the crew, and rumours are doing the rounds. I wondered if we might ask the Japanese when they come aboard today, if there's any official news of him.'

The flag lieutenant shook his head decisively. 'The commodore's orders are very clear for today's meetings: the negotiations are not to be jeopardized by the introduction of any extraneous topic whatsoever.'

'Has the commodore offered no comment on the private information I passed to you on Sunday morning?' asked Armstrong in a slightly offended tone. 'Is it of no interest at all that Lieutenant Eden was spotted above Uraga, and was pursued inland after some skirmish?'

'Nothing whatsoever has been said,' answered Rice doggedly.

'But why?' demanded Armstrong with some heat. 'Why is everybody seemingly indifferent to Eden's fate?'

'The subject is extremely delicate, Mr Armstrong, as you must know. And the information you gave was quite informal. Perhaps that has something to do with it . . .'

Armstrong made as though to reply, then seemed to change his mind. Standing in the doorway he lifted his head to listen to the echoing crash of hammers that was still audible amidst the background clamour of gongs and drums.

'The war drums seem to be getting louder again,' murmured the missionary. 'And more persistent.'

Lieutenant Rice listened for a moment, then rose from behind his chart table, his expression suddenly more conciliatory. 'For all practical purposes, Robert Eden and the Japanese castaway remain listed as "missing overboard". If they returned to the ship they would be placed under close arrest for disobeying orders. In the absence of any official word about them, perhaps the only way we can deal with the matter is to ignore it.' He paused, looking searchingly at the missionary. 'Have you learned anything further from the Japanese interpreter?'

Armstrong sighed and shook his head. 'No, nothing. I did try to talk to Mr Haniwara yesterday, although they were only on board a few minutes. But he behaved very strangely. On Sunday morning he had listened carefully to what I had to say about Eden, and gave me the information I passed to you. This time he ignored my questions and stared through me as if I didn't exist. His manner was most uneasy . . . It made me feel he was hiding something.'

A flicker of alarm appeared in the flag lieutenant's expression but, before he could answer, footsteps were heard clattering quickly down a nearby ladder and a moment later Midshipman Harris appeared and saluted as he came smartly to attention.

'Excuse me, sir,' he broke in excitedly, addressing Rice. 'The Japanese delegation is arriving! Their boat is approaching the port gangway.'

'Thank you, Mr Harris,' said Rice crisply. 'Return to the upper deck and conduct the visitors to the captain's cabin, as before. We'll follow you.'

As the cadet officer hurried off to comply, Rice smiled and buckled on his ceremonial sword, gesturing for the missionary to precede him. 'Just as we expected, Mr Armstrong, the response has come quickly. I think you'll agree this proves that the commodore's strategy is working well.'

'Before offering my own congratulations I'll wait until the exact nature of the Japanese response is known,' replied the civilian, moving quickly out of the cabin. 'And I'll be surprised if matters proceed quite as simply as you hope.'

38

The governor of Uraga stirred the air before his face with gentle movements of a bamboo-and-paper fan, and bowed his head formally towards Flag Lieutenant Rice to indicate he had finished speaking. Beneath his shiny, black-lacquered bonnet the governor's features remained impassive and he stared unseeingly ahead as Haniwara Tokuma, who was seated beside him, began to translate his words diffidently into the Dutch language. Dressed as before in a robe of green silk emblazoned with an embroidered peacock, the governor was supported by the same retinue of silk-clad civilian officials who had accompanied him previously. Their faces were devoid of all expression too, but their dark eyes were watchful and wary as they perched uncomfortably on the unfamiliar upright chairs around him, waiting for the translation to be made.

A few feet away across the captain's cabin Samuel Armstrong was concentrating hard, his head bent over a sheaf of writing paper. He was again seated at the end of the flag lieutenant's table, flanked by the same four watchful marine guards, Midshipman Harris and two other young trainee officers, who were armed as before with cutlasses. Armstrong had taken some notes while the governor was speaking, and now he added further careful jottings as he listened intently to the translation into Dutch. In each interval of silence the unceasing throb of drums and gongs from the shore became more audible, and some trace of tension was visible in every face in the cabin as all waited for the missionary to complete his notes.

'The governor's speech was couched in complicated official language that was sometimes difficult to untangle,' said Armstrong at last, leaning confidentially towards Rice with a faint frown of exasperation. 'In a long and roundabout way he said that his superiors are prepared in principle to accept the letter from our President—but they're trying to hedge the acceptance around with a lot of conditions and provisos.'

'What are those conditions?' asked Rice brusquely. 'Do they spell them out?'

'Yes, they do,' said Armstrong, consulting his notes. 'They say first of all that while the letter can be received here, a reply could only be given later through Dutch or Chinese intermediaries at Nagasaki. They're also resisting the commodore's wish to hand over a duplicate of the letter in advance of his own formal presentation of the original.'

'Do they explain why?' asked Rice with a frown.

'No, not exactly. But they seem to suspect there's something underhand behind this demand.'

'Possibly they suspect the truth,' said Rice, moving closer to the missionary so he should not be overheard. 'It's perhaps obvious that the commodore is still trying to force them to accept delivery of the President's original letter in Yedo itself.'

'Perhaps,' agreed Armstrong in an undertone. 'They're certainly insisting that they will only consent to receive the duplicates, translations and originals at one and the same time. And they also seem unable to understand the rank of commodore, because they refer repeatedly to our commander-in-chief as "the honoured admiral".'

The flag lieutenant drew a long slow breath to cover his own exasperation, then pulled a sheet of paper towards him to write out a quick summary of what had been said, and handed it to Midshipman Harris.

'Take this to the commander-in-chief immediately,' he said quietly. 'And wait for his reply.'

As soon as Harris had departed, an uncomfortable silence fell between the two groups. The morning was already hot, and a large honeybee drifted in through one of the cabin's open scuttles to float erratically back and forth above their heads in the still air; the lazy drone of its flight contrasted sharply with the more urgent rhythm of drums and hammers coming from the shore, and several pairs of eyes nervously followed its meaningless progress around the cabin. The Japanese, accustomed lifelong to kneeling or squatting without support on soft tatami-covered floors, shifted uneasily on the straight-backed chairs and fanned themselves more vigorously, taking care never to meet the gaze of their American counterparts.

'You may inform His Excellency that, because of the unexpected obstacles he has raised, we have been forced to refer these questions directly to our honoured "admiral",' said Rice at last, addressing Armstrong. 'And make it clear it will be necessary to wait patiently while the admiral considers what steps must now be taken in response.'

Neither the governor nor any member of his retinue spoke, or betrayed any other visible reaction, as Armstrong and Haniwara Tokuma interpreted the lieutenant's words. If anything, they sat straighter in their seats, but in the stillness and stiffness of their postures there was a hint of growing disquiet. The uneasy silence endured for several minutes more before Midshipman Harris was heard returning at a fast pace. When he re-entered the cabin, he was seen to be carrying a sheet of paper bearing detailed written instructions, and there was an anticipatory rustle amongst the men of both sides.

'Sir, the admiral's orders are that this memorandum should be translated into Dutch and read to His Excellency at once,' said Harris, saluting smartly and placing the paper on the table before the flag lieutenant. 'The admiral also says it should be explained at the outset that his terms are not negotiable.'

Rice thanked the midshipman and read quickly through the memorandum before showing it to Samuel Armstrong. When the missionary nodded to indicate that he was ready to translate the contents, the flag lieutenant cleared his throat and looked directly at the governor.

'Your Excellency,' he said, speaking slowly and very clearly, 'I am instructed by the honoured admiral to tell you four simple things, and they are as follows. First, the admiral will never go to Nagasaki *for any reason whatsoever*, nor will he ever consent to receive any comunication of any kind through the Dutch or the Chinese . . . Second, the admiral has a letter from the President of the United States to deliver to the Emperor of Japan, or to his Secretary of Foreign Affairs, or to a high official of equivalent rank. This original letter he will deliver to nobody else.'

Rice paused and waited for the translations to be made, watching the faces of the Japanese officials closely as they absorbed this information. Outwardly they continued to show no emotion, but some members of the delegation glanced sideways at each other as they listened.

'Thirdly, the admiral has already said he expected a reply of some sort within three days—and he will receive that reply nowhere other than in the neighbourhood of Yedo Bay.'

The flag lieutenant saw the governor's eyes narrow slightly as the third clause was translated for him, and he waited for several seconds, allowing the silence to lengthen significantly before reading out the conclusion to the memorandum.

'Finally, the admiral commands me to say that if this friendly letter from the President of the United States to the Emperor of Japan is not received and duly replied to, he will consider his country insulted. And if his country is so insulted, he will not hold himself accountable for the consequences.'

Lieutenant Rice had matched his voice to the uncompromising tone of the final words, and Samuel Armstrong delivered his translation in a similarly forthright manner. As he made his notes, a pained frown suddenly shadowed the scholarly features of Haniwara Tokuma, and the frown deepened when he turned to the governor to render the closing statement into Japanese.

For several seconds after absorbing the significance of the thinly veiled threat, none of the Japanese moved; but their expressions had become uncertain and the governor suddenly raised his fan in front of his face and spoke to his interpreter in an undertone. A flurry of urgent whispers followed, then all the members of the delegation stood up as one man and bowed perfunctorily in a parting salutation. The next moment they followed the governor out of the cabin and climbed rapidly up the companion-ladders to the entry port below which their boat was waiting.

'His Excellency wishes me to inform you that he must return immediately to the shore for further consultations with his superiors,' said Haniwara stiffly, inclining his head a fraction towards Rice. 'He wishes me to add that he is not at present authorized to agree to the demands you have made. If there is anything more to tell you after the consultations have taken place, we will return in two or three hours.'

Without waiting to hear Samuel Armstrong's translation, Haniwara hurried from the cabin and climbed quickly to the upper deck to join the rest of the delegation. When he arrived at the entry port, the governor led the way down into the boat, and as soon as they were seated its oarsmen began to pull swiftly towards the shore, where the drums and gongs of war were still sounding in the same steady, unflagging rhythm.

To his surprise Samuel Armstrong awoke on his bunk three hours later to find that a strange silence had descended on the bay. The drums and gongs were no longer audible, and the distant ringing of the hammers had also ceased. In the still heat of the early afternoon the soft slap of wavelets against the *Susquehanna*'s stern was the only sound that reached into his cabin.

He sat up on the bunk, feeling an overwhelming sense of relief that he had fallen into such a deep refreshing sleep after the wearying nightmares of the pre-dawn hours. During the meeting in the captain's cabin his head had throbbed intermittently from a mixture of tension and tiredness, but now he felt alert and clearheaded again. Pulling a pocketwatch from his waistcoat he saw to his amazement that he had slept for two blissful hours. Since the abrupt departure of the Japanese had produced an atmosphere of high tension on the *Susquehanna*, he had not expected to sleep at all when he eventually returned to his own cramped cabin. That under those circumstances he had enjoyed the solace of such deep slumber seemed like something close to a miracle.

At the conclusion of the meeting he had rushed up to the spar-deck hoping to find an opportunity to question Haniwara Tokima discreetly about Robert Eden before the Japanese disembarked. But their boat had already cast off by the time he reached the entry port, and he could only stand and watch helplessly as it was rowed rapidly back towards the shore. During the following half hour he had deliberately kept himself to himself, pacing the decks of the *Susquehanna*again while he pondered on the strained exchanges with the Japanese, and wrestled with the ambivalent feelings that pricked his conscience more acutely with each passing hour.

Yes, he told himself, his belief that the Christian gospels were mankind's chief hope of salvation remained fundamental. Therefore those teachings needed to be carried clearly to every race and nation on earth—and that would be the finest outcome of this effort to draw Japan into the world from its ancient state of isolation. But his personal involvement, day after day, in the increasingly threatening acts of armed intimidation was making him feel more and more uneasy.

Could he be sure any longer that the end justified such hostile means? Christianity urged brotherhood between all races and peace between nations, so was it really laudable to risk war—and hundreds or even thousands of deaths—to ensure the success of this expedition? And if the answer to such questions as these was 'No', then wasn't his own role in these historic events becoming thoroughly dishonourable? He was only an interpreter, but wasn't he in truth being duped and used as a cat's-paw to help cow and subjugate the Japanese? And wouldn't it be more honourable to withdraw his services and play no further role? Or was the most honourable course to carry on and try in some way to influence and modify the course that events were taking—as, in a different way, Robert Eden had done? This reflection made him realise he was increasingly disturbed that Eden's fate seemed to count for nothing against the dubious goals of the expedition. Motivated spontaneously by the injustice of the unfolding events of which he was a part, the young officer had courageously acted on his convictions; but his reward was to find himself abandoned, as though his individual life was of no value and Christian principles did not apply to those who disagreed with the official methods being employed.

All these thoughts had whirled endlessly through his mind as he paced the flagship's decks with the thud of the drums and gongs resounding in his ears. But, because he had found it impossible to reconcile the welter of conflicting emotions, he decided to seek some respite from them by applying his mind instead to a practical task, and had returned to his cabin to spend twenty minutes preparing the translation of the commodore's new letter to the Japanese Emperor. When he had finished it to his satisfaction, his mind felt a little easier and he took out a large folio notebook in which he had regularly recorded his impressions of the extraordinary voyage. In his small, careful hand he wrote a brief account of his latest feelings, then took off his jacket and stretched himself wearily on his bunk, intending to rest merely for a few minutes. The next two hours had seemed to fly by in an instant, and on waking he had risen to dash water over his face, feeling a quiet sense of elation at having found the relaxation he so sorely needed. He had eaten a snack of dried fruit and ship's biscuits, still wondering at the strange silence that had fallen over the bay, but he had not been surprised when a knock at his cabin door was then followed by an excited announcement from a midshipmen messenger that the Governor of Uraga had just returned to the flagship with his retinue and was being conducted to the captain's cabin.

When Armstrong took his place at the table beside Flag Lieutenant Rice, the tableau of that morning's tense meeting had reformed itself exactly as before: the demeanour of the governor was as grave and impassive as ever, and at his side the face of Haniwara Tokuma was composed in a similarly expressionless mask. Each member of the uncomfortably seated Japanese delegation also stared blankly ahead, but Armstrong felt he could detect an underlying tenseness in each of them that had not been apparent in the morning.

After the flag lieutenant had said a few words of welcome which Armstrong translated, the Japanese governor again launched into a slow, convoluted speech which he delivered without looking directly at his American counterparts. Haniwara Tokuma also avoided Armstrong's eyes when delivering the translation and, just before he finished speaking, the mystifying noise of hammer blows became audible again, ringing loudly in the distance.

'I'm afraid the governor is still repeating what he said this morning,' murmured Armstrong, leaning towards Rice. 'He says it will take a great deal of time to send the copies of the letters to Yedo and to send the originals afterwards. He therefore proposes that the originals and copies be delivered together to a very high official.'

'Tell His Excellency this can't be done,' replied Rice, bristling in his chair. 'Tell him that our admiral wishes the copies to be sent to the Emperor along with his own personal letter that you have translated today. This will inform the Emperor that the admiral is empowered to deliver the President's letter either to the Emperor in person or to a properly accredited official of his own rank. Tell him all that in no uncertain terms!'

As Rice spoke Armstrong watched the governor's face closely; his features had stiffened into an expression that was a mixture of defiance and apprehension, and he was growing noticeably pale. The features of the other Japanese officials had also become taut and strained and, even though they had not understood Rice's meaning fully, it was clear that the manner of his speech had alarmed all of them.

'Lieutenant, before I translate your remarks, I'd like your permission to put a few questions directly to their interpreter,' said Armstrong. 'Do you agree?'

'What purpose will that serve?'

'I sense that some common ground might be found if we were to go more lightly,' replied Armstrong. 'I believe they're frightened, but like us they have a fierce pride. Also, like us, they're determined not to allow themselves to be humiliated.'

'The commodore's orders are clear,' said Rice briskly. 'We are to be uncompromising.'

'Let me just try,' insisted Armstrong. 'If they leave again it may be impossible to avoid hostilities.'

The flag lieutenant hesitated for a moment, then nodded. 'Very well, but keep me informed of all that's said.'

Armstrong smiled his thanks and addressed Haniwara Tokuma in Dutch. 'His Excellency the Governor said some moments ago that a very high official is prepared to receive our President's letter, along with copies, and another letter from our admiral. Is that correct?'

'Yes, that is correct,' replied Haniwara guardedly. 'A high official representing the Emperor is already on his way here to receive the letters—but he is authorized only to accept the originals and the copies at the same time, not separately.'

'Will the high official bring written proof to show that he is properly authorized by the Emperor to receive these letters?' asked Armstrong in the same confiding tone.

The Japanese interpreter nodded again and raised one arm to show that he carried a small sealed scroll inside one of his loose sleeves. 'We already have in our possession this letter bearing the Emperor's seal, proving that he is properly authorized.'

'And will that high official come here to the ship to receive the letters?'

'No, he will not come on board. He will receive the letters on the shore.'

'Where exactly on the shore do you propose the meeting shall take place?' asked Armstrong. 'It's important that we know in advance.'

'A special ceremonial pavilion is at present being built close to the beach a short way from here.' Haniwara paused and lifted his head, listening to the noise of hammering. 'You have perhaps already heard the sounds of our carpenters hard at work on the pavilion.'

'Indeed we have,' said Armstrong, feeling a curious sense of relief flood through him. 'Indeed we have.'

'At the pavilion our high official will be able to give the admiral a suitable reception,' added Haniwara, still avoiding the eyes of the missionary. 'But because Nagasaki is the proper place to receive all missives from foreign nations, he will not be able to converse or enter into any negotiations with the admiral after the ceremony.'

'I see,' said Armstrong, nodding. 'I will explain all that now. Thank you for the clarity of your answers.'

Turning back to the American officer, the missionary quickly outlined what had been said. But, as he listened, the face of the flag lieutenant clouded with suspicion.

'Their pavilion may be a clever trap,' he snapped. 'They may be trying to lure us ashore so as to attack us. Before agreeing, we need more information about where it's being built.'

'But at least they've conceded to the commodore's demand for a ceremonial reception of the President's letter,' insisted Armstrong. 'Wouldn't it be worth finding out how the commodore sees this? While you're talking with him, we could seek more information.'

The flag lieutenant considered the question in silence, then stood up suddenly. 'We need to discover the exact location of the pavilion, Mr Armstrong,' he said very quietly, 'so that we can send a cutter to make a survey. When you've established that, Mr Harris is to take the information to the commander of the *Susquehanna*. It's vital to find out if we can anchor close enough to cover the pavilion with our guns. I shall go now and confer with the commodore.'

When the flag lieutenant had bustled out, Armstrong again addressed Haniwara Tokuma in Dutch. 'I am hoping our admiral will react favourably to what you've already told me. But first we should like you to give us the exact location of the pavilion.'

'It's being constructed south of Uraga,' said the interpreter, after a whispered exchange with the governor. 'Before the village of Kurihama.'

'Why has that site been chosen?' enquired Armstrong. 'Why couldn't you have built the pavilion here at Uraga?'

'Because foreign ships are not normally allowed to proceed beyond Kurihama,' replied the interpreter, keeping his eyes averted.

'How far from this ship is it?'

'It is not far—less than one Japanese mile. You can't see it from here because it lies between two small headlands.'

Armstrong broke off to pass this information to Midshipman Harris, and waited while he hurried off to find the commander of the flagship. When the cabin was quiet again he turned to Haniwara Tokuma once more. 'May I ask you which high official is coming to receive our President's letter? Can you give me a name?'

'His name is Prince Toda of Idzu.'

'And what is his rank?' asked Armstrong, making a written note. 'What position does he hold?'

'Prince Toda is First Counsellor of the Empire. He will be accompanied by Prince Ido of Iwami.'

'When will Prince Toda be available to receive the letters?'

'I'm not entirely certain. Possibly tomorrow or the day after . . .'

The sound of hurrying footsteps broke in on the exchanges, and Flag Lieutenant Rice reappeared and seated himself once more at the table, looking directly towards the governor.

'Please tell His Excellency that I had a conversation with the admiral,' he said firmly, glancing at Armstrong. 'And the admiral has said that His Excellency appears to have wholly misunderstood the matter of receiving the original letter and copies. But if written proof can be provided that a high officer of the Emperor has now been appointed to come here and receive them, the admiral is prepared to waive the matters in dispute, and deliver on the same occasion the President's original letter along with its translated copies and a letter from himself . . .'

'Does this mean the commodore is prepared to abandon his hope of delivering the original letter personally in Yedo?' asked Armstrong in a surprised whisper.

'Quite so,' replied Rice. 'But simply translate what the commodore directed me to say.'

Armstrong nodded quickly and complied, conveying the information in a neutral tone. On hearing the translation into Japanese, an expression of relief appeared fleetingly in the eyes of the governor; then almost immediately his face became impassive again and he inclined his head to acknowledge what had been said.

'Before the letters can be delivered ashore,' continued Rice briskly, 'the credentials of the Emperor's high officer must be translated into Dutch, signed with the proper signatures, and sent on board for our inspection—is that clear?'

The governor again inclined his head in acknowledgement.

'At the meeting itself, the admiral asks me to say that there will be no need for any discussion whatsoever. Only civilities and compliments will be exchanged. And, despite what was said earlier, the admiral will not now insist upon waiting here for an immediate response to the original letter of the President. He will require only some form of receipt and will return later to receive the Emperor's full answer.'

'When will the admiral come back?' asked the interpreter anxiously after a prolonged discussion with the governor. 'How soon?'

'He has asked me to say he will return after a few months,' replied Rice. 'And next time he will bring with him a bigger fleet of warships.'

A new flurry of uneasy discussion amongst the Japanese greeted the translation of this response and, while the whispering continued, the flag lieutenant touched Armstrong's sleeve lightly to gain his attention.

'The commodore has decided not to wait for an answer, because it would give them another chance to delay and deceive us while our supplies run low,' he murmured. 'So tell them that if we approve of the meeting place, after making a survey of the site, we will anchor both steamships close to the ceremonial pavilion. Although you won't say so, this will allow us to bring our heavy guns to bear on the pavilion during the ceremony. But you *can* say that the admiral will land and march formally to the meeting with his retinue and a large armed escort. All this is to take place no later than the day after tomorrow.'

Armstrong nodded, and waited until the Japanese whispering died away before making his announcement. On hearing of the commodore's intention to land with a large escort under the cover of his warships' guns, the governor and Haniwara conferred again with other members of the entourage, speaking at length in anxious undertones.

'It only remains to be decided when the Emperor's representative will receive the admiral,' prompted Armstrong gently. 'Will the day after tomorrow be suitable?'

'Yes, the First Counsellor of the Empire will be prepared to receive the President's letter the day after tomorrow,' said Haniwara after more whispered consultation. 'At eight o'clock in the morning. As soon as we see your flag hoisted, the governor will come aboard to guide you to the ceremony.'

'Excellent,' exclaimed the flag lieutenant, rising to his feet. 'Then this meeting is successfully concluded. I should like to thank His Excellency and his companions for their kind attendance here on our ship.'

The governor, his face still expressionless, bowed in response, then turned and led his delegation from the cabin, escorted by the remaining midshipmen. Samuel Armstrong, determined not to delay too long this time, hurried after them and caught up with Haniwara Tokuma as he approached the companion-ladder leading to the upper deck.

'Have you received any news at all of Lieutenant Eden?' murmured the missionary, keeping his voice low to avoid the risk of being overheard by the other Japanese. 'Rest assured I'll treat anything you say in the strictest confidence.'

'You must not try to speak to me like this!' hissed the interpreter, turning his back pointedly on the missionary and trying to push past him. 'Please leave me alone.'

'I'm sorry, I must press you,' whispered Armstrong, blocking the way forward. 'It's three whole days now. Surely there's been some new word of him?'

Unable to proceed, the interpreter raised his head to look directly at Armstrong for the first time. His face had become very pale and the missionary was shocked by the depth of fear that he saw suddenly in his dark, narrow eyes.

'By trying to make me talk to you privately, you're threatening the lives of my wife and children,' muttered Haniwara in a desperate voice. 'You should stop. There's greater danger than you realize . . . But you must speak to nobody of this!'

With a sudden lunge, the interpreter forced his way past the astonished missionary and clambered onto the rungs of the companion-ladder. The other members of the governor's retinue had already reached the upper deck and he scrambled frantically after them without looking back, his expression strained and all trace of his normal, scholarly composure gone.

39

From a dense fog of unconscious silence the indistinct murmur of human voices materialized only very slowly. Because he heard them through a returning haze of pain, Robert Eden could not be sure whether the voices were coming from outside his head or inside. Unrelieved darkness surrounded him but he gradually became convinced he could also hear the subdued clop of horses' hoofs moving steadily at walking pace across soft ground. The horses snorted quietly from time to time and their harness jingled as they moved, but something elusive prevented him from establishing beyond any shadow of doubt whether the noises were real or imaginary.

The pain he felt was flaring back into existence with a surprising swiftness both inside his skull and below his waist. He could smell dried blood, he realized suddenly, and a dusty, acrid odour also filled his nostrils. His whole body, if it existed at all, was cramped in a near-horizontal position as though it had been tortuously confined. He was being shaken and jolted constantly and every movement sent a new wave of pain coursing through him. In the blackness of the void in which he seemed to exist, he wondered whether he might already be dead or dying. His memory was frighteningly blank and he scoured its smooth, featureless surfaces in vain for some recollection of the immediate past.

An all-engulfing numbness gripped him and he knew instinctively he was not capable of independent movement. He was not even sure he could feel his arms or legs; his body seemed to consist of an inert trunk, an immobile head and nothing more, all swathed in a cloak of the deepest blackness. He could hear the faint sound of someone breathing slowly and rhythmically far off, and somehow knew that it was his disembodied self. In this state of utter helplessness and passivity he strained all his five senses to their limits in an effort to establish his whereabouts; but no matter how hard he tried to penetrate the darkness, success eluded him and, after what seemed like an eternity, he stopped trying and allowed himself to drift downward again into that deep, dense fog of unconsciousness.

The moment he released himself from the act of attempting to understand, vivid images swept into his mind, momentarily dazzling him. At first he was not sure what he was seeing; then he recognized that he was surrounded by Indian teepees made from animal skins, and smoke was curling from their open vents. The sounds of horses' hoofs that he could hear were bringing old squaws and younger women running from their shelters to watch the passing procession of ponies and mounted Iroquois braves. The braves wore feathers in their hair, their faces and bodies were daubed with brilliant war paints and they carried lances, tomahawks and bows in their hands. Quivers filled with arrows were slung around their naked shoulders and they wore broad-bladed knives tucked into their belts.

In the same instant that his senses ceased their desperate search for evidence in his surroundings, Eden became aware of who and where he was: struck down in a battle with the white marauders who had come to rob the Iroquois of their lands, his dead body was being solemnly transported to the tribe's ancient burial grounds. Bumping unceremoniously over the rough ground, he was being dragged behind an ageing horse on a rough litter of birch branches. The voices he could hear were subdued and indistinct because a tangible atmosphere of shame and dishonour hung over the funeral procession.

From the wizened faces of the old squaws and the dismayed stares of the younger Iroquois women who carried their babies strapped to their backs, he knew immediately that his corpse was the cause of their shame. They were looking, without doubt, at the passing body of a traitor who had been killed by his own tribe for consorting with their direst enemies. He had been killed because he had seen that the great tide of white settlers would soon inevitably overrun the Iroquois lands and change them for ever. He had been killed because he had seen before anybody else that his tribe could not save themselves by fighting the intruders. He had met secretly in the forest with a soft-spoken white settler who had quietly kid his weapon aside after they first surprised each other beside a pool where they had gone to water their horses. He had continued to meet the white settler secretly, because he wanted to find a way to stop the senseless killing and try to understand how their two peoples might live in peace—and for doing that he had been killed by warriors of his own tribe.

He opened his mouth to cry out in his own defence, but a burial shroud already seemed to cover his face and he could not make his despairing voice heard. Many of the Iroquois squaws hissed and spat in disgust as his dead body was dragged past them and he felt his despair deepen unbearably. Only one of the younger women, her beautiful face tragically stricken, stood aside, weeping silently without tears. The small baby at her shoulder stared in his direction too, its eyes round and wondering, and Eden felt his heart breaking within him. He knew he was right and those who hissed and spat were wrong; but equally he knew that he would never make them understand what he had tried to do.

The effort he had made to shout out had drained something from him, and the pain in his head and body suddenly grew more intense. Paradoxically, although he could see every last detail of the encampment through which the burial procession was passing, the darkness all around him also remained total and unrelieved. Within that darkness the painful jolting and shaking of his living body was continuing, the unseen voices were still murmuring and he could hear the steady continuous clop of horses' hoofs. From all these tangible sounds and sensations he knew he was not dreaming. The images visible in the midst of the darkness, all his instincts told him, were of a higher reality than dreams. He continued to look around himself and, without any feeling of unease or surprise, he realized that he was somehow experiencing two levels of conscious existence simultaneously: in the selfsame instant he was perceiving two different fragments of time. With an equal certainty he knew that the two different experiences were directly connected with each other but he could not begin to guess how, because in the blackness, his memory remained bafflingly blank and empty of all clues.

He tried to raise his head and shoulders but felt himself restrained by the invisible bonds which held him prone. He tried again to cry out, but his voice was scarcely a croak and he knew nobody had heard him. A new wave of despair surged slowly through him, leaving a deeper desolation in its wake. He seemed to be suspended in a state of mental muteness, robbed of all forms of cognition, and how long he remained in this state he could not tell. Then very slowly a new understanding began to suffuse his mind, and he knew he was not after all experiencing another era but that some fleeting vestige of inherited memory locked deep inside the very tissues of his body was echoing and reechoing into his conscious mind along the shadowy corridors of time.

He tried hard to sharpen the focus of this fresh understanding but failed. The effort left him utterly exhausted and he felt himself falling towards the brink of sleep. As he did so a bright radiance suddenly filled his vision. It quickly became dazzling, and from its centre emerged the figure of the lovely young squaw he had seen earlier. Her dark eyes burned with love for him in the tragic mask of her amber face, and she looked at him unwaveringly. She was carrying fragrant, oil-bearing berries and herbal plants in her hands and with great reverence she knelt beside him to anoint his racked and broken body.

The familiar, loving caress of her hands eventually revived him and, sitting up, he rose effortlessly to his feet. On seeing this, her tragic countenance was instantly transfigured with joy, and she stood up too, staring at him in wonder.

'Only men capable of great love are capable of great daring,' she whispered softly, moving close to him. 'You never need be ashamed.'

He did not reply but stared at her, astounded anew by her beauty, and allowed her to take him by the hand and lead him away from the litter of birch branches. The bright radiance continued to surround them, shielding their bodies from the gaze of those watching the burial procession, and they walked away unobserved. When they reached the nearby bank of a deep, fast-flowing stream, she quickly slipped out of her doeskin garment and beckoned to him to follow her into the rushing waters. He immediately flung off his burial shroud and with a shout of elation plunged after her.

The stream soon emptied into a broad lake and, on entering it, they both dived silently into its still, green depths. Following her down, he swam joyously in her wake, moving easily and watching the rhythmic movements of her naked limbs ahead of him. She had removed the decorated thong of leather which she wore around her forehead and, as she swam, her long black mane of hair swirled out around her shoulders like dark wings. The fragrance and taste of the oil-berries and herbs with which she had anointed him swirled past him in the water and he closed his eyes, following her invisible trail by his sense of smell alone.

He realized he was breathing the water unthinkingly like air, inhaling the scents of the herbs and the scents of her body simultaneously without harm. She began to tumble and somersault slowly and gracefully ahead of him in celebration of his miraculous resurrection, and he swam purposefully closer, dazzled by the flash of her golden limbs in the clear green waters.

Recognizing his intention she smiled back at him with her almond-shaped Iroquois eyes and rolled lazily onto her back, kicking her legs slowly and languidly as she watched him approach. Very gently he kissed her moving feet, her calves, her knees, then pressed his mouth more fervently into the soft apex of her thighs and held this fierce kiss of deep passion for a long time. Her long hair flowed in the water all around them as they spun and turned together; he caressed her face, her neck, her breasts, her haunches with his hands, his feet and every surface of his body. She returned his caresses with an equal avidity, her hands and her mouth closing around him again and again. They frisked like children and teased each other, they soared and swooped in the water, he entered and re-entered her, sometimes with great tenderness and sometimes with a loving ferocity. They chased and pursued each other in turn, sighed unending streams of air bubbles to the distant surface, and cried out silently in the deep waters when the long, sweet pain of their passion at last overwhelmed them.

As they spun and drifted clenched together in a wordless ecstasy, he looked up through the waters of the lake towards the immensity of the wide heavens above and felt his heart swell with gratitude. In those moments when their bodies were fused as one, he knew suddenly that he and she were joined in harmony to the universal source of truth that existed simultaneously in the heavens and in all created things. Their minds and their bodies were joined as one with the waters and fishes and weed fronds of the lake, with its sandy bed and its grass and tree-covered banks as well as with the infinitely broad sky and the clouds above that were reflected in the lake's placid surface. Because of this understanding, a deep feeling of peace stole over him, an infinite sweetness that spread rapidly through all his limbs, dissolving the last of the pain from his wounds. Without looking at her he knew that she too was experiencing those same profound feelings, and that there was no need for words to pass between them to confirm what he sensed.

When at last he turned to look at her he was not surprised to find that her beautiful Iroquois squaw's face was also that of Matsumura Tokiwa, that they were one and the same woman. In the slow swirling of the lake's natural undercurrents her long dark hair had momentarily piled itself above her head in a loose semblance of a Japanese chignon, and the faint, enigmatic smile in her eyes showed him that she too was aware of his moment of recognition.

Deeply moved, he embraced her with a renewed tenderness and as they swung slowly in the water, entwined in each other's arms, he saw that a gigantic, cone-shaped mountain was becoming visible in the fathomless shadows below them. They began to drift towards it and he noticed then that a great black chasm gaped open at its snow-covered summit. He recognized Mount Fuji in the same instant that he realized his memory of recent events was reviving, and as he stared downward into the dark crater he was seized by the feeling that he was gazing into the very soul of the earth. They seemed to accelerate in their spiralling plunge and he began to fear that they would be swallowed up into the terrifying void of the crater. But when he turned in alarm to look at her, he found that the Iroquois squaw who was also Tokiwa was still smiling gently at him.

'The more you love, the more you will understand,' she whispered softly. 'And the more you understand, the more you will love—you and all men.'

Her soothing words calmed his fears and he glanced quickly up at the immensity of the sky still visible above the lake, before turning his eyes down towards the ominous crater of the volcano again. This time he felt his understanding expand, and he knew that the universal source of truth was as much to be found in the hidden depths of the volcano as in the heavens overhead. Reassuringly, both were merely aspects of an infinite progression which continued endlessly in both directions above and below them, and he suddenly also understood that they were themselves an eternally inseparable part of that truth.

In looking down he also caught sight of a squadron of menacing black ships anchored on a distant bay, with their guns pointed at the defenceless shore. Nearer at hand he could see several groups of moving Japanese figures swarming around the snow-covered peak of the gigantic volcano. Most of the figures carried swords, tasselled lances, bows and arrows, and as he and the beautiful Iroquois-Japanese girl drifted lower in the green waters, they could see that on the mountain the armed men were skirmishing fiercely with one another. Some fell, pierced through with arrows, others stumbled and died from lance and sword wounds. One ordinary, defenceless Japanese without armour or weapons was attempting to flee from the fighting, but as they watched he was overhauled and brought down with an arrow. His blood spread quickly on the snow, forming a bright red halo around his head; then his enemies came up with him, lifted his lifeless body in their arms and tossed it brutally over the lip of the yawning crater. The body spun in slow circles like a sycamore wing as it sank into the blackness of the terrible abyss and, watching it fall, Eden's head spun dizzyingly too.

'It's Sentaro!' he heard his own hollow voice saying. 'It's Sentaro.'

Beside him the Iroquois-Japanese girl ceased to smile and her face grew serious. She nodded once very gravely, then again. 'Yes, Sentaro tried to understand too—and he tried to make others understand. Just as the Iroquois brave who was your ancestor did long ago. Sadly they have suffered a similar fate . . .'

'But why?' asked Eden in an agonized voice. 'Why?'

The corpse of the brave, simple Japanese peasant-fisherman was still spinning down into the darkness of the crater, almost lost to sight, and they both watched until it disappeared.

'Because there's not enough love of brother for brother,' she said softly. 'All human beings are of one family. Whether their skins are white or yellow or red, they're all of the same clan . . .'

From somewhere far off a deep and awful rumbling noise began, and grew rapidly louder. A brilliant flash of light momentarily blinded them and a great explosive force filled their ears; they heard the fierce sound of a rushing wind, and the waters all around them were churned and filled suddenly with dreadful showers of dark ashes and debris. The whole earth was shaken alarmingly and Eden, anticipating that Mount Fuji was erupting, turned his eyes downward to watch the awful crater in fearful trepidation.

But to his astonishment he saw that the great volcano lay dormant and still as before: the devastating convulsions of the earth and the rumbling explosion were coming from far off, where a great city was disintegrating and rising into the air, and Eden knew suddenly by some inner instinct that this destruction was caused not by the spontaneous forces of nature but by man. He knew too that it was obscurely linked with the violent death of Sentaro on Mount Fuji and the death of the Iroquois brave that he had seemed to be, although more than a century in time and thousands of miles separated the two events. The ominous black ships he could see riding at anchor, with their banks of heavy guns trained on the naked shore, were also part of the invisible chain of responsibility stretching back into the past and forward to the future.

'The strong have always oppressed the weak because there is too much fear, too little love, too little compassion,' whispered the Iroquois-Japanese girl, again speaking close to his ear amidst the darkness and turmoil. 'Humiliation and killing breeds the desire for revenge. Such emotions are nursed secretly through many generations, until they can be fanned into new and terrible flames of hatred. More killing always follows . . .'

When he turned to face her he could see only hazily through the smoky blackness of the falling debris. He was astonished to discover that the small baby she had been carrying on her back, when he first caught sight of her beside the funeral procession, was again swaddled at her shoulder. As before, its eyes were round with wonder as it stared at him, and once more Eden felt his heart breaking at the sight of such purity and innocence.

'Mankind will one day destroy itself unless those who love greatly continue to dare greatly,' she whispered imploringly. 'They must dare to bring understanding where there is none. Don't give up. If you do all will be lost . . .'

He kicked his legs to swim closer, reaching out his arms lovingly towards her and his child. But, as he did so, new explosive blasts churned the darkened water, and mother and baby were snatched violently from him. Whirling and somersaulting, they turned end over end as they were swept away, and she cast one last beseeching look in his direction before the black turbulence finally swallowed them up.

He wailed loudly in despair and, as they disappeared from his sight, all the pain of his wounds rushed back into his body once more. With the pain, the blackness around him deepened and the roaring gradually diminished before ceasing altogether. A brief period of silence ensued, then he started to hear again the quieter sounds of horses walking at a steady pace across soft ground; he heard the muffled impact of their hoofs, their gentle snorting and the faint jingling of their harness. He strained his eyes desperately, trying to see again the burial procession, the teepees, the women and children of the Iroquois village—but he could no longer distinguish anything in the black void around him, and knew his eyes must be covered.

He realized fully then that he was physically restrained by tight bonds, and was lying on his back. Bound and blindfolded, he was being held helplessly captive in some cramped conveyance that was jolting along amongst a procession of quietly moving horses. But it was not, he realized, the Iroquois burial procession. The sounds were similar but distinctively different in a way he could not define. He struggled to make coherent sense of all that had passed through his mind in a very short space of time—but he found his strength was not equal to the effort and with a muffled exclamation of pain he lapsed unknowingly into total unconsciousness once more.

Reining in his horse beside a black windowless *norimono* carried by six semi-naked bearers in the middle of his troop of samurai cavalry, Daizo Yakamochi gestured peremptorily for the bearers to halt. When they stopped he waved forward a lantern-bearer, and ordered the barred door of the *norimono* to be opened.

Leaning down from his horse, Yakamochi peered inside by the light of the lantern, and studied the inert form of Robert Eden in silence for several seconds. The blindfolded American officer was slumped in the well of the conveyance, bound tightly with ropes from head to toe. The bandage around his head was caked with dried blood, and one of his legs was roughly bandaged too; but he did not move or respond in any way to the light that was shone on his face.

'The foreign barbarian is still breathing, my lord,' said the lantern-bearer, bowing low and speaking very respectfully. 'But he continues to slip in and out of consciousness.'

'It doesn't much matter what condition he's in,' snapped Yakamochi. 'The important thing will be to produce him on time at tomorrow's ceremony before Uraga. And that will be the signal for one hundred thousand warriors of Nippon to attack the treacherous American invaders! Close the door now—and continue to guard him well. We've got no time to waste.'

Yakamochi watched the lantern-bearer bar the door of the *norimono* again; then he wheeled his horse and spurred it at a gallop into the darkness, to take his place once more at the head of the moving samurai troop.

40

In the garden pavilion from which Mount Fuji was dramatically visible by day, Matsumura Tokiwa glanced down curiously at her naked body. Was she imagining it, she asked herself, or could she really feel strange new sensations moving within her? Might it simply be the effects of the perfumed bath she had just taken—or was it something more?

Closing her eyes, she focused her mind inward in an attempt to establish once and for all whether the feelings were real or imaginary. They seemed to start in her toes, then flow gently up her legs and thighs, before flooding onward with greater strength through her belly to the tips of her breasts. The sensations seemed at some moments to suffuse her whole body with a warm, gentle sense of fullness—yet they remained disturbingly and tantalizing intangible.

She had just bathed in a bath-house adjoining the garden pavilion, prior to retiring for the night, and was being dried by her peasant maid. Outside in the moonless darkness the distant cone of Fuji was invisible, but the quiet splash of the miniature waterfall tumbling into the carp pool was a gentle reminder of the garden's soothing charms. As she listened to the tinkling cadences of the water, Tokiwa wondered whether her maidservant Eiko was in any way aware of what her mistress might be feeling. But when she glanced at the peasant girl who had helped her escape from the village *yadoya*, Eiko's placid features betrayed no sign that she had noticed anything unusual.

During the past day or two Tokiwa had experienced these vaguely pleasing sensations with increasing frequency. But while she paced agitatedly back and forth in the formal garden, or in the pavilion itself, awaiting news from Yedo Bay, she had not allowed her mind to dwell on them. Her thoughts instead had been focused constantly on the black ships and the many thousands of Nipponese warriors who had gathered on the shores of the bay to confront them. Anxiety continued to pervade all her senses, although she no longer felt directly endangered, and she found herself wondering constantly about what might have happened to the blue-eyed foreign barbarian she had encountered with such shocking suddenness in the middle of an extraordinary night.

She'd had no contact with anybody except the peasant maidservant since Prince Tanaka's departure three days earlier. Eiko had been brought to the pavilion by a group of Tanaka's samurai within hours of Tokiwa's request being made, and they had embraced warmly on her arrival. The fact that they had shared the danger of Tokiwa's secret flight from the *yadoya* had forged a strong bond of affection between them, and Eiko had shown her gratitude for the honour of being appointed as Tokiwa's personal maid by meeting her everyday needs with fastidious care and devotion. But, despite the comfort provided by Eiko's presence, Tokiwa had found herself growing more anxious whenever she tried to imagine where Prince Tanaka might be searching for the foreign barbarian, and what the outcome of his search might be. She also found that her brief taste of freedom during that nighttime dash from the *yadoya* had left her feeling permanently restless and she had not been able to settle quietly into the long hours of emptiness and waiting at the pavilion.

Although she was not as closely guarded as before, she had noticed that the samurai guards and sentinels of her host were still keeping watch on the pavilion—but more subtly, from a distance. In addition the high walls and closed gates of the estate confined her completely, heightening her sense of unease. Eiko was quartered away from her, with the other servants of the castle, and Tokiwa had quizzed her constantly about events taking place beyond its walls. But Eiko had not been able to relate anything more than vague gossip and rumours that ever greater numbers of Nipponese fighting men were gathering on the shores of the bay, preparing to attack the foreign invaders.

'Have you learned anything about the foreign ships tonight?' asked Tokiwa, without much hope, as the maid gently dried her shoulders with a soft towel. 'Is there any fresh news at all?'

'No, O Tokiwa-san, I've heard nothing new,' said Eiko politely as she continued her task, 'but perhaps Prince Tanaka will soon be able to tell you more.'

Tokiwa turned and looked sharply at the maid. 'Why do you suddenly mention Prince Tanaka? There's been no information about him either for days.'

'I am very sorry, O Tokiwa-san,' exclaimed Eiko apologetically, 'but I thought you knew. Prince Tanaka rode into the castle about an hour ago with a group of his samurai. Some were wounded, and all of them looked travel-stained and weary. I assumed you would already have received a note to say he would be visiting you tonight, after he has bathed and rested.'

'I've heard nothing yet,' murmured Tokiwa, turning away.

They lapsed into silence, but as the vague sensations in her body became noticeable again, Tokiwa brushed one hand across her ribs and touched the soft under-curve of each of her breasts in turn. She felt almost sure this time that she could sense a new fullness and ripeness in herself, and she put her head back and closed her eyes, luxuriating in the curiously pleasurable feelings.

'You are very beautiful, O Tokiwa-san.' Eiko was patting away the last traces of moisture, her face alight with admiration, and when she had finished she moved away a pace and gazed at Tokiwa wide-eyed. 'I understand very well why every guest at the Golden Pavilion falls in love with you—and why Prince Tanaka has made you his favourite. I'm sure you will not have to wait too long before he calls on you.'

'I expect you're right.' Opening her eyes, Tokiwa turned to face the maid, her hand still resting lightly on her naked bosom. They looked at each other in silence for a moment, then Tokiwa frowned. 'Do you notice any difference in me from other days, Eiko?'

'Any difference, O Tokiwa-san?' asked the maid in surprise. 'Why should there be any difference?'

'Unless I'm imagining it, my body feels a little strange.'

'In what way does it feel strange, Tokiwa-san?' asked the maid, drawing the towel with a gentle finality down her mistress's slender back. 'You look just the same as before.'

Tokiwa frowned and let her hands fall across the flat curve of her belly and down to her loins. She stared at them for a long time, then her eyes shifted slowly across the contours of her lower body, as though she was searching for some clue without knowing what it was.

'I don't know how to explain what I feel. It's as if my body knows some kind of secret that nobody else knows—not even me.'

'Do you feel as though you are suffering from some malady, O Tokiwa-san?' asked the maid anxiously. 'Do you think all your frightening experiences have brought on some invisible illness?'

Tokiwa shook her head. 'No, it's not a sickness. I feel as though I'm suddenly full to overflowing with something pleasant. But I don't know what.'

'Is it near the time of the moon for bleeding?' asked the maid in a whisper, although they were quite alone in the pavilion.

Tokiwa nodded her head. 'Yes, it is. In fact the normal time of the moon has already passed by a few days.'

The anxious expression of the peasant maid relaxed suddenly and she smiled. 'I think I understand, O Tokiwa-san . . .'

'What do you understand?'

'I remember my older sister having feelings like these. Not quite so strong as yours perhaps—and she did not express them as gracefully.'

'What do you mean?'

'She felt as you describe each time she was found to be with child.'

Tokiwa looked silently at the peasant maid, her expression showing that she was not greatly surprised.

'This is probably your body's secret, O Tokiwa-san—that for the first time you are with child.'

Tokiwa nodded slowly, her face serious, her eyes bright with emotion.

'Is the father Prince Tanaka Yoshio?' whispered the maid excitedly, laying the towel aside and gazing eagerly into Tokiwa's face. 'If you are bearing his son, his future will be assured . . .'

Tokiwa did not reply but instead stared down at herself again, wondering how her slender body would change and alter its shape during the coming months. Then a fierce surge of instinctive excitement and apprehension coursed through her at the prospect of bringing forth new life for the first time. For a moment or two she felt faintly dizzy at the thought; then her mind sped back to those harrowing moments when Prince Tanaka—while continuing to bark orders at his samurai leader—was rising and plunging harshly above her, drawing sharp cries of pain from her with his every movement.

'Prince Tanaka may not wish to father a child with me,' said Tokiwa, speaking in a faraway voice. 'His anger might exceed his pleasure if he knew.' She fell silent for a while, then turned back to the maid. 'I trust you to keep my secret, Eiko. You must say nothing to anyone.'

The maid looked startled, then nodded vigorously in assent. 'Of course, O Tokiwa-san. You can rely completely on my loyalty.'

Eiko had brought a night kimono of transparent white gauze to the bath chamber, and she solicitously helped Tokiwa into this before leading her back into the pavilion. She had already laid out a sleeping pallet beside a softly glowing *andon* but, in case Tokiwa wished to strum the *samisen* and sing quietly for a while before retiring to sleep, she had also laid out the instrument and her midnight blue kimono decorated with silver stars.

'I have washed and mended your favourite garment,' said Eiko quietly. 'It had become muddied and torn on your terrible journey. But it's now ready for you to wear again.'

Tokiwa looked down at the kimono. Its lustrous silk shimmered in the dim light, and the sight of it brought back memories which she had successfully held at bay during the past few days. She remembered wrapping the kimono hurriedly about herself during her frantic dash from the Golden Pavilion in Yedo. She had shivered with fright in it during that long, jolting ride through the terror-filled night inside the curtained travelling chair. After her foolhardy flight from the inn and the shocking encounter with the foreign barbarian by the waterfall, she had been grateful to feel its soothing comfort about her when she finally reached the protection of the half-ruined barn. But all these recollections paled into insignificance when she remembered the barbarian's halting description of the magic cloak of stars which he had drawn about himself at the top of Mount Fuji in his dream.

The distant moonlit image of the real Fuji-san, which had been visible in those moments through the open grain-doors of the barn, had seemed to cast a spell on them both and, closing her eyes, Tokiwa shuddered slightly on reliving the intensity of the moment. She wondered anew at her own actions in removing the kimono so unhesitatingly to drape it around the barbarian's broad shoulders, as he stood looking down at her with his strangely penetrating blue eyes. A curious breathlessness tightened her chest as the memories tumbled rapidly one upon another, and she heard again his hypnotic foreign voice gasping and murmuring the strange, unintelligible words of his own language at the height of their passion.

These remembered sounds brought with them an echo of the powerful sensation she had then felt that something was dissolving and melting dizzyingly inside her, and in that instant she knew without any doubt that there was a direct link between those extraordinary moments and her present distracted feelings. This new knowledge struck her with such force that she opened her eyes at once to find the peasant maid patiently holding out the blue kimono towards her.

'I didn't tell you all of my story, Eiko,' she said in a faltering voice. 'I mentioned the great panic among the crowds fleeing from the hideous aliens—but I left out one very important thing.'

'What did you miss out, O Tokiwa-san?'

She stared at the maid uncertainly for a minute or two. 'I know it would be wiser for me to keep my own counsel,' she said at last, 'but I need so much to tell somebody I can trust.'

'You honour me with your confidences, O Tokiwa-san.' The maid moved forward quietly so that she could slip the dark blue kimono around her mistress. 'I won't ever betray that trust.'

Smiling her thanks, Tokiwa settled herself in a comfortable kneeling position and gestured for Eiko to follow suit. Taking up her *samisen*, she strummed it reflectively, then looked up at Eiko, still playing softly.

'While bathing at the waterfall I was being observed without my knowing it. I told you only that Gotaro, the chief guard of Prince Tanaka, came to recapture me—but the truth is different. Although

Gotaro *tried* to make me his prisoner again, he was thwarted unexpectedly by another fighter.'

'Who was that?' whispered the surprised maid.

'A foreign barbarian!' Tokiwa stopped playing and looked up, her eyes burning with a sudden brightness. 'I was rescued by a foreign barbarian!'

The maid's eyes grew wide, and she stifled a cry by raising a hand to her mouth. 'You must have been terrified, O Tokiwa-san!'

Tokiwa bent her head and began playing the instrument softly once more. 'I'd spent two mights being terrified at the prospect of meeting a hideous alien, so I thought I would die at the very sight of one. But after I got over my shock I found there was very little of which I needed to be afraid.'

'How could a foreign barbarian rescue you?' asked Eiko incredulously. 'They are all on the black ships in the Bay of Yedo.'

'He had swum ashore secretly. A great manhunt was mounted to capture him. Thousands of warriors were marching and riding in pursuit.'

'Then how did you encounter him?'

'As I've said, he was watching unnoticed as I bathed in the moonlight. He saw I was in danger when Gotaro appeared and rushed out of hiding to fight him off.'

The peasant maid gazed at her thunderstruck. 'Didn't he have long fangs like an animal as we've been told, O Tokiwa-san? Was his body enormous and covered in long black hair?'

Tokiwa shook her head and smiled indulgently, while continuing to pluck a plaintive melody from the *samisen*. 'He was taller than most of the men of Nippon . . . and also broader at the shoulder. He fought furiously with his sword . . . He was very strong.'

'But you weren't frightened of him?' breathed Eiko.

'He had a Nipponese companion, a fisherman who had been shipwrecked far from our shores. He had sailed home to Nippon in the black ships. He told me he had known the barbarian for a long time and they had become true friends.'

'But how did he look?' asked Eiko with a desperate curiosity.

'His eyes were blue like the sky,' said Tokiwa closing her own eyes briefly, as though to remember better. 'And his hair was the colour of the leaves in autumn . . . He had learned something of the language of Nippon, so we were able to talk. But he was not curt and formal as the men of Nippon so often are. His manner with me was gentle and courteous.'

Something in the tone of the geisha's voice caused the maid to look sharply at her. 'O Tokiwa-san, were you ever alone at any time with this foreign barbarian?'

Tokiwa stopped plucking the *samisen* and gazed out into the darkened garden of the pavilion. 'Yes, we were left alone in a ruined barn when the fisherman climbed to a hilltop temple to pray. The barbarian was exhausted, and fell asleep in the loft. I felt moved by gratitude to take him up some rice to eat. As I climbed the ladder I could see Fuji-san shimmering beautifully in the moonlight through the open loft doors . . .'

She broke off and fell silent, still looking towards the garden. The maid waited impatiently for her to continue, shifting restlessly on her haunches. When she could contain herself no longer, she leaned forward and touched Tokiwa's arm lightly.

'And what happened then?'

Tokiwa drew in her breath very slowly. 'He woke suddenly and flew for his sword. I believe he thought I had come to attack him. It was dark up there. For an instant I feared he might kill me—but he realized his mistake just in time. He laid aside his sword and apologized . . .'

'Did he eat the rice that you had brought him?' whispered Eiko. 'Did the foreign barbarian like the food of Nippon?'

'Although he had said he was very hungry, he never ate any of it.' Tokiwa put down the *samisen* on the floor beside her and sat back again, drawing one hand thoughtfully across the silken folds of her outer garment. 'For a long time he just stared at this kimono, with a strange look in his eyes. Then at last he told me that the night before he had dreamed of climbing Mount Fuji in the dark. On the summit amongst the snows he had reached up and pulled down the starlit sky into his hands. The stars and the heavens were all made of silk, he said, and he wound them softly about his naked body like a robe . . . There was also a great mirror of ice on the summit. But on looking in it he had seen only the image of a very beautiful girl of Nippon—and she was wearing the dark silk of the night heavens . . .'

Eiko gasped aloud but said nothing.

'I could still see Fuji-san itself sparkling in the moonlight,' continued Tokiwa. 'And there was a strange feeling in the ruined barn. It was almost as though I was living in the ancient times of our myths, when the *kami* walked among us . . .'

'And what happened next, Tokiwa-san?' asked the maid in a tense whisper. 'What did you do then?'

'Looking back now I am very surprised by my actions,' murmured Tokiwa. 'But because I was deeply moved by his dream, I took off this kimono with my own hands although I was wearing nothing beneath it. I drew the silken darkness around his bare chest and shoulders . . . I think he was surprised too. But because of the magic of the night I could feel no shame . . .'

'In those moments you turned the dream into reality,' said Eiko softly. 'What you did was very beautiful. Perhaps the *kami* of the mountains and the night wished it so . . .'

Tokiwa looked up, her eyes alight suddenly with emotion. Faint spots of colour rose in her cheeks and she leaned excitedly towards the peasant maid.

'Yes, our most sacred volcano was so white and pure in the moonlight! And before leaving the inn I had prayed as never before to the *kami* of Fuji-san. I had made promises to them, if they would help me. I made my escape without mishap—so what happened afterwards seemed like an omen. It was as though it was all meant to be . . .'

Tokiwa's voice faded and she lowered her eyes. The maid shifted restlessly on the tatami, watching her transfixed, hardly daring to breathe in her impatience to know more.

'The passion of the foreign barbarian was fierce,' whispered Tokiwa at last. 'But he was tender too. He was not like the men of Nippon whom I have known. There was great gentleness in him.'

'Did he not have the strength of ten men, as we've so often been told, Tokiwa-san?' whispered the maid.

'His body was powerful—but it was also kind in its way with me. I felt things I had never felt before . . . If what you say is true about how I feel, and I am truly with child, I think it must come from the time I shared with the foreign barbarian in that ruined barn.'

The eyes of the maid widened in shock as she absorbed the enormity of what she had heard. 'Then you don't think Prince Tanaka is the father?'

The geisha shook her head emphatically, but did not raise her eyes.

'Are you not afraid for the future, O Takiwa-san?' asked the maid tentatively after another silence.

'This is a time of such great turmoil,' said Tokiwa, lifting her hands suddenly to cover her face. 'I'm not sure yet what I truly feel. But whenever I think of the foreign barbarian, above everything I remember his gentleness . . .'

Tokiwa continued to hold her hands over her eyes, and for a long time the splashing of the miniature waterfall in the darkened garden was the only sound to disturb the stillness of the night.

'Does Prince Tanaka know anything of what happened there?' asked Eiko at last.

Tokiwa dropped her hands and looked directly at the maid, her expression suddenly anguished. 'I lied to him! He asked me if I had unfastened my sash for the foreign barbarian, and I swore I had not.'

'How did he know about your meeting with the barbarian?' asked Eiko in surprise.

'Gotaro and Prince Tanaka intercepted the Nipponese fisherman when he went to the temple nearby. They took him prisoner and forced him to lead them back to the barn. They burst in at a moment when the barbarian was on the point of embracing me . . .'

'Oh no!' Eiko stared at her aghast. 'Then the prince saw everything?'

'Not everything,' whispered Tokiwa. 'But enough to make him furious. I was only partly clad, and I told him later that he had arrived just in time to prevent the foreign barbarian violating me.'

'Did he believe you?'

Tokiwa hesitated, fighting to hold back tears that sprang to her eyes. 'I hope so. After I told the lie he looked very angry for a moment. I was afraid my life might be in danger.'

'Then it was right to say what you did, O Tokiwa-san.' The peasant maid reached out impulsively and laid her hand on the geisha's arm. 'You truly didn't deserve to die for what you did. Perhaps you saved your own life by telling an untruth . . .'

'But I have dishonoured myself by lying,' said Tokiwa, choking back a sob. 'I am so ashamed . . .'

'You showed great fortitude,' said Eiko quietly, leaning closer. 'It took courage to follow the instincts of your heart—and you felt it was the will of the *kami*, remember. I'm sure it was not the will of the *kami* that you should die. There's no dishonour in that.'

Tokiwa bowed her head, and her shoulders shook as she wept silently. Eiko watched her with an expression of extreme concern etched on her simple face, and waited patiently until she had become calm again.

'Was there more fighting when Prince Tanaka and Gotaro burst into the barn, Tokiwa-san?'

She nodded mutely. 'Gotaro leapt upon the barbarian, who was unprepared for action, and would have killed him—but Prince Tanaka intervened.'

'Why?'

'Because the barbarian had helped Prince Tanaka, and the officials of Nippon, in some way when they first visited the black ships.'

'And this saved his life?'

'Yes. To repay this debt of gratitude, Prince Tanaka set the barbarian and his companion free. He ordered them to return immediately to their ship, under pain of death—but I think they disobeyed that order. Three days ago a messenger arrived here saying they were seen riding inland. Prince Tanaka left immediately with a troop of warriors, to go in search of them again . . .'

A soft footfall in the garden outside caused her to break off suddenly, and they looked up in time to see Prince Tanaka stride into the pavilion. His unsmiling face showed signs of fatigue but he was wearing fresh body armour, a new red cloak, and twin swords thrust into his waist sash. On catching sight of him, both Tokiwa and the maid rose quickly to their feet and bowed low in greeting. Then the maid withdrew from the pavilion, leaving them facing each other in an awkward silence.

'Greetings, O Tokiwa-san,' he said shortly, inclining his head a fraction in her direction. 'Unfortunately my visit must be brief. Matters of great importance demand my attention. I came merely to satisfy myself of your well-being.'

'I am well, thank you, O Kami-san, as you can see,' she said quietly, keeping her eyes lowered and avoiding his gaze. 'And I'm very glad to see that you too are safe.'

'I hope you've been comfortable and well treated,' he said in the same stiff tone, deliberately keeping a distance of several feet between them. 'If there's anything further you need, I will command it before I leave.'

'I need nothing more for my physical comfort, O Kami-san,' she said slowly, lifting her head to look at him. 'But it is a great strain living here in total ignorance of all that is happening.'

'You know very well you are being kept here for your own safety,' he broke in sharply. 'Our enemies have already kidnapped the wife and children of one important official, to force him to do their bidding. They would not hesitate to kidnap you too . . .'

She looked at him with startled eyes. 'Has fighting already broken out with the foreign barbarians?'

'No, not yet,' he said grimly. 'But the crisis will reach its climax early tomorrow morning. Within a few hours we shall know whether there is to be war.'

'What is to happen tomorrow morning, O Kami-san?' she asked anxiously.

'The foreign barbarians are to land a powerful armed force on the beach at Kurihama. That force will be led by their admiral. We've agreed to allow them to present a letter addressed to His Imperial Majesty . . .'

'I don't understand,' she said hesitantly. 'How could such a ceremony lead to war?'

'Because they are heavily outnumbered, they are going to sail their ships in close and train all their heavy guns on the shore. We have more than one hundred thousand warriors drawn up along the coast, ready to give battle, many of them hidden from sight. Their barbarian force can only be a few hundred strong, but one false step by either side could be a spark that ignites the gunpowder keg . . .'

'If fighting begins, what will happen, O Kami-san?'

Tanaka's face darkened. 'In an all-out fight we would possibly kill all their fighting men through our vast weight of numbers. But it would be a bloody and costly battle, because they have superior weapons. And we could not stop them destroying all our coastal cities and villages with their guns. This would cause great loss of life. They could also return soon with many more guns and ships . . .'

As he spoke, Tokiwa noticed that his left hand flexed and unflexed unconsciously on the hilt of his long sword, betraying the extreme tension he felt. Although he made no effort to move any nearer, his eyes never left her face and she sensed that despite the coldness of his voice, he was fighting an inner battle to conceal his true feelings. In her turn she felt seized by a new sense of inner turmoil; seeing him face to face again seemed to churn up the unfamiliar and confusing tangle of emotions that had arisen during the past few days.

A silence lengthened between them and she had an irrational urge to blurt out to him that she believed she was with child, just to see how he reacted. But she bit back the temptation, realizing suddenly that she ached above all else to know whether his search for the foreign barbarian had been successful—whether the barbarian had been killed or was still alive. Yet she sensed instinctively that this unspoken question was a large part of the reason why he now held himself aloof, stifling a desire to come close and embrace her.

'Has your latest mission been successfully concluded, O Kami-san?' she asked at last in a diffident voice, attempting to disguise the real aim of her enquiry. 'You were gone much longer than I expected.'

Tanaka's eyes glittered more brightly. 'I did not succeed in recapturing the foreign barbarian, Tokiwa-san, if that is what you are asking. He and the castaway foolishly disobeyed my orders. They rode inland and attempted to scale Fuji-san unaided. Unfortunately they were pursued also by our worst enemies, led by the son of Lord Daizo. There was much bloodshed and fighting on the mountains . . .'

Tokiwa stared at him aghast. 'Were they killed, O Kami-san?'

'The castaway was slain with arrows,' replied Tanaka, watching her face closely. 'His body was tossed into one of the high craters.'

Tokiwa closed her eyes briefly but regained her composure after a moment. 'And the barbarian himself?'

'The barbarian was about to be butchered when I led my samurai in a surprise attack on the forces of Lord Daizo. He started off down the mountain—but some of Daizo's warriors caught him and cut him down . . .'

'So you saw him killed?' asked Tokiwa, struggling to keep her voice steady.

Tanaka shook his head. 'I think he was carried wounded from the mountain by Daizo's men. My force was too small to defeat them. I had already lost many warriors and we had to retreat to avoid annihilation . . . We tried to follow them down the mountain but they lost us in the darkness.'

'Where is the foreigner now?'

Tanaka's stony expression became more severe. 'I've spent the past three days trying to find him. I enlisted the aid of local clansmen who helped me search in all directions between Fuji-san and the Bay of Yedo. But we've been unable to find any trace at all.'

'What could have happened to him?'

'I believe the son of Lord Daizo has been concealing the barbarian by day, and moving him secretly each night under cover of darkness towards Kurihama.'

'Why has he done that, O Kami-san?'

Tanaka sucked in his breath sharply and his dark eyes glittered. 'Because Lord Daizo is the most rabid advocate of all-out war against the foreigners. We've picked up rumours that he plans to produce the captive in chains at the very moment the ceremony begins at Kurihama . . . He will denounce the treachery of the foreign barbarians and cry out loudly to all the assembled samurai of Nippon to launch an immediate attack . . .'

'How awful, O Kami-san,' whispered Tokiwa.

Tanaka nodded quickly. 'Now perhaps you understand why I have no time to waste. I still have the support of some regional clansmen and I must continue to organize their warriors in the search for the foreign barbarian. We shall ride all through the night—we must intercept him before morning if war is to be avoided!'

Tokiwa lowered her eyes. 'I wish you success in your quest.'

He half turned, making as if to leave, then hesitated. 'You seem somewhat pale, O Tokiwa-san. Are you feeling unwell?'

She looked up at him uneasily, seized by an irrational fear that by some freak of insight he could understand her suspicions about her body and the strange feelings she had been experiencing. 'I have felt a little tired for the past few days, O Kami-san,' she said evasively. 'But I don't really know why.'

He turned back, staring intently, and her feelings of anxiety intensified under his gaze. His features were impassive but his eyes glittered suddenly, as though some deep inner anger had momentarily got the better of him. Drawing in a long breath, he took two quick steps towards her.

'These are times of great upheaval, O Takiwa-san,' he said coldly. 'I wished you to remain quietly in seclusion but you chose to defy that wish. And now your questions to me indicate that your mind is still restless with curiosity . . .'

'What do you mean, O Kami-san?' she asked haltingly.

'I think you know what I mean,' said Tanaka in the same cold tone. 'And you should perhaps consider whether it is wise to concern yourself so much with the fate of a foreign barbarian spy who has been the cause of so much conflict.'

'I meant no offence,' she began, alarmed by his rising anger. 'My questions were first and foremost about you and your affairs, in which I am naturally most interested . . .'

'Your encounter with the barbarian has already brought you close to death,' he said sharply, ignoring her protest. 'So do nothing that will resurrect that risk.'

'I don't understand you,' she said unsteadily.

'When I asked if you had unfastened your sash willingly for the foreign barbarian, you insisted you had not. I can only hope you were telling me the truth.' Tanaka moved a final pace nearer. 'If your reply had been "Yes", I would have had no choice but to kill you instantly, with my own sword. Do you understand?'

'Yes, O Kami-san,' she whispered, lowering her head. 'I understand.'

He stared hard at her in silence for a moment. 'Furthermore, if it should emerge later that you were not completely truthful about these events, O Tokiwa-san, you will still face that same danger. Do you understand that also?'

'Yes, I understand that also,' she whispered without looking up.

'I'm very glad to hear it. Now I must resume my urgent duties. I bid you farewell.'

Swinging on his heel, he strode out into the garden the way he had come and, as soon as his footsteps had faded into the darkness, Tokiwa sank slowly to her knees on the tatami. Her body, she was suddenly certain, felt truly different; there was a lightness as well as a sensation of fullness in her limbs but these feelings, she realized, were recognizable only to her instinct, not to her physical senses. Burying her face in her hands, she began to sob loudly, and went on sobbing, even though Eiko, on hearing her, rushed back to the pavilion and knelt to embrace her with both arms.

41

'The responsibilities you and I carry, Haniwara-san, will be very grave,' said the Governor of Uraga in a low voice, leaning close to the ear of his interpreter. 'Prince Toda of Idzu and Prince Ido of Iwami will be seated on stools facing the foreign barbarians when they come ashore. But both honourable officials have been ordered to comply rigidly with our laws, which forbid all forms of verbal communication between high imperial dignitaries and foreign barbarians.'

Haniwara Tokuma's thin face, already pale and drawn, tautened further. 'Thank you for informing me of this, Shacho-san. Does this mean Prince Toda and Prince Ido will not speak at all during the entire ceremony?'

'That is correct, Haniwara-san,' replied the governor quietly. 'The Council of the Shogun has issued an edict insisting they may not utter a single word here in presence of the foreign barbarians. They have been authorized to rise and bow silently in greeting and farewell, that is all. Only you and I will speak.'

The interpreter glanced anxiously around the hastily constructed ceremonial pavilion in which they were standing. Midnight had long passed and perspiring artisans clutching hammers, saws and other tools were working by paper-lantern light to put the finishing touches to two airy, high-canopied chambers built of striped red-and-white canvas and timber. Erected on the beach at the head of a sandy, crescent-shaped bay close to the straggling village of Kurihama, the pavilion was carefully screened from the sea by high canvas barriers and ringed by hundreds of guards carrying every form of weapon from flintlock muskets to swords and lances.

Haniwara and the governor were standing in a large entrance hall where the floor had been covered in white cloth. A pathway of red carpet was being fixed in place leading across it and up three shallow steps towards a larger, more sumptuously adorned inner chamber. The floor of this inner chamber was entirely carpeted in red, and the high walls were draped with violet and white silken hangings on which the Tokugawa shogunate's coat of arms had been embroidered. Vivid green-and-gold silkscreen paintings of wooded landscapes with cranes and other birds depicted in flight were being stretched from the floor to the draped ceiling on all three sides of this inner reception chamber and at the far end a large, scarlet-lacquered chest with gilded feet was being moved into a central position by sweating labourers.

'That box,' said the governor, pointing towards the scarlet chest, 'will play two important roles—one of them ceremonial, one of them secret.'

'What is it for, Shacho-san?' asked the interpreter agitatedly, stepping round a group of loin-clothed workers to hurry after the governor, who had started up the three broad steps to the inner chamber. 'Is the letter of the foreign barbarians to be placed in the box?'

'Not *in* the box, Haniwara-san,' replied the governor carefully, 'but ontop of it. When the admiral and the other foreign barbarians have arrived and seated themselves, your first duty will be to announce to them the names of our imperial representatives. Then you will ask them if the original letter and translations are ready for delivery.'

'And what do I reply, Shacho-san, if they say yes?'

'You will indicate that Prince Toda is ready to receive the letters. But he will not touch them and he is not to be approached under any circumstances. You will make it clear that the correct receptacle for such communications is the lid of the scarlet chest. And you will invite the barbarians to place them on its lid themselves.'

'I understand, Shacho-san,' said the interpreter, glancing nervously towards the chest which, like a grand altar, had been shifted into place close to the centre of the chamber's rear wall. 'I shall memorize each of those steps very carefully.'

The governor nodded his approval and stopped in front of the chest, gesturing with one hand towards two keg-shaped stools of white porcelain decorated with blue mountain motifs which had been positioned to the left of it. 'Throughout the ceremony, Prince Toda and Prince Ido will remain seated on these stools. The admiral and two other leading foreign barbarians will be invited to sit facing them here on the right side of the chest . . .' The governor paused and waved his hand towards three heavy, hand-carved, wooden chairs with raised sides which gave them the appearance of small thrones. 'These are the nearest pieces of furniture that could be found resembling the seats used by the barbarians in their own country. They have been brought here specially from a Buddhist temple, where they are normally used by priests when conducting funerals. . . .'

'What will happen after the foreign barbarians have deposited their letters on the red chest, Shacho-san?' interjected the interpreter nervously. 'Will the ceremony then be at an end?'

'No, not quite,' replied the governor. 'When the letters have been placed on the chest, I will go to make a low obeisance before Prince Ido. I will then receive from his hands a sealed imperial receipt for the letters. I will bring it to the foreign barbarian admiral and, after offering similar formal respects to him, I will hand it over. You will be given a copy and will make its contents known verbally at that moment.'

'What will the imperial receipt say, Shacho-san?'

'After acknowledging that the letter has duly been received on behalf of His Imperial Majesty, the note will reiterate that all business relating to foreign countries should normally be conducted at Nagasaki. It will also say that the letter has been received here in opposition to the laws of Nippon. Finally it will state that, as this is not a place to negotiate or offer entertainment, the barbarians, having delivered their letter, should leave our shores forthwith.'

'Those terms sound extremely forthright,' said the interpreter, staring distractedly at the scarlet chest. 'Is that the intention?'

'Yes, that is the deliberate will of the Council of the Shogun,' said the governor emphatically. 'You are to convey the sentiments in very firm tones.'

The interpreter nodded obediently, his face clouded with concern. 'And how exactly will the ceremony be concluded, Shacho-san?'

'I will return to the chest to draw and fasten a scarlet cloth about the deposited letters. This will mark the closure of the proceedings. At the same time you will tell the barbarians that there is nothing more to be done.'

'And when I have said that, what then?'

'You and I will then walk from the chamber towards the front entrance, indicating that the foreign barbarians should follow in our footsteps and return quickly to their ships. As they leave, Prince Toda and Prince Ido will rise to bow silently in farewell . . .'

The interpreter was still staring down distractedly at the scarlet chest, but now he raised his head and looked up at the governor with a perplexed expression in his eyes. 'You haven't yet told me what the secret purpose of this large box is, Shacho-san. Will you explain now, please?'

The governor nodded, his expression grave, and walked slowly to the rear of the chest, beckoning for the interpreter to follow. In the space between the chest and the silk hangings of the rear wall, he bent down and pulled aside a separate section of the red carpet to reveal a hinged trapdoor set in the wooden floor. Tugging it open, the governor stood back so that the interpreter could see the flight of rough steps that led down steeply into a dark cellar-pit dug out beneath the pavilion.

'The *secret* purpose of the scarlet chest is to conceal this entrance,' said the governor, glancing significantly at the startled interpreter and starting down the steps. 'Follow me. I will show you. There is space for ten fully armed samurai to hide down here—and they will be able to rush out unexpectedly to make a surprise attack at any moment during the ceremony.'

The interpreter did not move at first, but stared down with frightened eyes into the gloom of the underground hideout.

'What is it, Haniwara-san?' enquired the governor in a puzzled voice. 'Why are you so alarmed?'

'I did not expect there to be any violence here,' said the interpreter in a horrified voice.

'Come down and look for yourself,' repeated the governor, beginning to descend. 'And I will explain fully.'

The interpreter took a hesitant step towards the trapdoor, then stopped on hearing a stir of commotion from the open side of the entrance hall. Turning his head he saw a group of several grandly dressed *daimyo* were arriving.

Each feudal lord was accompanied by an elite entourage of twin-sworded samurai who were wearing braided leather and bamboo body armour as well as their branched helmets and fearsome fighting masks. The group of *daimyo* had stopped at the entrance to talk with the gowned official who was supervising the construction and preparation of the pavilion, and among them Haniwara caught a glimpse of the ominous, stocky figure of Lord Daizo. A sudden fist of fear clutched at his vitals as he recognized the face of the man who only two days ago had so shockingly revealed that he was holding Haniwara's wife and children hostage. For a long moment he stared numbly across the pavilion, the colour draining from his face, his heart pounding erratically as he wondered for the thousandth time whether his family was safe; he fought down pessimistic feelings that they might already have been harmed, and he turned his head towards the governor again only when he repeated his invitation in a more insistent voice.

'Come down quickly and look for yourself, Haniwara-san,' the governor urged him, following his gaze towards the entrance chamber. 'The *daimyo* have arrived for an inspection visit—but they won't come over here for a minute or two, so be quick!'

Haniwara hurried down the boarded steps into the hot cellar-pit to find it lit by a single paper lantern. Some planks had been laid on its hastily excavated floor, and pine props had been wedged into its walls. Clusters of long killing swords and lances hung from the rafters and shields, helmets and lacquered bamboo armour suits were piled in heaps in the corners. A second reinforcement tunnel led into the rear of the cellar, apparently from outside the pavilion, and a dozen flagons of drinking water had been brought in.

'What purpose is this to serve, Shacho-san?' asked the interpreter in an uneasy whisper, gazing round at the shields and weapons. 'Is it our plan to try and murder all the barbarians by surprise at a single stroke?'

"The Council of the Shogun has decided to take no risks,' said the governor in a low voice. 'So at least ten fully armed samurai will be hidden in here well before the ceremony begins.'

'But what will their role be, Shacho-san?' asked the interpreter insistently.

'They will be acting under strict orders from Prince Toda. They won't attack without reason. But if the foreign barbarians show any sign of resorting to violence, our samurai will swiftly rush out and slay the foreign admiral and his staff. . . .'

The interpreter shuddered and peered round at the shadowy walls, which seemed to bulge dangerously inward. The damp air smelled strongly of the sea and, because he could scarcely stand up straight under the ominously low ceiling formed by the wood-plank floor above, the interpreter felt suddenly panicky as though he was trapped in a mass grave.

'If there is a necessity, Shacho-san,' he asked shakily, 'who will pass on the orders for the samurai to attack?'

'It has fallen to the two of us to be the joint master of ceremonies,' said the governor slowly. 'So we shall be closest to the foreign barbarians. Therefore, Haniwara-san, I fear, if it becomes necessary, one or both of us will be designated to pass on the final orders through the trapdoor.'

'But surely we shall be given a signal by someone of higher authority?' enquired the interpreter in a desperate tone. 'We shall not have to make up our minds about it ourselves?'

The governor, noticing his sudden pallor and the panic in his voice, looked hard at his subordinate. 'Of course, Haniwara-san, of course. Don't be so afraid . . .'

The sudden sound of voices above the trapdoor reached their ears and the governor motioned silently for them to ascend. When the interpreter reached the top of the rough flight of steps he found his superior already bowing low in turn to each of the four or five *daimyo* who were grouped around the lacquered chest with their ferocious-looking samurai. They were discussing the procedures for the ceremony with the gowned official in charge, and Haniwara Tokuma in his turn bowed very low to each of the noblemen, reserving his last, deepest and longest prostration for Lord Daizo. He deliberately avoided looking the burly nobleman in the face at first but when, on straightening up, he darted a nervous glance in his direction, he was disconcerted to find Daizo staring intently at him, his eyes as cold and hard as they had been during their recent meeting at his castle.

'Since we need an individual of the highest integrity to convey the vital order if an emergency arises, I propose Haniwara Tokuma,' said Daizo suddenly, still staring hard at the interpreter. 'He will be closer to the hidden trapdoor than anybody else, and is known for his absolute reliability . . .'

The gowned official, the other *daimyo* and the helmeted samurai all turned incuriously to look at the interpreter, on hearing Daizo's proposal. None had noticed the pointed nature of the nobleman's stare and there was a general murmur of disinterested approval. After glancing briefly at each other, the gowned official and the governor nodded their agreement.

'Are you agreeable to Lord Daizo's suggestion yourself, Haniwara-san?' asked the governor formally. 'Do you accept the honour of this responsibility?'

To hide his dismay Haniwara quickly lowered his eyes. He could feel the coldness of Daizo's gaze upon him, and inside his chest his heart had begun to hammer painfully. But after a moment's hesitation he silently conveyed his acceptance by bowing deeply again in the general direction of Daizo, the other *daimyo*, the gowned official and the governor.

'Good. Then it is time to practise the secret procedure,' said the official, gesturing for the samurai to move towards the open trapdoor. 'I will seat myself in Prince Toda's position. I will give the signal for the attack by lifting my right hand across the front of my body to touch my left shoulder. You, Haniwara-san, should then move behind the lacquered chest to the closed trapdoor, and tap on it sharply three times with your heel . . .'

Their leather and chainmail armour creaked and their swords clanked quietly at their sides as the dozen samurai moved away swiftly down the steps into the concealed pit. The last one lowered the trapdoor behind him and an aide of the gowned official straightened the red carpet over it before retreating. The group of *daimyo* moved to stand in a semicircle behind the porcelain stool on which the gowned official seated himself, playing the role of Prince Toda, First Counsellor of the Empire. The hammering and the bustle of activity in the rest of the pavilion decreased suddenly, then stopped altogether as though by some silent command. The loin-clothed labourers and artisans paused in their work to stare towards the lacquered chest and the dignitaries ringed around it, aware from their demeanour that something of dramatic moment was being rehearsed.

The governor motioned to Haniwara Tokuma to kneel with him in formal fashion before the imperial stools. The interpreter, still very conscious of his fast-beating heart, tucked up his legs and tried to settle into the familiar posture, turning his head slightly so that he could see the seated senior official. Although he did not look directly at him, he was conscious of the burly figure of Lord Daizo standing among the other *daimyo*, and he could feel that his dark eyes were still staring fixedly at him.

'Remember the foreign barbarians will be watchful,' whispered the governor at his side, nodding faintly in the direction of the Buddhist funeral thrones a few yards away. 'So when the signal is given, move in a slow measured way so as not to arouse suspicion.'

The interpreter nodded tensely and looked towards the empty chairs, imagining that they were occupied by the tall, haughty figures of the Americans whom he had met on the *Susquehanna*. The fist of fear inside him seemed to tighten further at the prospect of being involved in attacking them, and at the same time his apprehension for his family's safety also grew more intense. An expectant hush had fallen over the interior of the pavilion, and no sounds came from beneath the trapdoor. When the gowned official at last moved his right hand to make the signal, it was done casually and unhurriedly and, because of his anxiety, Haniwara remained frozen for a moment in the kneeling position. Then he rose to his feet, trying not to hurry, and moved a few paces to the rear of the lacquered chest, where he tapped nervously three times on the trapdoor with his right heel before standing quickly aside.

At first nothing happened and he worried that he had tapped too softly and had not been heard. He was on the point of moving back onto the trapdoor to repeat the signal when it flew open with a crash and the hideous horned fighting mask of the first samurai appeared close before his face. He recoiled backwards in alarm as a bloodcurdling scream rang out from behind the mask and the warrior flung himself past the lacquered chest, his sword already in his hand. He lunged fast towards the three carved seats and slashed viciously left and right through the air above them, simulating killing strokes over and over again with great ferocity.

Half a dozen more warriors leapt from the cellar close on his heels to charge forward en masse, each one yelling and flailing his sword at the imaginary enemies. For a few seconds their steel blades glittered and flashed furiously under the light of the paper lanterns, then, on a sudden shouted command from the first samurai, all the warriors became still and replaced their swords in their scabbards. Within moments they had run back to the steps and disappeared again into the cellar-pit. Following them, their leader quickly hauled the trapdoor closed, and almost at once orderly calm returned to the pavilion. As one man, the watching labourers restarted their work and the sound of hammering and sawing quickly filled the air again.

'Quite satisfactory,' said the gowned official, rising from his stool and glancing round at the assembled noblemen and the governor. 'It is of course to be hoped that the foreign barbarians give us no cause to implement these purely defensive plans.'

Haniwara Tokuma, from his place beside the lacquered chest, watched the group fall into conversation about other aspects of the ceremony; but his heart sank suddenly when he saw Lord Daizo detach himself from the deliberations and walk towards him. In a loud voice the nobleman offered his congratulations on the efficient working of the plan but, on a pretext of asking a question about the trapdoor, he motioned for the interpreter to follow him behind the chest. When they were out of earshot, Daizo lowered his voice to speak more quietly and again, as at the castle, his tone was heavy with menace.

'I have something important to tell you, Haniwara-san. Are you calm and listening carefully?'

'Yes, my lord,' said the interpreter miserably. 'I am listening.'

'Then I can inform you that we have captured the hideous alien who came ashore secretly from the black ships to spy. Have you understood?'

The interpreter stiffened with shock, then nodded numbly without looking at the *daimyo*. 'I have understood, my lord.'

'Good. Because we intend to bring him to this pavilion by surprise, at the height of the ceremony. There will be a commotion at the sight of him. At that moment I shall appear in the entrance to the pavilion, and you are to be watching carefully. Is all that clear so far?'

'Yes, my lord,' murmured the interpreter.

'I shall make the same signal that you reacted to just now—and you will go unobtrusively to the trapdoor, and tap three times to order the attack on the other hideous aliens. If you do not obey these orders, your wife and children will all die within the hour.' Lord Daizo paused and looked at the interpreter through narrowed eyes. 'Are you quite sure you've understood everything?'

'I am sure I've heard everything very clearly, my lord,' replied the interpreter in a hoarse whisper. 'I have no wish but to obey.'

'Good, Haniwara-san,' said the *daimyo* with mock politeness. 'I am very glad. You are, as I thought, a very wise man.'

Without speaking further, Lord Daizo turned and hurried back to join the other noblemen. They were inspecting the mural pictures of cranes and other great birds which were being fixed in place above the ornate seats to be occupied by the visiting American naval officers. A quiet discussion about the artistic merits of the silk scroll paintings was in progress, and Lord Daizo immediately joined in, nodding and gesturing naturally with the others and betraying no hint that he had just issued secret orders of his own to assassinate the leading foreign barbarians in the midst of the ceremony.

42

On the quarterdeck of the *Susquehanna* Samuel Armstrong raised a telescope to his eye shortly after dawn and looked apprehensively towards the shore. Billowing mists still obscured the distant valleys and ravines, but the rising sun was beginning to break through in patches and he swept the glass slowly along new stretches of canvas that had appeared overnight on the nearest clifftops. Larger throngs of fighting men than he had seen before were becoming visible, patrolling briskly back and forth behind the blue-and-white screens with lances and muskets on their shoulders. Additional panels of canvas had also been erected around the forts and gun emplacements giving them a more substantial appearance.

He noticed too that scarlet streamers and flags bearing a variety of emblems and heraldic devices had been suspended from the tall posts supporting the screens. The new contingents of armed men he could see through the telescope wore a loose-skirted fighting dress—dark brown in colour, which he had not seen before—and they had broad sashes about their waists. At first glance these splashes of colour seemed merely to add a fresh dimension of ceremonial pageantry to the visible coast; but then he noticed that the soldiers were bare-armed, and after studying their movements closely he decided that the briskness of their demeanour indicated a new readiness, even an eagerness, for action. The unfamiliar banners and screens, he concluded, seemed more likely to have been erected for purposes of defence than for show.

No breath of wind stirred the glassy waters of the bay and, from beyond the headland to the south, the noises of hammering and construction were still continuing intermittently. Armstrong listened for a moment, wondering anxiously again what would be revealed on landing. But his thoughts did not dwell long on the prospect because the decks of the *Susquehanna* and the other three warships anchored abreast before Uraga were already a-bustle with noise too, as they prepared to move smoothly to their battle stations.

The recently started engines of the flagship were throbbing steadily and black smoke was beginning to drift lazily from its tall black funnel.

Neat piles of shot had been re-stacked beside each cannon and more carbines and pikes had been grouped in small pyramids, ready for use. Sailors dressed in freshly laundered white blouses, blue bellbottom trousers, blue collars and black neckerchiefs were dashing up and down the ladders between decks, tugging on new blue caps issued specially for the occasion. These caps were decked with bands of red, white and blue stripes—and thirteen blue stars representing the states of the Union had been emblazoned on the white stripe. The marines had donned their traditional blue jackets and white trousers, and were busy brushing their plumed shakos and whitening the gleaming bandoliers they would wear across their chests. Glancing back and forth from the ship to the shore, Armstrong reflected sadly that if the day were to end in killing and butchery, the fighting men on both sides would have the satisfaction of being arrayed in their best military finery to perpetrate these terrible deeds.

On hearing a quiet footfall behind him, Armstrong turned to find Commodore Matthew Perry himself approaching. Although he was hatless and wore no sword, the commander-in-chief was also partly garbed in full-dress uniform. Gilded epaulettes enlarged the broad set of his shoulders, and the twin rows of gold buttons on the dark bole of his chest were augmented by an impressive cluster of decorations and star-shaped orders. His dark, curly hair flowed over his collar as usual but his leonine features were impassive as he scanned the fortified shore minutely without the aid of a glass.

'Good morning, Commodore,' said Armstrong quietly, gazing in the same direction, towards the clifftops. 'There seems to be more activity around those forts than ever before.'

Matthew Perry grunted an inaudible greeting, but made no other reply. After peering hard into the mists for a long time he raised his head cautiously, like some big animal scenting the air, and looked up towards the brightening sky. 'There's no wind at all this morning, Mr Armstrong,' he said absently, without looking at the missionary-interpreter. 'That means the sail frigates can't move closer inshore. So the *Plymouth* will stay here, and its guns will command Uraga.' He paused, scanning the shore again towards the north. '*Saratoga* will be able to direct its cannon at the next town and the forts surrounding it. . . .'

'I think it's called Humai on the charts, sir,' said Armstrong.

'Just so, *Saratoga* will command Humai.'

The commodore fell silent again, turning his attention back to the nearest fortifications and the growing number of warriors moving above Uraga. His eyes narrowed as he watched, but he still offered no comment.

'Are you expecting trouble, Commodore?' ventured Armstrong tentatively. 'To me there does seem to be a new sense of purpose and urgency in their movements.'

'I have no serious apprehension that there will be a warlike termination to today's ceremonies,' said Perry sharply. 'Our best chance of security will lie in our capacity to put on an impressive display of power.'

Armstrong knew that late the previous evening the commodore had summoned the captains of all four warships to an urgent conference on the *Susquehanna*, after sending a scouting party in a cutter to Kurihama bay. The party had taken soundings and carefully surveyed the location of the ceremonial pavilion and its surrounding fortifications; armed with this knowledge, the commander-in-chief and his officers had mapped out their strategy for the vital day. No information had so far been passed to Armstrong himself but from what he knew of Perry's character he was certain that personal boldness and a forthright courage, which were the hallmarks of his career, would be stamped very clearly on the proceedings.

'May I ask exactly how you propose, Commodore, to "display" our power?' asked Armstrong respectfully. 'Knowing might help me pitch my interpreting at the correct level.'

'Soon, Mr Armstrong, we shall weigh anchor along with the *Mississippi* and steam the short distance to the entrance of Kurihama bay,' said Perry brusquely. 'We shall anchor across its mouth, with our guns primed and springs on our cables. That way we can threaten the landing place unwaveringly with the full power of our broadsides. I shall place additional howitzers in fully manned boats, which will be held alongside the frigates when we go ashore. These craft will be kept at a constant state of alert, ready to go into action at a moment's notice.'

'And how many men will you take ashore?'

'Three hundred or more! A hundred and ten marines, a hundred and twenty sailors, forty musicians from the two ships' bands, and a large body of officers. Each man will be armed with a sword and a pistol or a musket. All firearms will be loaded. There will be a thousand charges of ball in the party—and each of the fifteen boats will carry extra cartridge boxes!'

'Those numbers might be seen as excessive to support the peaceful delivery of an official letter,' said Armstrong dryly. 'But, if hostilities break out, our most conservative estimates say the Japanese have at least ten thousand visible armed men ranged against us.'

'But armed with what exactly, Mr Armstrong?' asked Perry dismissively. 'Nothing remotely dangerous to us, I'll warrant.'

'Since I shall be at your side, Commodore, I hope you're not underestimating the fighting spirit of the Japanese. They have a reputation as fierce warriors.'

'Talk to the men, Mr Armstrong, if you still doubt,' cut in Perry peremptorily and lifted his telescope to his eye to survey the clifftops. 'Every Yankee I've spoken to believes we can scatter any number of men with one broadside, one war-whoop and a single determined rush with cold steel.'

'I wonder if Robert Eden would be able to confirm that opinion as sound,' remarked Armstrong mildly. 'Provided he's still alive, of course, to confirm anything at all.'

The interpreter turned his head to look enquiringly at the squadron commander, but if he had heard the reference to his missing lieutenant he gave no sign. For a full minute Perry continued to study the shore intently through his telescope; then he snapped it closed with a decisive gesture.

'I have every confidence in the valour of the men presently under my command,' he said, looking directly at the missionary. 'And in our superior firepower. I trust your work as interpreter today for this expedition will also reflect that total confidence. Now, if you'll excuse me, I must go and prepare the day's orders. We must weigh anchor very soon.'

The burly figure swung briskly away across the quarterdeck, heading for his cabin, and Armstrong watched him until he went out of sight. Turning to look towards the shore again, the missionary felt a new shudder of apprehension run up his spine. He wondered once more about the fate of the missing lieutenant who had disappeared overboard so dramatically six long days ago and, try as he might, he could not dismiss the feeling that there was something ominous in the almost total absence of information about him during all that time.

The billowing mists that he could see still clinging to the hills and gorges inland also seemed to intensify the nagging anxiety he felt about his own safety. Standing at the rail, he tried to calm his fears by imagining himself stepping ashore and moving with unflustered dignity amidst the great multitude of feudal Japanese soldiery. But such thoughts, far from soothing him, served only to heighten his nervousness and he started suddenly when the *Mississippi* blew a piercing blast on her whistle to announce that she was preparing to move.

As he listened to the clank of the *Mississippi*'s anchor-chain and watched her giant paddle-wheels begin to churn, he resolved suddenly that before landing he would do something he had never done before. He would borrow a blue officer's jacket and for the very first time in his life strap on a sheathed sword! Because of Christ's agonized exhortation to Peter to put away his steel in the Garden of Gethsemane, he knew at once that he would never be able to draw and use such a weapon himself, even in self-defence. But if he carried one with him, he reasoned inwardly as the *Susquehanna* too began to weigh anchor, at least he would not stand out as the only defenceless target in the entire American landing party.

For a few minutes longer he stood alone on the quarterdeck, mulling over his astounding decision. Part of him felt he should change his mind and he tried to tell himself several times that his faith in God should be sufficient protection. But this logic, he found, was not sufficiently reassuring, and his disquiet persisted. Then, as he watched the bows of the two great smoke-belching warships swing slowly to point south towards Kurihama, he shook his head once in a gesture of finality and hurried below to seek out the ship's armourer and request that he be provided with a suitable blade.

43

Prince Tanaka heard the *Mississippi*'s shrill whistle split the stillness of the early morning as he raced his horse at breakneck speed along a narrow, woodland track high above Kurihama. He was riding at the head of his samurai guard troop and when they reached a wider road winding along an open ridge a few minutes later, he slowed his mount to a walk and turned in the saddle to look down towards the coast. Through holes in the patchy mist he could see the two massive black ships of the foreign barbarians, and both were sending long smudges of smoke skyward as they steamed south on the mirror-calm waters of the bay. Because there was no wind, all the canvas of the steamers remained furled, and he could see that the two sailing sloops-of-war had been forced to remain stationary at their anchorages.

'We have almost run out of time,' he said grimly over his shoulder to Gotaro, who had reined in beside him. 'We have only two observation posts left to check—and the black ships are already preparing to aim their guns at Kurihama.'

Both men were breathing hard from the exertion of the ride and the guard captain nodded wordlessly as he gazed down into the bay. With the onset of the day, the winding dirt road onto which they had come out was beginning to fill up with reserve columns of infantry moving quickly and silently to new locations around Kurihama. Military mule-trains heavily laden with food were also beginning to appear among local peasants hauling their farm produce to market on their backs. Occasional civilian palanquins bobbed among the tramping columns, and when Tanaka and his escort got moving again, some of the bodyguards had to ride ahead of him shouting and gesticulating with their swords to cut a passage through the growing swarms of men and animals.

'Our next post is about a mile from here,' snapped Tanaka at the men around him, as he turned onto a deserted woodland track again and urged his horse into a gallop. 'After that there is only one left. Follow my example! We must ride as hard as we can!'

The guards leaned low over the necks of their mounts as they spurred furiously forward through the woods at Tanaka's heels. It was the third time since midnight that they had checked the string of observation posts which he had set up in a last act of desperation along the high escarpment overlooking the bay. Twenty or thirty of his best cavalry samurai had been stationed in discreet bivouacs at the junctions of all known tracks leading down to the coast. They had been given strict orders not to attack but to inform him immediately of any suspicious armed column that might be transporting the captured foreign barbarian to Kurihama. But, as the night dragged on and dawn broke, no sightings at all had been reported. At first he had waited at a central camp to which messengers were ordered to bring information; then, as the empty hours ticked by, he had himself begun patrolling impatiently back and forth along the observation posts at a rapid gallop, followed by his hard-pressed guard troop. But as each bivouac was approached, the disconsolate attitudes of the waiting warriors had always told their own story, even before they were questioned. Despite his mounting inner tension, however, Tanaka's outward demeanour had remained unemotional in the face of each new disappointment, and when he reined in his sweating horse at the penultimate post set up in a roadside copse, he watched with an expressionless face as the post's commander bowed elaborately low in greeting to compensate for having nothing to report.

'Have you seen nothing at all suspicious?' asked Tanaka in a tight voice, glancing towards the nearby road where peasants were straggling past in groups. 'Are you quite sure?'

'Unhappily I am quite certain, O Kami-san,' replied the post commander in a regretful tone. 'We have scrutinized every passing column and every individual most carefully. There has been no sign at all of what you are seeking.'

Tanaka nodded curtly in acknowledgement and the commander began to bow low again, but was distracted by a sudden commotion of galloping hoofs approaching along the road from the south. Both men turned their heads sharply as two Kago clan samurai from the last observation post a mile away swung their horses into the bivouac in a swirl of dust. A scrawny, half-naked prisoner, bound hand and foot, was slung across the neck of the leading horse, and its rider leapt from the saddle and bowed quickly on recognizing Tanaka.

'What is this?' demanded the nobleman, a gleam of hope appearing suddenly in his eyes. 'Who is your captive?'

The leading samurai pulled the hobbled prisoner from his horse and forced him roughly to his knees in front of Tanaka. 'He's a chair-bearer,

O Kami-san. We captured him a few minutes ago in the hills above our post, where we were patrolling.' Breathing quickly, the samurai turned and gestured with one arm towards the steep, tree-cloaked heights above the road. 'We spied a long guard column, wearing the crests of Lord Daizo. They were escorting a single *norimono*down a wooded gorge. In the mist we got close without them seeing us. There were many reserve bearers, and this man was among them. He stopped to relieve himself among the trees, so we swooped to capture him without being seen. He has told us they are escorting a very important prisoner to Kurihama—but he says he will be killed by Lord Daizo's warriors if he says any more!'

'He will be killed instantly, where he is kneeling, if he remains silent,' said Tanaka, drawing his long sword and approaching the cringing captive with deliberate steps.

The bearer, who wore only a loin-cloth and a sweat-grimed turban, looked up in terror at the gleaming blade. His eyes rolled in fear as the nobleman swished the sword suddenly before his face in a lightning movement which would have beheaded him if it had come six inches closer. Standing perfectly still, Tanaka rested the razor-sharp edge of the weapon against the base of the bearer's neck and applied a gentle pressure until a slow trickle of blood began to appear on the steel.

'Tell us all you know,' said Tanaka urgently.

Trembling, and paralysed with fear, the bearer gaped up mutely first at Tanaka then at the watching ring of hostile samurai. Realizing that blood had begun to flow down his chest, he opened and closed his mouth convulsively but no sounds emerged.

'Is Daizo's prisoner a foreign barbarian?' prompted Tanaka quietly, increasing the pressure of his blade. 'Tell me now, or you are dead.'

The bearer began to nod frantically. 'Yes, O Kami-san,' he croaked at last. 'The prisoner of Lord Daizo is indeed a foreign barbarian.'

'Good. Very good,' breathed Tanaka, a gleam of triumph appearing in his eyes. 'And he is still alive, yes?'

'Yes, he lives, O Kami-san,' blurted the bearer. 'He is badly wounded . . . and also bound and blindfolded. But he lives.'

'Where have you carried him from?'

'From the region of our sacred mountain, O Kami-san,' said the bearer desperately. 'But we travelled mostly by night to cloak our path.'

'Good,' said Tanaka again, easing the pressure on his blade. 'And what is the exact condition of the foreign barbarian?'

'He has wounds to the head and in his leg, O Kami-san. They are bandaged but still bloody.' The bearer shifted gingerly on his knees, easing his neck fractionally away from the sword. 'He has been given water, rice and eggs during the rest stops. But he lapses often into unconsciousness. He's constantly blindfolded and when allowed to stand, he is very weak and unsteady on his legs.'

'Is he still wearing the garb of a peasant of Nippon?'

'Yes, O Kami-san, he is.'

Tanaka looked up quickly at the samurai who had brought in the captive. 'Is all the terrain wooded and steep where the armed column is descending?'

'It is, O Kami-san—densely wooded and very steep.'

'And the paths are narrow—with only room for men and horses to pass in single file?'

The samurai nodded vigorously. 'Yes, mostly so, O Kami-san.'

'And what sort of carriage was being used to transport the foreign barbarian?'

'It was impossible to see clearly in the mist,' said the warrior, shaking his head apologetically. 'It seemed to be a simple civilian carrying-chair—a black *norimono*.'

'Forgive me for interrupting, O Kami-san,' said Gotaro suddenly. 'Shouldn't I begin rallying our forces from the other observation posts, so that we can launch a lightning attack before it is too late?'

Tanaka shook his head decisively, without taking his eyes from the shuddering captive. 'We can't attack openly amongst such a great concentration of forces. If we did, we might start a terrible civil war—and that would give Daizo just the excuse he needs to attack and slaughter the foreign barbarians. If we are to succeed now, we must employ subterfuge . . .'

'Whatever you say, O Kami-san,' replied the guard captain, bowing his head respectfully. 'But how can we help you?'

Tanaka looked desperately about himself, his intense expression indicating that his thoughts were racing. On the road another supply train was passing at a rapid jog-trot, and two or three enclosed carrying-chairs had halted for a moment to allow the long line of animals and their drivers to pass.

'What kind of *norimono* exactly is being used to carry the foreign barbarian?' demanded Tanaka, again pressing his sword against the bearer's shoulder. 'Is it anything like those that are passing us now?'

The bearer turned his fearful eyes towards the road, then nodded hastily. 'Yes, O Kami-san. Something like the black one. It was just an ordinary *norimono* like that.'

'Commandeer it at once, Gotaro!' ordered Tanaka over his shoulder. 'Hold the bearers and its occupant here—and capture a few other passing bearers, too. Bind them all and hide them under guard among the trees.'

Without a moment's hesitation Gotaro drew his sword and signalled to half a dozen other guards to follow him. Yelling loudly, they spurred their horses towards me the halted chairs and surrounded it, brandishing their weapons. One of the samurai wrenched open its door and hauled out its shocked occupant, a grey-bearded official in a silk gown. Then the guards began shepherding the bearer-coolies, the *norimono* and the official back into the shelter of the trees.

'Wipe away the prisoner's blood with his turban, and replace it on his head,' snapped Tanaka, motioning forward the samurai who had brought in the original captive. 'Leave his bonds in place, and bind some other blood-soaked bandages about his legs. Stop a passing peasant and steal some clothes to dress him in. Then blindfold him and place him inside this *norimono*. Is all that clear?'

'Yes, O Kami-san,' called the samurai, rushing to obey. 'Your orders are perfectly clear.'

While the prisoner was being trussed further, Tanaka looked searchingly round at his remaining guards. 'I want six volunteers to join me . . . Six volunteers strong enough to help me carry a *norimono* a good distance on our bare shoulders—and brave enough to risk combat against fine swordsmen without any arms of our own.' He looked each bodyguard in the face in turn. 'We can disguise ourselves with the loin-cloths and turbans of these captured coolies. Now, who will join me?'

All the remaining guards instantly raised their clenched fists in the air and, after selecting half a dozen, Tanaka jumped down from his horse and began to remove his *jimbaori* and his armour. Two or three minutes later he and the six chosen guards stood ready beside the commandeered *norimono*, naked except for the borrowed loin-cloths and the towel-turbans which hid their samurai topknots. They watched as the prisoner, dressed now in peasant clothing, was bundled inside the carriage, blindfolded and swathed in bloodied bandages; then, at a command from Tanaka, they bent to hoist the single long carrying-pole onto their shoulders.

'How far from here is the track where Daizo's men are descending?' demanded Tanaka, addressing the samurai who had captured the bearer.

'About two *ri*, O Kami-san.'

'Then lead us there now as fast as possible!' He turned and motioned to Gotaro and the remaining twenty samurai to follow discreetly. 'Ride at a distance behind us! We shall try to approach silently through the trees, without being seen.'

He waved his free arm and, as one man, he and the six disguised samurai broke into a jog-trot, carrying the *norimono* on their shoulders. Following in the wake of the single mounted warrior, they hurried away into the mist, heading quickly towards the most southerly track leading down to Kurihama.

44

As the Susquehanna and the *Mississippi* rounded the jutting headland which had previously concealed Kurihama Bay from American eyes, a sudden hush fell over both ships. The seamen and marines, who had been busying themselves with the preparation of their weapons and equipment, fell silent and crowded to the open gunports and other vantage points to stare towards the shore. To their astonishment a great mass of Japanese fighting men was already waiting in full view, drawn up in spectacular ranks on the beach along the entire length of the bay.

Thousands of infantrymen, archers, pikemen and lancers, standing motionless and silent on the sands, glared seaward from amongst forests of fluttering feudal banners and pennants. The brightening sun glinted on spears, pikes and the bayonets of brass-bound muskets and, all round the margins of the crescent-shaped bay, hundreds of boats filled with armed guards had been anchored in parallel groups to face the American ships. Higher up the beach, partly concealed behind long canvas screens, large bodies of cavalry samurai could be seen moving quietly to and fro on spirited, brightly caparisoned horses.

A steep valley gorge, walled in with thickly wooded hills, rose abruptly above the beach, and the watching Americans could see that swathes of early morning mist still clung to its gullies and ravines. The steepness of these hills provided a dramatic backdrop, both to the mass of medieval soldiery gathered below and the ceremonial pavilion which was now fully visible at the centre of the bay. Constructed of blue and white canvas, and rising in three pyramid-shaped roofs only a hundred yards or so from the waterline, the pavilion dwarfed the humble houses of the nearby village of Kurihama. Like the forts on the heights above Uraga, and the gun emplacements around the bay itself, it was flanked by long canvas screens designed to conceal troop movements, and these too were emblazoned with the imperial Nipponese crest. A temporary wharf jutted into the sea at the mid-point of the bay, built from bags of rice-straw and sand, and a path had been cleared from it to the pavilion's entrance.

'It truly looks as though we're being invited to stick our heads in the lion's mouth, Major Pearsall, don't you think?' murmured Samuel Armstrong in amazement as he gazed out at the extraordinary scene from the quarterdeck beside the senior officer of the US Marine Corps, who was preparing to lead the contingent of armed men ashore. 'All that remains to be seen, surely, is how badly we get bitten.'

'There's no real cause for alarm, Mr Armstrong,' drawled the major, who was scanning the shore through a telescope. 'Look close and you'll see their lines are very loose. That means they lack real good order. And their men look squat and effeminate.' The broad-chested marine officer, who stood ramrod straight and well over six feet tall, lowered his telescope, passed it to the missionary and waved a white-gloved hand proudly towards the spar deck, where junior officers were beginning to marshall together squads of the brawniest men who had been hand-picked for the landing party. 'Man for man, Mr Armstrong, we're much bigger and stronger—and we're much better disciplined. If this lion tries to bite, we'll do more than tweak his tail.'

Armstrong looked through the glass then handed it back, his dubious expression indicating that he did not share the marine officer's supreme confidence. 'The feudal past is clashing with the new power of the modern world right before our eyes,' he said quietly. 'There's no telling what repercussions this will have—now or later. I for one will be praying very hard.'

'I trust in the Lord myself, Mr Armstrong,' grinned Major Pearsall, tapping the missionary lightly on the shoulder. 'But I trust also in the steady aim of my men, in their strength and their training.'

Swinging on his heel he hurried down to the deck below, where some of the chief participants in the landing party were beginning to rehearse their drills, and Armstrong moved nearer to watch. On the assumption that no such men had ever been seen in Japan, two powerful-looking black sailors with broad shoulders and bulging biceps had been chosen by Commodore Perry himself to march at his side as personal bodyguards. Both were nearly seven feet tall, and they gave an ominous impression of strength as they stood stock-still on the main deck, clutching the newest revolving rifles across their chests as well as carrying pistols and cutlasses in their belts.

Two strapping white seamen, almost as tall, were lined up ahead of them, bearing the United States flag and the commodore's blue pennant. In between stood two ship's boys who had been given the ceremonial responsibility of bearing the letters of the American President and the commodore's credentials. Dressed in new blue and white uniforms identical to those of the seamen, their flushed faces betrayed their excitement as they took up their places, and Armstrong watched two midshipmen enclose the vellum letters carefully in their gilded rosewood boxes, then wrap them in large envelopes of scarlet cloth before handing them to the young sailors.

The ship's band was drawn up ahead, and when all were ready the column marched a few dozen practice paces around the deck with Major Pearsall striding between the two black bodyguards in place of the commodore. Perry himself had made no appearance on deck since they had rounded the headland and Armstrong wondered whether this was evidence of his total confidence in the situation, or whether he might have been secretly surveying the heavily guarded beach from some invisible vantage point below decks. These reflections aroused new feelings of apprehension in his mind, and he let his hand fall tentatively to the unfamiliar sword hilt that dangled uncomfortably against his left hip. Whenever he moved, the sword and scabbard seemed to knock clumsily against his leg or the skirt of his blue frockcoat, and with a nervous gesture he adjusted its belt to another position.

'We are about to anchor, Mr Armstrong,' said Lieutenant Rice, breaking in on his thoughts suddenly as the *Susquehanna* began to swing broadside to the beach. 'The Japanese officials who will guide us ashore are to be piped aboard soon.'

Armstrong turned to find the flag lieutenant at his shoulder, staring out towards six Japanese boats that had been keeping station with the warships on a parallel course since the moment they weighed anchor. Two of them flew the now familiar black-and-white striped flag of the Governor of Uraga, and Armstrong had already identified the governor and his interpreter, Haniwara Tokuma, among the group of sumptuously gowned officials who were visible aboard the leading boat. Their four escort boats flew the same red pennants as other guard craft and, on seeing the great paddle-wheels of the *Susquehanna* begin to slow down, the oarsmen of all six Japanese boats changed direction abruptly to head towards the flagship's already lowered gangway.

'Does the commodore wish me to attend at the gangway to greet the Japanese dignitaries?' asked Armstrong, still fumbling distractedly with his sword. 'And to entertain them while they are aboard, perhaps?'

The lieutenant shook his head decisively. 'No. They will be greeted by my midshipmen. They alone will conduct them to chairs by the taffrail.' He turned and gestured with one hand towards several seats already in place. 'It's the commodore's wish that nobody shall have any verbal contact with the Japanese entourage on this ship this morning. All communication must take place exclusively ashore.'

'Why's that, Lieutenant?' asked Armstrong, raising his eyebrows in surprise. 'Is he concerned I might try to ask some more awkward questions about Robert Eden?'

'The commodore feels his orders are necessary in view of the delicacy of the moment,' replied Rice, carefully ignoring the question. 'Nothing must be allowed to jeopardize the situation now, and strict formality is to be observed by everybody.'

'All this will enable our Japanese guests, no doubt, to watch without interruption while we clear our decks, prime our heavy guns, and run them out towards their shores,' said Armstrong with mild sarcasm. 'It will help them clearly understand our war readiness.'

The flag lieutenant allowed himself a half-smile. 'Yes, Mr Armstrong, that of course had occurred to us. But after that they won't be aboard very long. In one minute's time I shall order a signal to be hoisted summoning all cutters from our sister ships. As soon as they're assembled, our hosts will be invited to re-embark in their own boats and we'll follow them in convoy to the beach. You'll travel in our first boat with Major Pearsall and the commander of the *Susquehanna*. Commodore Perry will follow the main convoy at a distance in his official barge, accompanied by myself and the commander of the *Mississippi*.'

'Thank you, Lieutenant,' said the missionary hesitantly, struggling to hide his dismay at the prospect of approaching the heavily guarded beach in the first boat. 'It will be an honour . . . to be among the first ashore.'

Noticing that the grey-whiskered missionary was still fiddling agitatedly with his swordbelt, the flag lieutenant smiled and gestured towards the main deck, where the drilling of the landing group had just finished. 'Perhaps you should try to relax a little, Mr Armstrong. You might even try taking a stroll around the ship to get used to this strange business of walking with a sword at your side. Try it this way.' The flag lieutenant bent quickly to adjust his belt and scabbard for him, then grinned encouragingly before hurrying off to execute his other orders.

Because the Japanese boat had already reached the gangway, Armstrong waited on the quarterdeck until the Governor of Uraga and his entourage had been piped aboard. When they were escorted to their appointed seats, he noticed that the governor was more extravagantly garbed than previously in a shimmering gown of multi-coloured silk brocade trimmed with bright yellow velvet. His family crests were embroidered in gold thread on its back and also across the garment's broad sleeves, inside which he clasped his hands invisibly as he walked. Like his similarly dressed suite of officials, he wore broad silken trousers that hid his feet, and a black-lacquered winged bonnet lent a new gravity to his serious features.

At his side, Haniwara Tokuma was more sombrely clad in darker robes trimmed at the cuff and hem with a scholar's official black satin; he wore a softer hat of black silk too, but it was his tense demeanour not the sombreness of his clothing which made Armstrong stare hard at the Japanese interpreter. Noticeably paler in the face than before, even at a distance across the quarterdeck, he seemed to Armstrong to be hunched with tension as he perched uncomfortably on the unfamiliar western chair and, as the minutes ticked by, his evident agitation served to heighten the missionary's own growing unease. On catching the governor's eye, Armstrong had bowed low in greeting and was gravely acknowledged in the same fashion, but the interpreter kept his eyes fixed steadfastly on the deck before his feet and never once looked up.

Even when the urgent drumbeat of 'general quarters' was sounded from the spar deck below, and gunnery officers began barking orders to prepare the flagship's massive sixty-four-pounders for action, Haniwara still did not raise his head. The governor and the rest of his entourage watched with near expressionless faces as the American gunners raced efficiently back and forth, loading, priming and heaving the muzzles of the great wheeled guns out through their firing ports; but through all this the Japanese interpreter continued to gaze unswervingly in front of himself, as though his mind was focused deliberately in another time and place.

When the commotion subsided to the sudden quiet of the ship's battle-preparedness, Armstrong found he could no longer stand inactive on the quarterdeck, and he descended quickly to pace back and forth along the spar deck in an effort to quell his own increased uneasiness. He stopped now and again to stare out through a port towards the crowded shore, but felt himself further disturbed by the apparent calm of the assembled Japanese forces. As the time drew nearer for the landing, they seemed, to his anxious eyes, to grow more intent in their determination to resist invasion.

On a broad stretch of raised ground behind the beach he saw a great throng of civilians had gathered to watch. They seemed to be standing unnaturally still, too, as they peered down towards the landing area, and this sight made him think suddenly of the great Roman amphitheatre where helpless Christians had been cast before ravenous lions under the eyes of the baying crowd. He shivered involuntarily, despite the warmth of the summer morning, and began walking again, finding that he had quickly learned how to hold his sword with one hand so that it did not impede his steps. But when at last he heard the clatter of the *Susquehanna*'s boats being lowered, and officers began shouting orders for the landing group to embark, he climbed slowly back to the appointed entry port with the greatest reluctance.

By the time he reached the top of the gangway, the flotilla of fifteen American cutters was bobbing in line alongside the flagship. Most of them were filled with their quotas of blue-jacketed marines and seamen, and the two ship's bands were already settled in separate craft. The Governor of Uraga had also re-embarked with his suite in the two leading Japanese boats, and soon after Armstrong hurried down into the barge of the *Susquehanna*'s commander the whole flotilla began to move away towards the shore.

The Japanese oarsmen, who were stripped to the waist, hissed vigorously at each stroke as was their habit and pulled ahead. Provoked by this challenge, the American sailors began to dip their own oars with greater rapidity in order to keep up, and the long flotilla sped forward across the glittering waters, slipping easily over long tendrils of seaweed that grew close to the surface. As they went, Armstrong noticed that some of the young Americans were staring towards the beaches, their serious faces showing that they too were wondering anxiously how the day might end. Others, however, joked and bantered boisterously with each other to keep up their spirits.

Although some mist still clung to many of the green ravines above Kurihama, the sun was becoming brilliant over the sea. It dazzled on the white plumes of the marines, gilded the caps and gold braid of the officers more brightly, and flashed on the steel of the many carbines and cutlasses which bristled in each boat. The spray from the fast-moving oars began to whip Armstrong's face and, despite his deep Christian abhorrence of all forms of warfare, he suddenly felt an illogical surge of exhilaration in his breast. The two bands struck up a cheerful sea-shanty, as if the danger of the Japanese shore batteries opening fire on this aggressive American flotilla was non-existent, and Armstrong let his body relax for the first time that day against the gunwale of the barge. At that moment one of the *Susquehanna*'s massive cannon exploded with a deep roar that shook the whole bay. A second gun roared a moment later, and the great crowd of Japanese civilians at which Armstrong had been staring began to break up and flee in all directions. A third gun boomed from the flagship and the missionary instinctively ducked lower in the barge, looking fearfully about himself.

'Don't worry, Mr Armstrong,' said Major Pearsall affably. 'It's just a thirteen-gun salute. The commodore is now leaving his flagship.'

Armstrong straightened sheepishly on his seat and looked back to see that the commander-in-chief of the US Navy squadron was in the act of stepping down into his barge. A resplendent figure wearing a gold-tasselled cocked hat, white gloves, ceremonial sword and his full-dress uniform of blue and gold, he paused and appeared to survey the shore haughtily for a moment, before embarking and taking his seat. The sixty-four-pounders continued to boom deafeningly across the bay as his craft began to respond to its oarsmen, and Armstrong turned back towards the shore to find that the crowds of Japanese civilians were hurrying back to their vantage points above the beach, having quickly realized that the roar of the foreign barbarian guns was merely symbolic, and that no damage or casualties were yet being inflicted.

None of the thousands of Japanese fighting men ranged along the shores, however, seemed to have moved a muscle. Each line stood as immobile and impassive as before, and he sensed instinctively that he was absorbing a lesson of vital importance about a nation that was still largely a mystery to him. Even the samurai cavalrymen, he noticed, had drawn their horses quietly into line behind the screens, and although a few of the animals shied and bucked briefly on hearing the guns roar, all were being quickly and efficiently quietened by their riders. Even though their lines might not have been as well drawn as a unit of United States marines, the unflinching devotion to duty evident in their stillness was eerily impressive and the missionary-interpreter continued to scan their ranks with apprehensive eyes as the American flotilla sped towards the beach.

45

What are those guns, O Kami-san?'

A young samurai, who was racing at Tanaka's heels through the misty woods above Kurihama, gasped out his question in a startled voice as the *Susquehanna*'s cannon continued to boom across the unseen waters of the bay below.

'I don't know,' rasped Tanaka without turning his head. 'Until this mist clears and we can see what's happening below, we must be patient.'

The samurai's bare right shoulder, like Tanaka's, was already rubbed raw from the unfamiliar friction of the *norimono*'s thick carrying-pole, and he was grunting loudly with exertion as he struggled to keep his footing on a steep slope above a gully. Under the rear section of the pole two other samurai were grimacing and grunting too as they strove to manhandle the cumbersome conveyance as quickly as possible down the sharp inclines, watched anxiously by the mounted bodyguards and reserve samurai carriers who were following closely behind.

'Do you think, O Kami-san, it means the foreign barbarians have begun to attack?' persisted the young man. 'Are we too late?'

Tanaka waved his arm to indicate they should stop, and lifted his head for a moment to listen. 'The guns are firing in a regular rhythm,' he said uncertainly. 'It could be a signal of some kind.'

As he finished speaking, the guns also ceased to roar, and an unnatural hush descended over the wooded hillsides, as though every tree and every living creature moving among them had paused to listen in terror.

'Perhaps the barbarians have just left their ships to advance to the shore,' whispered the young samurai. 'Which would mean our time is running short.'

'Perhaps you're right,' agreed Tanaka. 'So we must carry on as fast as we can!'

He raised his arm to give the command and they started downward once more, picking their way carefully over gnarled and knotted tree roots which jutted from the sloping ground. Ahead they could see that the mounted samurai who was guiding them had halted on the brink of a ravine too steep for a horse to negotiate. Mist still swirled in the bottom of the ravine, and he had dismounted in order to peer down its steep sides.

'I believe this is the lower part of the last track into Kurihama, O Kami-san,' he said quietly when the *norimono* reached him. 'Soon it forks and there are two ways down to the village, which is not far now. Although you can barely see it, the track runs through the bottom of this ravine.'

'Where did you encounter the armed column?' asked Tanaka quickly.

'We took our prisoner about four *ri* above this point, O Kami-san.'

Tanaka thought for a moment, then signalled for the *norimono* to be lowered to the ground. Standing absolutely still he stared down into the mist, listening carefully; but no sound came from below and he shook his head in a gesture of uncertainty.

'Perhaps they've already passed. They may be in Kurihama by this time.'

'We could run fast along the top of the ravine, O Kami-san, and see if we can overtake them,' said the young samurai eagerly. 'It may not be too late . . .'

Tanaka closed his eyes, focusing all his senses on the natural stillness of the forested hills around him. He knew that every second he delayed might be vital, if the armed column had passed and was already approaching the beach at Kurihama; but, equally, if he raced away down the hill and the armed column was still above them, he would lose his last opportunity to intervene by surprise in the concealing mist.

He knew intuitively that events must now be rushing towards a climax at the beach, but he still felt unable to move. Something held him rooted to the spot and he stood motionless with his eyes closed in an agony of indecision. Then in the deep silence he heard a faint and distant clink of metal; a few moments later the muffled sound of horses' hoofs moving through grass reached his ears. After another long wait he heard more quiet jingling of harness, more rustling from the foot of the ravine, and eventually the occasional murmur of men's voices. He knew then why he had not been able to stir himself before and, as the faint noises became continuous, he opened his eyes and saw that all his samurai were listening tensely.

They looked at one another but nobody spoke, and they obeyed instantly when Tanaka motioned for them to stretch themselves soundlessly on the ground. Looking round, he gestured urgently for Gotaro and the mounted guards to remain still and silent on their horses; then crawling forward to the lip of the ravine, he looked over in time to see the unmistakable figure of Daizo Yakamochi emerge from the mist below, riding slowly at the head of a large troop of Makabe samurai.

Tanaka counted thirty warriors moving in close attendance on their leader, then after a gap of twenty yards an ordinary black *norimono* emerged silently from the mist, carried by four turbaned bearers. Tanaka drew in his breath silently as he watched the *norimono* pass directly beneath their hiding place. It was closed and gave no hint of who might be journeying inside, but there was no doubt in his mind that he had at long last tracked down his quarry. A further thirty-yard gap separated the enclosed chair from another seemingly endless column of guards, and Tanaka measured the intervening distance carefully with his eye before drawing back suddenly from the edge of the ravine and gesturing to the samurai who had led them there.

'How far from here is the fork in the track?' he whispered urgently.

'Perhaps one *ri*, O Kami-san,' murmured the samurai in reply.

'And are both ways down the same?'

'No. To the right, the track passes over a broad stream that flows onto the sea. But to the left the track goes directly to the village and the beach.'

Tanaka's eyes narrowed thoughtfully, then he turned quickly to his chief bodyguard. 'Send a man immediately to our own Kago guard-boats that are standing by at the beach. Have one boat rowed upstream as far as possible!'

'Yes, O Kami-san!'

The chief bodyguard murmured orders to one of his subordinates, who dismounted and led his horse stealthily away from the edge of the ravine before remounting and riding swiftly off into the trees.

'Does the track between here and the fork run straight?' demanded Tanaka, turning back to their guide.

'No, it twists and winds all the way!'

'Then we must move fast now! If we can get to the fork ahead of them, we'll have one last chance of averting disaster!'

Rising cautiously to his feet and bending double to ensure he was not seen from below, Tanaka signalled silently to the three loin-clothed samurai who had been held in reserve, and between them they lifted the *norimono* to their shoulders. As before, he took the leading position at the front end of the pole and when they had all settled themselves, he gestured silently to the mounted bodyguards to follow quietly, making sure that they never became visible to the riders below. When everybody was ready, he waved his arm in a forward direction and they set off along the sloping borders of the ravine, carrying the *norimono* downward through the trees at a fast pace.

'The mist is beginning to clear, my lord. Look! I believe we can see the foreign barbarians making their way ashore!'

Yakamochi's new samurai guard captain, who was riding down the ravine at his master's shoulder, lifted one gloved hand from his reins and gesticulated ahead. Through patchy holes that the onshore breeze was beginning to tear in the mist ahead of them, the flotilla of American boats was becoming visible as it neared the shore.

'They will land in another five minutes, my lord,' said the guard captain anxiously. 'Shouldn't we begin moving faster?'

Through narrowed eyes Yakamochi peered down towards the bay for a moment; then he slowly shook his head. 'No, Sawarasan, there is no need. My father's orders are that we should appear suddenly towards the end of the ceremony. Then everybody's attention will be on what is happening. It is important not to show ourselves too soon.'

'But it will take at least another fifteen minutes to reach the ceremonial pavilion from here, my lord,' exclaimed Sawara.

'That's precisely right,' replied Yakamochi calmly. 'And we shall arrive in accordance with the plan I laid.'

He turned in his saddle to glance back past his bodyguards to where the black *norimono* was bobbing into view around a bend in the track. Its bearers were grunting rhythmically in time with their steps as they jogged—'yo-ho, yo-ho, yo-ho, yo-ho'—and he could see the top of their turbaned heads as they bent forward, concentrating hard on their physical task. Looking up at either side of the ravine he saw that mist still clung to the slopes above, enveloping the track in a shroud of silence.

'And this morning the *kami* of these hills are helping to protect their sacred homeland from the foreign barbarians,' added Yakamochi, allowing himself a rare smile. 'Instead of the *kamikaze* "divine wind" that destroyed the Mongols, the weather gods have sent a "divine mist". So the approach of our barbarian prisoner will remain concealed from all prying eyes until the very last moment . . .'

'Yes, my lord, you're right,' replied Sawara dutifully. 'The *kami* of the hills have indeed favoured us.'

Yakamochi nodded slowly, peering down towards the bay again. The haze below was continuing to disperse and he was able to see that the line of American boats was nearing the beach.

'What is more, the foreign barbarians are also co-operating perfectly,' he said smugly to himself. 'They are about to walk right into our trap . . .'

46

As the leading barge of the American flotilla touched the makeshift jetty of rice-straw and sand, the commander of the *Susquehanna* stood up. Many thousands of eyes stared fixedly at him as he scanned the beach, and from his seat amidships in the barge Samuel Armstrong was struck anew by the silence and utter stillness of the massed Japanese forces. The nearest ranks consisted of helmeted footsoldiers garbed in ribbed armour of iron and leather, and they clutched pikes and lances in their hands. At close range Armstrong could see that their dark faces were scowling and hostile, and twin-sworded officers positioned in front of them at intervals also glowered menacingly towards the jetty from beneath horned helmets.

After pausing for a moment, the commander of the *Susquehanna* stepped lightly and confidently over the gunwale. Seconds later Major Pearsall drew his sword and leapt ashore. As the booted feet of the two American officers sank into the soft sand of the beach, a slow growl of anger rumbled from the throats of the watching Japanese warriors—but still none of them moved.

'You'd best be quick, Mr Armstrong,' called the major. 'And try to keep your head high as you alight.'

The missionary, who had remained pale-faced in his seat until that moment, stood up abruptly and strode forward with an outward confidence not matched by his inner feelings. He realized suddenly that the massed ranks of Japanese were watching the first foreigners they had ever seen step down officially onto their soil, and he took care to ensure that his sword did not entangle his legs as he jumped down from the barge.

'Christopher Columbus must have felt something like this when he landed in Jamaica four hundred years ago,' murmured Armstrong, nervously glancing up at the tall medieval pennants and banners which swept fluttering to the ground amidst the dense concentrations of soldiery.

'Maybe,' replied Major Pearsall dryly. 'But unlike the cacique chieftains, I don't think these particular natives will be much impressed with a handful of glass beads.'

With his hand held tentatively on his sword-hilt, Armstrong moved to take up position between the two ramrod-straight officers. Glancing seawards, he was glad to see the reassuring black hulk of the two towering steam frigates anchored broadside across the mouth of the bay. Because they were ready for action, thick smoke spiralled skyward from their tall stacks, and the gaping black eyes of their cannon kept an unblinking watch on the shore. Although he felt comforted by their presence, Armstrong also realized, as he stood defenceless on the sand, just how ominous and fearsome the ships must look to all those Japanese at his back who were armed only with puny bows, spears and ancient flintlock muskets.

He felt suddenly ashamed, too, of his confident assertion, made a few days earlier on the flagship, that good would certainly flow from the venture if it led to the further spreading of the Christian gospel in this new region. From the beach, he could see for himself just how malevolent the American threat of force seemed and, although he was directly endangered by them, he realized that he sympathized strongly with the Japanese in making such emphatic preparations for war.

'We shall wait here, Mr Armstrong, until the commodore has landed,' said Major Pearsall as he glanced appraisingly around the beach. 'Then we shall fall in behind him to march in procession to the pavilion.'

The missionary nodded, and began to breathe a little easier as he watched the hundred-strong contingent of marines spring nimbly ashore. They shouldered their carbines, fell quickly into their allotted ranks and marched briskly over the jetty to form up into two lines on either side of it. They were followed by a similar number of armed sailors and two bands who advanced jauntily along the jetty, carrying only their musical instruments. Some two dozen officers had taken up their places on either side of Major Pearsall and the commander of the *Susquehanna*, and a complete hush fell over the Americans and Japanese alike as all eyes turned to watch the approach of the barge occupied by the US Navy squadron's commander-in-chief.

The Governor of Uraga and his entourage were standing apart on the beach, waiting to lead the parade to the reception pavilion, and Armstrong saw the governor crane his neck to stare intently towards the barge as it neared the jetty. The fact that, during several visits to the warships, neither he nor his staff had ever caught a single glimpse of the American first described to them as the 'Most High Lord of the Interior' was evident in the undisguised curiosity of his usually impassive face. Around him most of his extravagantly robed aides were also raising themselves on their toes to catch sight of the man who, as far as they were concerned, had previously surrounded himself with an emperor-like screen of secrecy. But, with a start, Armstrong saw that again Haniwara Tokuma was not among them. Standing slightly apart, the interpreter was not looking towards the jetty. His shoulders still sagged in what looked like dejection, his head was lowered and he appeared to be staring listlessly at the sand in front of his feet. Glancing round, Armstrong realized that the interpreter was the only man on the beach whose eyes were averted from the momentous landing of the foreign barbarian chieftain, and in that instant he felt his unease turn to a deeper and more certain foreboding. Something in Haniwara Tokuma's manner spoke silently of his utter despair, and the missionary felt a cold shiver of fear crawl up his spine.

But the next moment a voice yelled, 'Present arms!' and hundreds of American hands slapped in unison against the stocks of their loaded carbines. Armstrong turned back towards the jetty, in time to see the oarsmen of the commander-in-chief's barge sweep their blades erect and allow their craft to glide accurately to rest. A flurry of drums and brass instruments then crashed out the familiar opening strains of 'Hail Columbia', and Commodore Matthew Calbraith Perry rose to his feet to step majestically ashore.

The breeze fluttered the gold tassels of his cocked hat as he strode along the jetty, followed by his flag lieutenant and the commander of the *Mississippi*. He paused with his head held proudly erect while Major Pearsall and the *Susquehanna*'s commander saluted and offered the customary honours; then his officers fell into place behind him and his two towering black bodyguards moved to flank him protectively on either side. The two young sailors clutching the scarlet-covered letters of the President were already waiting in position behind the bearers of the United States flag and the commodore's blue pennant. They watched expectantly while the Marine Corps major paced to the front of the leading contingent of bluejackets with his sword drawn; then, when a loud command was given and the two bands in the rear of the parade struck up a boisterous march, they swung briskly forward, taking great care to keep strictly in step with the other three hundred uniformed Americans, as they bore the official letters proudly towards the reception pavilion.

Marching a few paces behind Commodore Perry, Samuel Armstrong watched the Governor of Uraga and the other Japanese officials closely. Their role was to guide the parade towards the pavilion but, as they walked on ahead of the marines, he could see that Haniwara Tokuma's mind was elsewhere. Remote and distracted, the interpreter looked about himself constantly, giving Armstrong a strong impression that he anticipated some unscheduled interruption to the proceedings, and every so often he glanced up nervously towards the hills rising behind the bay.

'Don't be surprised, Mr Armstrong, if we don't follow precisely in the governor's guiding footsteps,' murmured the commander of the *Susquehanna* at the missionary's side. 'Major Pearsall has orders to lead us to the pavilion by a broad, circular route. So, for a few minutes, our weapons and our discipline will be clearly exhibited for the benefit of the watching natives—and it won't be lost on them that our men are manoeuvring just as if they were marching into enemy territory.'

As the well-ordered column of three hundred armed Americans curved away across the beach beneath their fluttering national flag, Armstrong tried to memorize every detail of the extraordinary scene around him, realizing he was living through unique moments. Close up, he could see that the watching Japanese fighting units were drawn up in battle brigades, each composed of units of infantrymen armed with ancient muskets, pikemen, archers and cavalry. On the tall, multicoloured banners and pennants that curled overhead in the breeze he could see a variety of heraldic designs—rings of stars, castles, emblematic leaves and flowers—which confirmed that the troops had been drawn from armies of several different *daimyo*. Ranged on either side of the reception pavilion itself, he could see contingents of sentinels garbed very differently in white turbans, broad sashes of yellow silk and flowing grey tunics and trousers drawn in tight below the knee. Evidently the personal guards of the imperial dignitaries, they were armed with antique matchlock muskets, and the missionary could see that they carried fuses for these old-fashioned weapons coiled on their right arms. On either side of the entrance to the pavilion, which was flanked by long, funnelling screens, equally ancient four-pound cannon of apparent Spanish design had been set up; nothing within the shadowy interior was visible and, with the sun shimmering on the two brass cannon at its mouth, the pavilion to Armstrong seemed suddenly as inviting as the gaping, gold-fanged jaws of a dragon.

'Try to look as though you're enjoying it, Mr Armstrong,' remarked the commander in a jocular undertone as the bands struck up a new march. 'It's unlikely that you'll experience anything like this ever again.'

The missionary nodded quickly but made no reply. Ahead of him, filling his vision, were the broad, confident shoulders of Matthew Calbraith Perry; beyond him, the massed white plumes of the marines moved rhythmically as the tempo of the music increased and every marcher, relieved to be ashore after many long days at sea, swung his limbs with renewed vigour. Feeling the raw, pent-up energy of trained fighting men flowing all around him, Armstrong lifted his head and quickened his own step. But although he marched with his eyes open, he had begun to say a fervent prayer inside his mind, and he went on praying hard as the armed column swung across the beach in a broad arch, heading towards the pavilion.

'Keep very still and make no noise,' hissed Prince Tanaka, pressing himself deeper into a thicket of low-spreading trees and bushes that sprouted from the side of the winding ravine. 'We won't have long to wait!'

His bare chest heaved from the intense physical effort of scrambling halfway down the ravine at the front end of the *norimono*, which was now concealed beneath the trees. His six disguised bearers, who were crouching closely around him in the thicket, were also gulping air gratefully into their lungs after their fast run with the cumbersome carrying-chair and a desperate, slithering descent of the near-precipitous slope. Once they reached the thicket they had quickly torn branches from some of the bushes to camouflage the *norimono*, and now all were staring anxiously through the mist towards the track which zigzagged downwards in a double hairpin through a narrow, rocky defile no less than twenty feet below them.

'By running straight, instead of following the curves of the ravine, we may have gained two or three minutes on them,' gasped Tanaka, staring fixedly at the rock around which he expected the Makabe armed column to appear. 'But it can't be more.'

Now that they had stopped running, they could hear the insistent thud of drums, and the stirring martial strains of the two American bands, rising from the beach. In the still morning air the noise from the unfamiliar instruments rang strangely in their ears, and they looked at one another mystified as they waited.

'The foreign barbarians have certainly landed now,' whispered Tanaka. 'There's very little time left!'

He glanced up over his shoulder to a high outcrop of rock above them where he had stationed the samurai who had acted as their guide. Lying prone amidst the scrub ontop of the rock, the man had a bird's-eye view of both the narrow defile below and the following hairpin bends that led ontowards the fork in the track above Kurihama. Around those double bends Gotaro and the rest of his troop of Kago guards had concealed themselves in another clump of trees that jutted from the steep slope. They had tethered their horses a safe distance away above the ravine, and were now waiting tensely for a signal that the men of the Makabe clan had come in sight.

'We shall have very little time to do what is necessary,' murmured Tanaka, lifting his hand towards the rock in a prearranged signal to indicate that both the *norimono* and his men were ready. 'So our actions must be calm and natural in every way.'

He continued to watch until he saw the samurai lookout raise his head briefly above the edge of the rock and wave once in acknowledgement of the signal. The mist around the heights, Tanaka noticed, was beginning to disperse more rapidly, and he turned back to watch the track below, hoping desperately that the sun would not break through too soon. Across the entire hillside the natural noises of the morning remained muted; no birds sang and no animals moved among the trees. The curious marching music from the bay remained the only intrusion on the strange stillness, and Tanaka and his loin-clothed samurai strained their ears in vain for some sign that the Makabe warriors were approaching.

'Could they have taken another route we don't know about, O Kami-san?' whispered the youngest samurai, who was crouched beside him. 'Could we have missed an earlier fork?'

Tanaka shook his head decisively, glancing up again towards the overhanging rock. 'Our lookout knows the region well. He's certain there is no other junction . . .'

A loud, long-drawn-out groan of anguish broke the stillness suddenly close at hand, causing them to start and, on realizing its source, Tanaka gestured for the door of the *norimono* to be opened. When the young samurai hurriedly obeyed, they found that the terrified captive lying inside had somehow loosened the binding around his mouth; his head rolled agitatedly from side to side, his eyes were wild and staring, and he was moaning uncontrollably.

'Silence him!' commanded Tanaka. 'Refasten the gag securely—and make it clear he'll die immediately if he makes another sound!'

The young warrior grunted menacingly, drawing the short sword he had concealed inside his loin-cloth. Kneeling roughly on the captive's chest, he held the blade to his throat while a second samurai retied the gag tightly. After muttering fierce warnings in his ear and checking his other bonds, they closed the door of the *norimono* again. As they did so, the leading horseman of Lord Daizo's armed contingent moved into view at the head of the rocky defile forty yards away.

'Wait for my command,' breathed Tanaka, watching Yakamochi and his guards advance towards the sharp bend directly beneath their hiding place. 'And keep low.'

The lingering mist was still sufficient to blur the faces of the riders until they came close, but Tanaka could see the dampness of the morning air glistening on the forehead and topknot of Yakamochi as he swung his horse sharply below them and began riding away towards the next turn.

'Get ready!'

Tanaka mouthed the words in less than a whisper as the last of the leading group of samurai turned the corner below them and the black *norimono* came into sight. Its bearers were still moving comfortably twenty or thirty yards behind the vanguard, and Tanaka noted that they trotted in the same formation as before: the two biggest men supported the front and rear ends of the carrying-pole, two slighter men were running in between them, and two others were jogging empty-handed in reserve.

'Note their positions and their bearing,' Tanaka hissed urgently as they bobbed nearer. 'Be ready to imitate their movements exactly.'

Holding his breath, Tanaka watched intently to see if the Makabe guards following the carrying-chair had moved any closer; but by the time the *norimono* was turning below their hiding place, the track behind it was still empty.

'Take the front and rear positions,' he commanded, pointing at his two brawniest bearers. 'You and I will fill the support places,' he added quickly, turning to the youngest samurai. 'Now let's uncover the chair!'

In an instant the branches and foliage were tugged aside, and laid carefully on the ground where they would attract no attention from below. As soon as this was done, Tanaka motioned for the conveyance to be raised but he delayed his final order as he watched the Makabe *norimono* move slowly away from them towards the next bend in the defile. At any second, he knew, the following group of guards could appear—but he also feared that if he moved too soon and too noisily the bearers themselves would turn round and all would be lost. Forcing himself to remain calm although his heart was pounding in his chest, Tanaka waited until the softly chanting Makabe bearers were some fifteen yards distant, then lifted his arm suddenly towards the rock high above them in a final signal.

'*Now! Forward!*'

Taking his place under the carrying-pole, he urged his men out of the trees and down the nearly vertical incline. They slipped and slithered under the weight of their swaying burden, clutching wildly with their free hands at the long grass and bushes in an attempt to slow their descent. To Tanaka they seemed to slide with an agonizing slowness over the intervening twenty feet, and all the time his eyes flicked back and forth towards the projecting rock around which the Makabe rearguard was about to appear.

Stones and dirt cascaded all around them as they descended, and one bearer fell and slid painfully down to the track on his back. Tanaka feared their noise might betray them, even if they were not seen, but they reached level ground moments later and to his great relief the bearers of the Makabe *norimono* went on jogging obliviously forward until they went out of sight around the turning ahead. Catching a fleeting glimpse of the first horse of the rearguard moving into view through the mist behind them, Tanaka quickly helped the fallen bearer to his feet and rushed their own chair onwards a few paces, until it was concealed by the rocks of the bend. Once they had steadied themselves, however, and were moving safely along the centre of the track, he slowed the pace.

'Go very easily now,' he hissed. 'Run exactly as you saw the others running—but even slower. It's important we should be seen soon by the guards behind.'

They rounded another sharp bend, to find that the *norimono* was still in sight, and they watched on tenterhooks until once again it disappeared along the winding track. Glancing up towards the high rock, Tanaka saw his lookout signalling to indicate that they had succeeded in entering the column without causing any evident alarm—but he was also making urgent gestures for them to move less quickly, and Tanaka acknowledged this with a quick hand signal of his own.

'Slow right down,' he ordered sharply, dropping to little more than walking pace. 'We're approaching the area where the track forks—where Gotaro and our guards are lying in wait! We'll only have seconds to act . . . So we must hold back the warriors behind us . . .'

Within a few moments the Makabe rearguard came into sight behind them, and Tanaka braced himself for an outburst of shouting that would signal the discovery of their deception. All around him the faces of his men became tense as they lowered their heads and concentrated hard on imitating the lolloping gait of the real bearers. Moving more ponderously, they slowed the rhythmic 'Yo-ho, yo-ho, yo-ho' pacing chant to less than half speed, and from their expressions Tanaka could see that they were intensely aware of the eyes of Yakamochi's samurai boring into their backs.

'Try to keep your nerve now!' he commanded tersely as they approached yet another sharp bend. 'In the mist they won't notice any difference.'

They could hear the casual mutter of the following guards' voices growing in volume as they drew closer, but still no alarm was raised and Tanaka murmured urgent new words of encouragement to his men. Glancing up towards the lookout, Tanaka saw him signal decisively with two raised hands towards the place where the Kago samurai were concealed. As ordered, he had judged from his vantage point which moment would be most favourable for them to go into action, and Tanaka knew that within seconds Gotaro and the others would hurl themselves from their hiding place into the ravine. Seeing that he and his bearers were approaching a bend which would hide them briefly from the eyes of the enemy guards behind them, he signalled surreptitiously to one of the reserve runners to prepare to take over from him.

'Hold this pace for another half minute,' he commanded. 'Then speed up. If all goes well and you reach the fork without being recognized, make sure you follow Yakamochi to the left—down towards the bay!'

The moment they rounded the bend and were bidden temporarily from the eyes of the following guards, Tanaka ducked away from beneath the carrying-pole.

'You've all done well,' he whispered fiercely, looking at each man in turn. 'Play your roles as long as you can. When you're discovered, fight to the death—or flee for your life! Each of you is free to choose!'

After glancing back quickly, to ensure that they were still unobserved, Tanaka dashed away at full speed and within seconds disappeared beyond the next curve in the track.

At first sight Samuel Armstrong thought that two life-sized effigies had been set up beside the scarlet chest at the far end of the ceremonial pavilion. Already formally seated on the stools of decorated porcelain, the two imperial delegates held their straight-backed postures uncompromisingly in the manner of lifeless statues as Commodore Matthew Perry and his three-hundred-strong escort marched jauntily towards the pavilion's entrance, with bands playing and colours flying. The inside of the pavilion was shadowy in contrast to the sunlit beach but the shaven pates and oiled topknots of the two delegates gleamed softly in the penumbra.

Both the high officials were wearing wide, stiff-shouldered jackets of rich brocade, bound with brown sashes from which twin swords jutted; flowing trousers of purple silk almost hid their black-lacquered clogs, and their respective clan insignia were embroidered in brilliant colours on wide sleeves inside which their hands lay concealed. Their narrow eyes were focused unseeingly in the middle distance, as though nothing of interest was visible before them and, like the eyes of stone statues, they remained blank and unblinking even after the parade had come to a brisk halt before the entry vestibule.

The moment the marchers halted, the bands also ceased to play, and another dramatic hush fell over the beach. The thousands of armed men and the watching civilians seemed to hold their breath again, unsure of what might follow. The turbaned sentries around the pavilion entrance gazed uncertainly at the first foreign barbarians they had ever seen close up—but none of them moved.

As the parade drew nearer, Armstrong had noticed that the governor and Haniwara Tokuma were waiting diplomatically beside the entrance. Because he was under scrutiny from so many eyes, the interpreter appeared to be making an effort to disguise his earlier unease, and he stood straighter, gazing expressionlessly ahead. But at close quarters his pale nervousness was still evident to the missionary and inside his mind Armstrong suddenly heard again the anguished warning that the Japanese had muttered aboard the *Susquehanna* during their last private conversation—'*You should stop . . . There's greater danger than you realize!*'

The memory brought Armstrong's own growing agitation to a sudden peak and acting on an impulse of the moment, he stepped forward and bowed elaborately, first to the governor, then to his interpreter.

'Perhaps Your Excellency would wish now to inform us of what formalities are planned,' he said deferentially in Japanese. 'We can then endeavour to help things proceed as smoothly as possible.'

'There's no need for any prior explanation,' replied the governor. He nodded towards the carved wooden funeral thrones that had been set up to the right of the scarlet chest. 'I am about to lead your admiral and his officers to their seats.'

'And thereafter?' Armstrong turned his head to look at the interpreter, trying to indicate by the intensity of his glance that he wished to exchange a few private words with him. 'What procedures will be followed?'

'It will become clear,' replied the governor impatiently, beginning to move up the steps leading into the pavilion. 'We shall indicate how and when your letters should be presented. An imperial receipt will be offered—but no discussions of any kind can take place. Let us now take up our places.'

Turning quickly, Armstrong explained this exchange to Lieutenant Rice, then watched Commodore Perry, the two frigate commanders and the flag lieutenant follow the governor up onto the red carpet that led through the vestibule to the inner chamber. The Japanese interpreter began to move forward at the same time, but Armstrong surreptitiously tugged at one of his sleeves and with a gracious gesture beckoned another group of American officers to proceed ahead of them.

'Confide in me, please, Haniwara-san!' whispered the missionary urgently, falling into step beside him but speaking Dutch this time so nobody around them would understand. 'You can trust me. I know we're all in great danger. I promise I'll help, if it's in my power.'

The diminutive Japanese interpreter walked in a dogged silence for a few paces, his gaze fixed dully on the carpet. 'How can anybody help?' he whispered at last, without looking up. 'It's too late.'

'You and I are both men of goodwill,' insisted Armstrong. 'It's our human duty to act together for peace!'

Glancing ahead, the missionary saw that they were approaching the high-ceilinged inner chamber where the walls were decked with long silken drapes and giant mural paintings. As the American officers moved to take up their places around the Buddhist funeral thrones, from the opposite side of the pavilion groups of topknotted Japanese nobles and officials were entering. All wore twin swords and one by one they ranged themselves along the wall, kneeling, in support of the still motionless imperial delegates.

'Your officer Eden has been captured,' whispered the interpreter. He looked up quickly, and the missionary saw from his haunted expression that fear had suddenly overcome his native caution and reserve.

'Then he's alive!' exclaimed Armstrong, feeling a surge of elation. 'Where is he now?'

'Not far away,' whispered Haniwara frantically. 'But one of our most hostile *daimyo* is bringing him here in chains. When he arrives, nobody will be able to stop the killing . . .'

Before Armstrong could reply, there was a sudden stir in the pavilion, and the procession in which they were moving halted. Armstrong looked ahead to see the two imperial delegates rising stiffly from their stools. Without focusing their gaze on anyone in particular, they bent forward from the waist in deep, formal bows to acknowledge the arrival of the American commander-in-chief. The governor, who had stepped to one side, prostrated himself on the red carpet facing the two imperial delegates and pressed his forehead against the floor for several seconds. Commodore Matthew Calbraith Perry, however, barely disturbed the elegant gold tassels of his chapeau, as he lowered his chin a mere few inches in response.

A flurry of hostile whispering broke out among the watching Japanese and there were murmured comments too among the American officers as they moved onto take up their places. At Armstrong's side the Japanese interpreter had prostrated himself in the fashion of his superior and the missionary had to wait until he had risen before moving forward alongside him again.

'Is the *daimyo* you spoke of present, Haniwara-san?' he asked quietly, casting his eye quickly over the groups of nobles now assembled along one side of the pavilion.

'Yes,' replied the interpreter in a frightened whisper, staring again at the floor. 'But you can say nothing of this. He has taken my wife and children hostage, to ensure my compliance with his orders . . . They will be killed if I don't obey him . . .'

All the Japanese nobles were staring grimly at the arriving foreigners but Armstrong encountered for a fleeting moment the deeply malevolent individual gaze of Lord Daizo, who was standing apart from the others close to the entrance of the pavilion. His narrow eyes were focused chillingly on the two of them, and Armstrong knew that he had instinctively identified Haniwara's tormentor.

'What are your orders?' asked Armstrong in a frantic last whisper, as they mounted the steps to the inner chamber and prepared to separate to their respective sides. 'What must you do?'

'For defensive reasons armed warriors are stationed in hiding here,' murmured the interpreter. 'To save the lives of my family I must give them a secret signal to attack . . .'

He broke off abruptly on seeing that the American officers in front, who had been shielding them from the gaze of the imperial delegates, were moving aside. Proceeding more briskly, they took up position behind their commander-in-chief, who was already seated regally on one of the carved thrones. Commodore Perry's back was ramrod straight, one hand rested significantly on his gilded sword-hilt, and his eyes were fixed haughtily on his hosts. Left with no alternative, Armstrong reluctantly parted company with the interpreter and turned aside to assume his own place, standing a respectful pace or two behind the commodore's seat. He watched Haniwara Tokuma kneel down beside the governor, wondering desperately about the man's unfinished words and when an awkward silence fell in the chamber, he looked about himself anxiously, trying without success to discern where armed warriors might be hidden behind the sumptuous wall coverings. He felt a strong urge to lean towards the commodore and whisper a warning about the danger they faced—but at the last moment his promise to respect the confidences of the terrified Japanese interpreter stopped him. Waiting and watching in an agony of suspense, he tried to think how he might otherwise help; but no obvious course of action suggested itself, and he resorted again to a fierce, silent prayer.

'*Toda-Idzu-no-kami to Ido-Iwami-no-kami de guzaimasu*,' said the governor suddenly, bowing towards the seated Americans. '*Toda-Idzu-no-kami wa dai-rochu de guzaimasu!*

'Toda, Prince of Idzu, and Ido, Prince of Iwami, are your hosts,' said Haniwara Tokuma, translating the governor's words into Dutch in an unsteady voice. 'Prince Toda, on the left, is the honoured First Counsellor of the Empire.'

In the curious, strained silence that again followed Armstrong's further translation into English, nobody else attempted to speak. The two imperial delegates, both grave-faced men in their late fifties or early sixties, continued to sit unmoving on their stools and, directly opposite them, Commodore Perry and his two senior commanders had become equally immobile. No vestige of expression appeared on the faces of the two

Japanese dignitaries but, after scrutinizing them carefully, Armstrong felt that in their remote manner there was more than a hint of apprehension.

At the foot of the red-carpeted steps in the outer vestibule, the two young sailors from the *Susquehanna* stood as still as they were able, holding in both arms the pouches of scarlet baize which contained the boxed letters from the President of the United States. Beside these diminutive messengers, the two black bodyguards flanking them appeared taller than ever. With their revolving rifles slung about their shoulders, they too stared ahead expressionlessly, dwarfing everybody else in the pavilion. Beyond them, among the nobles grouped by the entrance, Armstrong again picked out the squat, fierce-eyed *daimyo* whom he had noticed watching Haniwara Tokuma earlier. Lord Daizo's scowl had not changed and the missionary noticed that his eyes rarely shifted from the figure of the kneeling interpreter. From time to time, however, he cocked his head as though listening intently for some sound from outside the pavilion and, on noticing this, Armstrong knew beyond any shadow of doubt that the Japanese interpreter had been telling the truth.

'Are your official letters and the translations and copies now ready for delivery?' asked Haniwara Tokuma suddenly in Dutch, after whispered prompting from the governor at his side. 'If so, Prince Toda is prepared to receive them.'

The interpreter avoided Armstrong's eyes as he spoke, but the missionary could see that the tension inside him was increasing. Feeling his own sense of helplessness grow, Armstrong made the translation quickly and watched Commodore Perry signal with one white-gloved hand for the young American bearers and the black bodyguards to stand by.

'We wish to make it clear that Prince Toda will not touch the letters,' added the Japanese interpreter hastily, rising to his feet and gesturing to the cloth-covered tray laid out on the lacquered chest. 'Prince Toda should not be approached . . . Your letters are to be placed here after your bearers have knelt to show their respect.'

'In our country we show our respect by standing,' snapped the commodore, on hearing Armstrong's translation. 'There will be no kneeling here—by me or any of my men!'

After listening to Perry's reply, the governor rose slowly from his knees and took up a position beside his interpreter, leaving clear the approach to the lacquered chest. A moment later the commodore beckoned for the bearers of the letters to advance into the inner chamber. Followed closely by their tall escorts, the boy sailors marched proudly forward in silence. Their faces shone with the excitement of the moment and inside their minds as they moved they could still hear the commodore's ringing words addressed to them earlier that morning: '*You will have the honour of bearing the President's letter ashore. You will carry the very key that will* open *Japan*.'

On reaching the scarlet chest the boy sailors halted, turned smartly and passed their ornate packages reluctantly into the hands of the two black bodyguards who had moved up beside them. Removing the gold-encrusted rosewood boxes from their pouches of scarlet baize, the bodyguards opened them for all to see. Taking out the President's letter to the Emperor, and the commodore's letter of credence, they held them aloft for a moment so that the watching Japanese could see that they were beautifully written on vellum, and bound in blue silk velvet.

Each of the presidential seals, attached to the letters by cords of interwoven silks, was encased in a large, finely-wrought, circular box of pure gold fully six inches in diameter, and a buzz of subdued comment rose from the watching Japanese as the bodyguards leaned forward to place the ornamented letters and their containers in the tray. From the baize pouches they then extracted two further letters, from the commodore to the Emperor, as well as copies and translations of each communication, and positioned them with equal care on the lid of the chest. Having completed their task, the bodyguards drew themselves up to their full height and saluted the documents with great solemnity. Then, after glancing enquiringly towards their commander-in-chief, and receiving his curt nod of approval, they turned and marched briskly back to the outer chamber to resume their places beside the boy sailors.

'Inform His Highness Prince Toda that the communications from the President of the United States and myself are duly delivered,' said the commodore grandly, rising from his seat and nodding in Samuel Armstrong's direction. 'Ensure also that His Highness understands that copies and translations into both the Dutch and Chinese languages have been provided for his convenience.'

Armstrong complied, and they watched Haniwara bow low to the governor before murmuring his translation in a halting voice. In his turn the governor prostrated himself in front of Prince Toda, to whisper an account of what had been said. But the imperial delegate made no gesture of acknowledgement and, in the silence that followed, Armstrong heard the first sounds of a distant commotion beyond the pavilion's canvas walls. Several voices were shouting and chanting angrily in unison, and the noise grew in volume as the voices drew nearer. If Commodore Perry heard them, however, he gave no outward sign and he again gesticulated for Armstrong to translate.

'Inform His Highness further that in summary the President's letter expresses our wish that the United States and Japan should trade with each other for mutual benefit,' declared the commodore ringingly. 'And that coal and provisions should be commercially supplied to all our passing steamships whenever required. And that civilized protection should invariably be granted to any Americans shipwrecked on Japan's shores . . .'

Perry paused for the two sets of translations to be made, then straightened his shoulders a further fraction, to lend additional emphasis to his words.

'In addition, my own letters to the Emperor reiterate that we wish to live in peace and friendship with Japan—but they also point out clearly that no friendship can long exist unless Japan ceases to act towards American citizens as if they were her worst enemies! No more shipwrecked American seamen shall be publicly exhibited in cages! No more visiting US ships should be forced back to sea! Tell His Highness my letters state that, as evidence of our friendly intentions, we have come this time with only four of our smaller warships—but, should it become necessary, we can return very soon to Yedo Bay with a much larger force!'

While he was translating this declaration, Armstrong was aware that the commotion from outside was increasing. Haniwara Tokuma clearly noticed this too and in his distraction he stumbled several times over his translation. Around the pavilion, many seated Japanese and some of the American officers were beginning to listen frowningly to the noise, although the imperial delegates themselves remained unmoving and statue-like on their stools. From the corner of his eye Armstrong noticed a sudden flurry of movement by the entrance to the pavilion and, looking up, he noticed that the scowling face of Lord Daizo had disappeared.

'We should like you next to read to the imperial delegates the full texts of the letters,' whispered Lieutenant Rice at the missionary's shoulder, while the governor was completing the translation to his superior. 'And don't pay any attention to the noise outside, whatever it may be. It's the commodore's wish that we should all continue to preserve an appearance of absolute imperturbability. So take all the time you need. There's no hurry.'

Riding at full gallop through the outer ranks of archers and pikemen drawn up to the rear of the pavilion, Lord Daizo grunted with satisfaction when he caught sight of moving pennants bearing his own insignia. They fluttered above a long line of samurai cavalrymen descending through the dunes at the foot of the hills, and he recognized immediately the erect figure of his son riding at their head. In the same moment he saw too the black *norimono* bobbing down the broad path fifty yards or so behind Yakamochi, carried on the shoulders of the turbaned bearers. A growing crowd was gathering on the beach to watch the column approach, and chanting civilians were already running downhill alongside the *norimono* and its escort.

The chanting, which had prompted him to rush from the ceremony and mount his horse at the rear of the pavilion, was swelling in volume and as he drew nearer, a smile of grim satisfaction spread slowly across Daizo's face. He had given his son instructions to encourage the shouting of anti-barbarian slogans as his column approached the beach, and now he could hear angry voices yelling, over and over again, *Son no Jo-i! Son no Jo-i!*'—'Revere the Emperor! Expel the hideous aliens!'

Spurring his horse forward, Lord Daizo entered the dunes, followed closely by three personal bodyguards. When they met and halted, his son bowed dutifully from the saddle in greeting, as did Sawara, his new guard captain, who was riding at his side. On catching sight of the *daimyo* of the Makabe clan arrayed in his finest formal silks and brocades, the chanting spectators who had been escorting the column fell silent and gathered in awe around the stationary *norimono.*

'You've done well, Yakamochi,' said Lord Daizo, nodding approvingly. 'You've arrived just at the necessary moment.'

'Thank you, O Kami-san.' Yakamochi bowed low in acknowledgement of the compliment. 'I'm glad to have carried out your esteemed instructions successfully.'

'Have you already displayed the barbarian prisoner to the people?' enquired Daizo, glancing calculatingly at the throng pressing curiously all around them. 'Have they had their first glimpse of him?'

'Not yet, O Kami-san!' replied Yakamochi deferentially. 'But they are aware that we have a treacherous foreign barbarian inside—and you've already heard the angry outcry which greeted this!'

'Let those inside the pavilion hear more of Nippon's anger this very moment!' commanded Daizo fiercely. 'Show him to them now!'

Yakamochi nodded to Sawara who dismounted and strode purposefully to the standing *norimono,* from which its bearers had retreated a few paces. Pulling open the door he leaned inside—then froze, staring into the carrying-chair with an astonished expression on his face. For several seconds the new guard captain stood as though paralysed; then, after glancing anxiously over his shoulder towards his waiting masters, he dragged into the daylight the trembling figure of the anonymous Japanese bearer who had been taken captive at dawn by the Kago samurai of Prince Tanaka Yoshio. Still blindfolded, and bound hand and foot, the scrawny Nipponese bearer swayed unsteadily on his feet while Lord Daizo, Yakamochi, all their assembled warriors and the watching crowd gazed at him in stunned disbelief.

'Who is this?' roared Lord Daizo suddenly. 'Identify him!'

Reaching out with one hand the samurai guard captain tugged off the blindfold and the bloodstained cloth which had been wound around the captive's head by Tanaka's men as a rough disguise. Confused further by the sudden, blinding sunlight, the terrified prisoner tried to cower away, and would have fallen if the guard captain had not seized him by the shoulder.

'Where is the foreign barbarian?' demanded Daizo, his voice shaking with barely controlled fury. He urged his horse forward, peered for a moment into the empty carrying-chair, then glared round at his son. 'He seems to have disappeared into thin air!'

Speechless and white-faced with shock, Yakamochi dismounted and hurried to stare incredulously into the empty *norimono*. 'I don't understand,' he stammered, looking up at his scowling father. 'I can't imagine how—'

'This is one of our own bearers, O Kami-san,' exclaimed Sawara suddenly, staring hard at the shuddering captive. 'But where are the rest of them?'

'There!' said Daizo sharply from his saddle, pointing over the heads of the crowd. 'They're running away!'

The disguised Kago samurai, who moments before had been standing unnoticed a few yards from the carrying-chair, had slipped quietly away through the crowd and were now dashing through the sand dunes towards the hills. But they were not fleeing in disarray, like fearful men. Instead they were running purposefully, in a disciplined group, making for a track that led up into the nearest belt of trees. Some of them had lost their turbans or cast them off deliberately and their warrior topknots were now clearly visible as they ran.

'Samurai in disguise,' breathed Yakamochi in astonishment. He stared after the fleeing men, then turned suddenly to his guard captain. 'Send men to cut them down! But try to capture at least one of them alive for questioning!'

As two dozen yelling Makabe warriors spurred their horses towards the hills, scattering the crowd before them, Yakamochi drew his sword and seized the terrified captive by his hair.

'What happened?' he rasped, jerking the man off his feet. 'Tell the truth!'

'Please be merciful, my lord,' wailed the bearer in terror. 'I was captured in the mist at dawn—'

'Who captured you?'

'Men of the Kago clan, my lord . . . They threatened to kill me. They made me tell them about the barbarian prisoner . . .'

'And you told them?'

The trembling bearer nodded despairingly. 'Yes, my lord. And they seized a *norimono* just like ours . . . They tied me hand and foot and put me inside . . . Then they followed you down the ravine, watching for their chance to switch the carrying-chairs and deceive you.'

As comprehension dawned, Yakamochi released the bearer's hair and let him sink sobbing to his knees. For a brief instant he stared down at the cowering man, his eyes ablaze with anger and frustration.

'You betrayed the Makabe clan and the land of the gods,' he said quietly.

'I deeply regret it, my lord!' whined the bearer. 'Please forgive my weakness.'

'There can be no forgiveness for such abject cowardice,' breathed Yakamochi, and in the same moment swung his sword downward with great force, severing the man's head from his shoulders. He watched dispassionately as the headless body rolled sideways, gushing blood into the sand; then he stepped forward and wiped his crimson blade on the dead man's tattered clothing, before thrusting it back into its scabbard.

Looking up, Yakamochi sought the eye of his guard captain. All colour had drained from Sawara's face during the ruthless execution, and he understood instantly the significance of Yakamochi's grim expression. Drawing a quick breath, he nodded briefly to his nearest Makabe warrior, then sank slowly to his knees in the sand. He tugged his body armour aside, fumbled briefly with his clothing below the waist, then very slowly drew his short sword from its scabbard. The finely honed blade gleamed in the sun, and Sawara stared at it for only a second or two with a strangely calm look in his eyes.

'I, Sawara, have failed in my duties towards the Makabe clan,' he said, speaking very softly. 'Therefore this action is inevitable.'

Leaning quickly to the ground, he tucked the wide sleeves of his fighting kimono securely under his knees to avoid the humiliation of toppling backwards when he no longer had control. As soon as this was done, he grasped the hilt of the short sword in both fists, placed its sharpened tip against his lower abdomen on the left-hand side, and jabbed it deeply into his vitals. With an expressionless face he drew the sword steadily across to the right-hand side, before turning it in the long wound and cutting sharply upwards. As he removed the sword, his face betrayed its first signs of pain and he stretched out his neck. In this instant the warrior hovering at his side drew his own long sword from his sash. For a second, the blade hung in the air, then it flashed downward, and the ugly thud of the blow striking home was followed by another softer sound. At the moment of his decapitation the guard captain uttered no sound, and died silently.

A fearful stillness had fallen on the watching civilian crowd. For several long moments they stood and stared blankly at the lifeless remains of the bearer and the samurai guard captain, lying only yards apart. Then, as if by some unspoken agreement, they began one by one to turn and move quietly away.

In the distance, at the foot of the hill, the galloping Makabe samurai were beginning to catch up with the running men. Their swords flashed repeatedly in the morning sun as they struck again and again from the height of their saddles; two Kago warriors fell before they could reach the protection of the wooded slope, then both pursuers and pursued disappeared among the trees.

'It's not yet too late,' whispered Lord Daizo fiercely. He had sat unmoving astride his horse, watching without emotion as his son decapitated the hapless bearer, then the guard captain performed the expected, ritual self-disembowelment; now he turned his back on the distant skirmishing and gesticulated towards his son. 'Send more men quickly into the hills to search again!'

'Yes, O Kami-san,' said Yakamochi, bowing low in response. 'I will do that at once!'

Lord Daizo watched his son despatch a larger number of warriors to begin combing the hills, then leaned down towards him from the saddle. 'We can still launch the lethal attack in the pavilion! Even without the barbarian prisoner, warriors hidden under the floor will obey my signal through the interpreter. Bring the rest of your men and follow me!'

Pulling the head of his horse round towards the sea, Lord Daizo dug his spurs sharply into its flanks and sent it springing forward, in the direction of the ceremonial pavilion once more.

47

Prince Tanaka glanced repeatedly over his shoulder as he raced downhill on foot beside the captured Makabe *norimono*. There were no immediate signs or sounds of pursuit from the winding, wooded track to their rear but, because he could still scarcely believe how perfectly his deception had worked, he felt an irresistible compulsion to check behind every few moments. Close around the *norimono*, Gotaro and a dozen Kago guards who had quickly retrieved their horses were riding with drawn swords in their hands, determined not to make the same error as their enemies. They had gained their prize unseen, by emerging from the mist above the ravine like silent, fleet-footed ghosts, and from time to time they brandished their blades wordlessly before the faces of the frightened Makabe bearers to remind them of the continuing need for silence as they hurried the chair down towards the bay.

'Look, O Kami-san!' exclaimed Gotaro excitedly, pointing ahead as they rounded another bend in the track. 'There's the bridge!'

A quarter of a mile below them, half a dozen unrailed planks had become visible, straddling a narrow rushing stream. Just below it, the stream widened into a turbulent but navigable creek, where water that foamed down the hillside swirled onward more slowly, heading for the sea. Tanaka nodded wordlessly as he ran, then exclaimed aloud himself as a guard-boat rowed vigorously by a dozen Kago samurai oarsmen came into sight, pulling hard upstream.

'That's our craft. Let's speed up!'

Although one of the rearmost guards was now leading his riderless horse, Tanaka had chosen to run down the hillside on foot in order to supervise the progress of the *norimono* more closely. Because he still wore the loin-cloth and turban, when he arrived at the bridge where the Kago guard-boat had moored, its occupants did not at first recognize their master. Only when Tanaka tugged off the turban and tossed it aside did the boat commander bow apologetically low, along with all the startled members of his crew.

'You've made excellent progress against this fierce current,' called Tanaka from the bank, raising his voice above the roar of the water. 'Now I have a special mission for you. Are you ready to conquer any difficulties you may face?'

'Yes, of course, O Kami-san,' replied the commander, bowing again. 'What is the mission?'

Tanaka darted a last wary glance up the hillside as the bearers lowered the *norimono* to the ground beside the bridge. 'You are to row as swiftly as possible to the nearest of the black ships, taking with you the body of the foreign barbarian prisoner. It's vital that you keep the body concealed from all eyes, and once you reach the ship, make absolutely sure it is taken safely aboard. Then row away fast, without offering any explanation. Is that clear?'

'Quite clear, O Kami-san,' replied the boat commander gravely. 'Where is the body?'

'Wait a moment!'

Tanaka strode over to the samurai guard who had tended his horse and carried his armour and weapons down the hill. After a moment's hesitation he drew a long sword from its scabbard. Hurrying back to the *norimono*, he motioned for Gotaro and another guard to take up positions close to the carrying-chair. When they were ready, he unlatched its door with his sword-tip, and stood back. He had opened it only once previously, just after successfully snatching the chair from the Makabe, to satisfy himself that the blindfolded figure inside was without any doubt the foreign barbarian whom he knew; during the frantic dash downhill, the door had remained firmly closed but now he motioned for Gotaro to swing it back on its hinges and lift the prisoner into the open.

'Hold him upright,' commanded Tanaka, as Gotaro and the other guard dragged the trussed figure of Robert Eden out of the chair.

Stepping forward, Tanaka stretched out his sword and sawed quickly through the bonds around the American's feet and legs. Eden sagged in the arms of the guard captain for a moment, then straightened to stand shakily unaided. Reaching upward with his sword, Tanaka sliced through the blindfold with a single deft movement and whisked it away. With his hands still bound behind his back, Eden blinked round uncertainly at the ring of samurai facing him. His peasant clothing was in tatters, the bandage around his head was caked with dried blood, and his eyes were hazed with pain; but when his gaze came to rest on Tanaka, recognition showed immediately in his expression.

'Last time we met, Eden-san, I told you that spying in Nippon was punishable with death,' said Tanaka grimly. 'To honour your earlier actions,

I freed you to return to your ship—why did you choose to disobey my orders?'

Swaying on his feet, Eden straightened his body, trying to flex his cramped muscles as best he could with his hands still bound behind him. For a moment he looked uncertainly at Tanaka, then he lifted his chin defiantly. 'I rode inland . . . to climb . . . your sacred mountain, O Kami-san. That is all.'

Tanaka frowned in puzzlement. 'In the midst of preparations for war that was a foolish thing to do.'

'It was done . . . on an impulse.' Eden shrugged, speaking with difficulty. 'Perhaps I hoped it might help me understand . . . your country and its people. If that makes me a spy . . . then I am a spy.'

Tanaka took a step nearer and lifted his sword menacingly. 'In the barn I warned that if you were recaptured, there would be no escaping execution. You've acted very unwisely.'

Eden stood his ground, eyeing Tanaka and the surrounding warriors without flinching. 'I've spent days . . . anticipating my death, O Kami-san. Why have you waited so long?'

'You don't understand,' snapped Tanaka, taking another half-step forward. 'Until a few minutes ago you were a captive of Lord Daizo. And it's Daizo's insane wish to start a war with your country. He planned to use you to help him gain his ends.'

'How could he do that?' asked Eden unsteadily.

'Your admiral and three hundred other Americans landed half an hour ago to take part in a ceremony near here. Lord Daizo's men captured you on Mount Fuji and kept you alive so that they could display you there by surprise, as a treacherous spy. That would have provided a reason for all the assembled forces of Nippon to launch an immediate attack.'

'And now you've stopped him,' said Eden slowly, understanding for the first time. 'Why did you do that?'

Tanaka's eyes glittered angrily. 'Because I believe it would be madness for us to engage in war with well-armed barbarians—at least until Nippon has ships and guns that are just as powerful!'

'But you're also guilty, O Kami-san, of the same sort of madness as Lord Daizo,' said Eden. 'I did learn something, climbing Fuji-san . . . although not what I expected.'

'What do you mean?'

'On Fuji-san, Lord Daizo's men ruthlessly killed one of their own countrymen—and cast his body into the volcano. Sentaro was a simple man, but he understood something vital—that there *can* be true friendship between men of different races and nations. He was killed because he was a man of goodwill.'

'Of what importance is that to me?' demanded Tanaka coldly. 'I didn't kill him!'

'No, but I heard the orders you just gave to your boatman,' continued Eden in the same subdued tone. 'You want to send my dead body back to the black ships—even though I've told you I came ashore in peace. Until this moment I thought you'd tried to save my life on Fuji. But I can see now—you too wanted to kill me quietly . . . Your blindness is as great as Lord Daizo's.'

Tanaka lifted his head angrily but did not reply. For several seconds the two men stood staring at each other in complete silence. Around them, Gotaro and the other guards shifted and murmured, watching warily.

'We have spoken enough,' said Tanaka at last, still holding Eden's gaze. 'It is time for action.'

'I agree, O Kami-san!'

As Eden spoke, he tugged his hands from behind his back and threw aside his loosened bonds. Lunging sideways he snatched a long sword from the astonished Gotaro's sash and backed away towards the bridge, holding the weapon at arm's length in front of him.

'I've had nothing to do . . . for days . . . except feign unconsciousness . . . and work at loosening my bonds,' he gasped, breathing heavily from the sudden exertion. 'I won't be executed by you . . . I'll die fighting.'

As one man, the ring of Tanaka's bodyguards unsheathed their swords and began to move forward. Scowling furiously, Gotaro drew his own remaining short sword, and made to spring at the American. But before he could move, Tanaka raised his arm to signal restraint.

'Wait, Gotaro! Leave him to me! He hasn't the strength of a baby!'

Eden continued to back away until he reached the end of the bridge, where he stopped, swaying precariously. The crew of the boat, moored a few feet below, watched in silence as Tanaka approached, still holding his sword steadily in front of him. All who were watching could see that Tanaka's assessment of Eden's condition was accurate. Greatly weakened by loss of blood and the long, cramped days and nights in the *norimono*, his face was set in a grimace of pain and it was clear that he remained upright only by a supreme effort of will.

'Your reckless bravery has not deserted you in the face of death, Edeh-san,' said Tanaka approvingly, as he stopped little more than a sword's thrust away. 'Yet a single light blow will finish you now.'

Eden's blade was wavering and his sword arm began to shake as he stared fixedly at Tanaka, half standing, half crouching by the end of the bridge. His eyes were blurring with exhaustion, and his expression suggested that he was aware how the sudden exertion had sapped nearly all his remaining strength; but still he held his racked body in a posture of defiance, readying himself for the attack.

'Perhaps you're right,' said Tanaka softly, looking past his raised blade and into the American officer's high-cheekboned face. 'Perhaps we share some ancient ancestral blood. Perhaps your wild courage rises from the same fountain which has nourished the finest swordsmen of Nippon.'

'The Iroquois wise elders used to say . . . "All men of this world are kinsmen",' grunted Eden, grimacing and shifting a step nearer the stream. 'Knowing this, the greatest warriors always stood for peace . . . It seems in Nippon you haven't learned this vital truth yet.'

'I've learned another truth, though, Eden-san,' said Tanaka grimly, lifting his sword higher and taking another step forward. 'That concerns a foreign barbarian who claims he wants peace above all else—but then does so many rash things that he almost brings about a war single-handed!' Tanaka paused, his expression darkening. 'The land begotten by the sun will be a much safer place without you! Your death will be one victory you can't deny the people of Nippon . . .'

'Killing me . . . won't be a victory for you,' panted Eden, staring defiantly back at Tanaka. 'You'll win only if you make me hate Nippon and its people.'

Frowning, Tanaka continued to stare at him uncertainly.

'Hatred thrives on ignorance . . . And you want to destroy what little knowledge I have now of your country . . . You want to stop me taking those few shreds of understanding back to America, don't you? You want to snuff out any faint hope of peace and friendship between our nations.'

Eden swayed again and almost fell, but recovered his balance with an effort. He continued to stare defiantly at Tanaka, who held his ground but did not move nearer. For some time, neither man spoke; then slowly Tanaka straightened up from his fighting crouch. Without taking his eyes from Eden, he used his free hand to summon the guard tending his armour and his horse. After another pause he suddenly handed over his long sword for re-sheathing, and signalled to the boat commander to step ashore.

'You will take the foreign barbarian back to his ship now,' he snapped. 'Make sure he remains hidden at all times from the view of those in other boats.' Turning again to Eden, he gestured for Gotaro to come forward. 'Eden-san, you may restore that sword to Gotaro. In recognition of your valour, I've decided to return you to your ship alive.'

For several seconds Eden's eyes remained wary, and he gazed round suspiciously at each Japanese in his range of vision. Only when he was confident that no trickery was intended did he slowly lift the sword into a vertical position before his face, and incline his head in a formal salute—first to Tanaka, then to Gotaro. The two Japanese waited until he had returned the sword hilt-first, then both bowed their heads similarly in acknowledgement.

Turning away, Eden allowed himself to be helped down into the boat by its commander, and he was led respectfully to a place of concealment inside the high, curved prow. By the time the boat had cast off from the bank, Tanaka was fully dressed once more in his *jimbaori*, armour and a horned helmet. Standing with his feet astride on the narrow bridge, he watched the crew row Eden swiftly away towards the sea, aided by the fast current. The nobleman made no gesture, but continued to watch the boat in silence until it disappeared from view round a bend in the stream.

As soon as it went out of sight, however, Tanaka leapt into his saddle and urged Gotaro and his guards to mount up. 'We must ride fast now to the pavilion,' he called over his shoulder as he set off rapidly in the direction of the beach. 'Lord Daizo and his warriors will already be there!'

48

Samuel Armstong paused in his formal reading of the American letters and carefully turned over the last sheet of vellum in his hands. Raising his eyes, he glanced round the hushed pavilion, and saw that Commodore Perry had become as stiffly immobile on his seat as the two imperial princes opposite him. His jaw jutted pugnaciously above his uniform's high collar and he stared stonily ahead, clutching the hilt of his sword with one hand as he listened to the missionary's rendering in English of the last few lines of his own letter addressed to the Emperor of Japan.

'Our admiral further states: "American commerce with all this region of the globe is rapidly increasing and the Japan seas will soon be covered with our vessels,"' said Armstrong, enunciating his words slowly and clearly. '"With the aid of our steamships we can reach Japan in eighteen or twenty days. Therefore, as the United States and Japan are becoming every day nearer and nearer to each other, the President desires to live in peace and friendship with Your Imperial Majesty—but, as it has already been pointed out, no friendship can long exist unless Japan ceases to act towards Americans as if they were her enemies. However wise this policy may originally have been, it is unwise and impracticable now that contact between the two countries is so much more easy and rapid than before."'

Armstrong paused and waited while Haniwara Tokuma, working from a Dutch text, provided a nervy rendition into Japanese. His delivery had become increasingly staccato and unsteady, and Armstrong noticed that, in between the passages of translation, he had begun to glance up repeatedly towards the pavilion entrance. The chanting which had broken out in the distance had now died away but, while it lasted, it had heightened the atmosphere of tension within the pavilion. As a result, in the intervals of silence between the translations, the expressions of Japanese and Americans alike remained alert and watchful, suggesting that they were listening for further unusual sounds from outside.

'The admiral concludes his letter with great clarity,' continued Armstrong, glancing down at the parchment once more. 'He says: "In my capacity as commander-in-chief of the United States naval forces in the East India, China and Japan seas, I set out these arguments in the hope that the Japanese government will see the necessity of averting an unfriendly collision between our two nations. To do this, they need only respond favourably to the propositions of amity which are now made in all sincerity. Many of the large ships-of-war destined to visit Japan have not yet arrived in these seas. As evidence of our friendly intentions we have brought but four smaller ships, designing, should it become necessary, to return to Yedo in the spring with a much larger force. But it is expected that the government of Your Imperial Majesty will render such a return unnecessary, by acceding at once to the very reasonable and pacific overtures contained in the President's letter . . . With the most profound respect for Your Imperial Majesty, and entertaining a sincere hope that you may long live to enjoy health and happiness, the undersigned subscribes himself Matthew Calbraith Perry."'

Armstrong watched tensely as Haniwara Tokuma began to translate again, but before he had gone very far there was a stirring at the entrance to the pavilion. The missionary looked up in time to see the glowering figure of Lord Daizo step silently inside, accompanied by an equally dark-faced young Japanese wearing the travel-stained armour of a samurai beneath a nobleman's red *jimbaori*. The demeanour of both men was tense and hostile, and Haniwara Tokuma stumbled again over his words as he lifted his head to dart an uneasy glance in their direction. After a moment he recovered himself, and Armstrong saw Lord Daizo and his companion shift to a position from which they could be seen clearly by the interpreter.

As soon as the translation ended, the Governor of Uraga rose and stepped respectfully towards the grave, impassive figure of Prince Toda. In front of the prince's stool he suddenly prostrated himself full-length, pressed his forehead to the red carpet, and remained in this position of absolute homage for several seconds. Feeling his own anxiety mounting, Armstrong moved unobtrusively to the side of the Japanese interpreter and leaned close to his ear.

'What is happening, Haniwara-san?' asked the missionary in an urgent whisper. 'Is His Excellency about to deliver your receipt to the admiral?'

'Yes,' replied the Japanese in a frantic undertone. 'I have a translation for you . . .' He paused, took a text in Dutch from his sleeve, and handed it over. 'Now, please return to your place.'

'I wish to help you avert a disaster,' whispered Armstrong, glancing at the translation and pretending to point enquiringly to something on the page. 'What must you do to unleash the attack?'

The Japanese caught his breath and looked up with a haunted expression in his eyes. Then his face clenched suddenly and some dam of inner reserve gave way, broken at last by the heavy burden of fear he had nursed alone for so long. 'When given a signal, I should strike the trapdoor three times with my foot,' he whispered hoarsely. 'I *must* do it.'

'Where's the trapdoor?' hissed Armstrong, pointing to his translation again, but glancing desperately around the pavilion. 'Where exactly is it?'

'Behind the red chest,' murmured the Japanese, bending forward to make a show of looking more closely at Armstrong's sheet of paper. 'It's very near to your admiral's seat.'

The governor had raised himself from the carpet but was still kneeling deferentially with his head bowed, in a waiting posture. Very slowly, without otherwise moving, Prince Toda pulled a scroll from one of the deep sleeves of his gown and handed it wordlessly to the governor. After prostrating himself once more, the official rose and backed slowly away from the First Counsellor of the Empire, bowing repeatedly at each step. Finally, at a distance, he turned and began to cross the pavilion towards Commodore Perry, carrying the scroll which was bound with an imperial yellow ribbon. As he watched him go, Armstrong glanced quickly towards the pavilion entrance and saw Lord Daizo staring hard at Haniwara Tokuma, as though willing him to look in his direction.

'I will go and stand on the trapdoor myself and block the way,' whispered Armstrong, making a sudden decision. 'Then you'll be unable to reach it to give the order to attack!'

The Japanese interpreter's eyes grew suddenly round. 'No! No! Please don't, Armstrong-san! If you do, you could be the first to die!'

Armstrong felt a sudden chill of fear deep inside his bowels and he hesitated; then he noticed that a glimmer of hope had appeared in the stricken eyes of the Japanese interpreter. 'It's only right I should take some risk myself after all this time,' muttered the missionary and moved off towards the lacquered chest, trying to make his action seem casual.

Walking very slowly, Armstrong paused before the chest and looked over the formal documents and their containers, as though assuring himself that every last formality had been complied with. Then he stepped sideways and shuffled back a pace or two, clearing his throat and glancing down at his translation of the imperial receipt. Noticing for the first time the seams in the floor-covering which defined the trapdoor, he took a deep breath and stepped squarely onto one end of it as if he was seeking a less obtrusive standpoint from which to observe the rest of the proceedings. Watching the governor begin to prostrate himself in front of Commodore Perry, Armstrong steeled himself not to look towards Lord Daizo, and at the same time he tried not to think about the hidden cohort of armed warriors waiting to spring into action a few feet beneath the soles of his boots.

'What is being presented now, Mr Armstrong, please?' asked Flag Lieutenant Rice suddenly as the governor straightened up from his prostration and offered the parchment respectfully to Commodore Perry.

'This is the imperial receipt for our Presidential letter,' replied the missionary hastily, lifting the paper in his hand into view. 'I've been given this translation in Dutch, which I shall read out in a moment. It's quite in order for the commodore to accept it.'

The throne borrowed from the Buddhist temple creaked in the silence as Perry leaned down stiffly to accept the scroll from the governor's hand. Once he had taken it, the governor lowered his face to the floor once more, then rose and backed away, bowing at each step until he had resumed his place beside his own interpreter on the opposite side of the pavilion. Haniwara Tokuma's hands were shaking as he lifted his translation into view and began to read it aloud; but it was also noticeable that he no longer allowed his attention to stray to the pavilion entrance, where Lord Daizo and his son still stood staring fixedly at him.

'The imperial receipt states that the letter of the American President is "hereby received and will be delivered to the Emperor",' said Armstrong, glancing up from his text towards Commodore Perry, who was looking enquiringly in his direction. 'It further says, "Many times it has been communicated to you that business relating to foreign countries cannot be transacted here in the Bay of Yedo but only in Nagasaki. However, it being observed that the admiral, in his capacity as ambassador of the American President, would be insulted by these arrangements, the justice of this has therefore been acknowledged. Consequently the above-mentioned letter is hereby received on this day and at this place, Kurihama, although such acceptance is quite contrary to the general laws of Japan."'

Armstrong paused in his reading to look up, and saw Commodore Perry nod haughtily in acknowledging that he had succeeded in forcing an unprecedented concession from his reluctant hosts. The commanders of the *Susquehanna* and the *Mississippi*, who were seated close behind, also leaned forward to nod and murmur approvingly. From the corner of his eye, however, Armstrong saw Lord Daizo move a pace or two further into the pavilion, so as to become directly visible to Haniwara Tokuma. Seeing this convinced Armstrong that a moment of crisis was approaching, and he looked down quickly again at his translation.

'There's one last paragraph, Commodore,' he said in a more urgent tone. 'And it's very brief and to the point. It says simply: "Because this is not a place where negotiations can be conducted with foreigners, neither a conference nor any entertainment can be permitted. Therefore as the letter has been received, you will now leave here immediately.'"

Perry bristled on his seat. Then he frowned and turned to confer in a confidential undertone with his two commanders. At that moment Armstrong looked up towards the entrance of the pavilion and saw Lord Daizo lift his right hand slowly across his body to clasp his left shoulder in a deliberate gesture; he had already fixed his hostile gaze on Haniwara Tokuma, and the missionary knew instinctively he was seeing the prearranged signal being made. Inside his chest his heart began to throb wildly, and he held his breath as he watched for the interpreter's response.

For a long time Haniwara seemed to stare back at the *daimyo*, as though hypnotized. He did not move but Armstrong could see that his hands, which still clutched the translation of the imperial receipt, were shaking more than ever. Then abruptly he turned to look towards the American missionary; his expression was agonized and beseeching in the same moment, and his eyes burned with a terrible indecision. Wondering what he would do if the interpreter decided to rush towards the trapdoor and push him aside by physical force, Armstrong felt sweat break out on his own brow. He was trying wordlessly to convey encouragement and compassion in equal measure to the Japanese as he looked steadily back at him but, fearing he was not being successful, he began to pray desperately inside his head.

The indistinct murmur of the commodore's voice merging with those of his senior officers was the only sound to break the strained silence in the pavilion, and all eyes were focused intently on them. Nobody but Armstrong was aware of the terrible battle of wills being fought out silently by the *daimyo* and the scholarly interpreter, and only the missionary witnessed the decisive moment when the struggle was lost and won. Outwardly the appearance of the interpreter scarcely changed; his face remained very pale but Armstrong noticed that a curious calmness seemed to descend upon him as he turned again in the direction of the *daimyo* with a new sense of resolution evident in his bearing. His eyes were lowered, and the missionary saw that he did not raise his head to challenge Lord Daizo directly; but his determined defiance of the nobleman's intimidation was silently and unmistakably expressed in the total immobility of his small, slender body.

As the moments ticked by, Lord Daizo had become visibly more impatient, but Armstrong saw his face darken suddenly with rage when he recognized the interpreter's defiance for what it was. Dropping his right arm to his side, he lifted it very deliberately across his chest in a last, furious repetition of the secret signal, while glaring anew at the interpreter, willing him to obey. But, instead of reacting, Haniwara Tokuma slowly turned his back on the *daimyo* and glanced towards the governor who was standing at his side, making it clear he was patiently awaiting the instructions of his immediate superior.

For a moment Lord Daizo stared across the pavilion with an expression of outright disbelief on his face. Then Armstrong saw him lean angrily towards his son and whisper urgent orders in his ear. While listening, Yakamochi glanced towards Commodore Perry and the other senior American officers who, in defiance of the order they had been given to leave, were still conferring in low voices. Yakamochi's eyes narrowed in concentration as he listened, suggesting to Armstrong that he was memorizing positions and measuring distances in his mind; then he bowed quickly to his father and rushed from the pavilion.

The exterior entrance to the tunnel which gave access to the secret underground chamber was situated a hundred yards to the rear of the ceremonial pavilion. The entrance itself and the approaches to it were all heavily screened with blue and white canvas barriers, and groups of sentinels drawn randomly from different regional clans were stationed at intervals along the narrow canvas corridors. An expectant hush had fallen over the whole beach, and the thousands of Japanese fighting men and civilians drawn up around the crescent-shaped bay seemed to strain their ears in a vain effort to detect what was going on inside the marquee.

On emerging hurriedly from the outer vestibule, Yakamochi stopped and beckoned to his chief bodyguard, who had been waiting discreetly in the shadow of the pavilion. Lifting a hand to shade his eyes, Yakamochi scanned the nearest groups of sentinels, searching for signs of Makabe emblems on their battle-dress.

'What are you seeking, my lord?' asked the bodyguard. 'May I be of assistance?'

'Yes,' hissed Yakamochi. 'We need the correct passwords to gain immediate entry to the underground chamber! One of our samurai sentries could tell us!'

'What is our aim, my lord?'

'A signal to attack the foreign barbarians inside the pavilion has been ignored. We must lead the assassination force ourselves!'

Without hesitation the bodyguard ran to the nearest group of sentries and drew aside a Makabe samurai. After conferring briefly with him he returned quickly to Yakamochi's side.

'The password for the screened areas and the tunnel entrance, my lord, is *kurufune*—black ships! And for the door of the chamber itself at the end of the tunnel it is *kamikaze*—divine storm!'

'Excellent! We must move quickly. Follow me!'

Yakamochi set off rapidly along the outside border of the screened zone, followed closely by the guard. When they reached the guardpost nearest to the tunnel entrance and gave the password the sentries bowed low and allowed both men through without further questions. The narrow, low-roofed tunnel, shored up with pinewood props, was lit only feebly with a few paper lanterns, but Yakamochi led the way through it at a crouching run. Outside the wooden door of the chamber, two samurai sentries again bowed deferentially low on hearing the whispered code-word, and stepped aside after indicating that strict silence should be observed inside the underground chamber itself.

As Yakamochi pushed open the door and stepped quietly over the threshold, the alert eyes of a dozen fully armoured warriors turned to look at him. By the light of a single, flickering lantern he could see that some of the samurai were crouching warily by the flight of wooden steps that led up to the trapdoor; others were standing or kneeling beside the earthen walls, and all without exception carried long killing swords, as well as shorter daggers in their sashes. It was evident from their alert postures that all were ready to spring into action at a moment's notice and that every swordsman was listening attentively for the slightest sound from above.

'The signal for action has already been given!' rasped Yakamochi, looking quickly around the chamber. 'But a treacherous official failed to carry out his orders! I've been sent to lead you in the attack!'

He drew his sword with a flourish and stepped towards the wooden steps.

'Follow me, now! Death to the foreign barbarians!'

He lunged towards the steps, but as he did so Prince Tanaka Yoshio ducked silently out of the shadows beneath them to bar his way, his naked sword already raised in his hand. Behind him, Gotaro was also dimly visible and Yakamochi could see that he too was holding an unsheathed sword.

'If you wish to attack the foreign barbarians, you will have to kill us first!' said Tanaka softly, positioning himself with care on the lower step. 'We shall not let you pass.'

Looking Yakamochi in the eye, Tanaka stood very still, his sword as steady as a rock before him.

'Why do you love the foreign barbarians so much, O Kami-san?' snarled Yakamochi, moving slowly towards him. 'What is the reason for your abject treachery?'

'It would be madness to attack the barbarians now! With their superior weapons and ships they can invade us and make us their slaves for centuries to come.' Tanaka paused, measuring the distance between them with his eye; then very quickly he moved two steps higher. 'If we provoke them, they will do just that—and our proud nation will be ruined . . . perhaps for ever!'

'And if we don't?' demanded Yakamochi in a harsh whisper, moving slowly forward once again. 'Do you think they won't see us as weak and cowardly—and treat us even worse than slaves?'

Watching the young Makabe nobleman intently, Tanaka lowered the tip of his sword until it pointed directly at the centre of his chest. 'With their guns and mighty ships, the foreign barbarians are the overlords of the whole world at present. But it's the divine destiny of our great Emperor to become the chief of all nations . . .'

'We agree on that, so we should kill now—to show them our courage!'

'No! We must deceive the foreign barbarians long enough to learn all their secrets. Then some day we shall exceed their strength—and lead the world in their place!'

'You're wrong, O Kami-san,' sneered Yakamochi, taking a sudden step forward and dropping into a crouch by the bottom step. 'It's always best to attack first—and by surprise! Your body will be trampled in our attack!'

Yakamochi dodged suddenly to the left and his sword flashed towards Tanaka's head in a feint designed to throw him off balance. But, to his astonishment, Tanaka remained absolutely motionless on the higher step, watching his opponent's blade calmly as it passed within a few inches of his face. Caught off balance himself, Yakamochi tried to lunge to the other side, slashing ferociously upwards at Tanaka's throat. But Tanaka leaned forward with lightning speed, and in the same movement plunged his sword hilt-deep into Yakamochi's chest. He withdrew the weapon just as swiftly and Yakamochi froze in his tracks, his eyes staring sightlessly, his arms held high in the air. His sword fell first to the sandy floor of the chamber, then he sagged down silently beside it, his mouth opened wide in a soundless scream of agony.

'Does anybody else favour attacking the foreign barbarians now?' asked Tanaka softly, looking first at Yakamochi's stunned bodyguard, then glancing round slowly at the face of each samurai warrior in turn. 'If you do, please say so.'

Nobody moved or spoke. In the deep silence Tanaka came slowly down from the steps and wiped his sword with great care on Yakamochi's red cloak. After one further quick glance around the shadowy chamber he returned the clean blade emphatically to its scabbard.

In the main hall of the pavilion above, there was a rustle of anticipation as Commodore Perry finished his murmured consultations and turned back to confront the two grave-faced Japanese dignitaries. Rising to his feet, he looked sternly across the room, and the silken tassels of his cockade shivered as he drew himself up to his full height.

'It is my intention to leave the Bay of Yedo at a time of my own choosing,' he declared sonorously. 'My squadron of ships will probably depart two or three days from now, when our nautical surveys of the bay are complete.'

The commodore waited while Armstrong translated his words and Haniwara Tokuma in his turn conveyed their meaning in sibilant Japanese to the governor and the two imperial delegates. An expectant hush followed, but neither the impassive First Counsellor nor Prince Ido made any comment or reply, and Commodore Perry glanced pointedly at Armstrong to indicate he should be prepared to translate further.

'In conclusion,' he continued in the same booming voice, 'I hereby announce my intention to return here in the approaching spring, perhaps in April or May—or even sooner. This will be for the purpose of receiving what we trust will be a favourable reply to the letter from the President of the United States of America. That is all I have to say.'

The commodore resumed his seat and, after the translation had been made, a hurried conversation ensued in whispers between the governor and his interpreter, who remained on their knees in front of the lacquered chest. When they had finished, Haniwara Tokuma looked up diffidently towards Armstrong and the commodore.

'Will the admiral return with all four of his vessels in the spring?' he asked tentatively. 'That is the governor's enquiry.'

'I shall return with all of them,' replied Perry ringingly, when he had understood the question. 'And probably more.' He paused and turned towards Armstrong. 'Leave them in no doubt that the four present ships are only a small proportion of the entire squadron.'

On hearing this reply there was another brief flurry of conversation between the two Japanese; then both men bowed simultaneously from the waist in Perry's direction, before rising slowly to their feet. The governor walked to the lacquered chest and with ostentatious care wrapped the American letters about with the scarlet cloth on which they had been laid out. Then he turned and bowed again towards the commodore, murmuring a single brief sentence in Japanese.

'The governor says: "There is nothing more to be done here,"' said Armstrong after listening carefully. 'And he invites us to follow him out of the pavilion, since the ceremony is now concluded.'

The missionary watched the governor and Haniwara Tokuma move off together side by side, leading the way towards the outer vestibule.

The interpreter was still very pale but, despite the signs of strain, his features remained composed. Armstrong tried to catch his eye but he kept his gaze focused before him on the red-carpeted floor of the pavilion, and it was with a muffled sigh of relief that Armstrong himself stepped away from the trapdoor to fall into line behind the commodore and his senior commanders. At times the soles of his feet had seemed to burn in anticipation of the floor beneath him being thrown violently open by a horde of sword-wielding warriors and, as he looked towards the sunlit beach beyond the pavilion entrance, he breathed deeply again and allowed himself to hope for the first time that all would end well.

To acknowledge the departure of the Americans, both imperial delegates rose stiffly from their stools. When the commodore paused to incline his head in their direction, they again bowed gravely in return, but otherwise their faces remained without expression and they still uttered no audible sound. In total silence the procession of American officers passed out of the main vestibule, scrutinized closely by all the watching Japanese. As the front ranks drew abreast of Lord Daizo near the outer entrance, Armstrong could see from his expression that the nobleman was seething with a barely suppressed anger. His eyes never left Haniwara Tokuma, but the interpreter did not raise his head to look at him as he passed.

As soon as the commodore and the head of the procession emerged from the pavilion onto the beach, a flurry of exuberant commands rang out as marine and naval officers ordered their waiting men to present arms in honour of their commander-in-chief. Eager, well-drilled feet stamped the sand, and a forest of carbines glittering with fixed bayonets were shifted expertly onto shoulders as the parade formed itself up quickly around its nucleus of senior officers. Within moments the ships' bands had again launched enthusiastically into 'Hail Columbia' and, soon after the parade began to move, this was succeeded by the strains of 'Yankee Doodle' which enlivened and cheered the uniformed marchers as they stepped out gladly across the beach.

Samuel Armstrong responded with equal enthusiasm to the music and began to swing his limbs vigorously in relief. As he marched, he peered anxiously into the surrounding throng of curious Japanese, seeking a parting glimpse of Haniwara Tokuma. But he could not immediately pick out the interpreter among the dense crowds now pressing around the pavilion. The closeness of the staring faces reminded every marcher how easy it would be for the assembled Japanese force to converge suddenly in overwhelming numbers, even at that late stage in the proceedings and, as he fell into stride at the rear of the commodore's party, Armstrong sensed he was not alone in wrestling with his lingering feelings of unease.

The procession moved away in a slow curve, making for the temporary jetty, and Armstrong at last caught sight of the diminutive figure of Haniwara Tokuma standing beside the Governor of Uraga about a hundred yards from the pavilion. His face looked gaunt but he was scrutinizing the parade intently, and Armstrong saw his expression tighten when their eyes met. As they exchanged glances, something indefinable in the stoical demeanour of the Japanese interpreter moved the missionary suddenly to the depths of his being. Fears for the safety of his family were etched into every line of his narrow, intelligent face, but in his stance Armstrong also saw something else—a hint of fierce pride that, no matter what terrible consequences might follow from his actions, for the sake of a higher aim and for his country he had refused to yield to a terrible personal tyranny.

On recognizing this, Armstrong bowed his head spontaneously in the interpreter's direction as he marched, feeling more than he had ever done before that the gesture was deserved and appropriate. Haniwara Tokuma's expression did not change but he waited until Armstrong looked up, then lowered his own head slowly in a brief but equally emphatic bow. He straightened up again just before the Americans turned away down the beach, and as Armstrong marched ontowards the jetty and the safety of the massive warships riding at anchor on the bay, he carried away with him above all else the haunting image of Haniwara Tokuma's brave but stricken face.

49

In his tiny aft cabin above the *Susquehanna*'s rudder, Samuel Armstrong bent low over his makeshift writing table, hurrying to complete a concluding entry in his journal. Neither the rumble of the flagship's steering mechanism nor the noisy churning of its great paddle-wheels interrupted his concentration as his right hand worked a quill pen rapidly back and forth across the pages of the large folio notebook. Through an open rear scuttle, the sloop-of-war *Saratoga* was visible gliding silently in the flagship's wake at the end of a towing hawser, its sails furled neatly on their yard-arms. Astern of the *Saratoga*, to port, the *Mississippi* could also be seen, towing the *Plymouth* with similar ease, and all four ships were proceeding at a majestic nine knots down the centre of Yedo Bay, heading for the open sea and Hong Kong, Canton and Shanghai.

Carefully maintaining regimented distances between themselves, the war vessels were giving a final demonstration of the unprecedented power of steam to the thousands of Japanese civilians and soldiers lining the cliffs and beaches. It was the early morning of Sunday 17 July 1853, and no breeze was yet ruffling the flat, shimmering waters of the bay. Because of this, the crews of becalmed Japanese fishing junks, in particular, were watching in awe as the great black warships passed southward, belching spirals of thick smoke and leaving wide paths of churned white water in their wake. Hundreds of heavily laden boats rowed by standing oarsmen were putting out from the beaches too, carrying peasants and townsmen who were eager to catch a last glimpse of the fearsome foreign barbarians and their all-powerful machines.

After the ships weighed anchor five miles above Uraga, Armstrong had stood quietly watching these crowded boats from the rail of the quarter-deck. At first he had felt an immense sense of relief that the squadron was departing from Japan and all its dangers, after ten long days of tension. He was greatly relieved too that his demanding role as interpreter, which had given rise to so many conflicting inner feelings, was finished—at least for the moment. But, to his dismay, quietness of mind otherwise eluded him and he had soon hurried back to his cabin to try to order his racing thoughts in his journal.

He wrote furiously for several minutes, then something made him raise his head from his task, as the *Susquehanna* swung its bows a degree or two eastwards in adjusting its course down the bay. The western shore became temporarily visible through the rear scuttle, and Armstrong was struck afresh by the beauty of the undulating green hills and the manicured rice terraces sweeping gently down to the beaches above Uraga. Steep, bare mountains were becoming visible far off and then, as though it had silently signalled its presence in advance, the thrillingly symmetrical snow-capped cone of Mount Fuji materialized silently from a long rift of white cloud, to stand supreme above the morning landscape.

The volcano's broad base was shrouded in low cloud as usual, and its purple-blue flanks and dazzling white summit again seemed to float unsupported in the distant heavens. Seeing the vision-like mountain had always pleased the missionary before, but now the sudden sight of it caused him to stop writing and he laid his pen aside. Standing up, he went to the open scuttle and stared pensively out. Unexpectedly, the simple purity of the mountain's beauty soothed his anxious mind to some degree, and he watched it unwaveringly until the flagship adjusted its course again and robbed him of his view of the western shore. Feeling calmer as a result, he returned to his table, but instead of making further notes, he sat down and slowly read over the several pages he had already filled with neat, methodical handwriting.

> *My greatest joy of the last three days was the discovery, on re-embarking from Kurihama, that Robert Eden had returned mysteriously to the flagship during our absence, he had written. It seemed to me then that my most fervent prayers had been answered on at least two fronts. A major conflict had been narrowly avoided onshore and the brave young New England lieutenant had been miraculously restored to the ship alive, after being missing for seven days. My joy of course was quickly tempered by the discovery that Lieutenant Eden had been gravely wounded, and this morning he's still fighting for his life on the lower deck in a special partitioned-off area of the ship's infirmary. He had collapsed on the starboard companion-ladder after being delivered to its foot by an anonymous Japanese craft, and had to be carried bodily below by two startled sentries. At present, three sailors armed with carbines and cutlasses are standing guard twenty-four hours a day around his special sick berth, which adjoins the ship's prison. This arrangement has been made because strict orders had long since been*

given that he should be placed promptly under close arrest if he ever set foot on the ship again. From Flag Lieutenant Rice I've since learned that the wounded lieutenant has given only a sketchy outline of what happened to him, and no information at all is being given out on this. If he recovers, he'll face a court martial on desertion charges. The outcome will surely be a spell of imprisonment and the termination of his promising navy career . . .

Armstrong stopped reading, feeling a new surge of admiration and compassion for Eden. The young officer had clearly known what enormous risks he was taking with his life and his future when he struck out bravely from the ship. In comparison Armstrong suddenly felt that his own action of buckling on the first sword of his life, so that he did not have to go ashore conspicuously unarmed, had been doubly timid and unworthy, and he shook his head in a little gesture of self-disgust before returning his attention to his journal once more.

To make matters worse, Eden developed a high fever after the ship's surgeons operated on his head and leg wounds, he had written. The crisis point of the fever passed only late yesterday, and he's still said to be very weak from pain and loss of blood. I've sent repeated messages both to Eden himself and the surgeons, offering to visit and minister spiritually or otherwise to him—but so far I've received no response. All of this has illogically made me feel more uneasy than ever about my own role in the dramatic events of the last ten days. Robert Eden followed his peaceful convictions, risking all. But, despite my growing distaste for what I've been doing, I've continued to play a leading role as an accessory in these naked acts of armed intimidation. I can only hope that my secret efforts to help Haniwara Tokuma resist intimidation may have compensated in some small way. Whether that was so or not, I haven't really succeeded in modifying our latent hostility to the Japanese in any meaningful way . . .

Armstrong again broke off from re-reading the journal entry, remembering how Commodore Perry had been stung by the final undiplomatic words of the imperial receipt that had been handed to him at the ceremonial pavilion: '*Your President's letter having been received, you will now leave here.*'

His response, on returning to his flagship, had been to order all four warships to advance ten miles nearer to Yedo, sailing spectacularly in line abreast and taking visible depth soundings as they went. Later a dozen cutters were launched to make further soundings inshore, and when the alarmed and breathless Governor of Uraga had eventually caught up and come aboard to ask why the squadron was not departing as demanded, Armstrong himself had been directed to tell him that safer anchorages were being sought and planned for the much bigger squadron of warships that would return in a few months to receive the Emperor's response. Next day the commodore had transferred his pennant to the *Mississippi*, and sailed the steam frigate ten miles further up the bay, demonstrating with an unmistakable hostility that the American ships were capable of advancing to areas within cannon shot of the capital itself.

During intervals in this activity, the governor and his suite of officials had artfully been allowed aboard the *Susquehanna*. There had been no sign of Haniwara Tokuma and the governor had pointedly evaded all Armstrong's questions about his welfare, saying merely that he was 'resting from his duties'. Another interpreter had taken his place and the governor had remained invariably polite and gracious, despite the atmosphere of high tension created by the provocative manoeuvrings of the warships. After a lot of thought, Armstrong himself had decided to say nothing, for the time being, of what he knew about the intrigues and infighting that had surrounded events at Kurihama, in case they introduced new tensions into the remaining meetings. Before the squadron's departure, the whole Japanese delegation had twice been entertained with wines and whisky as well as ham and other American delicacies, which they had swallowed with great relish. They had also been shown the engines and all the ship's weapons, which had clearly fascinated them. The new interpreter had conveyed endless questions from the visiting officials and, to the surprise of the watching Americans, he had taken meticulous notes about the dimensions and methods of manufacture of the guns and the engine machinery.

There had also been a final impromptu exchange of modest gifts—American seeds and history books in return for Japanese fans, lacquered bowls and pipes. But Armstrong, as he had noted in his journal, had been unable to overlook the hypocrisy inherent in all this outward civility that had been offered side by side with the hostile and threatening deployment of the warships.

> *"The real truth behind these moves was summed up quite blatantly by Commodore Perry himself last night, he had written. The commodore said then on the quarterdeck in my hearing that the Japanese 'could only be brought to reason through the influence of their fears'! He also said he was confident that when they fully realized that their sea coast was entirely at the mercy of a strong naval*

force, 'they will concede all that will be asked of them'. Although the United States Congress alone has the power to declare war, and certainly has not done so over Japan, there have been times in the past ten days when an effective local declaration of war by the commodore has been implicit in all his actions—and I, to my great regret, have gone on aiding and abetting all this, despite my growing reservations. 'Japan has at last broken its own code of selfish exclusion to obey the universal law of hospitality,' said another senior officer last night—but my Christian conscience won't accept now that it is right to enforce such a 'universal law of hospitality' with sixty-four-pound guns . . .

Armstrong broke off from his reading, feeling again with renewed force the inherent flaws in the arguments that were being used to justify the US Navy squadron's actions. He wondered why he had not seen these flaws more clearly earlier in the voyage; then he realized that he had in fact been vaguely aware all along that his attitude was ambivalent. In the end, he decided, he had probably chosen subconsciously to ignore the more uncomfortable contradictions and with this shaming thought he returned to the concluding lines in his journal.

I suppose in truth Robert Eden had youth on his side in acting so bravely and decisively. Perhaps I couldn't really expect myself to be as fiercely uncompromising after long years spent trying to reconcile the many impossible conflicts between different religions. Perhaps compromise has long since become a way of life for me; perhaps that's what experience teaches; perhaps that's the great lesson of maturity that everybody must learn as they grow older. Or maybe not! Maybe in some situations, compromise is a form of cowardice of which we should be ashamed; important principles should never be compromised! Might the world be a better place if there were more purer, braver spirits—more Robert Edens—among us? His superiors, quite rightly, will say that, by rashly taking matters into his own hands without authority, he increased the risk of war and courted disaster for us all. But Eden, no doubt, would say in response that the actions of his superiors were wrong—and that he was trying to mitigate their effects. Whatever the answers to all these questions are, I hope in the years to come the Japanese won't smoulder with resentment over this hostile first approach by America, in which I've been so closely involved. They would certainly have every right to do so. I can only humbly pray that God will intervene compassionately to help end

Japan's self-imposed isolation—and draw her people into fellowship with the rest of the world without a violent and bloody collision.

A crisp knock on the door of his cabin interrupted Armstrong's reading and when he rose to open it, he found Midshipman Harris standing stiffly to attention on the threshold.

'Flag Lieutenant Rice presents his compliments, Mr Armstrong,' said the midshipman, saluting briskly. 'And I'm to tell you that your request to visit Lieutenant Eden has been granted.'

'Excellent!' exclaimed the missionary in surprise. 'Does that mean the lieutenant is out of danger?'

Harris shook his head quickly, his face serious. 'I'm afraid not, sir. If anything he may be a little worse. The surgeons say his chances are something less than fifty-fifty.'

'Is that why I'm being taken to him now?' asked Armstrong quickly.

'No, sir. I understand Lieutenant Eden himself has asked for you to make the visit.'

The missionary's face clouded anew with anxiety. 'So when may I see him?'

'I'm ordered to escort you there immediately, sir,' replied the young midshipman. 'Please follow me.'

50

The ship's infirmary was located near the bows of the *Susquehanna* on the lower deck and when they reached it, Midshipman Harris motioned for Armstrong to wait while he spoke in an undertone with the armed sentries. When they nodded their approval, he opened the barred door into the specially partitioned section of the prison sickbay where Eden lay alone with his heavily bandaged head propped against several pillows. The midshipman motioned the missionary towards a stool which had been positioned beside the bed, then saluted smartly again.

'You may stay five minutes, Mr Armstrong, that's all,' he said crisply. 'Those are the surgeon's strictest orders.'

'Thank you, Mr Harris. I'm very grateful.'

When the door had closed, Armstrong sat in silence looking at Eden, who had not moved or opened his eyes. The bulkiness of the bed coverings suggested at least one of his legs was thickly bandaged, and a film of perspiration shone on his cheeks. When at last he did open his eyes, the missionary could see from the expression in them that the young officer knew better than anybody else that he was fighting for his life.

'I'm very glad you asked to see me, Robert, because I wanted to tell you how much I admire your courage,' said Armstrong, touching Eden's shoulder gently in a warm gesture. "The US Navy, I'm afraid, won't look at it my way. They'll probably say you endangered the expedition by flouting their strictest orders. With some justification they'll probably use words like "foolhardy" or "harebrained" . . .'

Eden turned his head slowly to look at Armstrong, but he did not speak.

'But I understand the nobility of your motives. In God's eyes—and mine—you've proved yourself a true man of peace.'

Eden's expressionless face showed no sign of reaction but he continued to gaze steadily at the missionary.

'I prayed many times, Robert, for your safe return,' continued Armstrong quietly. 'But I hardly dared hope my prayers would be answered.

I'm overjoyed that you've been restored to the ship. Did you pray yourself at any time during your difficulties?'

Eden shook his head slowly.

Armstrong looked uncomfortable for a moment; then he spoke in a hesitant voice. 'I should like to say a short prayer now—to give thanks to God for delivering you from all your tribulations. 'Would you like to pray with me?'

'No . . . thank you . . . Mr Armstrong.' Eden shook his head again with an effort. 'My feelings . . . about such things haven't changed.'

After another moment of hesitation the missionary closed his eyes, bowed his head and murmured a heartfelt prayer of gratitude. A scuttle in the hull was open, giving a view of the green western shore of the bay, and Eden turned his head to look out through it while Armstrong prayed.

'Do you have any regrets now about what you did?' asked the missionary, after another long pause.

'None . . . at all,' replied Eden in a faint voice, still gazing out through the scuttle. 'For myself . . .'

Armstrong frowned. 'Do you regret it for somebody else's sake?'

'They killed . . . Sentaro . . . I very much regret that.'

Armstrong narrowed his eyes in a grimace of regret as he absorbed the news.

'That's why I asked you . . . to come to see me,' continued Eden weakly. 'Sentaro was a simple man . . . But he understood things wiser men choose to ignore . . . And he died because of that . . .'

'How can I help?' asked Armstrong, bending closer. 'I'll do anything I can . . .'

'Nobody who cares about him knows of his death . . . or where his body fell . . .' Eden paused to gather his waning strength. 'His wife and children . . . live in a village called Yurutaki on the western shore of this bay . . . They should know that he died bravely.'

'Do you want me to try and inform them?'

Eden nodded feebly. 'Sentaro used to pray to his own gods . . . Perhaps to honour his memory, you could also pray for him sometimes?'

'I'll gladly pray for Sentaro's soul,' said the missionary in a hushed voice. 'And I'll do all I can to inform his family. How did he die?'

'They beheaded him . . . and tossed his body into a side crater.'

Armstrong shook his head in dismay. 'Why did they do that?'

'For consorting with foreign barbarians . . . as he always feared they would.'

'Where is his body?'

Eden nodded towards the open scuttle and when he turned to look, Armstrong saw that the distant image of Mount Fuji had drifted into view again above the distant hills. 'We climbed the sacred volcano together . . .' Eden closed his eyes again and his face twisted with pain. 'But we never reached the top. They laid a trap for us.'

Armstrong stared incredulously at the young lieutenant, suspicious suddenly that his injuries might have made him delirious. 'Did you truly climb Mount Fuji, Robert? I can hardly believe it.'

Eden nodded. 'Before that I tried to send Sentaro back with a message for the commodore, describing what I'd found . . . Most of the Japanese guns on the cliffs are wooden replicas. They were terrified of us and their defences are pitiful . . . For my own reasons I wanted suddenly to ride to Fuji alone . . . But Sentaro disobeyed my orders and followed me . . . We'd almost reached the summit when we were discovered and attacked.'

Realizing that Eden was quite lucid, Armstrong looked wonderingly out through the porthole again, seeing the distant mountain with new eyes. 'How, in heaven's name, did you get back to the ship?' he whispered.

Eden lay silent for a long time and the missionary wondered whether he had enough strength to answer; then unexpectedly he stirred and opened his eyes.

'Many clans are fighting among themselves. Some wanted to attack us straight away. Others were trying to stop them. I became the prize captive and I was carried back to the coast, hidden in a sedan chair . . .'

'How did you escape?'

'I didn't escape. My captors were attacked by another clan. They seized me and brought me secretly to the ship themselves.'

Armstrong closed his eyes in relief. 'I can see now just how close we came to disaster. We've committed a grave error in trying to cow such a spirited people with unsubtle threats of war.'

Eden nodded in agreement. 'They may be very backward—but they are brave and proud . . . I think we're making the same mistakes here that we've made with the native Indians back home.'

For several moments Armstrong sat looking at the young officer in a reflective silence. 'Why did you want to climb Mount Fuji, Robert?' he asked at last. 'What possessed you to attempt such an extraordinary feat?'

'I can't explain it rationally . . .' Eden broke off, wincing with pain. Then he turned suddenly to look at the missionary again, as though his words had just triggered a deeply buried memory. 'When we first sighted land here, I caught a glimpse of Fuji. It looked like a vision in the moonlight. That night I had a very strange dream about the volcano which left very powerful feelings inside me.'

'What sort of feelings?'

'A strange new sense of understanding . . . On top of Mount Fuji, in the snow, I had pulled down the night heavens and wrapped them round me in a cloak . . . I felt totally at peace . . . I tried to write of that dream in my journal.'

'What was it you "understood"?' whispered Armstrong.

Eden's eyes narrowed with the effort of thought. 'That in the stars there's something more important than the "God" you preach about . . . They're part of us, we're part of them. And one day we'll make other voyages of discovery like this one—but to the unknown countries of the stars.'

Armstrong frowned and shifted uncomfortably on his stool. 'There can be nothing more important than God, Robert.'

'You don't understand, Mr Armstrong!' Eden raised himself up agitatedly from his pillow. 'I can see now—it was because of these very intense feelings that I swam ashore . . . And on Fuji and afterwards I felt other things which are just as hard to put into words . . . Will you listen to me?'

'Of course,' said the missionary gently. 'I'm listening.'

'After I was wounded I seemed to hover between life and death. I think I believed I was already dead . . . But then I felt I understood that we somehow carry all knowledge of the past and the future inside us . . . Perhaps locked up somehow inside the physical tissues of our bodies . . .'

Alarmed at his agitation, Armstrong placed his hands gently on Eden's shoulders and tried to guide him back towards the pillow. But the young lieutenant resisted with surprising strength and sat up, staring out through the scuttle.

'I felt certain we could unlock all these silent secrets if only we knew how to do it! And I saw how we had made the same terrible mistakes over and over again . . . Always we kill and maim one another without cause—because we haven't understood this simple truth . . . There's an evil side to our natures which relishes killing, but it can be overcome.' He stopped speaking and his eyes widened with anguish. 'In the end . . . I saw that all the beauty of life will be swallowed up in awful destruction and horror if we don't try to understand . . . And we'll never travel to those distant countries in the heavens unless we conquer our terrible urge to hate and kill.'

'Please, you must rest quietly,' insisted the missionary soothingly. 'You need to conserve all your energy to recover.'

As if the strength had drained out of him all at once, Eden sagged abruptly against the pillow. 'I know my wounds are severe,' he said weakly. 'And I'd like to make a last request of you, if I may . . .'

'Of course,' said Armstrong quietly.

'My journal of this voyage is among my belongings in my cabin. If I don't survive my wounds, I want you to take it. And when my son Jonathan is old enough, read it to him . . . and explain what you know of all this?'

Armstrong hesitated for a moment, then nodded. 'Of course, I'll do anything I can.'

At that moment the door to the sickbay opened and Midshipman Harris appeared, saluted and stood to one side.

'I'm afraid your five minutes are up, Mr Armstrong, sir. I must ask you to leave now.'

The missionary rose reluctantly and stood looking down at Eden, his face set in anxious lines. 'I shall continue to pray for your full recovery, Robert—and for Sentaro's soul. Meantime, may God's blessing be upon you.'

'Thank you, Mr Armstrong.' Eden's voice was weary and he did not turn his head to look at the missionary. 'Some day I hope to climb Mount Fuji again—in honour of Sentaro. And next time I'll reach the top . . .'

Armstrong touched Eden's shoulder lightly in a gesture of farewell, then followed the midshipman out of the sickbay. In the act of closing the door behind him, he turned to look back. Eden was lying very still against the pillow, his face deathly pale and Armstrong was suddenly afraid that he had stopped breathing. His eyes were wide open but unblinking and he appeared to stare fixedly at the snow-capped mountain peak floating high in the morning sky above Japan as the *Susquehanna* and the other three ships of the US Navy's East India Squadron ploughed steadily onward down the Bay of Yedo, heading for the Pacific Ocean.

Postscript

Such a novel as this one, based closely around a single historical event, may stimulate questions about where the line between fiction and history has been drawn. Since some very dramatic facts about this extraordinary first clash between Japan and America seem to be little known, it is perhaps worth identifying at least some of them.

For example, long after the event, a Japanese samurai who had been involved revealed that a concealed pit had been secretly dug beneath the ceremonial pavilion at Kurihama. So warriors armed with killing swords were in truth crouching beneath the feet of the lordly Perry as he forced unprecedented concessions from his frightened hosts. Another samurai also later claimed that he had been sent aboard Perry's flagship, albeit during the second trip, on what turned out to be an abortive assassin's errand. Furthermore, the extraordinary sphere of blue light that lit the heavens so brilliantly for so long on the historic night of the US warships' arrival was also a stranger-than-fiction reality, described in detail by several historical accounts. But then perhaps, at best, historical fiction is another, different form of history because professional historians themselves select and narrate their stories according to a subjective point of view—and none of us was there at the time.

But having identified some unlikely-sounding events that were real, I should add that all the named characters in this novel are fictitious. The only exception is the central figure of Commodore Matthew Calbraith Perry—although most of what is known about Perry makes him seem more like the creation of a novelist's imagination. I would like to emphasize, too, that even those individuals around him in the story who had counterparts in real life are purely fictional characters.

For my understanding of the time, place and context of this remarkable moment in history, I am indebted to a number of people and sources—and in particular to one coincidence of cosmic proportions. My greatest debt of gratitude is to Pat Barr, author of the outstanding book *The Coming of the Barbarians—The Story of Western Settlement in Japan 1853–1870*, first published in Britain and the United States in the late 1960s. Arguably the best popular history of Japan at that period, the book fell into my hands during early researches in London libraries. Only when visiting Norwich, the city of my birth, did a local bookseller point out to me that Pat was also Norwich-born. What was more, after many years living abroad including a long spell in Japan, she had recently returned to live in the city again. A meeting in Norwich was arranged and to our astonishment we discovered that for a time as children we had lived twenty yards apart on opposite corners of Whitehall Road. We had attended the same school for a year or two, our parents and families had known one another and we had even sometimes walked to that school in the same group of children. Pat survived a sudden, near-fatal illness which followed close on the heels of our 'reunion' and at many delightful meetings since in our natal city she has invaluably shared her perceptions of Japan, its history and its people with me. Pat has written a number of other books about China and India and had followed up her widely acclaimed first Japan book with another history, *The Deer Cry Pavilion—A Story of Westerners in Japan 1868–1905*; then she wrote a novel of the nineteenth century, *Kenjiro*. Both books provide further fascinating insights into Japan's astonishingly swift rise to international prominence. So this amazing coincidence opened up understandings I could hardly have obtained elsewhere.

Sometimes at our meetings we have tried to calculate what the odds might have been against two children from a small group of friends in an East Anglian city growing up to write—unbeknown to each other—a clutch of internationally published books and novels about Asia. So far we've not reached any conclusion.

There were of course other seminal histories of this dramatic period in Japan which provided vital background. They include the splendid antique volume *Narrative of the Expedition of an American Squadron to the China Seas and Japan—performed in the years 1852, 1853 and 1854* by Francis L. Hawks (New York, 1856); The *Mikado's Empire, Book 1, History of Japan 660 B.C. to 1872* (New York, 1887) by William Eliot Griffis; *India, China and Japan* (1857) by Bayard Taylor, who was an alert official scribe on board the black ships; and *A Journal of the Perry Expedition to Japan* published later in Asiatic Society of Japan Transactions by Wells Williams, one of the squadron's interpreters.

Among more modern publications, *Black Ships off Japan* by Arthur Walworth stands out, as do two excellent biographies of Matthew C. Perry, *Old Bruin* by S. E. Morrison and *The Great Commodore* by Ed M. Barrows. On wider issues, the acute perceptions of the remarkable Anglo-Greek writer Lafcadio Hearn opened wonderful windows on that time.

Hearn married the daughter of a samurai and immersed himself totally in the country at the turn of the century. His *Glimpses of Unfamiliar Japan* (1894), *Out of the East* (1895) and *Exotics and Retrospectives* (1898), in particular, provide unique revelations.

For other insights into Japanese history and culture I am indebted to Anthony Farrington, director of the Oriental and India Office Collections at the British Library in London. Hamish Todd and Mrs Yu Ying Brown, of the Japanese Department of that library, also gave me valuable guidance, particularly in the Japanese language. Ralph Smith, Professor of South East Asian History at the School of Oriental and African Studies, London University, again helped me with some important initial leads; a new friend, Charlotte Duke, later provided kind first-hand knowledge of Japanese customs and Lesley Isherwood and her daughter Lotte in Oxford triggered some rare inspirational images during the initial investigative phase of the novel at the Bodleian Library. Reginald W. Rice of Menlo Park, California, first encountered enjoyably on board the *QE2* in mid-Atlantic, led me into a new awareness of the intertwined history of native American-Indians and European settlers in New England by generously sharing details of his family's vivid history with me. Mavis Giles, with typical kindness, drafted and redrafted this manuscript—and the previous one—often at dawn, in the seventh year of assisting loyally and capably with so many projects. Justine Taylor, Elizabeth Murray, Ken Brown, Tony Davids, Chris Metcalfe, John Farrant, Pat Bolger and Frank Marsden also helped generously with essential background research in London. Ronald Titcombe very kindly sacrificed much time in offering expert advice on nautical terminology and seafaring matters.

I also thank Ian Chapman for his insight, understanding and friendship over what is now more than a decade of publishing collaboration; and I'm newly grateful to Peter Lavery for the astuteness of his editorial eye. Michael Sissons, stalwart agent and friend for some twenty-seven years, orchestrated his customary notes of creative encouragement at just the right moments during a longer than usual period of gestation. Enormous amounts of assiduous research in that same period were always willingly undertaken by Angela Hind. She also supervised the manuscript tirelessly through its several drafts. For this and very much more besides, I am greatly in her debt.

Finally and very sadly, Shirley, my wife of twenty-two years, lost a brave, harrowing and extended battle against cancer in the very last stages of this novel's preparation. During work on all my ten previous books from *Hostage in Peking* in 1969–70 down to *Tokyo Bay*, Shirley invariably provided a judicious blend of encouragement and constructive criticism.

This support continued even after our divorce—which thankfully led us into a new and increasingly warm friendship. So here I lovingly acknowledge once more her ever-wise counsel: invisible traces of this exist in every book I've published to date. She is, and always will be, greatly missed—both by me and by our daughters Clarissa and Lucy.

London, Spring 1996

About the Author

Anthony Grey became a foreign correspondent with Reuters after beginning his career in journalism in Norfolk, England, where he was born and educated. He reported on the Cold War from East Berlin, Prague, Warsaw, Budapest, Sofia, and Bucharest for two years before being assigned to China to cover the Cultural Revolution. There, his imprisonment by Red Guards in a house beside the historic Forbidden City of China's emperors attracted worldwide headlines for over two years. After his release, he was awarded the Order of the British Empire (OBE) for services to journalism, and was named UK Journalist of the Year. He has gone on to become a radio and television broadcaster, bestselling historical novelist, independent publisher, and frequent public speaker.

ANTHONY GREY

FROM OPEN ROAD MEDIA